HALF LIFE

A Novel

KRISTA FOSS

McClelland & Stewart

McClelland & Stewart and colophon are registered trademarks
of Penguin Random House Canada Limited.

Library and Archives Canada Cataloguing in Publication data is available upon request.

ISBN: 978-0-7710-3649-1
ebook ISBN: 978-0-7710-3650-7

Book design by Lisa Jager
Cover art: Donny Jiang / Unsplash images
Typeset in Adobe Caslon by M&S, Toronto
Printed and bound in Canada

McClelland & Stewart,
a division of Penguin Random House Canada Limited,
a Penguin Random House Company
www.penguinrandomhouse.ca

1 2 3 4 5   25 24 23 22 21

For Fehn

1993

✳

SEPTEMBER

K nock on wood.

The bedroom's filled with light. Sunday: the clock radio says 2:33 p.m. Elin strains for the sounds of someone shifting on the porch or leaving it. It's made of new pine and reverberates under heavy feet.

She can't recall a rattle. There would have been that. The front door's windowpane is loose, on the verge of breaking, in need of re-glazing. She lies still, buried under the uncertainty of it, coveting the duvet's warmth. If the knock occurred, its kind would matter:

loud

half-hearted

panicked

perfunctory.

Mette told her once that *knock on wood* originated from pagans seeking the protection of trees. To knock on the top of the table was to let good fortune fall to the floor where you couldn't reach it.

But a door. She wonders if its luck falls inward, retreating to the corners, keeping company with dust, dropped coins, torn fingernails.

Outside the window, the daylight softens: she's missed the best hours. Perhaps luck escapes out the edges of her door's loose windowpane.

Her head pounds as she moves down the stairs from her attic bedroom to the second floor, whose three rooms hold nothing but a few boxes, still unopened. The washroom blinks with sunlit porcelain.

She owns a house.

Its emptiness keeps the possibility fresh; she's afraid of unpacking, letting the old selves of books and torn winter jackets, tax documents and pans with burn marks invade the clean slate, the reinvented Elin Henriksen.

Another knock. This time she hears the definitive pane rattle. Her head winces: she should have come straight home after her closing shift. Instead, she crawled in after sunrise. Her feet sound brutish on the staircase to the lobby.

She's had a month of silence. The street is quiet, her neighbours are quiet, she hasn't unpacked the stereo. She gave away her television.

Now there are shadowed hands against the frosted glass, frantic as fighting birds. *Rap, rap, rap.*

A voice, throaty and familiar. The pleading, strange.

Elin pants as she undoes the deadbolt.

She swings the door open to an unexpected face, distorted and confused. Lilliana Henriksen has no jacket on; her body, aspen-thin, trembles in the ochre brightness.

Mom?

Her mother turns, careens toward the sidewalk.

Elin, I need your help. Come!

There's a cab idling.

Elin grabs a parka from the hallway hooks and slips her feet into unlaced sneakers that are damp, reeking of fry oil, spilled margarita mix, exertion. She is braless, sockless, wearing boxers; a late September cold snap rushes in from the open door, chastens her knees.

The house keys are not in the hallway, and Elin can't remember where she's put them. Her mother stands at the open cab door wearing a face like a freshly bombed church.

Driving away from her unlocked house, Elin tells herself a good robbery might be the impetus she needs: fewer things to put away, her cupboards draughty with potential.

though her face is puffy. She pulls herself up to a seated position and her eyes serrate over Elin's face.

Have you called Aunt Petrine? The newspaper? The funeral home?

Yes. Yes. Yes.

When will Casper get here?

Soon. He should be in the air right now.

Your sister?

On 94.

I hate being alone with this, she says.

Her mother gets up and starts rifling through a box that she pulls out from the bedroom dresser. Elin realizes she is already imagining the obituary and searching for a photo. A flattering one.

The Lilli's eyes linger over a snapshot and Elin is about to ask to see it when the lid closes. Before she can say anything, her mother places the box in the open drawer, shutting it with a practised hip.

I'll have a shower now, Elin.

The selected photo hangs at her mother's side, in the scissors of her long fingers.

You should wait for Casper, in the living room.

Five minutes after The Lilli shuts herself in the bathroom, there's a knock on the door.

Casper steps into the hallway, arriving from Boston before Mette drives in from Chicago. Elin puts a hand over her mouth and sobs at the sight of him. Casper, at twelve, had put a plank between two work-horses in the backyard then tested it by walking across, before he lifted himself into a handstand. She'd watched from the porch steps as his sneakers toed the clouds. Her invincible brother.

He's wan and his expensive dress shirt is wrinkled, yet even now he possesses something she doesn't: poise.

Casper wraps his warm hands on Elin's forearms. His eyes are shiny, red-rimmed.

Where is he?

She sucks in a breath.

They took him.

His face spasms.

Anger? It's hard to tell. She'd read somewhere that emotional and social control are two of the six factors associated with charismatic personalities. He shakes his head.

It's not real if I don't see him.

Elin holds her mouth open, wordlessly. The Lilli emerges, her head turbaned in terry cloth. She pulls her son to her.

Oh, Casper! He's gone.

Her mother's snot and tears darken her brother's shirt, its fine cyan houndstooth.

Elin retreats to the kitchen so they can cry and whisper together, and keeps vigil for Mette. The house phone rings. She moves to answer it, but Casper picks up in the other room, quickly impatient with the measured, too-kind voice from the funeral home. She listens to her brother finish the arrangements, afraid to hang up, signal her presence. The edge of the sink cuts into her lower back and the raw cold of the floor tiles moves up from her bare soles; the whole of her shivers.

And then her sister's headlights fluoresce the kitchen window. She plunks the receiver down and rushes to the door.

Mette, tears already streaming down her face, cinches her silently. Elin is grateful for the surprising strength of her sister's arms and then the chaos of scents rising from her hair and skin: cigarette smoke, balsam car freshener, beeswax, and damp cotton.

The Lilli does not cry out for Mette but receives the touch of her large hands as a benediction. When they are all seated, Elin rushes to get glasses of water and plates of cheese, rye toasts, and quartered oranges.

Mette pats the sofa seat beside her.

Come, El. Sit.

Before she can, Casper bites into a large section of orange and a dribble of juice slides past the webbing of his fingers toward the mitred cuff at his wrist. He looks at her with a helpless alarm.

Napkin?

Mette makes a sound.

But Elin is relieved to move. She fetches a damp linen serviette. Her mother smiles weakly.

You've done enough, Elin. It's late. Go home. You can come back tomorrow.

There's room for all of us, Mette says.

Elin shakes her head.

Left my house unlocked—could use some pants.

On the way out, Elin glances at her mother. Something in her eyes fastens complicity like a leash, tightens it between them: The Lilli won't mention the cab ride to her other children. Elin realizes she's wasted her chance to kiss her father's cheek to remind herself of the ways he made her who she is.

His death moves into her limbs like winter rain.

Four days pass. Casper and Mette both announce they can't stay: him, with an expensive last-minute return ticket and meetings that can't be missed; her, speeding back to an untrustworthy cat alone with a self-feeder and studio time that can't be cancelled. They clasp each other with awkward intensity: hands over wrists, palms at the back of necks. Elin breathes deeply for the first time since they arrived. She fills The Lilli's refrigerator with groceries and a fresh bottle of gin, and hesitates at the door.

I need to be alone with this now, her mother insists.

But only eighteen hours pass before Elin's answering machine is lit up.

Children, I'm leaving you each the same message. Your aunt Petrine and I are flying to Copenhagen in two weeks. Your father's ashes will be spread at the Forum. Can someone drive us to O'Hare on the twenty-third?

There's a hesitation followed by a cleared throat.

It's your mother, by the way.

Copenhagen's Forum was where their father, Tig Henriksen, watched Arne Jacobsen and Flemming Lassen build the House of the Future. Right inside the exhibition space. He was a tow-headed twelve-year-old, escaping a sad home, purchasing sandwiches and coffee with *krøner* he'd swiped before sneaking into the Forum, according to The Lilli, who told the stories he wouldn't.

The house was curved and chambered like a mollusc. There were winding staircases, a boathouse, a garage, a helipad with its own actual gyrocopter.

Imagine how that looked to a young boy in 1929: he thought Danes would design the future, she said. Including him.

The message ends and Elin's old house is quiet again. She dials The Lilli's number. It goes to her machine on the fourth ring.

Mom, it's El. Happy to drive you and Aunt Petrine to the airport. I'm the one who lives in the same city as you, remember?

Elin arrives at Burnham Avenue just before lunch. The Lilli looks both durable and delicate, a tall, slender woman embodying clean lines and defensible proportions, the good design and impossible standards that are—*were*—solder in the complex joints of her parents' marriage. Her carry-on is small, the urn tucked into a large leather tote.

Petrine is not there.

We're not travelling together.

In the car, her mother lists the things they'd fought over: timing, airline, Copenhagen hotels.

She wanted me to stay overnight with her in North Point so you could pick us up there and grab 43.

It *is* closer, Elin said.

Her mother's glare dances along Elin's bare neck.

My husband. I have lost *my* husband. I am not going to stay in his sister's house, surrounded by the money she married into, on the eve of taking his ashes home.

This is home, Mom.

Elin smiles to herself. Her mother reaches over, twists on the windshield wipers.

That window's filthy, Elin.

She'd hoped for a chance to talk to The Lilli about the cab ride. Why had her mother not called the paramedics first? Or Mette, Casper? Why had she come all the way to North Bremen? The police hadn't followed up.

When they take the exit to I-94 east, her mother turns the radio off abruptly.

Casper is coming with me instead.

She says this staring straight forward.

If you make good time, we can collect him at Terminal 3 arrivals, and you can pop us over to Terminal 5, so he doesn't have to wait for a shuttle.

Elin nods her head, taking in the new information.

Righty-o. Do my best.

Drive a little faster, Elin.

Casper is not waiting at Terminal 3. Elin keeps driving, despite her mother's protests, to Terminal 5, drops her off, and parks the car. The Lilli stands ramrod straight inside the concourse doors.

He's late and now we've gone ahead.

No, Mom, I just checked. His flight came early. He's here somewhere.

She turns around and sees her brother half a football field away, striding toward them on a diagonal, framed in a nimbus of airport light, carrying a tray with four coffees, a bag sweating pastry grease. He kisses The Lilli on the cheeks, and nudges Elin with his shoulder.

He looks handsome, impeccably casual, troubled only in the corners of his eyes.

Are you doubling up? she says, nodding to the extra coffee.

He's about to answer but doesn't need to because, behind him, Elin catches a distinctive swing of hair from a figure wheeling out of the bathroom, wearing a flounced poncho, bright as a poached quetzal.

Mette.

Her sister buffets them in succession with enthusiastic kisses, little grunts of pleasure.

For an awkward second, they sip their coffees in a silent huddle.

So, this is like a family trip now?

Elin can't help herself. The Lilli is stone-faced. Casper grimaces with irritation. Mette is chastened.

Total last-minute splurge for me, she says. I thought, fuck it, I'm going. Had some points. Literally booked seven hours ago.

Casper glances at his watch. Mette takes an exaggerated interest in the departures monitor. The Lilli fishes a travel-size hand lotion out of her bag and begins massaging a dollop into her fine hands.

Well, Elin says, I guess I'm holding down the fort here.

The Lilli gives her hands a final rub, then leans in and brushes a sandpaper kiss on her daughter's cheek. Elin smells the lotion's spearmint-and-camomile uprightness mingle with the concourse's ozone of dry-cleaned shirts, egg sandwiches, and cortisol.

We have to go, Casper says.

Mette reaches over and squeezes Elin's forearm, mouthing, I'm sorry.

They hurry together toward the checkpoint. After a few metres, Mette turns, with a stricken expression.

El, my cat, she yells. Assistant quit. Could you? I'll email the security code.

Elin gives her sister the thumbs-up.

Eat shit, she says under her breath.

They've already turned away, three tall, straight backs, leaning into a storm like ship masts.

And Elin smells petrichor—the fragrance released by rain falling on dry land. Less romantically, it's caused by spores, Elin thinks, lying dormant in the earth, stirred back to life.

While they are gone, Elin completes The Lilli's precise, if shakily written, lists. Her father's pension documents, death benefits, unpaid suppliers, old sweaters, new shoes, favourite aftershave, photos, preliminary sketches, unexecuted designs, are filled out, donated, discarded, and archived.

She opens the sympathy cards and arranges them on the honeyed oak of her mother's Peder Moos sideboard. An hour later, The Lilli calls from Copenhagen and says, Throw them away. I don't want those waiting for me when I get home.

She asks The Lilli for another task. The slightest pleading in her tone.

Time to go back to your own life, Elin. Casper will deal with the lawyer. I'll call in a few days.

The sound of the abrupt click sends an awful energy to Elin's fingertips. She stands outside her parents' house in the carport's cold air, ripping the cards hungrily so they fall like strange weather into the garbage can.

Back at North Bremen, Wisconsin's weird October light follows her inside, scattering its bleached bones into her hallway. The comfort Elin hoarded from being busy escapes out her front door into the afternoon's fugitive beauty.

What's left is a new feeling, a lightness that's also unhinged. As if the vocabulary of grief belongs to the old, and cannot account for her particular mania of sadness, the urge to dance wildly, the wish to stop breathing, intense and simultaneous.

And to talk. Who in her life was big enough to hold her troubles, not do anything with them?

She could move forward, as if everything was normal—working, unpacking, planning. But now there's something spent that she can't un-spend, those lumens of possibility that belonged to her only a week earlier. How to mark it? Who to mark it with?

She slows her breath.

There's an isosceles of sunlight on the wood floors. She has an urge to curl up in it like an old cat.

Elin taunts herself. Speak to him. She takes the answering machine into the living room.

What's a life but reflected light and radiation?

She lies down, opens her mouth. Out comes a nervous laugh. Elin hits Record.

Memo to a missing grandfather.

So he's dead.

Can I say a cruel thing? Felt fatherless before he died.

Elin sits up, turns off the recording, erases. She's not going to go in so hard, make a bad impression. And what does she want, anyway—sympathy, love even? Or wisdom: please, old dude, help me accept this big change.

I'm so sorry, she imagines him saying.

He's a good man, big-hearted. All her sources say so. The thing is, she wants to share her hurt with him, make it commensurate with his own. But how? He'd lost so many he loved.

This is the problem: you can't talk to an older person about what hurts. They can always trump you. They can always say, Oh, that's too bad, but here's what happened to me (insert truly harrowing devastation that dwarfs your picayune grief).

Her mouth is dry; the room fishbowls around her. She has no one else. Her finger depresses Record again.

I saw a movie once (might have been a documentary) and it had that strait between Denmark and Sweden in it. Kattegat, right? I've never been. So Denmark has always seemed a bit made up to me, a lost-empire fairy tale. Except that my family, what's left of them, is there right now. Weird, huh?

I didn't get an invitation.

Even in the movie, those waters surged. This little boat tipping like an injured seabird.

I thought: this is where you turned and a rogue wave pulled your seventeen-year-old kid off the sailboat's gunwale. Into that ugly water. God, I could feel it as if I was there.

Elin puts her palms against her forehead. She sees him screaming into the wind's maw. The kerchief around his neck taut as a semaphore.

Your friends held you back. Wouldn't let you jump in. You must have been pissed. But you'd have died too. They held you. And you're a strong man.

She wants to say, I don't know what to feel. I don't know how to be changed by this.

How did you tell her—your wife, waiting for you in that pretty cottage surrounded by heather and dunes, expecting a husband, a son, to walk through the door after a pleasant summer afternoon? Expecting to reach for your warm necks—him then you—for a kiss? The smell of wool, wind, brine: a good day. How did you walk through the door alone and get through the next moment?

It's true about losing someone. You feel responsible. Even when you couldn't have done a damn thing, even when you're innocent.

She stops talking. Watches the reel of the answering machine tape turn. Grief changes the way you experience silence, she wants to say. But the idea isn't hers: she'd underlined it in a *Psychology Today* article.

And she's done with silence. Her parents made a meal of it, washed it down with rye and gin.

How often did you feel your son's hand on your shoulder, and turn, expecting his big smile, those blazing eyes? she says instead.

You jumped in? your wife must have asked you. *Surely, you jumped in after him?*

Elin imagines him pulling ivy that has grown freely up a prim stucco edifice. He has bicycled back to his institution three months after losing his son. He loves his work. The ivy has taken advantage of his absence.

If you were here, would you hold me? she wants to know.

Would you hold me like your lost child?

I can't be alone. I can't always be alone.

She wonders what he'd say to her. If he'd let her call him *morfar*, mother's father.

I've always wanted a daughter.

He might say that.

Mette.

She is sipping a Pernod in Nessun Dorma, an old haunt, passing through Smallwaukee following a Minneapolis gig two months after their father's death. Elin sees her from the entrance: hair limp, eyes limpid, amused. She wavers but then advances.

Yoda, Elin says as she sits. I'm so sorry.

Yeah. In your cold bedroom. Watching the stars.

Mette takes in a deep breath.

He was yowling, dehydrated, pretty pissed off when I came back. His water bowl was empty. Had a tantrum in his litter box. Threw up on my bamboo *zafu*. My favourite.

Mette, I forgot. I got all the way home and I couldn't drive back. I had to go to work. Then it just slipped my mind.

Her sister takes a long sip of wine and locates an ethereal calm that Elin wants to poke, to see if it's filled with goo or hard as a peach pit.

Let's be honest. Four days: it was a bit of a fuck-you.

Peach pit, Elin thinks.

Pyt happens, her sister says, using her guidebook Danish.

Mette waves her hand.

It's forgiven. All done, offered up to the universe.

That smile again, its unnerving contrariness.

I should have bought you a ticket, El. Cheaper than the vet bill.

She taps her forehead, winks.

Sorry again, Mets.

It was impulsive going. Joining that twosome. They bicker incessantly, y'know?

Not surprised. He needs a good lay.

'Twas ever thus.

Why go, then?

Mette puts the end of her thumb in her mouth and chews, in the same way she did as a worried twelve-year-old who couldn't get to sleep. All her earlier cheer collapses into that thumb tip; her top tooth cuts angrily at the nail. And then another big gulp of wine.

I wrote a song. A good one.

For Dad?

Mette shakes her head.

For us. Breathing in the ashes.

2017

✳

JUNE

1

There are two plants in the principal's office. When she enters for a one-on-one Wednesday morning meeting, Elin checks and sees they are still there.

One is a *dieffenbachia*. It sits on a shelf in front of the window, in a yellow pot with rusty stains, neither thriving nor dying. Not quite green, and not quite happily variegated. She has come to this office to meet with eight different principals during her decade as V.H. Phillips Secondary's physics teacher and mentioned to only one that the window plant's folk name is "dumb cane." It was intended as an icebreaker.

That principal didn't laugh.

He folded and unfolded his hands over her file on the top of his desk and stared past her with a rheumy fatigue.

She didn't get her class trip money that year.

The other plant is called devil's ivy, *Epipremnum aureum*. It's on the top of a bookshelf behind the new principal, the one who arrived a few months ago. A jute plant hangar slouches around the pot. The vine is scraggly and the sparse leaves, dark green and waxy, trail down the side of the bookcase like a sad kite string. The folk name for that one is "money plant."

So, Ms. Henriksen, says Dilip Preet.

It is their first meeting.

He is handsome in his sharp eyeglasses, open-collar shirt and good herringbone jacket. She notes a Fitbit on one wrist, a *kara* on the

other. Two framed degrees lean into a bookshelf, and above his cur-
riculum binders sits inspirational reading: *The Audacity of Hope* and a
self-help book whose three-sentence title includes "getting everything"
and "out-think, out-perform and out-earn." A Milwaukee Wave coffee
mug and photos of a woman in hiking gear are on his desk. All of it
would fit in a single banker's box, every trace of him gone in under
twenty minutes.

There are schools in Whitefish Bay or Fox Point where all the
principals she's met would rather be.

How long have you been with V.H. Phillips?

Elin's eyes drift to the file under his folded hands. It's hers; she
recognizes the salmon pink, the coffee ring left by principal number
six. She makes eye contact.

Twelve years.

He looks at her with a charming, assessing glance. She's tempted
to save him the trouble and just say it out loud: I'm forty-eight.

And where were you before?

Perhaps the acting head of science had told the scrappy-ne'er-
do-well-makes-sorta-good version of her, in the way that he had of
making all his generosity barbed.

Teaching is my second career, Elin says.

The truth was, she'd made more money as a bartender; the North
Bremen house was purchased with three years' worth of tips—a
large cash down payment—something she couldn't imagine on her
current salary.

Principal Preet moves his hands.

Okay. You teach subjects other than physics?

Elin stares directly at the file now: would he have it there if he
hadn't read it? There's something about that bracelet on a man that
she's always found attractive. He does not fold and unfold his hands.

When I was a substitute, some biology. Now I teach the two senior
physics courses. And two maths.

And you're hoping for a three-quarters load next fall?

Yes, I'd applied for an accommodation. It's all in there.

She points to the file. Principal Preet swallows.

I wanted to take some courses.

Always a good sign when a teacher refreshes their credentialling, he says with a half-interested tone.

How to let him know she's the single parent of a teenaged daughter? She'd have to admit to sending Bets to an out-of-catchment high school because the academic standing of V.H. Phillips wasn't good enough. And also, perhaps, that her vigilance was for naught: Bets has become increasingly rudderless during a gap year.

Principal Preet tilts his head in a way that worries her, as if he can see inside the simple clockworks of her brain. What she wants to say is, I can't lose even a not-quite-full-time job right now. Bets may eventually come around, forget the sins of her parent, and accept one of the university offers.

She looks past Principal Preet and starts to count the devil's ivy leaves along the bookshelf. There are thirteen. Flightless leaves held above the earth by a tough, no-bullshit vine.

Ms. Henriksen, I called you in today to get to know you and talk about the class trip. Because your department's without a permanent head, the request seems to have been, er, lost in the shuffle. But there's a correct process, right?

Elin nods. She does know this; she has defended the class trip to eight principals.

Can you explain this trip to me? I'm struggling to see its relevance.

The trip is simple. She takes her senior-year students to Allis-Chalmers's former Hawley plant because it was part of the Manhattan Project. Allis was the only company in North America with machining large enough to produce the massive magnetic coils needed for purifying uranium in Oak Ridge, Tennessee.

It was, for a few years, a 400,000-square-foot secret.

Elin chooses her words carefully. She finds these hired-gun administrators have a short attention span if she doesn't quickly say something about STEM, so her second point makes the link: without narrative, the science, technology, and math aren't meaningful. Local connections bring them even more alive for students.

He leans forward, folds his hands, takes a deep breath.

So, you just go and look at a big building?

Yes. You have to see it to understand the scale of things: the height of the roof, the size of the overhead timbers. Mind-blowing.

Isn't there a Sam's Club there? A mattress store?

His voice has changed pitch: incredulity.

She redoubles her enthusiasm. The comment sections of her teacher ratings are filled with compliments about her storytelling, how it kept students going through senior physics.

There are also atria where it's still open, so you have a sense of the original plant. I get the students to circumnavigate it. Then we meet an actor who re-creates a scene about what it was like to work in the plant.

Actor?

And playwright. He's written a beautiful piece about how some of the coils were sent back from Tennessee after being used to make uranium. He recites a soliloquy. It's a Hawley foreman realizing he might be exposing his workers to radiation.

(She'd gone on an awkward date with the actor, Casimir. It ended with a dry-lipped, tongue-less kiss. She was unable to get past his insistence on being called Cas, like her brother, and declined a second date. Despite this, he still performed for her class trips. No one would mount his play.)

Elin doesn't wait for the principal to overthink it. She imitates the actor's gruff blue-collar caricature.

General Groves says he wants us to clean the coils and get it back to Y-12 pronto. Men ain't trained for that I says to 'em. Nobody listens. Seven of us cleaning, five dead of cancer in a decade. Young men with wives, children. I sent 'em down there. Got into the mix myself. The hours long. All of us under pressure. Knew disease was coming for me too.

Principal Preet's elbows dig into the pink file. Elin can't stop herself. She takes in a big breath to give the last lines *gravitas*.

You can't outlive a bomb. It's forever reaching backward and forward in time. Damn thing never stops going off.

When she looks up, Principal Preet is staring at his Fitbit. His temples twitch.

Flighty—you think that once about a woman and you never have to take her seriously.

Her mother had used the word to describe her years ago; Casper, whom Elin adored, nodded his head, repeated it. *Flighty* had bothered her more the way he'd said it, his tone implying something insubstantial, impermanent.

Elin's throat feels furry.

Ms. Henriksen, I apologize. But I'm struggling to understand. Show me how this relates to the learning outcomes of a senior-year physics class.

Elin searches for a concept, the one that principals like to hear. She hasn't been sleeping well. Her mind feels viscid. Flipped classrooms. Differentiated teaching. Blended learning. Multiple intelligences. Jesus, what was that term?

He's staring at her.

I have six girls in my senior-year physics class this semester, Mr. Preet. Six. It's a record for *this* school. And I'm going to work extra hard so every one of them qualifies for university science courses.

This school's retention in math and science is bleak, he says.

Retention. She'd wanted to say it first.

My retention rates are high, Mr. Preet.

Yes, but your classes are small, Ms. Henriksen. So, there's a recruitment issue on the other end, right? Perhaps your course has a bit of a reputation issue within the school.

Her face feels stewed-fruit warm. She remembers Bets studying calculus, and Bets studying algebra, printing formulas on flash cards, falling asleep with her lights on, her textbooks open, a grimy pink eraser between her fingers. Bets getting 89 in math, then 93, and finally 99. The umbrae below her big green eyes darkening like old bruises.

Principal Preet looks up with an apologetic squish in his forehead.

Okay, he says. Let me think about it. We're under a lot of pressure budget-wise. Our scores are low—dismal—in post-secondary placement. And you know, Ms. Henriksen, the catchment neighbourhood is gentrifying. This new crop of parents, let's just say, I'm getting to know them real well. They want their kids to be engineers, doctors, software developers just as badly as the moms and dads in Bayview, Greenfield. But failing that, they want them to get jobs. Scores are everything. Our students gotta know the formulas, the equations, solve the problems. Right? The stories are nice, but . . .

Elin nods.

It's an inexpensive trip, she says.

Principal Preet stands up. He's taller than she'd imagined.

My next appointment is waiting.

She extends her hand.

Damn thing never stops going off. That's a good line.

Principal Preet repeats the words as if admiring a weird melon he'd never buy.

Elin glances again at the *dieffenbachia*. A mature leaf droops toward her, zippered with decay. She wants to say something remarkable, to finish well.

She points to the devil's ivy behind him.

Y'know the race to develop a quantum computer?

Huh?

The model for it is right there in that plant. The way it makes chlorophyll is an act of quantum computing.

Principal Preet stares at her for an uncomfortable second.

I could explain, she says.

Have a good day, Ms. Henriksen.

———

In the staff room, Elin dumps stale coffee into a fresh paper filter.

She'd done a whole lesson once on coffee rings: how the liquid's viscosity and surface tension pushed the sediments to an outer sphere. An orbit. Why hadn't she impressed Principal Preet with this talent of hers? Making connections—finding the sublime in the commonplace.

Her phone burrs inside her cardigan pocket. Without checking the screen, she cradles it between her shoulder and chin and fills the coffee carafe with water.

A raspy feminine throat clears on the other end.

The phlegm-knowledgement, Mette calls it.

Mom?

It was unlike The Lilli to call her.

Oh. I didn't expect to get you.

I'll hang up. You can leave a message.

Don't be smart, Elin.

The staff coffee maker is a yard sale clunker. When she presses the button to start the machine, Elin sees she's failed to push the filter tray in properly. The heated water catches the paper edge of the filter and folds it; the liquid leaking into the carafe is speckled with grit. Reflexively, Elin reaches in to correct it. A tributary of scalding water pools in the crook of her thumb and slides along her forearm.

Shit!

Excuse me?

Mom, I'm at work. What is it?

There's no need to be rude.

Elin turns on the cold water, runs her thumb under it, and bites her lip.

You girls keep things from me.

A red tide spreads past her wrist. It throbs. She wishes she'd sounded smarter in her meeting with Principal Preet.

What are you talking about, Mom?

Your sister is going to sing. With her guitar.

Do you mean at the memorial thingy?

Don't act ignorant, Elin. I'm old but not a fool.

In an email sent to Casper and her, Mette had joked: if we've got to pay to name a gallery for Dad, we should be able to call it the Tig Modern, the Henriksonian.

It's not a memorial, Elin. It's a naming rights unveiling. And *now* she's coming a day ahead of time. And *now* she's telling us she's going to sing. You knew, of course.

Nope.

Whoosh, like a puncture. How long had it been since she'd seen her sister perform?

She imagines Mette onstage with her beat-up Gibson, her still-lean legs in ripped jeans tucked into square-toed Becks, her shoulder-length golden hair streaked now with a lambent grey. Wisconsin's Lucinda Williams. Milwaukee's love child of Emmylou Harris and Patti Smith. She'd sing that song, the one that made her famous and still paid some of her bills, to get it out of the way early, and she would sound good, even better than when she'd made it a hit. (Middle age, so ruthless with performers, added grit to Mette's tone. Typical of her, to get better as she got older, not worse.)

Well, her mother says. There's a small item in the *Journal Sentinel*.

Elin hears the snap of newsprint and imagines her mother at the kitchen table, all dressed for a luncheon, face sharp as a seabird's, long finger tracing underneath the lines of type. The last of a rare genus: print edition readers, *senex chartam lectorem*.

No, she has the Latin wrong.

It's a private event splashed all over the newspaper, Elin.

Read it to me.

Her mother clears her voice and recites six lines of staid copy.

Mom, that's a community events item. And most of it's about the gallery dedication. There's only one sentence about Mette.

Your sister has rented the café below Windhover Hall. Pure extravagance.

There are fifteen minutes left in Elin's spare; she'll have to remake the coffee before another teacher invades her space, comments on the wasted filter. The coffee was a public good; the staff tithed monthly and grumbled mordantly about the dangers of Communism now that Wisconsin was a red state again.

It's her way of remembering him. And she's paying for it.

There are proper ways to memorialize, Elin. Dignified ways. Like the dedication. Besides, your sister talks too much when she's onstage.

The staff room door opens. Elin moves to hide the failed coffee. With the phone crooked in her shoulder, she pulls out the filter, tips it into the garbage, then empties the carafe and lets her mother count down the seconds of silence.

We should throw a party, Elin says. Both Mette and Casper arrive on Saturday, right?

This comes out of her mouth before she considers it.

The dedication's the next day, Elin. You're not thinking.

How long has it been since we've all been together? Let's do it up. Celebrate it.

She pictures them, a little drunk, a little tired, cradled by a party's goodwill and laughter. After her aunt Petrine, and her father's former clients and suppliers, the ones still alive, had started nodding off and ordered cabs homes. Followed by the gradual exits of the museum staff, Mette's stalwarts, Casper's local connections, neighbours, the mid-century-modern collectors, friends. So many unsaid things, spinning toward the remaining four of them with a cratering force, and time running out. How could that go wrong?

I don't think so, The Lilli says.

Mette turned fifty last month, Mom. Did you send her a card or leave her a message? Let's combine all the celebrations. It's overdue. We could use some fun.

(Elin *had* sent a card. Elin *had* left a message.)

Your sister hates birthdays. And we have only ten days—it's not enough time to pull a party together.

Elin feels a small tap on her shoulder and turns to see the scolding eyebrows of Joy Francis, a biology teacher.

My mother, she mouths, and rolls her eyes. Joy grimaces and signals for her to move away from the mess she's made of the coffee.

Bets and I will just go ahead and do it anyway, Mom.

I won't let Bettina in my house if her midriff's exposed. I'm putting my foot down.

Oh, we're having it at your house?

Don't be smart, Elin.

Her mother clears her throat; the line goes click.

Everything has a natural frequency: the flap of a bird's wings, heart rates, the U.S. bank building, a full coffee cup carried through busy halls by an overheated teacher. All of them find their ideal rate to slosh and sway. Anticipating the jostle of students rushing to first period, slamming the terrazzo as if their knees had a cold-fusion abundance of elasticity, Elin has perfected her walking speed to match the peak amplitudes of the hot liquid's movement against the mug's insides, so she doesn't lose a drop over the brim.

Small successes get her through a day.

The physics room looks out on a tired lane of wood homes with flaking paint, yards strewn with old tires and plastic kiddie slides, bindweed reaching dendritically up chain-link fences. Bleak but for one huge European copper beech, *Fagus sylvatica purpurea*, which was not as old as the one dying in South Shore Park, but at fifty feet high arguably as magnificent, its branches heavy with deep-burgundy leaves tasselled with downy catkins. A beech could, in the right conditions, live past two hundred years. The things it would have seen. Elin had joked to her students that old trees were the short-term rental for visitors from the multiverse. You need an intervention, miss, one of the smartasses in the back row responded.

Before second period begins, Elin opens a red-flagged email in her inbox from the overworked student counsellor. She's concerned about Mabel Flores's sudden disappearance from all of her classes. There's a tight pull across Elin's chest. Mabel was her most talented student, and though she'd noticed her absence in senior physics, if she was perfectly honest she'd welcomed the break from the girl's nervous pencil chewing, her constant you're-boring-me-to-death eye rolls in the second row. All that young brain's rapid-fire abstractions reminding Elin of her petering neural network. She'd assumed Mabel's was a conscientious truancy—her prodigious talents better served by the Internet and Neil deGrasse Tyson. (True, she'd not thought twice about including Mabel among the six girls in senior physics she'd boasted about earlier to Principal Preet.) Was it possible she'd not only misread the situation but was guilty of negligence?

Weeks earlier, there had been a moment at the end of one of her classes when Mabel lingered, perhaps wanting to talk, and Elin had felt tired, resentful at not being a match for the girl's curiosity. She'd pretended her cellphone was vibrating in her cardigan pocket and looked at the screen.

Oh, it's my mother. She's really old. Gotta take it. Sorry.

Hey, Mom, she said into the silent phone, pretending it was the woman who never called her until, as it turns out, today.

Mabel, deflated, walked away.

Her second-period students congregate behind the closed classroom door, shuffling, cranky, and already overheating in the June warmth.

Elin looks at the beech again. Once, she'd seen the bright-orange flare of a Baltimore oriole sitting on its branches. Yellow-orange against purple: complements, almost. She stopped her lesson mid-sentence, pointing it out to the students and piking her body over the hip-high window ledge to get a better view. It's so beautiful. Can you see it? she asked twice.

For a few days, the Baltimore oriole was a meme that circulated among her senior-year classes. Whole lotta hashtags, one student told her, offering his phone. Elin refused to look.

She kept her admiration of the tree to herself after that.

Sometimes she imagines him under it, the man who has followed her much of her adult life, relaxing in the beech's shade—there'd been a huge one outside his home—with his outsized forehead, the straight, thick brows and flaccid mouth. Rugged, but not handsome. Tired eyes that smoulder with intelligence. He'd be smoking—sometimes a cigarette, as often a pipe—and overdressed for the Wisconsin spring. And watching her. So she wasn't alone.

Elin locks the door, fishes her phone out of her purse, and thumbs through the utilities until she is staring at a red button. She presses Record.

Memo, she says, facing the window. It's been a while, morfar.

She tells him she's bungled her meeting with Principal Preet and committed to a party she can't afford on the eve of a memorial she's ambivalent about. Now her most talented student is AWOL. And Mette is singing at the gallery dedication.

Bets is a worry.

He has no answers and she doesn't want any.

End memo, she says before she gets up to open the classroom door. The skin around her thumb starts to throb.

2

An aching tooth wakes Elin up around 2 a.m., Thursday.
She leaves the attic door open and the second-floor hallway light ablaze on the nights Bets works. Most every night, lately. There's a soft, beery glow where the ceiling slopes by the foot of her bed.

The tooth whinges and Elin uses her tongue to find it. Her saliva tastes fungal. Death, that little flirt, was showing up in a succession of winks and nudges—a rotting tooth, racing heart, memory loss—before it committed. Her eyes water.

I can't live in fear like you all the time, Mom, Bets said recently.

Sometimes Elin will turn—they will be gently poking fun at each other—and catch in the quick retreat of Bets's smile, her held breath, a dusting of sadness that reminds her of her own. She will be shaken by it, yet unfairly comforted too. They are alike. Other times, Elin watches Bets charge down the street or enter a room, a giant bearing her blessings—youth, beauty, self-knowledge—as daggers not roses. Her daughter, a stranger suddenly.

This is the young woman who calls out Elin's fearfulness, as if she could inoculate herself against having it.

A toothache is a worry, because it conjures a dentist in her future. A dentist means money, and she has opted out of full dental coverage. Elin grinds her molars. Usually, she can wait out the sensitivity.

She'll have to be more frugal if Bets gets an offer once the late-application window for university is over. She can remortgage the house for tuition, but there will be living costs to cover. Bets's insistence on taking a gap year meant turning down a full scholarship. Elin doubts such a generous offer will be made twice. Was it too late for Elin to withdraw her request for reduced teaching hours? Principal Preet might also think she's flighty; once it takes hold, that idea hangs tough in the face of evidence to the contrary.

Trucks grumble along North Humboldt, two blocks over.

The clock says 2:21 a.m.

Bets's plan for the gap year was to work at any job she could find, save, and spend this summer travelling.

Where? Elin had asked at the beginning of last summer, again in the fall, and once this past February. She wanted to be involved, to compare rates for flights to London or investigate voluntourism adventures: the sloth rehabilitation centre in Costa Rica or building a school in Lesotho. WWOOFing in Oregon.

Might start in Denmark, Bets said the last time she asked.

Elin couldn't help but accordion her face.

Oh, honey. It's so small and expensive. All those earnest cyclists. Flat as Kansas. Likely as xenophobic. Seriously?

Mom, we're from there.

Elin imagined a train full of *Jyllands-Posten* readers assessing her daughter's brown skin, green eyes, dark hair.

Well, my parents are. But us? Not so much.

You haven't even been. You should want me to go.

I do. Of course I do. But this is your first trip. And you only have so much money, so much time. Right?

I could travel longer. Maybe pick up some work.

Sure, said Elin. But you'll want to be back in time for the fall term.

Bets turned away from her mother with a small shrug. Elin couldn't stop herself.

I mean, that's why they call it a gap, honey, because it doesn't go on and on. It's a small, measurable break in a continuum.

Yeah. I suppose.

For the first ten months of her gap year, Bets worked at an independent coffee shop that had recently franchised. It sold twenty-dollar pounds of shade-grown, hummingbird-friendly coffee, espresso drinks and bourbon-peach-sage fritters for four dollars each. The uniform was black jeans paired with the shop's peach-on-black visors and T-shirts with slogans such as "Get Iced," the chain's summer promotion for frappuccinos and cold brews, or "Thank God It's Fried Day," a short-lived campaign to push fritters and beignets—we'll get yelled at for calling them doughnuts, Bets said—and "Express-OH!" when the chain introduced drive-through windows.

Each time Bets landed in the kitchen wearing a new promotional T-shirt, Elin grinned, tried not to laugh. Bets rolled her eyes. Once, when Elin giggled, Bets spit out her fruit punch Gatorade, spraying her mother's blouse from across the room. Elin was late to meet a friend because she had to change—her belly sore from laughing, her discarded top bagged like blood-spatter evidence.

In late March, Bets announced she'd quit the coffee shop.

I need to make more money faster, she said.

Why do you need so much?

There are things I want. I can't rely on you forever.

Bets softened and put her hand on Elin's shoulder.

Shorty.

Tall and pretty, Bets had no problem getting a job in a bar. So she got two. The first was a craft brewery with hand-stuffed bratwurst on Old World Third Street. The other one was a Brady Street cocktail lounge. Now, instead of morning shifts, she started work at 4 p.m. or 8 p.m. She came home after midnight, or later, much later. The sneakers she left on the front mat smelled of spilled beer and bourbon; the clothes she dropped on the basement floor reeked of absinthe and bitters. Elin found little shards of broken coupes and highballs in the cuffs of Bets's pants, and a variety of sunny streaks on her tops. One of her workplaces offered thirteen different mustard options. The other served sparkling wine and jasmine tea, each flute delivered with an opened blossom floating on a pond scum of bubbles. In the morning, Elin could sense a yeasty pong lingering in the house, as Bets slept late: the old-cheese reek of twelve-dollar bespoke pints. Alcohol's bright medicinal notes.

They argued when Elin found out Bets was walking home from Brady rather than spending the money to take a cab.

It's a few blocks, Mom.

Elin begged her.

I will pay you to take a cab. You can charge them all to my credit card. Joy's kid got jumped by three guys with a sawed-off shotgun. Just last week. In Yankee Hill. It was 8 p.m.!

She kept at the argument four days in a row. She wasn't sleeping imagining her daughter cross the North Avenue bridge in the dark.

Okay, okay. Geez, Mom. I'll take a cab. It cuts into my tips, y'know. It means I have to wait that much longer to get what I want.

Thank you, said Elin when she'd rather have asked, What *do* you want?

But stop waiting up for me, okay?

Elin's jaw spasms. She leaves her bed to look at the tooth. If she can see the object of her distress, it will torture her less.

The house has one bathroom, on the second floor.

She peeks around the corner into Bets's dark, empty room. The numbers on her alarm clock say it is 3:05 a.m.

Numbin' out, that's what Bets calls Elin's habit of losing herself.

She'll come up the stairs or turn a corner and find her mother frozen, eyes locked on some mark on the wall, or an object outside the window, mumbling to herself.

You numbin' again, Mom? Bets will say, something fragile in her playful timbre.

Finding my *drishti*.

The bathroom light is dim, and sodium-coloured. There's a wicker shelf on top of the toilet tank, and among other things it holds a box, made when The Lilli convinced Elin's father Tig there might be money in small, beautifully designed items.

Design, her mother had said many times, is a conversation between the object and the space it occupies, a unity flowing between creator and environment. Even a jewellery box, she insisted, is *Gesamskunst*.

The rosewood box has three compartments: a large one Elin uses for her spare makeup collection, another for elastics and hair clips. The third, narrow one holds her instruments of self-torture: nail clippers, tweezers, safety pins, razors, and her vintage dental tool kit.

The throb in Elin's tooth feels tolerable. She runs the hot water until it is really hot and puts her hands under it, just because.

Then she opens the rosewood box—there is an ingenious thumb imprint that lifts the polished top—to fish out her dental kit. Her plan is to slide the magnifying dental instrument onto her tongue until it is in position to reflect the crochety upper tooth in the vanity's mirror. Elin wants to know if it is cracked; a cracked tooth can be babied.

She thinks there might be clove oil in the medicine cabinet, or at least ibuprofen. Even a crushed Aspirin packed around a tooth can soothe a colicky nerve. She'd overheard this tip in the staff room, that think tank of doomers and survivalists.

The dental kit has a mother-of-pearl button. Elin smooths her finger over it and clicks it open.

A shard of mirror, the size of a katydid's wing, is loose inside. Broken. Oh no.

Elin nudges the stray piece back into the space of the cracked mirror. Her eyes tear up. She tries to remember how recently she'd opened the kit, counting on the pellucid smart of the tool's reflection.

When you are a kid, you want to break things. But Bets was no longer a kid.

Though over several weeks when her daughter was twelve, Elin discovered a crack, a chip, a missing handle in small items, thrift-store ephemera, that she loved and left on windowsills and shelves—a crystal salt shaker, a hand-painted porcelain teacup, a Fisher Brothers apothecary bottle.

They were left where they'd always been, but in a way that begged noticing. The teacup was upside down on the saucer. The apothecary bottle moved perilously close to the window ledge. The salt shaker's abalone-button top screwed off and placed beside it. Every three days for a few months: revenge through attrition. Elin fretted about how to confront the girl. She understood destruction in small doses had a sneaky satisfaction.

Out of the blue, she told Bets about her parents' long bouts of silence. She hadn't planned it, but they were eating dinner with a new quiet elongating between them.

The longest one was when I was thirteen, Elin said. The last time Cas, Mette, and I were all living at home together. Almost three weeks! Migod, The Lilli and Tig were stubborn. Acted as if we kids didn't notice. Both of them with these wax museum expressions. That house was tense.

Three days in and Aunt Mette had chewed the cuticles of her fingernails into bloody shreds. Uncle Cas got these pimples on his forehead that festered into sharp white points.

Gross, said Bets.

She scooped a forkful of pasta into her mouth, chewed, studying her mother.

What about you?

Bad dreams.

Elin remembers waking with eyelids dark as prunes.

Like what?

Wrecking things. Taking my father's manhattan glass and flinging it against the fireplace so a flying chunk speared his eye. Grabbing my mother's prized modernist lamps, wringing their necks—they really did look like ugly poultry. Tossing them aside, jerking with live current.

God, Mom, you're so violent.

Elin picked up her plate. She wanted to tell her daughter that she would do anything for her, forgive anything. Instead, she turned her back and started to wash up.

We all have that in us.

On the eighth day of their parents' epic silence, fifteen-year-old Mette refused to eat, a hunger strike, an attempt to get them to argue. Gelid-eyed, The Lilli gathered her elder daughter's plates, breakfast then lunch, as if they were empty, scraping full portions into the garbage. She flashed a wordless glance at their father. He returned one, curare-tipped with that most civil of sentiments: contempt.

By dinner, this unreality—Mette left hungry, excellent food wasted, both unimaginable when things were normal—broke Elin. She swallowed mashed potatoes with tears running down her face that pooled near her peas, making them saltier.

When the house lights were turned off, they gathered in Casper's bedroom. Elin was so grateful for her siblings' magi faces and warm breath in the flashlight and shadow under the tent of her brother's quilt, she started to cry again.

S'okay, El, Mette said. We've got each other.

Later, it was Mette who said at first, yes, abortion, absolutely, you're broke, you're not in contact with the father. Mette who didn't blink when Elin said, I've changed my mind.

And then Mette who made the spare bedrooms of a rambling Riverwest Queen Anne into something pleasant, livable, after Bets, a long baby, pink-brown with robust lungs, was born during an early summer heat wave. Mette, raising up an old futon on bricks, covering it with a gently used eyelet bedskirt so Elin could sleep in the second-floor bedroom with her baby on nights the attic got too hot. Fighting with a young woman over a garage sale rocking chair with large, rounded wicker arms that fit around the body like a shawl. Telling her, I need for it my sister who is having a *baby*. And she is *alone*.

Filling Mason jars with black-eyed Susans and flowering mullein so it felt like a homecoming, despite the oppressive humidity, the baby's angry heat rash.

Placing the rocking chair by the bedroom window at the right height so Elin could watch moths splatter the street light aureoles on hot, humid summer nights; her baby wild-eyed, resolutely awake.

Her sister is implicated in all that goodness, the first year of Bets's life, when Elin thought she'd atomized into the moths, lamplight, breastfeeding, and felt a new wholeness, particulate and joyful.

There's a footfall on the porch, followed by the sound of the key in the door.

Bets.

Elin listens for the motor of a leaving cab but hears none. She closes the case and places the dental kit back inside the rosewood box. She wants to stand at the top of the stairs and confront her daughter.

Did you take a cab like you promised?

She wonders if she was better at parenting a younger child, nimbler with the titrations of trust and candour. Had the twelve-year-old Bets stopped breaking Elin's things after that dinnertime story? Or had Elin stopped looking for broken things?

She flicks off the bathroom light and walks quietly back up the stairs to the attic.

From under her duvet, she hears the stairs creak. Bets is on the second floor. Elin looks at her clock. It's 3:31 a.m. Her alarm goes off in three hours.

There's no point trying to go to sleep, she tells herself.

She dreams she has a cat. And a dog she loves decapitates it.

It's the cat's fault. The animal dies knowing it, too.

The dog has a deep, ugly gash along her cheek. It's clear the cat struck first; but the other pet's justice is too ferocious.

The head rolls past Elin's feet, hits the corner of a door jamb, and turns up to her wearing a taxidermy kitten's expression: bloodless and a bit perplexed.

It looks as happy as any cat ever looks to Elin.

In the dream, she is back living with her siblings in the Burnham house. Casper and Mette don't yet know about the cat; Elin worries how they will react. The injured dog skulks about as if she's already in trouble. Elin aches for her sister and brother, for the pain that is about to divide them from the dog.

Her worry builds. They walk to and from the kitchen and the arches of their feet graze the cat's bloodied neck, yet they don't seem to notice. Elin's head tightens, throbs as Casper and Mette keep moving back and forth. Eventually, they will look down. But if seeing is believing, then perhaps, she thinks, not seeing is another kind of believing, equally powerful. When Mette finally glances at the strange sensation near her bare foot, its Elin's eyes that flicker wildly, seizure-like. Suddenly, she's floating above the situation, and all her feelings are gone. She is empty, barely even interested.

From this new distance, high above her siblings, the cat's head, and the skulking canine, Elin realizes she can close the lid. She does. It feels so much better. As far as she knows, the cat springs back to life (one down, eight to go) to become great friends with the dog. And Casper and Mette remain unwitting, certain of a world where no such indecency is possible.

Elin is surprised to have slept. And to open her eyes at the precise moment she'll recall her dream: Schrödinger's Cat. And Dog.

A thump brings her hand to her jaw: she listens for pain. But the tooth has gone quiet. The thump repeats. It's coming from below her bedroom.

There's no counting on Bets to wake up; that girl sleeps with the luxury of the oblivious.

She pulls her feet out from the comforter, checks the sky, ties on her robe, and grabs her eyeglasses. It is not yet 6:30 a.m.

On the last step from the attic, Elin sees that Bets's second-floor bedroom door is open. The C-shaped curve of her daughter, sitting up in bed, bowed around her laptop, makes her start. So much of the child who once clung to her still there in that profile. Elin feels a lift, followed by a new pressure. Bets is getting ready to leave. This uncharacteristic early rising yet another symptom of its inevitability.

She stands at the bottom of the attic stairs watching her daughter typing: the loose waves of her dark hair tremble with each stroke. Bets licks her bottom lip then pins it with her front teeth. She has plants in the window, suspended in exquisite blown-glass terrariums, lucent spaceships with cacti and succulents in layers of pink and white pebbles, heading to a new planet. A velvety green fern reaches up to them from the windowsill.

You're up early.

Hmmm.

Did you hear the door?

Nnn nnn, Bets says without looking up.

Elin hesitates. She wants to ask what she is working on, but her daughter's mumble has a new modulation, a tonal Do Not Disturb.

A quarter of the way down the stairs to the first floor, the front door is in full view. Sunlight pours through the loose glue-chip glass pane unobstructed by shadows. Elin walks softly into the living room; its bay windows look onto the porch. The sheer curtains freckle with sunlight.

She is wrong.

There is no one there. The sound was imagined.

Her shoulders relax; she loosens the tie of her bathrobe. She is glad to be up early on a weekday morning. No need to rush to school.

Elin turns on the kitchen radio, hears the drawl of the bathroom shower from above, the pitchy pressurization of the heating kettle, and something else still, a plangency that doesn't belong. She lowers the radio volume, listens, and it comes again, a bewildered moan. For an instant, what she hears is her own disembodied worry.

When Bets leaves, there will be nothing left to do but get old. How many times had the thought crossed her mind?

But the sound continues outside her head. Elin removes the kettle from the burner and waits.

There it is once more: long, sonorous, achy.

She peeks back into the front hall. There are no new shadows. She marches forward on sock feet and swings open her front door, exasperated by the tricks she plays on herself. The loose pane settles with a costume-jewellery *tink tink*.

The porch looks empty.

Except not quite.

A thin white dog—muscly, with caramel patches—is tied by a leash to the wood column at the bottom of the porch steps. It has a drooping bow around its neck, a brown envelope hanging from a violet ribbon. Its shoulders stoop at the surprise of her, its ears pinned with a lowly, robust fear.

Elin is unused to dogs. She sits on the open door's ledge and considers the animal. The dog squeezes its eyes as if in pain.

Hello.

Her intuition—that unscientific word again—tells her this is a former stray. It's not a beautiful specimen, not with that diamond-shaped head and those oddly yellow eyes, wide and unctuous.

She's about to offer her hand when Bets thumps down the stairs, bringing a waft of damp hair and laurel-scented soap with her. She pushes past Elin with a familiar, playful roughness.

Oooh, who's this?

With not an ounce of her mother's wariness, Bets untethers the strange animal, leads it up to the porch, where she sits cross-legged and cooing as the dog moves into her lap, licks her face, thumps its tail.

Mom. This dog is so beautiful. These eyes. These eyes. I've never seen anything like them.

Bets unties the silly bow, unthreads the note card. Elin reaches for it, but her daughter is already tearing it open. She flips it around, her forehead scrunched.

It's from Aunt Mette. Cool.

The new animal watches her in a slanting, amphibious way as Elin plucks the card from Bets. The envelope's kraft paper has an ink stamp of a bluebird in the corner.

Inside, in black felt-tip, are Mette's large, looping upstrokes, the kind graphologists attribute to extroverts:

Em,
> This is Mitzi.
> Keep her well.
> Back in time.
> Xoxo
> Me
> P.S. I'm assuming you're better with dogs than cats

Elin stares at the note's few lines. Her sister, notorious for taking on rescue animals despite rarely staying longer than a week in her Chicago townhouse, has left her with a dog, a part lizard named Mitzi. Which means Mette had been in Milwaukee that very morning, and left again, without calling. Or hired a driver. Footsteps on the porch, yes, the knock unlikely. The pane un-rattled. Avoiding conversation? There was a time she'd barge right in, help herself to tea or wine, tell a story then leave.

Back in time, she wrote, as if Mette set the parameters for understanding time.

Does this mean Auntie's coming before the dedication?

Bets's face is buried in the dog's neck, her voice muffled.

A day early.

Awesome. Can't wait to see her 'n Uncle Cas.

For an instant, Elin finds it hard to forgive her daughter's excitement.

3

Elin's last period on Thursdays, Introduction to Secondary Mathematics, or ISM, a course the other teachers call pre-math with a pity-face smirk, begins routinely.

The students are twitchy. The teaching straightforward: concept, example, practice. Rinse, repeat. She doesn't really have to plan, only follow the text and the exercises, a course-in-a-box. The enrolment is small, the regular class duration shortened to accommodate the students' lower concentration levels.

The class starts with a dilemma of scale: In her haste, she has grabbed legal-, not letter-sized, grid paper. They are working on $y = x^2 + b$. She wants them to use half-inch squares; they're easy to count, and each student can visualize the parabola, understanding it first as physical movement along the axes, a beautiful shape, finally a calculation. Faraday, then Maxwell.

Elin turns to see Aliyah holding up a legal sheet with a scolding intensity. She is the unofficial spokesperson for an informal subset within the class who won't acknowledge they are a group: the tidies.

Yes, Aliyah.

Are you gonna hole-punch this for us? How will it fit in our binders?

There are seven tidies in this class, randomly scattered among its four rows. Theirs is a particular distress she understands; she remembers the way Bets could not start her homework until papers, notes, pens, calculator were laid out at right angles to each other. For a few months she would dissolve into tears if Elin rushed this setup before helping her with calculus.

She recognizes the tightness in Aliyah's voice as a deep fear of material chaos, a need to exert control over her small bit of real estate in the cosmos, specifically her ISM binder.

Right now, the other six are as worried about how to fold an 8½-by-14-inch sheet of paper so it doesn't tear its single hole punch and the fold won't bunch up their other pages, with their colour-coordinated dividers.

Rico in the back row rotates the awkward paper so it can take three-hole punches. A dew of sweat gathers above his lip as he works out folding a flap at the top to avoid excess sticking outside the binder. His brow wrinkles.

The remaining students will take a picture of the completed parabolas with their phones, leave the grid paper crumpled on the floor. But the tidies have an archivist's reverence for source material. They want it; they just need it tamed.

Agreed—it's a bit awkward, Elin says. If you want, I brought a few packages of these along.

She holds up a sample. It's an 8½-by-11 card stock pocket with three holes. She raises all the packages so they can be assured there are different hues. Elin demonstrates.

A single neat fold and it slips right in. Or you can just use it for whatever you want.

Aliyah relaxes visibly; she is close to the front of the room, so she's assured of her desired colour.

The class grows quiet: crisis averted. The pencils are out. The exercise explained, and an example at the front for them to reference. She can relax.

Einstein, warmly wrinkled and framed in a corona of white hair and smoking a pipe, watches her from above the whiteboard.

She wonders if he too has grown tired of the quote, a banner of typewriter font that cuts him off at the neck:

Everybody is a genius. But, if you judge a fish by its ability to climb a tree, it will spend its whole life believing it is stupid.

Elin contemplates the quote weekly, wondering if it is true, never arriving at a definitive position.

You're all about that Niels Bohr, miss. That's like the third time you've gone off about the poster thing.

It's Bones from the second row. She'd been talking out loud.

She *had* looked for a Niels Bohr poster for thirty years. Though posters of Bohr are much harder to find. He was preternaturally unquotable, suspicious of any idea reducible to a few clear sentences. Bohr and Einstein were, unsurprisingly, intellectual combatants; more surprisingly, affectionate friends.

It's just frustrating, she said. That you all know who he is and not Bohr.

Cuz Einstein's the genius, right?

Elin could say the consensus is yes, that Einstein was more singularly gifted. But he himself compared Bohr's thinking to music, his highest compliment. (Not knowing, perhaps, that Bohr was tone-deaf.) The first time Einstein came to visit Bohr's Institut Fysik Teoretik, already nurturing the luminaries of quantum mechanics, Bohr, a lifetime cyclist, came on foot to pick him up at the train station and they took the bus back together, becoming so engrossed in their mutual interests, they passed the institution and were far from it before noticing, getting out of the bus to take another heading back, only to dive back into their conversation and miss the stop near the institute again.

That was too inside for most students.

How do you know that, Bones?

He points to the poster.

Exact same picture. Genius Bar, Apple Store.

Oh.

Elin hunches her shoulders, pulls the skin around her jaw to approximate jowls. Titters rise from the back of the room.

You know, Bohr wasn't the greatest in front of a room of students—any room. He wouldn't have believed a quote from one of these posters, because he didn't trust ideas that were too tidy. Honestly, have any of you found a poster quote that really worked out in your life? That was right for every circumstance?

No one answers, but there are eyes that are up. She wonders if they're listening or avoiding the graphing exercise.

How to make physics students out of them? Tell them Bohr was a low-talking, hopeless lecturer whom Schrödinger compared to a tentative theology student when they first met? Or that Heisenberg thought Bohr was more Faraday than Maxwell, more philosopher than physicist, while Ehrenfest loved him unreservedly?

He wasn't confident about math, Elin says. I mean, he needed math, but it didn't come easily to him. So he got help for his proofs. Yet this guy won a Nobel Prize, a year after Einstein.

The ISM classroom is quiet.

Sounds pretty humble, miss, says Bones.

Music comes from a phone behind him.

Humble baby girl, humble baby girl, gonna be
Shut up, baby girl, shut up, humble me

The laughter that follows sounds relieved; she's taken them down a tangent and this is a way out.

Okay. Phone muted. NOW.

Perhaps she takes Bohr too personally. Not only because he's Danish.

They get down to work and this gives her time to think. She jams the dry-erase marker cap into the top of her hand to carve petri dish outlines in her skin. She fills these in with intricate fine-point amoebas. Sharpie pox, she'll say if Joy, who teaches biology, notices with an arched eyebrow.

I get it, miss!

It's Clayton, second row from the back with DIY bangs, late-night-gamer eyes. Elin drops her marker and walks over. His grid paper is spread over the desk. Within the quadrant of an x-y axis is the faint outline of a perfect parabola, a sensual curve cradling a handwritten equation in its bowl; form and formula. As she looks, he takes the sharpened pencil and shows each point to her, as if they are pinprick stars, illuminating the galaxy inside his own head.

He is grinning.

Has she copped out with the rote exercises, the workbooks, the doodling sessions at her desk? Clayton has seen patterns, solved equations, felt wonder.

Excellent, Clay.

She hears an uncomfortable shift, exasperated sigh beside her.

Can you help Myra?

Articulation was the central dilemma of science. That's what Bohr thought. Someone fresh with discovery might say it better than her.

Her students had laughed too when she told them how she couldn't understand fractions. How her grade six teacher drew a flat, round circle on the blackboard and divided it up into pieces like a pie. But Elin couldn't see a pie, only a poorly drawn circle, squished like a cartoon lasso, because she came from a house where an exegesis on whether a curve was perfectly executed was dinnertime conversation. For her parents, mostly.

The teacher handed out an exercise sheet. The other students started working. Elin moved her pencil over the paper, but its sharp tip didn't make contact. She didn't understand. She thought something was wrong with her.

That night, she sat alone at the kitchen table with the exercise sheet and the same pencil, still sharp. Her parents, busy in the studio, debated ideal pencil leads and paper with enough tooth for dark blacks, before battling the proportions of Tig's dining room set. She willed herself to understand the skinny symbols, her own incomprehensible tables, their little ledges with ones on top and fours and twos underneath, like hiding children, and how they added up to numbers without ledges, or worse, some with, in this new, topsy-turvy world where a bigger number under the ledge did not correspond to a bigger quantity in the flat circle, but the reverse.

She'd pushed the heels of her palms into her temples as if comprehension were something she could muscle into her cranium. Her nails pressed so hard against her scalp that brushing her hair would sting for the next two days.

Mette found her in the kitchen and took one look at her face before stealing a few cigarettes from her mother's pocket, and two oranges from the kitchen fruit bowl. In the backyard, they smoked, coughed, and Mette peeled each orange so the skin stayed in one long piece. Before they ate them, Mette divided one into four equal piles of sections, assigned each section a number from Elin's exercise sheet. Then she put the orange back together, rewrapped in its snaking peel. Parts. Whole. After an hour of touching, smelling, and tasting fractions, the whole orange, its pliable divisions, Elin understood. The exercise sheet smelled of smoke and oranges in her backpack the next day; all her answers were correct.

Now Elin meanders between rows of her students, chiding the slowpokes to finish drawing their x-y axes and start plotting their lines, when there's a violent pounding on the classroom door.

The ism room is on the ground floor, in the west wing of the school, where she has an angled, more distant view of the copper beech and the residential streets behind it.

Elin's first instinct is that she's missed something, failed in some necessary vigilance.

Guilt forever jumping the queue, getting ahead of itself.

The students murmur with a bilious excitement. Elin moves to the closed door. The pounding starts again. She can see it shake on its hinges.

There's a face pressed into the door's small pane of glass—bloodshot blue eyes, cheeks dark as plums.

In her decade of teaching at this school, there have been numerous violent fist fights, several stabbings, a few teacher assaults, some gunplay in the parking lot. Students of hers had died while walking across the street, or at the hands of brothers, uncles, friends, enemies, police. But not on school property. This school has avoided that gradation of tragedy.

The boy whose face is pressed against her door has passed through a metal detector and can be seen right now on a CCTV camera by V.H. Phillips's two-man security team. Elin reminds herself of this as she gets up to the little window, turns to it squarely, and quietly reaches with a shaky hand for the button that locks the door.

Rosa Wyzcowski! I need to see her. I need to see her now!

There's a shrillness to the boy's aggression: his cheeks have red blooms that move like manta rays under his skin. Elin has seen this before, the seizure-like rage, the animal state of disinhibition. There's little room for reasoning.

You have to report to the office. Please leave and report to the office. Her voice wavers.

It's a fucking emergency!

He pounds on the door again. She can imagine the skin splitting on his baby finger. Elin sees movement in the handle. He's twisting it and she wonders if he is strong enough to break it. She walks back to her desk, grabs her cellphone, and punches in the security code number. Three of her students also have their phones out. They are filming the whole thing. Faces lit with alertness.

Put those away! Elin points. Spit flies from her mouth. A drop lands on a front-row student's wrist; he stares at it and looks at her with worried eyes.

Rosa Wyzcowski stands up. She's shoving her workbook, pencil case, and grid paper in her backpack; her breath hiccups.

Rosa, sit down. You're not going anywhere.

Elin moves toward the door and faces the boy. He's pulled away a few inches, just enough for her to see that he's a big kid with football shoulders and a mop of oily hair, a wide, pimpled forehead. His face is blotchy, slicked with emotion.

I need to see Rosa. We have to go. Pleeaassse. PLEASE.

How many of her young students, girls all of them, had said to her, I can't help who I fall in love with, miss. Her well of empathy feels cracked as a salt flat.

The door's windowpane has his greasy cheek print.

Back away from this door and report to the office immediately.

A desk scrapes on the floor. Rosa Wyzcowski is right behind her. Elin hears her apnea breath and turns.

Miss, miss, Jeezus, that's my brother. My jaja's sick, miss. Let me go, please. Please.

She's crying now. Her face the same quilt-work of pinks as the one pressed into the pane a moment earlier. Elin hears the security guards arrive in the hall. She blocks Rosa's view.

The sounds of struggle reach them muffled. A body thuds against the door. Rosa yelps. The boy cries out then goes quiet. A gargled panic fades down the hallway. Elin's hand shakes when she unlatches the lock ten minutes later.

Go to the office, Rosa. Wait for me there.

She turns to her class. No one makes eye contact. A girl in the back row has been chewing her sweatshirt cuff. The wet stain, Elin notes, is in the shape of $y = -x^2$, the inverted parabola, tomorrow's lesson. There are twenty minutes left in the period. V.H. Phillips has rules about dismissing students early, freeing them in the hallways before the other classes, then into the city before their parents come off shift or expect them home.

Okay, she says. We're done for the day.

Her students move as if the classroom's tight membrane has been punctured. They empty as one large gush. The quiet they leave is disconcerting.

———

Jaja is specific in its familiarity, Elin thinks, looking out toward the beech at the end of the day. Like *morfar.*

Her hips rest on the window ledge. Science had new things to say about trees, some of it controversial. Including how they knew their offspring, and the elders protect those related to them, and even those who were just close by.

Other kids go stay with their grandparents, Mette had said when she was fifteen and their parents weren't talking to each other. Why don't we know ours?

They knew tidbits about their father's parents because Aunt Petrine made fun of them.

Mette had a lighter that she flicked and flicked: its small blue flames filled the space under Casper's quilt with a sharp butane-and-carbon reek, the smell of espionage.

Not hers. Not The Lilli's. She doesn't even have pictures. Weird, right?

Possibility, its Ouija board planchette, moved in front of their eyes.

Elin's holding her phone in one hand, her thumb hovering over it, when she hears the chiding shush of good leather soles on linoleum. Principal Preet, his hands tucked behind his back, stands a foot inside her door and stares.

Everything okay, Ms. Henriksen?

She squints, and rights herself. He crosses his arms, leans against a desk. Away from his office with its maddening houseplants, he seems more like someone who belongs: his jacket is off, his sleeves rolled up.

So, he says, how might that have gone better?

Elin shakes her head, moves back to her desk, bewildered. Had she already started recording when the principal entered?

Today. What happened in class. Your class.

Elin sighs.

Look, he says. We sort of have to make this place a little friendlier.

Friendlier?

Yeah. Y'know, more welcoming. Lots of good research showing that makes a difference in these sorts of schools.

These sorts?

So about today, the incident, he says.

Elin gestures to the hall, where the small, vitreous eyeball of a cctv camera looks back at them.

Bit of a mixed message, right? The welcoming part.

Not ideal.

I followed the protocols.

She doesn't mention the early class dismissal or leaving Rosa to find her way to the office alone.

It was a family emergency, he says. The grandparents are their guardians. Sad situation. Granny's not doing well.

Grandpa. *Jaja* means grandpa.

Principal Preet surveys Elin's desk: there's a flattened muffin wrapper beside her laptop, an action painting of crumbs over the keyboard.

The kids and their social worker are pretty upset about the way it went down. So, we need to find a workable compromise with these situations, Ms. Henriksen.

Call me El.

Principal Preet stands up and gives her the smile of an indulgent parent.

All right then, El. Let's do better.

He turns to leave. At the door, he bends to pick up a stray piece of graph paper, turns, and hands it to her with a nod.

Elin looks down. The name *R. Wyzcowski* is pencilled in the right-hand corner. There is a grimy footprint over another perfect parabola.

Rosa had understood the exercise too.

4

At the end of the day, a package, thick and orange, sticks out of Elin's mailbox, visible from her parking spot across the street.

The first time Bets ordered something online, she was ten. The junior detective kit that came in the mail was put on Elin's credit card after Bets stacked up nearly twenty dollars of single bills and quarters from squirrelled allowances and slid them across the kitchen table to her mother like a poker debt. That envelope was larger and duller. But when Bets saw it, she held her breath, and clasped it as if it was the worst kind of surprise, getting something she wanted, before disappearing to her bedroom, opening it away from her mother's eyes.

Later, Elin popped her head in, saw Bets's small desk cleared for the kit's items, now laid out with forensic tidiness:

magnifying glass
notebook
fingerprint brush
ink pad
cornstarch
black light pen
crime scene tape

It reminded Elin of when Casper, balancing on a garbage can, denting its metal top, pulled a nicotine-coloured canvas rucksack from their parents' carport rafters. She couldn't help herself. She stood in Bets's doorway explaining how Mette undid the tarnished buckles and

a time-travel odour vented into the day's heat. With the same reverence as Bets had, they'd laid out that package's contents on the cement
floor: French cigarettes, a yellowed newspaper, a flare, a paint-flecked
bandage tin. Casper found the bone-handled pocket knife, and a small
canvas change purse with tiny, dull aluminum coins.

Elin stopped. Bets sat at her desk with her back to her mother, her
shoulders rounded as if to shield her detective kit from a parent's
magic-embezzling eyes.

What mystery will you solve?

Bets shrugged, not turning. Elin waited, then collected the torn
envelope and walked away, wishing she'd keep her stories to herself.

Later, when Elin passed Bets's bedroom again, the magic kit was
put away and stowed out of sight. She could hear the television on in the
living room downstairs, recognized the PBS after-school-special jingle.

Wanna watch?

Bets called out when she hit the bottom stairs.

Elin didn't. There was dinner to make, laundry, lesson planning, a
heap of marking.

It's sea otters.

Bets used her tone for making things okay again: a peace offering
of agile mothers and pups, with their uncanny adaptation of tools. Elin
sank into the sofa beside her, just as a zoo handler held up her arm to
the camera, displaying an otter bite that snapped her wrist, left her
forearm ballooning with bacterial infection. There was footage of a
male otter kidnapping a pup, holding its head underwater, until its
mother gave up her dinner, a ransom of sea urchin viscera and cracked
abalone. Another female was missing half her nose—an injury sustained during mating. The special ended with gleeful otters diving and
playing, and a link to the World Wildlife Fund's website.

Bets was unperturbed.

Mom, what did you expect? They're related to wolverines.

More online purchases followed, the detective kit giving way to
band merchandise, obscure skate-punk toques, vintage denim arriving

in rolls, boxes, and squishy plastic sleeves. Each new package lit up Bets's face as it had when she was ten. Elin had learned not to ask. So when her daughter arrived at the dinner table wearing a new T-shirt or holding a decal she was excited about, looking for her mother to share in the fun, it was a windfall. It was better.

This was not how she'd felt when Casper, whose adaptation was for burying things as well as exhumations, sent Elin packages during the five years when he, his mother, and Mette stopped speaking to her.

Those large envelopes arrived monthly that first year of their estrangement, then less predictably. Six months after the last one was delivered, they all started talking again.

At the very most, Casper scribbled *FYI—C* on the top of a photocopied stack. Otherwise, there was no trace of her brother in the contents. The address label was typewritten. There was no return address.

His envelopes stuck out of her mailbox on North Bremen—she'd painted it bright red—so she'd see the brown tops as she pulled up in her car. She might have the radio on or be singing aloud to a song that revived her sense of possibility when a peripheral glance at the front of her house would register the small detail, the visitor who'd ruin the party.

Elin gets out of the car, grabs the large orange package without looking at it, holds it against her chest. Her mouth is dry.

She sits on the front porch in a disintegrating wicker chair.

Mom, that chair is disgusting, throw it out, Bets says every spring, after it has weathered another year outside, suffering the assaults of Wisconsin snow and rain, fraying like a septuagenarian's webworm eyebrows.

At the first ray of warm-enough sun, Elin retrieves the outdoor cushion from the basement, reunites it with the wicker. She's waiting for the seat to rot through, for her bottom to land on the porch, for the unremarkable chair to announce it's done.

It wheezes and lists slightly under Elin's weight. A zebra spider moves along the arm, using her wrist as an expressway. She tucks the package under her feet.

It won't be from him.

Plenty of time.

For the years they didn't speak, such packages became Casper's side of a one-sided shouting match.

The late afternoon sun is warm. Poppies and lupines swell open in her neighbour's yard. Someone's lilac tree is in bloom. The air's already boozy with summer.

Elin's walkway cuts through a tangle of periwinkle and golden Jenny. Manitoba irises push up their chartreuse stalks in search of sunlight. Whatever else grows there does so at the whim of the dense ground cover. There are surprises: spiderworts and primulas seeded by the larcenous little paws of squirrels arriving from the neighbours' front yards. Years earlier, a chocolate tulip streaked with bright gold blossomed in her garden; the autumn before, she'd watched her neighbour tear open a special order of Dutch bulbs and kiss them as if they were his toddler's cheeks.

Casper found the rucksack on a June day much like this one, when Elin turned seven, after Tig drove off in the family's cream-coloured Corvair with its red-licorice interior to teach a summer semester at the Minneapolis College of Art and Design. The days leading up to his departure were marked by a low, rumbling tension at the dinner table, their mother's words extra-barbed, their father sinking further behind his newspaper. The heat set in. And Elin, Mette and Casper took shelter in the carport.

They'd passed the rucksack items to each other, pressed them to their noses, turned them around in their fingers: the coins' unfamiliar lightness and holes, the softness of the cigarette's faded teal package and its stale tang, the knife handle's delicately veined glamour, its blade that flicked and unflicked with gritty resistance.

They weren't listening for the door that opened into the garage. Mette had just drawn a velvet sachet from an interior pocket and was about to loosen its drawstrings when The Lilli's heels ripped across the cement floor, fast as a torn seam.

What are you doing?

Mette yowled when her mother's long nails dug into the side of her neck.

Move.

Her face raw with betrayal, The Lilli shoved each item back inside the rucksack, glared into the eyes of her children, and said only, It doesn't belong to you, before disappearing with it into the house. They were locked out until dinner. They hadn't had lunch.

Elin had admired the chocolate tulip's contrary beauty against the sentimental Easter colours of her garden's other misfit blossoms. But she gave in to the stress of having something that didn't belong to her; she eventually dug it out, tossed it over the fence into her neighbour's garden under cover of darkness.

When she and Casper resumed talking to each other as adults, she told him that story, and he howled.

In a flash, he was his old self, as jubilant as he'd been when they were young and played ferociously—card games, hide-and-seek, capture the flag—and loved each other without saying so.

Don't try a life of crime, El, he said. You'll starve.

The bulky envelope comes out from under the desiccated wicker chair where Elin confronts the address.

She sighs with relief at the large, life-affirming black felt-tip.

Mette's handwriting, unmistakably. Skyward, heart-forward loops, swift downstrokes, open e's, round a's.

Extrovert

Celebrity

Loyal Friend

Creative Genius

That's what a graphologist had told her, one who claimed not to recognize her face or to ever have heard of Mette's ubiquitous "He Looks Good Leaving," covered and covered again, by everyone from Vegas headliners to hair metal bands to lonely girls with Casio keyboards and a YouTube channel.

The graphologist reminded Elin of the old Polish lady who came over to babysit when they were small, and made a slurping sound when she drank tea, watching them over the lip of her china cup.

Mette Eleonara and *Elin Margrethe,* she'd said, eyeing the sisters. Your mother named you to feel clever. Made you mirrors of each other. Maybe *she* wanted one. A mother looking for herself in her daughters won't always like what she sees. Worse is not seeing herself at all.

Elin does a Bets: She squishes and prods. She shakes and pinches. Inside the package are at least three things. One is rock-hard and spiky, intriguing. The other is soft and lumpy. A third squeaks, loses air, refills, squeaks again.

This is the Mette she adores: spontaneous, generous, whimsical. The same sister who'd taught her about fractions, and by her high school years was skipping classes to cook at Outpost Natural Foods, where she had an affair with an organic farmer ten years her senior so most of her adolescence was spent exhausted from overwork, saving money for studio time, and swerving from despair to hope with every café delivery of free-range eggs and baby spinach.

Laughing, Mette has filled this package for Elin. High on dope or mantras, alone or not alone, in a sketchy motel or a five-star hideaway, she's written the note. (Elin can feel the card; there's always a card with a bird, and she is grateful for this predictability.)

Elin takes a big breath and rips. The quilted envelope's contents spill in her lap:

A squeaky bath toy

A bag of organic vegan dog treats

A large velvet sachet holding something hard, prickly, and palm-
sized

A greeting card with a roseate spoonbill on its front and inside:

Em,

    Mitzi gets toy and treats. You, the rock.

    Work it out, old gal.

    Soon, soon, soon,

    Love and popsicles,

    Me

The rucksack Casper found was not seen again. Elin never forgot that day's humiliation of peeing in the back garden in full sun, already dehydrated, pants down for the neighbours to see, head swooning. But it was leavened by a delicious revelation: how things hid inside other hidden things, an undiscovered universe of nesting dolls.

Later, when they were adults, Elin kept each package her brother sent. She opened it, read it, and worked herself through a bottle of wine, a piccolo of champagne, and, painfully, two miniatures of Grand Marnier hoarded from a motel minibar. The next morning, she threw up and went to an 8:30 a.m. Advanced Differential Equations class with a cranky Bets clutching a Barney sippy cup.

The reports Casper sent were neatly printed, stapled, and collated. Elin lay awake at night imagining if he'd asked an assistant to do it, or if, in some squall of shame, he'd waited until others left the office.

She cried, but did not drink, after opening the second package with its new stack of scientific and certain-looking studies, a lacework valance of Ph.D.s casting a shadow to mid-page.

When the third package came, she didn't open it. She called her brother. He didn't pick up; perhaps it was better that way.

If she imagined what she'd say to him, she'd start sounding clear, logical. Inevitably, that wouldn't last.

Cas, why are you doing this to me? Why?

Instead, she slipped the reports back into the envelopes in the exact order they came in and wrote with her Sharpie on the left-hand corner of the flaps—the dates they arrived, the number of reports contained therein, and total number of pages. Doing this made the envelopes her study subjects, dispassionately observed, measured, and recorded. It separated her from them.

With Mette's packages, Elin is free to be as disorderly as she likes. She collects the items, drops them back into this other envelope, and makes a sloppy fold of the ripped opening.

She remembers that sea otters sleep in forests of kelp, the plant sea urchins would decimate unchecked by the otters' appetites. They do this together, sometimes dozens of them, and they hold each other's paws, so no one drifts away in the night, an entanglement of plant and otters that's called a raft by the people who study them.

She reaches for her key, but the door handle gives.

The house is open. Inside, Bets is singing.

5

Twelve unread *New Yorker* magazines are piled up on Elin's bathroom floor, beside a lit aromatherapy candle Bets gave her for her birthday, and a glass of wine.

She slips into the bergamot-lychee-scented bath already regretting having to leave it, willing the evening to slow down, expand into an infinite languor of warm water, glasses of wine, and quiet, one thin and delicious layer of the space-time's *mille feuille*.

The magazines each have a Post-it Note sticking out the top; she's marked that issue's must-read with a bright, optimistic tongue of sticky paper.

The articles she's chosen are invariably long reads on topics such as Silicon Valley's failure to recruit women or weather manipulation in China or weird parasitic wasps invading the Midwest. Up until a year ago, she'd read the political articles. Now they give her arrhythmia.

After an hour, only one of the Post-it Notes has been removed. That issue is dimpled from her wet fingertips. A corner drips from when she fell asleep mid-read and the magazine listed into the bathwater. Now a folded page has tattooed her thighs with type. She starts rifling through the other issues, ignoring her own recommendations. The water cools and she turns the tap on with her toes. She reads the film reviews, the Briefly Noted books, and stares at the back-page cartoon caption contest, willing herself to come up with a winning line, fearing her wit's already outmatched by subscribers from Halifax and

Portland, who no doubt also tackle the long reads, especially the political ones.

She holds her breath at the sound of loud *thunks* from downstairs, as if bodies were doing a rowdy square dance on her front porch.

Bang, shuffle, bang.

Knock on wood.

Elin wishes she hadn't had the wine. She pulls herself out of the bath and a swoon of low blood pressure forces her to grip the cool edge of the pedestal sink to steady herself.

The bangs repeat—thunderous, a bit panicky.

She pulls on underwear, reaches for her robe, ties it loosely, and moves to the stairs. There's water running down the back of her neck, her knees. She makes footprints on the hardwood.

Part of the way down, she sees the silhouette of Bets's head, the hair and height so distinct, yet there's a tilt that looks unnatural, wrong. And another shadow too, one she does not recognize.

Earlier that evening, when Bets was leaving, she'd tried to slip past Elin. She was wearing her Doc Martens with a black miniskirt, fishnet stockings, and a T-shirt emblazoned with the Baroques' *Purple Day* album cover. (Mette had given her the shirt. For a short while, she'd gone out with the lead singer.)

You look so cool, Elin said.

There's a party at a friend's.

Work friend? Someone I know?

Bets shook her head.

Elin missed the promotional T-shirts and the boxes of day-old pastries showing up on the kitchen counter, when Bets's café friends hung out. The bar friends have not been introduced to her.

I'll be late, Bets said. Don't worry about me.

She emphasized the last phrase wryly. At eighteen, Bets was three years under drinking age. The rules allowed her to work in a bar as long as she didn't consume.

A day earlier, Elin heard a talk show therapist call low expectations a toxic offshoot of permissive parenting. They're just as much a prison as overly high ones, the woman had said, her tone nasal and hectoring. It nibbled at Elin during the day: had she failed to give Bets the space to be ambitious?

On the way home, she'd noticed a new gluten-free bakery, Grain Relief, was opening up in Murray Hill. She mentioned it casually, or so she thought.

You'll learn how to bake and there'd be tips, and you would have evenings free. Then, if you wanted to get a prereq out of the way at Marquette or UWM, you'd be ahead of the game. Even do something fun—music, programming, dance.

Bets had listened, her smile a bit shaky.

Okay, Mom. I'll think about it.

Now, as she moves down the stairs, she loathes herself for the tiny whirr of vindication—her fears had been right—that wheedles into her rising panic.

Whatever has happened, Bets has come home. She can stand up, which means her limbs must work. There are no sirens, no screaming, no shots being fired in pursuit. Whatever it is can be endured.

When she swings the front door open wide, she wants to throw up.

Bets's head lolls on her neck weirdly. Her face is quilted with puffy welts. One eyelid is shut. Her bottom lip is split. Her mascara is running. The collector's item T-shirt is torn, the fishnets are ripped. One of her boots is gone. No purse.

She is being held up by an acne-scarred guy, not a boy, a man who is old, too old to be anywhere near a girl Bets's age. He's wearing a white T-shirt under a leather motorcycle jacket with black skinny jeans and army boots. He has a scruffy beard, silver rings on too many of his fingers, and smirking, calculating eyes.

And he's just about to say something when Bets falls into her mother's arms.

Elin stumbles backward under her daughter's weight.

Cotton pads

Hydrogen peroxide

Ibuprofen

Polysporin

Elin can't find them fast enough. As she snaps ice cubes out of their trays, her hands shake uncontrollably. She reaches for the bowl of ice and sends a dirty water glass near the sink's edge flying to the floor, where it smashes, a small carnation of shards arcing around her that she sees but cannot register, her bare feet already rushing to her daughter's side.

The trajectory that stretches out for them now includes painful examinations, horrible questions, skeptical law enforcement, trauma counsellors, nightmares, fear of going outside, fear of being alone, fear of never feeling safe or whole or lovable again, and the hollowing back and forth to courtrooms with their degraded notions of justice.

Tears drip off the edge of her nose.

She does not let the man come inside her house. He is still there on the porch smoking while Elin kneels by the couch where Bets lies and presses ice into her daughter's beautiful messed-up face, wipes away streams of mascara, dabs her lip with Polysporin.

Oooh, says Bets, as if her tongue has been stung by hornets. Hurts.

Elin eases the remaining boot off Bets's foot and wraps a blanket around her body in its torn clothes. She wants to ask, what happened?

She does not want to know.

After she opens the door, stands in its jamb, takes a deep breath that doesn't quell her sobbing, notices the man still there, registers him dropping his cigarette onto a pilfered allium and starting to say something, Elin lunges.

She goes at him for a good three minutes, even after Bets cries out from the couch for her mother to stop. The man lets her scratch, punch, and knee him, until finally saying, Hey, ease up.

I didn't do anything to her, he says. I didn't touch her. I brought her home. Hold up, lady, I brought your kid home.

A neighbour comes out and intervenes, pulls Elin off the man, suggests he leave.

Elin has his skin under her fingernails. Her bathrobe has come open.

6

On Friday morning, after they get through a night of concussion watch and Elin finally lets Bets sleep, she calls the school to cancel her first period via voice mail.

Bets wakes up before 9 a.m. The secretary who listens to the school's voice mail will have already reported Elin's absence to Principal Preet.

Mom, you have to apologize. Big time. I mean, that was some crazy shit.

Her face is discoloured, less swollen. She is unexpectedly animated, hungry, and talkative.

Stay calm, Mom.

Okay.

I started a brawl.

The house party was dud, she adds.

She'd left with her new friend Maya for a retro '80s Battle of the Bands at Mad Planet. There was a lineup.

These girls in front of us, Mom, I mean, you should have seen them. Total Tosa basics.

Tosa basics? When did you start talking like that?

Bets ignores her.

White jeans, flat-ironed hair. Giggling, like it was super-edgy to be slummin' it in Riverwest. They were with two beefy guys in custard–coloured Lacostes. So, whatever, hilarious, right? But these girls start throwing nickels at a homeless man who'd asked for change. He was out of it, leaning up against a post. They toss nickels at him like they're throwing peanuts at a zoo. Like he's not human.

Mom, that's so wrong, right?

Elin nods. She's still stuck on something unrecognizable about Bets and wondering if the changes had all come during her gap year or started before. All of this culture's problems, Mette once said, are problems of attention. (Her sister had just finished her first retreat at the Shambhala Centre in Murray Hill.) Why hadn't she noticed sooner how her daughter had changed?

I call them out, nicely at first, says Bets.

Hey, ladies, what you're doing is, well, pretty fucking rude. Either hand the gentleman the change or don't give him anything.

They just look at me and laugh and roll their eyes. And then one of them—you know, total cheerleader type—starts it up again.

So, I step out of line. I stand between them and the homeless guy and I look right at them and say, I asked you to stop.

Oh, Bets.

But Mom? You want me to stand up for what's right. You taught me that.

Of course. But there's a difference between being principled and being reckless, putting yourself directly in the way of danger.

A nickel, Mom. I put myself in the way of a nickel. Maya was right behind me. She's compact, all muscle, you know, training for MMA. They realize no one in that line is on their team. Even the beefy guys. So, they stand down.

I tell myself to forget it and have a good time. The bands are decent, the place is packed. Maya and I are having a laugh, dancing a bit. But those girls are watching me, because when I go to the washroom, two of them follow. I'm putting on some shimmer when the cheerleader leans in right beside me and pulls at one of my curls.

She touched your hair.

It gets worse.

Love your hair, she says. Isn't her hair beautiful, Ash?

Don't touch me, I tell her.

Oh, jihadists have such lovely hair.

She said that?

Yeah. The racist bitch.

What did you do?

I laugh at her. This girl is just so stupid, she doesn't realize that she doesn't know anything. She's too stupid for me to feel insulted.

I move to leave, and she stands in my way, so I push past with a little shove. It wasn't even hard, but she hits the hand dryer with a little squeak, like a plastic bath toy. Such a joke.

Now the whole night's kinda wrecked. I'm ready to go, but don't want to abandon Maya without saying goodbye. So I'm looking for her, and suddenly I'm grabbed from behind. It's one of the beefy boyfriends, the one in the pink shirt. He gets me in some varsity-wrestling-champ armlock, and he drags me into a corner away from the bar and the dance floor, where the collection of Barbies are waiting. That chickenshit holds me down while they just have at it. Kicking and scratching and punching. The cheerleader rips my T-shirt.

Oh, Bets. Oh, damn.

That's when Curt shows up. Sees the whole thing. He crunches the guy in the temple using his fist with all those rings. The dude lets me go. By then the bouncers have been alerted and they're moving in. And Mom, I couldn't help myself. That idiot girl who ripped my T-shirt, pulled my hair, I turned around and decked her. She went sailing back. She flew.

I didn't know I was that strong. Of course, that's what the bouncers see: the Persian kid taking down the Wisconsin milkmaid.

Persian? Since when are you Persian?

Bets ignores her.

Curt grabs my hand and pulls me through a back hall; he knows the place, he sets up for the bands, and we're out in the alley, and he's calling for a cab. I'm confused. Like, why do I have to run away, slink out the back?

It's not till I'm sitting in the cab that I start feeling it, the adrenalin wears off, and my head starts to throb.

We can lay charges, Bets. We can ask for footage.

Bets goes quiet.

You don't understand, Mom. The punch I threw was the one that really landed. It was a good punch, Mom. That one must have hurt.

Oh.

Alone in the kitchen, Elin sweeps up the broken glass from the night before, when a shard had landed point first in the soft hollow beside her big toe, and she was too distressed to notice. Bits of glass wink among bloody footprints on the tile floor.

She sees her father on a rooftop, staring along Rosenørns Allé, when Copenhagen's Forum explodes, the very place Arne Jacobsen had built the House of the Future years earlier. The original Forum's glass roof shattered upward, into the heavens, so it hailed slivers.

What was it her mother had said? That summer Casper found the rucksack?

Danes cannot ruin Danish things.

According to The Lilli, Tig said it first. But of course, she told the story.

The Holger Danske saboteurs planned to bomb Copenhagen's Forum rather than let the Germans take it over, use it for barracks.

He stayed up all night arguing about it. He broke blood vessels; the whites of his eyes ran with red.

They didn't listen.

The next day, a young boy on a Long John bicycle carrying a crate of Tuborg with a hundred pounds of explosive tucked inside it rode past the German guards. It was done.

Bad weather, The Lilli said. The kind of rain cement and broken glass make.

Slivers knit themselves into her father's open palms. Blood pearled around them before it ran down his wrists.

Elin empties the dustpan and imagines an entitled girl from a rich suburb where a mom and dad may be friends with a Republican governor, the same one who was systematically gutting funding for inner-city education, a girl with a once-delicate nose forever misshapen by a punch.

Or a jaw that needs wiring.

Other than this stranger named Curt, no one had seen what had happened to Bets. But the girl taking the punch—all her friends were witnesses.

This house. She's regretted the sharply gabled, workmanlike Queen Anne almost as long as she's owned it, believing it was the first of many she'd have: perhaps a cream-brick Federalist three-storey in Brewers' Hill was next, or an open-concept loft in the Third Ward's historic warehouses.

Restless nights, with Bets asleep on the back seat, she'd driven slowly through other neighbourhoods imagining her other homes. This one, if I meet someone who can help with payments. This one, when Bets is out of elementary school.

Over fifteen years, on a punitive schedule, she paid off a second mortgage, the one that financed her degree, the degree that was supposed to make their lives bigger. Now she's ready to do it again. For Bets.

The refused scholarship hurt, though. The space between Elin's eyebrows cramps thinking about it.

There will be no next house.

The Lilli once told Elin that a home was something you have a relationship with—it's possible to love it more than members of your family.

I go to sleep in a Frank Lloyd Wright house and wake up in one, The Lilli said. It doesn't matter to me if anyone knows or not.

In fact, it had mattered. Elin overheard Aunt Petrine yell out at a dinner party—they'd all gotten drunk and vicious—that the Burnham Avenue houses were part of an ill-fated partnership between Wright and a Milwaukee developer to create a low-cost suburb on the outskirts of the old South Side. The company, American System-Built Homes, went bankrupt after only five homes were complete.

Prefab kit houses were beneath Wright, her aunt said, her tannin-stained lips wet and vulpine. Besides this neighbourhood is getting dangerous.

Her mother uninvited Petrine to the next holiday dinner.

But not before Petrine dropped by North Bremen, and said only, Solid. Affordable. It will keep you dry.

She is still paying off the bathroom. The backyard needs landscaping. She's ignoring the slight lift in the roof tiles at the right corner. The eaves leak.

Now she wishes she'd loved it more.

We could lose it all, Elin thinks. Even a small life can shatter.

Hon, did you get your purse back from the bar?

Bets is eating a bowl of milk-soggy cereal. Her lip and eye are crusted. One side of her face is mottled: yellow-purple, green-brown. Despite being underappreciated, the house is generous with sunlight; the kitchen fills with the soft heat of early summer.

You might get your friend Maya to call for you.

Bets gives her mother a baleful look.

Nobody takes a purse to a club, Mom. I had everything I needed in my skirt pockets. I lost my house key and my fake ID in the ruckus.

Elin crosses her arms.

No, the ID is not traceable to me, in case you're wondering.

Relieved, still worried, Elin tries to be cheerful: she wants to ask Bets if she needs to talk through what happened, if she is angry or disappointed or newly afraid. But her thoughts keep getting sucked inward by the gyre of causality—a mother's nemesis. Did Bets work in a bar because Elin had? Had those few guilty glasses of wine when she was pregnant led them here? And what about the freezing February night when Bets teethed with pugilistic rage and a desperate, exhausted Elin dipped her soother in gin? Her own mother gave them gripe water when it still contained alcohol: poor parenting's damning epigenesis.

Paradoxically, this makes her want to yell at her daughter. How dare you? How dare you risk everything?

A glance at her phone tells her she can make her second-period class. Principal Preet's reproachful mouth, the impatient foot tap, are to be avoided.

Can you call a friend to stay with you today, hon?

For a fleeting instant, someone smaller and hurt stares out through Bets's eyes. As quickly, her daughter retreats behind the drawn bow of a pained smile.

Sure, Mom.

She may need space, Elin tells herself; this new Bets is someone she barely knows.

In the staff room at lunch, Elin keeps looking out the window at the copper beech, visible now from its east side. The leaves look brown-purple like settling bruises. Elin should be with her daughter.

She sinks far into the lounge's stained couch and pretends to be absorbed in something on her phone, though it is uncharged. Joy was supposed to meet her here, and Joy is the only one who will understand, tell her something wise and only half-true about parenthood, laugh at the absurdity of wanting a child to reflect back an amplified version of your character, your imagined better self.

The new art teacher, a thirty-something woman with a sleek chestnut ponytail, precise bangs, and bright-red nails, sits down across from her instead. Elin has been introduced to her twice and can't remember her name. The art teacher is keen to chat.

Elin puts her phone down, resists crossing her arms in front of her, though she wants to. She tenses into a smile. Her stomach is tight.

I hope this isn't weird, says the art teacher. But I was at The Art Museum on the weekend. They've got a show on mid-century modern design in America. And I noticed they included a few pieces from their permanent collection. There was a dining room set and a really sleek vase by a Milwaukee designer, someone I'd never heard of: Tig Henriksen.

Elin takes in a deep breath.

That's your name, isn't it? I was wondering if it's Danish.

Yes.

I thought so. There can't be many Danes in Milwaukee. I mean Racine, sure. But the city?

Swimming in Swedes and Norwegians.

Elin hasn't the stomach for a conversation about Milwaukee's endless summer festivals, whether there is a Danish one, or why all of them, even HmongFest, serve bratwurst and beer. Not today.

So, are you related?

He was my father.

The art teacher slams her mug on the coffee table and claps her hands.

No effin' way! That is the coolest. You're the daughter of a Danish modernist designer.

Elin sees her father bent over his drafting table in the second-floor bedroom converted to a sunny studio: his lips flattened midway between a grimace and a smile, his forehead pulled in toward one dent between his eyebrows. The light around him umber-gold.

The woman's eyes slide along Elin's wildly printed wrap blouse, jersey skirt, capri tights, and ballet flats. And she wants to say, yes, it's rebellion against all that structure, good tailoring, irreproachable taste.

So, where did he train?

He was a student at the Royal Danish Academy of Fine Arts. Before the war.

Like Arne Jacobsen!

She could tell the woman that very gallery would soon be named for him. Casper's idea; if Tig was alive, he'd turn one hundred next month. The exhibition would go, but her father's full name in eight-inch-high Weiss Antiqua font would embellish the lintel. His designs, donated by Casper, would be put into storage.

The gallery naming cost money. Most of it was Casper's and The Lilli's, though Elin suspects Mette contributed at the last minute. Only she had not helped pay for the dedication. There was Bets's future to consider.

They knew each other, Elin says. My father revered him.

Holy shit! says the art teacher. Jacobsen's iconic chairs—the Ant, the Swan, the Egg. The limited editions in perfect condition. Weren't you blown away?

The woman presses her hands to her lips. Elin can't admit she hasn't seen the show; she's avoiding it. Now she's dizzy with remembered sensations. Tig's warm-wool-and-benedictine-hair-tonic smell. Dust motes riding the studio's angled rays of light. The click of broken pencil leads. Paper fibres stuck to her father's fingertips like down.

His working posture was to push one palm into the paper while his free hand held a mechanical pencil with 4H lead so only a third of it appeared above the grip of his middle and forefingers.

You must have a house full of mid-century modern, the art teacher says.

Elin shakes her head. Her staunchly anti-*hygge* mother could not abide Elin's decor. She has not so much curated her possessions as allowed them to congregate haphazardly, something The Lilli read as a repudiation of the family's ideological good taste, the discipline of a singular aesthetic. Only the Narwhal worked. Tension without intention, Mette called it. As a result, it was the first thing visitors noticed.

Just one piece. A chair.

The first sketch appeared spindle-like to her child's eyes, something that would prick her, make her go to sleep. Its front and back legs, two contiguous arcs, flatten ever so slightly into armrests at their greatest diameters, held in place by the relaxed V of the seat. Its backrest squeezes like a raindrop into the narrowest arc of curved wood.

Joy arrives and stands listening to the conversation, eyes already scolding Elin.

Amazing, says the art teacher. I'd kill to see it. Y'know, sometime.

Sure, says Elin, and she can't help but add, Sometime.

The last two words have a precise clip, like a firmly closed door.

Elin counts to three slowly in her head. Then the art teacher glances at Joy, lifts up her mug, and leaves with a nice-talking-to-you nod, her faced stained with an awkward heat.

Elin lets out a sigh. Joy falls into the vacated spot on the couch.

That was generous, she says.

A few years earlier, on a grey weekend afternoon, Elin pressed the TV remote and stumbled on a documentary series called *The Giants of Modernism*. Her father's famous chair design flickered before her. A crisp BBC announcer with a Manchester inflection stood over the very drawing she'd seen as a child, now in an archivist's drawer in the Copenhagen Museum of Design.

In the late afternoon of Scandinavian cool, the announcer said, was a chair with the unlikely name Narwhal.

Its creator, the Danish-American Tig Henriksen, would not be a major name in mid-century modernism.

Henriksen fashioned himself after Jacobsen but couldn't quite achieve that man's balance of mass and space.

So, although it is exquisite, spatially gestural, the Narwhal does not stack, nor does it float. It lacks the functionality, the iconic simplicity and proportion, of a Jacobsen chair.

The announcer shut the drawer with her hip and her father's sketch disappeared.

Today it's a bit of a cult piece, more due to its ambition than what it achieves, the announcer said as she walked down the hall into the light of the upper galleries.

Elin threw the remote at the TV screen.

———

With fifteen minutes left in the lunch period, a message tracks around the staff room in a series of smartphone dings, hesitations, expletives.

> Dear V.H. Phillips' Senior Secondary faculty and support staff,
> After conducting a budget review, I've discovered that every department has overspent the monies allocated for supplies and photocopying before the fiscal year end.
> As of immediately, no further requisitions will be filled.
> Photocopy accounts that have exceeded departmental limits will be suspended.

Elin has a thumbtack in her cardigan pocket; she reaches in and presses the sharp end against the fleshy part of her thumb.

> We will have a new supply policy and procedure in place for the fall. In the meantime, get creative!

Get creative, echoes indignantly around the room. The exclamatory tone is mocked. Angry laughter follows.

> Each department has overspent in different categories. This is the time to collaborate and share remaining supplies to see us through to the end of the semester. To this end I've created a Supply Swap 'n Share discussion board on the learning platform. The link follows.
> Sincerely,
> Dilip Preet
> Principal

No way!

The gym teacher, a small, long-armed man, reddens. The staff room door slams: he's charging to the office. Elin feels sorry for the miscued optimism of Principal Preet's exclamation marks.

A half-dozen teachers remain. They simultaneously look up and around, assessing each other as potential exam-booklet hoarders, jealous guardians of a cache of unused quota on their photocopy accounts or fresh dry-erase markers. The fragrance of grocery store bento boxes, reapplied deodorant, and humid shoe leather turns sharp, suddenly hostile.

Elin presses down on the small metal point against her skin. After the acting head of science leaves the staff room, Elin, Joy, and the two other science teachers huddle on the springless couch and whisper with low voices.

Their department supply cupboard has been gutted for months. Just last week, Elin had furtively scooped up extra staples left behind by an English teacher using the ISM room.

I'll do it, she offers. I'll make a run after school. Photocopies early next week. Get your originals to me.

In return for what? says Gary, the chemistry teacher.

Coverage for my Friday classes, next week. My sibs are coming to town. Family thing.

Gary exchanges a curious look with Joy and Dez; Elin can see an algorithm of who'd have to do what being worked out with arched eyebrows and head shaking.

Elin takes out her phone, gets a list ready.

It's a good deal. Gimme your shopping lists, she says.

I want two packs of exam booklets, the good ones, says Dez, who teaches general science. Two hundred photocopies.

Highlighters, whiteboard markers, pencils, Post-it Notes—fluorescents please—and thumbtacks, says Joy. Grid paper. About three hundred photocopies.

Foolscap, says Gary. File folders. Sharpies. Exam booklets. Staples. I'll get back to you on photocopy numbers.

Keep track of what you spend, says Joy.

Not like she can claim it, says Dez. Unless you're incorporated? Are you a business, Elin?

Should be, says Gary. The shit we pay out of pocket for.

The morning bell sounds.

So, I'm covered for that Friday? You'll use your breaks.

They nod in unison.

That's going to be one expensive day off, says Joy.

Elin jams the corner of her thumbnail skin into the tack's sharp edge; there's an exquisite twinge. She shrugs.

She *is* worried about the money. A three-day weekend, she intones prayer-like to calm herself as she races between Teacher's Supply Outlet, Education World, and then, more desperately, the Piggly Wiggly and Walmart, the latter with an in-store McDonald's where she orders two McFish sandwiches and two Diet Cokes to go. Her hand plunges into her pocket looking for the tack, but it's no longer there: her fingers poke through a hole in her cardigan pocket.

Absence.

Her father used that word to describe what he aimed for in his design work.

Sounds like something's missing, she'd said to him as a young girl.

Exactly.

At twenty-four, she'd invited him out to lunch to tell him she'd bought the North Bremen house.

The deed was folded in her purse. The real estate agent had left flowers and champagne: she was his youngest-ever purchaser.

Twenty-four, the realtor had said, and shook his head, giving her some business cards to leave for her co-workers, smelling new opportunity where he'd least anticipated it.

She waited for her father outside a popular restaurant, one she'd picked especially for him. This new sense of independence and worthiness: its hum made living feel urgent. She owned something, earned through hard work, frugality, determination.

When Tig stepped out of a taxi that day, he was wearing a silk scarf, navy with small mint polka dots, tied at his neck, and a fitted vest over a chambray shirt, though the heat of summer lingered. She wished he hadn't worn the scarf: people noticed such a choice. He pecked her on the cheek, and she took his arm. They entered the restaurant and turned heads, both of them tall and lean, her father with his glacial eyes, the once-blond hair turned bright silver. She, ash-brown, grey-eyed, pretty in a handsome, unconventional sense of the word. The least Danish of my children, The Lilli said about her.

Others' admiration lit a candle in the Arctic of her father's face; this was a quality that was hard to miss.

The restaurant was Kwak Li's new spot, Taro, in Lower East Side. Li had a ponytail and a Norwegian ex-model wife. There were whispers of a cocaine problem. Elin called in favours to get the reservation, wanting to surprise her father because Li had created a new dish with *skerpikjøt*, a Faroese wind-cured mutton. It was something Tig had eaten as a child, one of the few details from his past he'd revealed directly. She would pay for lunch and her father would make that half smile he saved for things that delighted him.

The waiter looked at her and her father and back at her. Elin was unnerved by the ping-pong bounce of his glance. She chose a tempura dish; she was hungry for something rich. Her father ordered the mutton. The waiter suggested a vinho verde because it was light.

Little bubbles, he said. For the lady.

She didn't like the way he winked.

Full-bodied wines can slow you down, he said, patting her father's upper arm in a way that flustered Elin. Both men grinned.

The waiter brought extra plates after their entrees were delivered, in case they wanted to try each other's food.

No!

She waved her hand; his eyebrows arched at the abruptness.

Her father tucked into the mutton. He gulped his wine. A well-dressed man sitting alone in the booth diagonal to them, his lips wet with soup, nodded at Tig. She watched her father nod back, then adjust his silk scarf. He asked the waiter to compliment the chef.

Elin's sense of accomplishment cooled.

Tig was worrying a chunk of mutton with his knife, remarking that he preferred the dish with cold potatoes rather than the spicy angel hair noodles, when she cleared her throat.

I've bought a house, Dad.

Her father's knife stopped moving for a half second, then resumed.

But you still work at a bar.

He didn't look up before popping a chunk of meat in his mouth. The waiter came by and took her plate. Tig held up his hand, pointed to the remaining food on his.

A cup of coffee for me. Dad?

Tig was chewing. He brought his napkin to his lips, shook his head.

The waiter hesitated for a moment, as if he were about to speak, before thinking better of it, and disappeared.

Elin glanced at her father at the precise moment a tooth fell out of his mouth mid-chew. The tooth was grey and cracked. It landed on a rim of flawless china, making a clavichord clink. He reddened.

She looked away to spare her father's feelings, sensing him tonguing the jellied emptiness where the tooth had been.

Her father curled a finger over the bicuspid and wrapped it in his linen napkin before the coffee arrived. A chasm of silence and embarrassment grew between them. She peeked down at his food—there was a tumulus of angel hair in a moat of pepper sauce, and a stringy piece of meat the colour of dried blood.

The waiter arrived with the bill. Her father wouldn't let her pay.

She declined her father's offer of a cab ride home, insisting she wanted to walk. When she turned onto North Bremen, her house came into view. From that distance, it looked shabby: she'd failed to notice all the ways it was problematic.

———

On the Hyundai's passenger seat, a carton holds Elin's guerrilla run of teacher supplies, undistributed. On top is the box of bright thumbtacks for Joy, the ones with the hard plastic heads and the extra-sharp points.

Less than twenty-four hours has passed since Bets was jumped in the bar. And Elin is arriving home later than normal. The McFish sandwiches will be soggy by the time she gets them in the house. The Diet Coke flat.

7

They'll never forgive you, Bets says on Saturday morning.

She's sitting up on the couch taking selfies. A scratch that Elin hadn't noticed amid the swelling a day earlier now zigzags starkly from mid-forehead to left temple.

I, too, survived the Killing Curse, Bets says, using her Hermione Granger voice.

Elin wonders who's being sent the photos.

Who?

Uncle Cas, Aunt Mette, Grandma. You live in Milwaukee. There's no excuse not to have checked it out before the memorial. At least once.

But why? I'll be there in a week.

Mom.

Bets picks up a disposable chopstick beside her uneaten takeout and makes a figure eight in the air.

Evanesco!

Vanishing spell, Elin thinks. She's relieved to be spared one of the Unforgivable Curses.

Is it weird that Bets is so animated, even jokey?

Sitting in her parked car, staring at The Art Museum forty minutes before closing, Elin watches tourists, weekend gawkers, art students, and retirees dribble out before the city's restaurants fill up for Saturday night. She reapplies lipstick, unrumples her shirt, locks the car door, and heads for the entrance.

She'd argued with Casper about the museum's Quadracci Pavilion when it was still relatively new. She'd liked it back then, its streamlined spaceship-meets-yacht curves that seemed to be speeding out into Lake Michigan. Away. It felt exciting, a bit risqué for Milwaukee. Casper called the *brise soleil* gimmicky—opened, it looked like a flesh-less white bird drying its wings—the kind of architectural frill that's distinct, and gets talked about, but is ultimately a mechanical liability.

It won't age well, he said. It's no Sydney Opera House.

Elin noted his reference to a Danish architect. Old habits.

She walks into the nave of the great hall, its bleached ribs bowing like a postmodern cathedral. It looks out on the lake's grey-blue flatline that goes on forever, a horizon of water, the city's broad bay. Today, she cannot feel the edge-of-the-planet necessity of so much space squandered for an aesthetic immensity. She wants to tell Casper he is right.

They hadn't agreed on much as adults.

The furniture she's come to see—it was in Casper's New York City apartment a year earlier—is now part of the *Mid-century Modern Migrations: European Influence on American Design* exhibition.

She wonders if participating in the exhibition, organizing the dedication, meant he'd relaxed about the pavilion design. So much could change in sixteen years.

Her teacher identification gets her in for free. Elin politely refuses the exhibitions calendar, the coupon for an upcoming show, and the earphones for interpretative audio. Would Joy have begrudged her a single thumbtack? She wonders if she'll open the new box before handing it over on Monday.

The exhibition is small; it takes up a single gallery. The Jacobsen chairs are elevated on platforms in the centre of the room, so they can be viewed as sculptures, a fulcrum around which the other designers' works rotate. The art teacher is right: against the bright white of the room, the upholstery's perfect condition and pop-art colours sting.

Because he was Jewish, Jacobsen had to leave occupied Denmark during the war. Tig followed. Your father had Jewish ancestry too, The Lilli claimed, it was for his safety. Later, Petrine would smile at Elin, with eyes that could lance a boil. There's not an ounce of Jewish blood in our family, she said. Not an ounce. My brother was tired of being a resistance fighter. And he was opportunistic. There was Jacobsen. The genius designer who'd be grateful to anyone who'd worked in the resistance. Tig stalked Jacobsen around Sweden, trying to ingratiate himself into the great man's future commissions. While your mother stayed in Copenhagen, an adolescent risking her life.

Elin circles the Jacobsen chairs, reminded again of her father's ambition, his want of his idol's fluid, liberated lines. She recognizes the Ant is an original: its three metal legs would later be replaced by four when it was manufactured en masse. She reads the curatorial statement and bristles a little at the use of words such as *childlike* and *playful*: design was serious business in their house. The Lilli would see a problematic line at a distance and be shaking her head before she'd crossed the studio threshold, one hand landing first on her father's shoulder, the other on the drawing.

No, Tig, no, she'd say. This curve is too shallow; the balance is off.

Elin spies a Kem Weber airline chair—its cantilevered seat with butterscotch PVC cushioning and knock-down birch—and remembers a boozy lunch she'd had with her aunt, and the story Petrine told about her parents' arrival in the U.S.

He was so sure he'd waltz into Weber's Hollywood firm and get a job, Petrine said. He simply didn't have the portfolio or the credentials. Nearly twenty years—do you believe it?—they chased that dream. New York. Chicago. And after all that, they were mostly broke. They took a train to Milwaukee when my first husband, Evan, offered your father a job; Lilli insisted it was just for a few months. But she was in her late thirties and pregnant. Your mother never recovered from the disappointment.

Of motherhood?

Milwaukee, Petrine said. But then she tipped her head.

Both.

Elin rubs her temples, looks down at the carpet. Her eyes are tired.

It's weird, she says, as if whispering to a friend.

Lists of Casper's things came via text, when he, in a few short trips of cyclonic efficiency, arranged the gallery naming and rhymed off pieces of their father's work he might donate.

Elin texted back, asking elliptically about the Sørejse.

Gone, he replied. One of the first items they asked about. Important work. Also, they want to know if the family has a Narwhal we can part with?

Casper could have pressed her to donate the chair in lieu of contributing to the dedication fund. She'd stared at the text but did not answer. He let it go: in their family, silence was short form.

Now Elin pivots, surveying the gallery, until she moves toward it: her father's most successful dining room set. The Sørejse is a six-foot-long tongue of teak, gabled sharply at the end, a homage to the westwork of Grundtvig's Church, a shape that still strikes her as quirky, incautious, wholly original. It's held up by thin, dowel-like legs narrowed toward the floor into the daintiest of toes. The matching dining room chairs are a dream of simplicity, their striped teal upholstery complementing the teak's warmth.

She knows she will touch it: it will be impossible not to press her palms into the table's surface, or rock the chairs, and push her thumbs into the fabric, an enduring texture that held the peculiarities of her family's laughter, disapproval, and clammy silences.

Elin feels a swoon of ownership. The teak looks duller, darkened against the walls' unrelenting whiteness. Someone—the curator—has placed a set of Søholm earthenware, in corals and greens, on top of it.

She peers around: the room is empty but for her.

Leaning palms down into the Sørejse, she smells red—cabbage and caraway, currants dense as blood—feels her brother kicking her shins under the table, hears her mother's sonorous storytelling voice, and Mette singing, constantly singing.

She wants this table. It should be hers: the warm colour, low lustre, straight grain, held the very best of her childhood, held it fast against the drag of time.

Footsteps echo in the gallery and get louder. Elin divines the heavy, paramilitaristic swagger before she sees it. Dizzy, she lifts her palms, crouches, and crawls under the table where she can't be seen.

Let them tell her who this furniture belongs to.

Casper was newly married and completing his Ph.D. in the history and theory of architecture at MIT when, nineteen years earlier, Elin had visited, looking for comfort, finding this table instead.

He had a vast, airy apartment that overlooked the Broad Canal, where he lived with Shahrzad. They'd eloped two years after Tig's death. When Elin arrived, Shahrzad was out teaching a graduate seminar— Emerging International Legal Perspectives on Polygamy, Polyandry, and Polyamoury, Casper said. The two of them were "warp-speed" busy.

You would be, she said. All those capitalizations.

He ignored her and started chatting, as if he was being inter-viewed. The riverfront trail is perfect for a morning run. They are fight-ing about a dog: yes for him, no for her. He's investigating fractals and Mandelbrot equations as they apply to epochs of architectural design. Exciting stuff.

He gulped his espresso as if it were orange juice.

You look well, she said.

Married life is good for me.

He grinned and peeked at his watch.

Gotta go. Bunch of meetings. Necessary evil. Make yourself at home and we'll be back for an unfashionably early dinner. Spare key's on the hook behind the door.

He gave her a quick shoulder squeeze.

Pumped to have you here, kid. Give yourself a tour of the place.

He hadn't asked her a single question. And Elin was pregnant, something she'd come to announce.

Her brother left and she poked around. On the opposite side of the kitchen, Elin spied the outer rim of a curved glass ceiling and walls, old and funky as a Lord & Burnham greenhouse.

There were two broad steps down to a rectangular room, like a giant vitrine laid on its side, with a door of leaded glass. She peered through. A palm shivered in the corner beside a large flowering bougainvillea—bright as penny candy—and a row of orchids.

Elin gasped.

In the middle of the slate floor, sleek as a speedboat, was the Tig Henriksen Sørejse.

The table's surface had been recently refinished into a gemstone sheen. The six chairs—spoon-backed and elegant—were reupholstered to carefully match the aqua-and-teal-striped wool from the original.

She imagined the dining room set travelling to this riverside apartment eighteen hours from Milwaukee—the museum-quality packing, bonded movers, insurance, receipts, phone calls, gratitude. Her brother yelling, Careful! as the movers finessed it into the service elevator.

Elin pressed her cheek against the seat upholstery, ran her fingers across the table's surface. She'd expected to serve her own child a Sunday morning pancake, a plate of buttery noodles, at the very table where she'd eaten. She'd never considered she wouldn't have a choice.

Under that table, Elin feels an old sorcery. It's getting hot. Who would care that the memory still hurts, that it makes her throat sore?

Only morfar. Because he's reliable, calculable, family.

And he too had had a sister. (That was a welcome surprise. When they were looking for him, rifling through library books borrowed from the University of Wisconsin, Elin found the photograph. The one with Jenny in a stiff, expensive-looking dress of dark satin, square laced collar, her brunette hair swept up and her hands folded, sitting beside and slightly behind her two jowly, rugged brothers.)

Elin rifles for her phone. Opens her voice memo. Sees there are two recordings and hits the red button.

If you're listening, morfar, she says, try and see it through your sister's eyes.

After finding the Sørejse, Elin ran around Casper's apartment opening every door, peering into closets and cupboards, anticipating other looted and hidden family artifacts. The rucksack.

There was nothing else.

She was in a sweat when she called Mette on Casper's phone. She had to know if it was a conspiracy.

Calm down, her sister said. I can't make out anything you're saying.

Did you know about this? Did you know?

It was quiet on the other end of the line.

I wouldn't have wanted it, Mette said.

Maybe I would have!

Stop yelling. You're a mess of hormones.

She started to cry, and Mette stayed on the line listening to her sob.

You going to be okay, old girl? Lots going on for you.

Yup, Elin said.

Keep cool. Remember it's just stuff, huh? It's not who you are.

Maybe I like the stuff better than me.

Ah, El. Don't say that.

You know, I stared and stared at that photograph with your sister, Elin whispers into her phone, took a photocopy before the books had to be returned.

She won't say that neither he nor his siblings had been conventionally attractive, but Jenny's posture made her recede even more. What was it like for her? Born into comfort. Hard to make a problem of delicious food, fine dresses, big ideas, a professor for a father, a mother from an important banking family, an aunt who'd done graduate work in physics. God, how awful to feel dissatisfied with that. In the photo, Jenny stares away from the camera, with a small-eyed gaze that imprisons her in the moment. Her remarkable brothers, on the other hand, face outward, trampling time.

I kept a photocopy. Studied it like it was a piece of art.

Elin fidgets; she stops the recording. The museum floor is unforgiving. The subject of Jenny is a sore spot.

What was it like for her?

Finish the other story, he'll say. Lack of focus is epidemic right now.

Perhaps it *was* the hormones.

When Mette hung up, Elin peered into Casper's refrigerator looking for ketchup. There was none.

On the counter, there was a half-drunk bottle of wine, corked. She found a highball glass, filled it halfway, and went to the terrace.

Elin imagined they ate across from each other on the table's narrow middle, surrounded by ferns, dim stars perforating the velvet of city nights. It was too soon in their marriage for Shahrzad and Casper to take the opposite ends of the table.

She pulled out the chair at the far end, spilled the wine on the corner of the fresh upholstery so the aqua stripe darkened into an ugly brownish stain, two thumbprints wide, and the teal turned red-purple.

Elin used the paper towel to soak up the puddle on the slate tiles and the drips running down the leg. She pushed the chair so its seat was under the table and wondered how long it would be before it was discovered; she hoped they would argue about it, blame each other.

When the wine was recorked, the paper towels hidden beneath the coffee grounds in the garbage under the sink, Elin grabbed the spare key.

The Charles River was as beautiful as Casper had promised. There was a fresh breeze. Clouds, in thick folds, hung over the green ribbon of water. Elin walked for hours, sat at a riverside patio, watching the scrubbed goodness of cyclists, joggers, dog walkers, and stroller moms. The day's newness made it clear that staining the upholstery was criminal, slightly insane.

Casper was already in the doorway, laden with keys and bags and pulling a wheeled document case, when Elin returned with a can of plain soda water she'd hoped to use on the chair.

Shahr'll be back soon, he said, looking young and hopeful. She's always wanted a sister—expects to be great friends with you and Mette.

Join me for a glass of wine after you shower. I've got nice briny olives, a smoked Gouda to tide us over.

Elin stayed in the shower too long, took her time getting ready.

She hadn't thought through the *when* of telling her brother she was pregnant—pregnant, and between bartending gigs, and unsure of how to connect with the baby's father.

Rather than alert him to a change, she accepted a glass of wine. Cowardly. And thirsty. They sat across from each other, on matching armless divans. The coffee table was glass, the rug a rich red-and-blue shiraz. Elin couldn't sink back or rest her elbows.

Little sips, she told herself, promising to drain the glass into one of the orchid pots first chance. Casper held out the cheese tray.

Try the Gouda. Deadly.

I'm pregnant.

Casper had his face in the bowl of his wineglass. He put it down and glared at her.

You're kidding.

Naught but firmness gains the prize / Naught but fulness makes us wise.

Geez, El. What the hell?

It's Schiller. Morfar's favourite.

There is no fucking morfar, El.

The apartment's door handle rattled and there was a thud against it. Casper's head swung toward it, then back.

That's Shahr. Can you . . . Don't mention the pregnancy stuff. It's just that . . . We'll talk.

He stood up, opening his arms.

Buried deep, truth ever lies!

Quit that, El. I'm serious.

The woman who walked in the door in a persimmon wrap dress was tall with long hair that fell in dark whorls on her shoulders. She had a high, intelligent forehead, frank eyes, and a huge bouquet in her arms. The sight of their guest turned her face into a paroxysm of delight.

She wrapped her arms around Elin and the bouquet's cellophane crackled between them.

It's so good to meet you finally.

Casper chewed his bottom lip as his wife, her heels hitting the hardwood in an eight-syllable verse, hunted down a vase for the huge, eye-stinging gerberas.

Then she turned her attention back to Elin.

So? Have you seen it?

What's that?

Our glass terrace? Shahr said. C'mon, you couldn't have missed it. And what's inside. Best part.

Elin took a second large gulp of wine; it mixed queasily with hunger and fatigue. Casper reached for her glass, she dodged, and he pressed his hand against the back of her shoulders, pushing her forward. Shahrzad stood in front of the terrace entrance for a dramatic instant then moved away, with a corny game show elegance.

Oh, Elin said, pasting on a bright smile. The Sørejse!

She put her wineglass down on its surface and proceeded to rub her palms over it, smearing away the water marks from her earlier tears. Shahr gasped, swooped in to pluck the glass from the table's naked surface.

Shit, you must have paid a ransom: it's so rare and has so many memories. I can't believe The Lilli let it go.

Casper lost colour.

Well, no. Actually, Shahr admired it—can you believe it?—I guess Mom was so excited to have us visit, she gave it to us. A belated wedding gift or something.

And you took it! A family heirloom.

He exchanged a look of alarm with his wife. Her fingers tightened around the curved back of a chair.

What broke Jenny, morfar?

The voice memo is back on.

He'd be unlikely to answer that.

Elin thinks she understands how Jenny felt. The pneumatic tightness in the air each time her younger brother came home from boarding school (Jenny had a tutor). His head reeling with ideas. Perhaps she'd seen Eckersberg's nudes of servants at the National Gallery, noticed their red hands, wished she could wake up knowing what she had to do every day. Did she watch the maids refill the samovar, pour Cherry Heering into tinkling aperitif glasses, push the kitchen doors with their hips, slice the warm, brown sugar–scented *drømmekage* to serve with coffee after dinner, and see a productive imperative her own life lacked? Then her gifted brother—the one her father compared to a precious metal—would return and disappear into the workshop, specially built for him. With its own lathe. And a bench piled high with rusted sprockets and levers, old wheels, the primitive bones that convert energy to its world's work.

Elin imagines Jenny sitting by that bench, watching him take apart clocks and bicycles.

Is that where you first encountered the possibility of an orderly universe? she asks her morfar.

He'll shrug, look away.

Did she talk to you about it?

He won't say anything.

Oh, c'mon.

Jenny studied history, Elin thinks. Tried teaching. Nothing would stick.

Casper and Shahr were over-solicitous of Elin's preferences for Thai takeout. Green or red curry? Medium spicy? Sticky or coconut rice? Shahr put out dripless candles on a tasteful runner on the Sørejse. Elin insisted on helping set the table, arranging three woven flax placemats farthest from the stained chair.

Another bottle was opened—a *ripasso*. She held out her glass for a refill, and Casper turned away.

They moved around each other in a pantomime of friendly dinnertime anticipation. Elin sensed that her visit, like a tax audit or a dentist appointment, couldn't end soon enough.

The buzzer announcing the arrival of food made all three of them start. Shahrzad ran to the door waving her credit card. Casper found Elin seated at the Sørejse.

Let's slide everything down to that end. Shahr's favourite spot is there—and she paid for dinner. The view's better.

He winked, trying to get them back on track. Elin's guilt sharpened as she pushed the settings along the table's cool surface. Shahrzad came in holding a steaming tray. She'd emptied the food into pretty porcelain bowls and laid serving spoons across them diagonally. The candlelight on her face showed a stubborn hospitality; she was going to trump their earlier awkwardness with food and beauty. She set the tray down adjacent to Casper and together they placed the bowls on the runner to protect the table's surface.

Smell's gooooood, Casper said.

Shahr pulled out the chair, bent her knees to sit, and placed her palms on the seat edges to draw herself in. She stiffened and lifted the hand that had pressed into the stained upholstery. She rolled onto her opposite hip and stared, poking a long, manicured fingertip right into the fabric.

Faint with hunger, Elin almost confessed right there and then.

Casper lifted his glass.

Welcome! he said, looking across at her. C'mon, Shahr, sidle up. I'm starving.

Shahrzad pulled the chair in before raising her glass, some fresh blankness in her face, as if she were looking at Elin through a double slit. Wave or particle.

Welcome, she repeated.

For the rest of the dinner, Casper talked. He gave a long, excited description of his research, including a hilarious imitation of a colleague who pronounced *Rem Koolhaas* with excessive spit. He told all the best stories about the Sørejse—the arguments, board games, food fights, and dinner parties, though he left out the summer he found the rucksack and The Lilli held them captive to her past. Perhaps he sensed Elin's need to have some things belong only to them.

They laughed and ate, commenting on the reflections from the river, the candlelight in the glass, the smell of the sea grape's plate-sized leaves, anything to avoid a lapse into quiet. All through it, Elin sensed the two perverse wills—her brother's forced forgetting of her pregnancy and his wife's denial of the red wine drying under the warmth of her hip, a souvenir from the recipient of her generosity, a small stain in her otherwise unblemished universe reminding her that those who were hostile to the principles of justice and decorum are often closer than you think.

Elin drove home the very next day, after Casper and Shahr had gone to work.

The espresso maker was still warm.

———

Now Elin's face leans against one of the Sørejse's smooth teak legs.

It was never clear why your sister's life was so much unhappier than yours, morfar. Not from the books, anyway. You were suspicious of clarity, thought it was less interesting than truth.

Thou must tempt the dark abyss
Wouldst thou prove what Being is

Are they mutually exclusive? she whispers. Let me know.

But of course, he doesn't.

In the hallway outside the gallery, she hears the crackle of the security guard's radio, the falsetto of a concerned voice. Her cover's blown. She stops the voice memo, wiggles out from under the table and to her feet, placing her palms down once again on the Sørejse's surface to steady herself.

Ma'am, ma'am. Please don't touch the exhibit.

Elin pops her hands up. The security guard is beside her, pock-marked and too thin; his uniform slouches around him as if he'd had a sudden, dramatic weight loss and couldn't quite trust his changed body.

Sorry. It's such a lovely table.

Yes. I'm sure you know that touching's not allowed.

Of course, it's just that . . .

Ma'am. I'm going to ask you to back away from the table.

She won't tell him that Danes cannot ruin Danish things.

Ma'am, are you okay? Should I call someone?

Can I ask you a favour?

She turns to the security guard and recognizes a former student. There's a flash of synaptic activity in his eyes; he's struggling to place her.

We're closing in ten minutes.

Elin crouches so she has a view of all the chair seats under the Sørejse.

Do you see a stain on that chair?

The security guard bends obligingly; he may have made the connection.

No, ma'am. I don't.

He hesitates. She wonders if he wants to confess some small truth: how a bad grade or a kind word from her had altered him in a modest but irrevocable way.

She could tell him truth is slippery.

Well, wait, he says. I'm not sure.

He squints and crouches lower.

There might be something there.

8

On a Sunday afternoon, Zaffiro's is a comforting pungency of grease, oregano, yeast, and tourists, in this case a family of four, effulgent with Midwestern health and judgment, who crane thick necks as Elin enters.

It's as if they know she's argued with her daughter and slammed the door on her way out, uttering an intentionally piquant expletive.

Welcome to Milwaukee: Scream City.

They'll give away my best shifts if I don't go back, Bets had said.

But Elin was prickly with new fears, variables that couldn't be controlled: the dark unknowns of who her daughter hung out with, where she went, and when she might throw her next punch. There was no way to explain all the ways Elin had failed her.

You have to watch that business, she said. Keeps you up all night, sleeping away most of the day. Like vampires. And then all that cash, always having cash: hard to make choices about your future, the rest of your life, when your wallet's full, and you know you have a place to be. Solves the problem of uncertainty by making other options feel scarier, less sure.

Bets glowered with impatience. Elin noted her bruises, still visible, looked like hastily removed Halloween makeup.

Mom, you bought a house by the time you were twenty-four. You paid with rolled change!

Her daughter's changeability surprises her. How Bets, a rare alkali, could flare, as reactive as cesium, a latecomer to the periodic table.

By working at a bar. By wasting a decade.

You had me in that decade.

Yup, and I want the apple to fall a helluva lot further from the tree.

You don't get to decide that. You have to let me fall where I fucking please.

Seriously. The f-bomb?

Cesium plunged into ice water made hot sparks, magenta flames, plumes of steam.

I want to afford my own apartment. For me, my generation, you know what that's like? That's like being in the one per cent.

Oh, Bets. You're exaggerating.

I'll have roommates until I'm middle-aged. And a house—Jesus, Mom. I needed to start saving for that, like, ten years ago.

When you were eight? Before you got an allowance?

Bets's shoulders drooped.

I'm going back to work. Stop being a bitch about it.

Excuse me?

After the door slammed, after she called her daughter an unforgivable name under her breath, Elin remembered cesium is one of the softest metals, curling and cutting like room-temperature butter.

She plops herself down at one of Zaffiro's small tables covered in reassuring red-and-white-checked plastic and faces away from the four scrubbed necks to eat her mini-pizza, drink her beer, stare into her phone.

In a petulant fit, she'd driven first to the Bayview Pick 'n Save for a package of Moon Pies. They are in her purse, softening in the early evening warmth. Afterwards, she'd sat on a South Shore Park bench and stared at the copper beech that was dying. Wisconsin's oldest of the species, it had outlived its natural lifespan, starting out as a sapling on a farm that rolled up to the edge of Lake Michigan, breathing in soot from the steel mills that came later, enjoying the end of its days as park shade-giver before slowly wizening into a leafless skeleton. Death by fungus. Wasn't that another kind of life? A reincarnation?

There's a slight pressure on her shoulder.

El?

She starts. That touch and scent—pimento, geranium, and nutmeg—Marty.

D'ya mind?

He pulls up a chair. The waitress moves his pizza and beer over to her table.

Jesus, he says. Thank god for someone else in this town who's not at brunch.

Marty, it's almost 4 p.m.

C'mon. The city has a raging brunchification problem.

A rugged hand with cracked skin at the knuckles hoists his beer mug. His swig leaves a wide mouth of suds around his moustache and beard.

City of Festivals.

Cream City.

Machine shop of the world.

Smallwaukee.

She can't avoid the past in this city.

Been a while, Marty says.

She sees his slight grimace of discomfort.

Two years.

Three.

Marty's thick neck, the way his spackle-flecked flannel shirt tightens across his shoulders: she's forgotten how much comfort he offered.

How's your mom?

Holding up. She's tough.

She is that, says Marty. Remember she made tomato aspic for me when she found out I was vegetarian?

She left out the beef broth. Thought it was a crime against jellied salads.

There's a slight droop at the left side of his mouth; mirth jerry rigs it level.

She opened the door, looked me over—tattooed forearms, black Adidas, black rodeo shirt, earplugs, and a fade—and flinched.

She did not flinch. She asked you to take your shoes off.

But then she wanted to know what part of the city I was from.

You said south. And The Lilli said, Old South Side?

No, south of the airport, grew up in public housing. Now I'm a former anarchist living near a macaroon shop.

He remembers it word for word.

I asked if the aspic had gelatin in it and your mother snapped, Of course it does.

There's only one way to get that glisten, Elin says. You ate nothing but potatoes.

The Lilli had pressed her lips together, drained two Brennivins before dinner, and offered Marty a tour of the house.

And then, Marty says, the unforgettable Great Danes soliloquy.

Know it well. A Dane carved Mount Rushmore and a Dane invented the hamburger. And Lego? That caught you off guard.

No, says Marty. It was when she said the Danes had the most organized resistance in World War II. That's when the tides turned.

Christ, says Elin. You forgot, this was how my parents met. On those long, flat roads that had made it so easy for the Germans to roll over the place.

You know that story has more holes than Swiss cheese. Or Jarlsberg. Whatever it is your people eat, Marty said.

Which parts? The plane's engine? Big bags of guns, French cigarettes falling into the cabbage fields. My father arriving in the dark to pick up the airdrop. What insults your historic probity?

Marty tilts his head, takes a swig of beer. He's having fun.

She's not even thirteen, leaves home, works on a farm, and just happens to be there for an airdrop where she meets—wait for it—not just a regular guy, but a modernist designer and resistance fighter old enough to be her dad, who lets her talk her way into the movement. C'mon. Could be a movie.

So what if my parents lived on a larger scale than us?

If I had not pointed my flashlight in the sky, not met Tig Henriksen, The Lilli told Marty that night, I'd have hoped for nothing more than being the assistant at a nice shop selling small items of high quality in the back streets of Nyhavn.

He was unmoved.

Yeah, but more Danes volunteered to fight for the Germans than joined the resistance, he'd said. And the Danish government, they just outright collaborated, didn't they? I mean, they gave medals to Göring, von Ribbentrop, while Jews were being gassed. For Chrissakes.

Elin wanted to reach across the table and throttle him.

She remembers her mother rapping a bony wrist on the teak. The light-blue vein in her forehead pulsing a warning.

Marty imitates her: Not true! There was an apology.

Except that Rasmussen was part of the coalition of the willing a decade ago, Marty had said. You know—kinda tight with Wolfowitz, all ready to throw Danes into Iraq. So, the apology was nicely timed, right? Morally unjustifiable apathy toward a WW2 fascist becomes the morally justifiable bombing of someone else's fascism.

God. You really were a self-righteous bastard.

How could I forget?

You know, there was a part of me that liked how you didn't pander. Though you must have known you weren't going to be invited back.

Your mother stood up at her end of the table, looked at me, and said, Get out. *Exit, pursued by a bear.*

Marty laughs.

Geez, that woman is terrifying.

I'm sorry, Elin says.

He reaches his hand across to hers.

Do you want another?

She isn't sure if it will be her second or third half-pint. If only aging hadn't trapped her in a fetid tropic, turned her body into a weird insect living there, she might ask him to come home with her.

Sure, she says. Reverie is surprisingly thirsty work.

When Mette's predilections led her to a six-foot-seven cowboy and third-generation firearms engraver, Elin, the comet trail of her sister's tastes, discovered Moon Pies.

A bad habit, that years later led her to Marty.

Mette at thirteen was already a singer-songwriter, working hard to shed her family's pseudo-Scandinavian tics in order to pierce the very heart of Midwest pain with a sweet, raggedy tone that defied later categorization:

honky-tonk

alt-country

country rock

folk rock

psychobilly

outlaw country

American Cosmic.

It was Mette who found the song by Big Bill Lister.

After Saturday morning Danish lessons in Trinity Lutheran's basement (Elin refused to take them), Mette hopped on the number 20 bus with Danish conjugation exercise sheets crammed in her backpack and navigated an intricately mapped route of her favourite record stores:

Mean Mountain Music

Atomic

Radio Doctors

That's not your voice, Elin would say when her sister began applying her Library of Congress inexhaustibility to regional styles of lonesomeness and penury: two things Elin said nobody would buy from a girl who lived in a shrine to Scandinavian modernism on the outskirts of working-class Milwaukee. And took Danish lessons.

Sufferin', Mette said. You gotta have it in your tone.

But it's fake, Elin told her, frightened by how far Mette could go away from being recognizable.

Not if you feel it, it ain't.

Isn't, Mets. We're in Wisconsin. We say *isn't*.

One day, Mette brought home a 1951 Capitol Records forty-five of "RC Cola and a Moon Pie." Her record store friend said Big Bill Lister had worked as a rhythm guitarist for Hank Williams and was occasionally his opening act. The Moon Pie song had been written by a fishing buddy of Williams, though it was first associated with Lister.

It was a simple ditty about being poor, selling the calf for a dollar and change to pay the bills, and being happy with an RC cola and a Moon Pie. Mette said the pie wasn't actually a pie, but a large chocolate-covered cookie sandwich with a marshmallow filling that a coal miner could wash down with a cola for a quick lunch that only cost a dime.

Elin couldn't stop thinking about that: adult men sustained on the teeth-rotting fizz of soda pop and cookies. Given the pieties of their own desserts-on-weekends-only regimen. (Casper had his furtive stash of Slap Stix and Mette had a thing for Snirkles, a caramel-and-nougat concoction that yanked on Elin's fillings. She was always looking for something of her own.)

And so, the Moon Pie—rich crust, heaven of marshmallow, the universe's sweet metaphysical darkness holding it all together—became her signature indulgence.

Over the several weeks that Mette worked out "RC Cola and a Moon Pie" on her acoustic guitar with the loose b-string, leaning toward The Carter Sisters' vocals, Elin searched for a Milwaukee source of Moon Pies.

A kind clerk at the Pick 'n Save shook her head and said, The closest thing we got up north are Burry's Scooter Pies.

Elin bought a whole box using birthday money.

The woman arched her eyebrows.

Don't eat 'em all at once. Give you cankers.

Elin snuck the bag with its two bottles of cola past her mother and stored them under her night table until later, when the lights were off.

Guess what I got?

A two-foot hardwood gulf separated her and her sister's beds.

Mette groaned and turned away, twisting in the sheets. Elin held a bottle close to her sister's head so she could hear the clink of the opener against its glass rim, the cap's click, the gassy sigh.

The cola was warm, but Elin guzzled and slurped for effect, and then ripped the Scooter Pie packaging noisily.

Okay! Jeez, El.

She was ready for Mette's country-girl vexation: when her sister turned, Elin held out an opened bottle in one hand and, in the other, an unwrapped cookie sandwich, its bottom softening where it met the warmth of her palm.

RC Cola and a Moon Pie, darlin'?

Mette pulled herself up to sitting, adjusting her eyes to the darkness. A moment of disbelief stiffened her, followed by a short, sweet grunt of mischief. They ate the entire package that night in their shared bedroom—the crumbs dropping into their bedsheets, marshmallow sticking to their molars, chocolate settling in the corners of their mouths—crumpling up the wrappers and throwing them at each other, waking in the morning with fuzzy teeth, sugar headaches, garbage to hide, and, in Elin's case, a canker inside her right cheek.

Mette quickly moved on from the Lister forty-five—she found a copy of Loretta Lynn and Conway Twitty's "You're the Reason Our Kids Are Ugly," a song The Lilli yelled at her to please for the love of god stop singing.

But Elin would still lapse into the older RC Cola tune apropos of nothing.

It was their language. Though it wasn't.

Casper scowled at them. Tig retreated to his studio, shut the door. The Lilli began to hoard a confused hurt in her eyes, as if by creating stories only understood to them—Mette and Elin—they'd marked territory to exclude her.

Finely tuned to the silken mutabilities of The Lilli's face, Elin went out of her way to emphasize the impenetrable silo of sisterhood. Her mother had long since ceased to be reliable.

After Scooter Pies were discontinued, the maker of Snirkles was long defunct, and Pabst Blue Ribbon wasn't even bottled in Milwaukee anymore, Moon Pies got better distribution.

All the Walmarts carried them.

On principle, or nostalgia, Elin bought them at the Pick 'n Save, and if they only had banana flavour, she purchased Mallomars instead. Both delivered the comforting shock of sweetness she was looking for. Both reminded her of the shared bedroom on Burnham: Mette sourcing records, Mette learning chords, Mette finding her voice singing honky-tonk but hanging out with the scarified punks of Riverwest. Mette, the most loving of the three children, the one who ran away the most and the farthest. And came back expecting the family to be the same. As if she couldn't understand herself otherwise.

The adult Elin took lonely late night drives to buy Moon Pies.

She met Marty Flanagan this way. Wearing a ski jacket over sweatpants, unwashed hair tucked into a baseball cap, she was hovering her chafed, mittened hands over the Pick 'n Save's Moon Pie display when she first heard his voice.

Too many flavours now. Salted caramel. What the fuck.

Elin turned to see a large, round-faced man with a bristle of facial hair, his broad chest straining against a black, threadbare *Killdozer: For Ladies Only* T-shirt under his open jacket.

There was drywall dust on his skin.

He smiled at her. Elin wore lipstick, though the rest of her face was bare. She'd applied it without a mirror, out of habit. Her sibbersauce. That's what Mette called it.

Here's a free tip, Marty said. Cold night like this. Microwave that baby for five to ten. Like a warm pudding.

She looked at him blankly. Was he making fun of her? He had broad shoulders and a soft belly, a sugar-syrup shimmer to his eyes; she could tell by looking at him that he was uncomplicated, in ways that would charm and frustrate her. She hadn't been charmed for a while.

She left the Pick'n Save with two original single-decker chocolate pies and his name in the contacts of her smartphone. It was so unexpected, this meeting someone like this. Nervous, she'd thumbed in his name as Farty Managan. He laughed and corrected it.

Not my first time, he said.

She ran to her car. She couldn't eat those Moon Pies fast enough.

Two days later, he texted her.

I'm in Canada btw.

On purpose? she replied.

Ha! You've never been.

Cold, boring, smug. No thx.

Whaddya mean? Montreal = prettiest place in N.America.

She had no answer for that; flirtation shouldn't be work, she told herself, and she powered her phone off. Nobody does that, Mom, Bets told her later. She thought she wouldn't hear from him again.

He asked her out.

They met at the Oriental Theater on Farwell; she had a soft spot for its cinnabar carpeting, Mughal arches, elephants, and seated Buddhas in recessed alcoves, its confusion of taste, appropriations, and all the films she couldn't get at the mall.

Afterwards, he suggested a café, and there said, Close your eyes and open your mouth, which was not what she expected; they were in public. She'd already sourced the exits.

The first sensation was soft, sweet: too small for a Moon Pie, but familiar for its single layer of buttery cookie, more marshmallow, darker chocolate. She kept her eyes closed. He wanted to please her; it both delighted and burdened her.

What is it?

Whippet. *Pets de soeurs.* The Québécois Moon Pie. Or, for Milwaukeeans, nun's farts.

More of a Mallomar, though. But good.

I smuggled a whole package out of the country for you. I thought you'd appreciate the nickname.

Smuggled?

Sure. You wouldn't believe the tariffs on these little babies. My mother is French-Canadian. Papa, Milwaukee Irish. Mom moved back after they split.

So, you're one foot in, one foot out of being American?

Whaddya talking about? Pure Milwaukee. This city was founded by a voyageur—Juneau. Right?

Of course.

Appalling lack of history, young woman.

I can't imagine this city as anything but stubbornly Middle America.

Land's Potawatomi, beer's German, the steel made mostly by the Polish and Serbs, Black sweat building everything else and then there's that habit of voting in socialist mayors—the best ones we'd ever have— we're kind of as Canadian as the Canadians.

Elin nodded; she was about to say how ironic she found it that her parents, the resistance fighters, ended up in a city known as the German Athens. If only to prove she knew something about the city. She stuffed her mouth with a Whippet instead.

And took Marty home. Later, she would joke it was just to stop the history lesson. He was impressed she lived on North Bremen.

You know Vel Phillips lived nearby. On Booth.

I did.

She'd wait to tell him she worked at the high school named after Phillips, not only the city's first Black member of city council but the first female too. (And the first woman to wear a pantsuit in the civic chambers, a fact The Lilli surprised Elin with.) She'd use Marty's being a know-it-all to get back at him.

He inspected her house as if it were an injured pet.

Ugh, franken-fix on the washroom. Tragic—they must have pulled out the original pedestal sink, deco tile, for this chipboard-'n-plastic shit.

He wasn't much for booze, he told her, asking if she had any pot. She didn't. They settled on tea and Drambuie. She poured double shots.

He was a lightweight when it came to alcohol. Into their second nightcap, he was talking too much, in a way she was sure he'd regret the next day. She took advantage; poured him another drink.

Marty told her about his "group," a loose association of former punk 'n metal scenesters who found their way into construction, eventually becoming "defenders" of the city's architectural past.

He was all public-television enthusiasm for the different orthodoxies when it came to water damage and re-pointing brick and whether every fireplace should operate in its original form. His "group" maintained an invite-only website where they tracked "gutters," contractors who bought historic but shabby homes and did QDRs (quick-and-dirty renos), filling dumpsters full of walnut spindles and wrought iron grates, before reselling the houses grossly marked up. They had watch lists of condominium developers they suspected were lining the pockets of city councillors in order to raze historical blocks. They had watch lists of empty churches waiting like lame caribou—to be plucked and deboned by circling hardware privateers hungry for their slate roofs, hammered copper, ash pews, cream-coloured bricks, and brass knockers.

You sound like vigilantes, she said, knowing this would encourage him to say more. He was a kinder, gentler version of something already familiar, the bully aesthetic.

Oh, no, he said. We just watch over Milwaukee's buildings. Nothing illegal. Nothing violent. Straight edge all the way.

She didn't know why she wanted to bed him. He was exactly wrong for her—as rooted in Milwaukee as she was, but content about it, not stuck.

He was on a roll now, laughing at his own lexicon:

suburbia was the "MDF desert."

gentrifying neighbourhoods, "be-dumpstering."

houses with moisture issues, "Grim Seepers."

Elin half listened; she'd wait until he realized he'd gone too far. Once he felt the first shiver of sobriety, realization would follow: I should have stopped myself, asked her at least one damn question. She'd be in charge because he was doing himself no favours. She already saw it happening. He began laughing nervously, unsure whether to carry on with the story of his friend, a restoration arts college graduate who'd just purchased a small home that was technically in Harambee, though this friend—racist pirating twat—insisted on calling his neighbourhood Upper Brewers' Hill.

This whole town redrawn by white flight, white encroachment.

Shame has so many hues. Elin tracked its early colour, a cold, lightless flint that blurred into pinkness, crawling up his neck.

He went quiet.

Oh, fuck, I talked too much, he said.

She put down her drink, walked over to where he sat on the couch, straddled him, and shoved a Whippet in his mouth. He looked surprised and made a muffled laugh. As he chewed, she started licking his neck, biting his earlobe, another Whippet softening in her hand. This she smeared over his face.

She undid his shirt quickly, and he tried to regain some control, pushing his hands up her top, but she slapped them away. In quick succession, she slammed a Whippet in his forehead, another against his throat, and made an incontinent skid with a third along his chest hairs. He gasped. She shoved her mouth against his, bit, and sucked.

When she pulled away, his eyes looked afraid, the sight of which aroused her powerfully. Elin took a breath, stared back into those eyes, and waited for him to nod. When he did, she pushed him on his back. A few minutes later, Marty was naked on her living room floor, his hard-on covered in chocolate-marshmallow pudding. She slapped him on his belly with a force that teetered on the edge between violence and play, then told him to shut up so she could enjoy her dessert.

At the door the next morning, a few hours before Bets returned from her sleepover birthday party, Marty laughed at himself, referencing his own tangent from the night before, testing to see how much of her regard he'd squandered, trying to regain that earlier footing where he could be himself and be loved. He leaned into her neck, his breath warming the crook of her shoulder.

Just tell me you're not one of those cretins waiting for an Ikea to open in Oak Creek so you can Swedish-burn the character out of this place with that ready-to-dissemble shit.

She smiled. He'd fill her ears with words yet forgive her bad manners in bed.

Have a good day, Marty.

She kissed him softly under his chin where she imagined his carotid artery branching into its external and internal branches, feeding his mind and his mouth.

Be gentle, El, she whispered to herself as she watched him get into his car, turn, and wave at her, with an expression that said she'd surprised him, in a way that made him happy and afraid. As if this woman he might fall in love with was an unapologetic pickpocket.

Elin ate the rest of the Whippets in bed for breakfast and waited for her daughter to come home.

9

Let's go for a walk, Marty says. Work off the beer.

It's a warm June evening. The patio umbrellas clutter the sidewalks like noisy seabirds. Music thumps from open car windows. The streets hum with laughter, heckling, outrage, outrage, outrage.

Remember that BBC documentary crew that parked it here for a full summer? Mayor, police chief giving 'em full access. Convinced the Brits were the good journalists, wouldn't repeat the old tropes. And then it comes out.

He stops, pulls back the curtains of an invisible screen: MILWAUKEE: MURDER TOWN, USA.

I thought it was Murder Capital of America.

Look around, says Marty, all I see is peace, love, unity, and respect.

Somebody yells; a pop can is tossed from the open window of a moving car and bounces across their path.

We are misunderstood, he says.

Elin steers Marty toward the quieter part of North Prospect Avenue. She loves its low-rise art deco apartment blocks, one after the other, all the way to North Avenue. The lake winks between the foliage.

If I could do it all over again, this is where I'd live, she tells him. Graduate work in physics, maybe a Ph.D. I felt more alive, more urgent learning than teaching.

A younger couple walks past them, holding hands.

In my Advanced Survey of Theoretical Physics, I was like one of four female students. The prof, he'd look right at us. Tell us a story about the women who were important to the beginnings of quantum and nuclear physics: Lise Meitner, Maria Goeppert Mayer, Chien-Shiung Wu. I mean, nobody taught that stuff then, right? He wanted us to know that we were not alone. I thought he was talking right to me. Saying I could be great.

You *are* great, El.

Marty takes Elin's hand gently and braids their fingers.

But for you, it's not enough, right? Like you can't stop there, if others get to be geniuses.

You sayin' I'm not a genius, Marty?

The sound of his chuckle loosens an old ease, as if they hadn't stopped talking. For a brief moment, Elin thinks maybe she can do this. Again.

Oh, no.

She stops in the middle of the sidewalk.

What?

Mitzi. I forgot about the dog.

You have a dog?

Elin gets a mental picture of Yoda, two decades earlier, panting at the sight of her empty water bowl, searching the house for other ways to quench herself, voiding her bilious insides all over Mette's meditation cushions.

Mitzi had more muscle and jaw for vengeance.

I have to go. I've left her alone for hours. She hasn't been fed or outside. I'm sorry.

She gives Marty a peck on the cheek and runs back to where her car is parked.

Five minutes later, Elin's back on North Bremen, bursting through the front door calling for the dog.

She hears no response. She races up the stairs and checks Bets's bedroom, the second-floor office, and her room in the attic. Nothing.

Mitzi!

She yells with force, with authority: a voice a dog will respect. She hears nothing. She checks the kitchen. The dog's water bowl is full. She scans the backyard in case Bets let her out and forgot her there.

Elin sees the back gate to the alley is open, its door swung wide out into the yard.

Shit.

She doesn't know anything about this animal. She doesn't know if it will be friendly or fierce when confronted with another person. And what if that person has a dog of their own—a teacup pedigree out for its late night pee? Elin smells blood and liability.

Mette has a soft spot for animals that have suffered trauma. Yoda was fished out of a back alley in Cleveland with a maggoty gouge in her hip. For all she knows, the dog ran with a snarling pack of feral Houston red-noses or was plucked from an underground fighting ring run by fugitives from the American dream in leather vests with built-in concealed weapon pockets.

She grabs her keys and the leash from the hall closet and is reaching for the front door knob when she notices the smallest patch of not-right colour.

Elin stops. The early evening light refracts through the living room window into a blue-gold pool that lands on the Narwhal. Mitzi, curled with feline compactness, lies there, her nose tucked under her bent back leg.

Her yellowish eyes are open. She's not so much looking at Elin as considering her.

Elin recalls the sensation just before she'd sped down North Avenue: Marty's hand falling away from hers, slipping through her fingers.

Bets, at fifteen, had not liked Marty. She had not liked the way he tried to talk to her about music, or show her how to mince onions, or give her advice on getting her first tattoo.

He kept showing up, first on the weekends and then during the week. Elin didn't invite him to sleep over, and she refused invitations to stay overnight at his place.

Still, there hadn't been any boyfriends who lasted as long as Marty.

Elin kept asking Bets, Are you okay with this Marty thing? What do you think of him?

And she would shrug.

Then one day Bets asked about her real father.

They were at the kitchen table, her homework spread out before her as Elin washed the dishes. Bets wearing her oversized bathrobe, faded pink and printed with eyeless cats, over street clothes.

Elin turned and flung the dishtowel over her shoulder.

What would you like to know?

You always tell me things didn't work out, that he was this really good guy. He'd be proud of me, whatever. But I want to know more. I want to know *why* things didn't work out, *why* he would be proud of me. Do I sound like him, look like him, am I good at the things he's good at?

Bets closed her books, put her calculator away and her pen down. Elin watched her: how long had she been screwing up her courage, waiting? Her daughter's dormant curiosity had let Elin off the hook. She'd gotten comfortable.

The thing is, I told you before, hon, we didn't spend much time together. There's only so much I know.

But why didn't you spend more time together? Was he mean to you?

No, not at all.

Where did you meet?

Elin fills the kettle. She wants to slow things down.

At McGillicuddy's, where I worked. He was visiting from Chicago, catching a Brewers game with a few friends. He came up to the bar to order a round of beers.

Because there is so little story, Elin attenuates what details she has, while pretending to work a tea stain out of her favourite mug.

An amazing smile. Like yours. He kept saying funny things about Milwaukee, just silly things, y'know. You call this place Cream City? Where's all the cream? Not a cow in sight.

She looked out the kitchen window; for months she'd imagined him there, building a tree house for Bets, raised garden boxes for her. Tape measure, level, circular saw on the plywood placed over two work-horses. Rings of sweat under his arms. Adding details each time she rinsed dishes at the sink. A smear of dirt on his forehead. The way he grunted with focus. She'd thought about Bohr—how concentration emptied him, so he appeared lifeless, almost idiotic, before the flash, the scintilla of inspiration. And she gave those qualities to him, this new imaginary man, updated with the bleat of an expletive. It felt harmless until she started looking forward to it and told herself to stop.

You have to tell a lot of tourists that Milwaukee gets its nickname for the colour of its bricks, don't you? he said. What city is nicknamed for bricks? That made me laugh. I mean, it was corny. A joke I'd heard a hundred times. But his way was well-meaning, playful. A bit awk-ward. Which was adorable.

Bets shifted in her chair, turned to face her mother. The way she clasped her hands in her lap looked too grown-up, too attentive. Elin's chest felt sore.

I was going through a hard time: I'd been a bartender since I'd moved out of the house, almost a decade by then. My sister had a recording contract. My brother was finishing his doctorate from MIT. And here's this man from Chicago, the handsomest man who'd ever given me a second glance . . . It was . . . it was great.

Did you, like, go out on dates?

Elin drew in a breath. She folded the tea towel and placed it neatly over the stove handle.

Bets was more innocent than her peers, and sure to lose that soon. How easy to omit facts.

Yet her daughter held herself to impossible standards. If she expected less of Elin, she'd want, at minimum, honesty, full disclosure.

Once.

You went out on *one* date?

Yeah, sorta. He came back after the game. Just him. He had another beer. It was a slow night. I got off shift early.

You slept with him on the first date?

Well, it was the only date, love. He went home the next morning.

Bets looked down at her homework. She straightened the pages of her notebook, lined up her pen so it was flush with the edge of her scientific calculator. Elin watched and felt her pulse pound in her ears, the way it would after climbing the steep stairs to the attic too quickly.

Mom, were you a slut?

I don't believe in that word, Bets.

But I was conceived during a one-night stand, right?

Yes.

It's kinda slutty, though.

That's not how I think of it.

But if I did that, you would.

No. I wouldn't use that word.

Bets wouldn't look her in the eyes; her cheeks were rouged with disappointment.

So, if I slept with Sheldon Bailey, you wouldn't call me a slut.

I'd call you grounded. But no, not a slut.

Did you *want* to see him again?

Who is Sheldon Bailey?

Bets's eyes clouded.

I *did*.

So why didn't you call him?

We didn't exchange numbers.

Elin can see her daughter fighting tears. How much is too much information?

You could have looked him up.

The whole truth: she'd never had sex like that before, so completely selfish and reckless, and anonymous. She was run over by it. For two days afterwards, she smiled for no reason, her body shook. Food tasted exquisite. She hadn't so much as asked his full name.

No. He called himself Jay, she said. I'm sorry. I thought it was his name, but then I realized it could also be his initial.

Bets piled the calculator and notes on top of her textbook, gripped the pen and pencil in her hand, and pushed the kitchen chair backward so it screeched against the linoleum. The sugar pot lid slipped off with an accusing *tink*.

Great role model you're turning out to be.

Ouch, said Elin.

Hunched over her books, her daughter swung herself around, her hip catching the chair as she exited the kitchen without looking up. Elin felt the impact of her daughter's feet thwacking the stairs as if they were uppercuts to her ribs. Silence. She wanted to take back what she'd admitted, read a book on the teenaged brain, listen to a therapist on YouTube, sign up for a seminar, confess.

She'd simply had a great fuck, and hadn't thought much about it, until a few months passed.

Later that night, she called Marty to tell him it was over. She wasn't going to give him a long explanation, she said, she couldn't explain her feelings to herself.

10

A tack, green as spearmint, is suspended between Elin's forefinger and thumb with just enough pressure to feel a pinch. Her first Monday class has ended, and she stares out the window at the copper beech.

Buche, Elin whispers, the German word for beech, the origin of book, because beech bark was once used for paper. Someone has carved a large heart into the soft trunk of this one. Elin squints, she can't make out the initials, their runic message. She wonders if the writer cares that the carving will outlive the attachment it proclaims, then the two people themselves. Arborglyphs and ghosts, Elin thinks. The tree appears to do nothing yet knows more than she does. Should she tell Principal Preet that the beech is known as the Learning Tree?

A throat clears behind her.

Regina Williams is at the door, wearing a troubled expression and holding the hand of a small child.

Hello.

The boy beside her student cannot be older than four. He has on a short-sleeved madras shirt, neat khaki shorts, and brown chukka boots. His small hand is in Regina's.

Elin recognizes a mother's grip, its argument of competing impulses: cling, don't cling. Regina is older than her other students, perhaps by a year or two. Her loneliness, familiar.

Who's this?

This is my son Jordan, miss.

The boy looks at her wide-eyed. He is wordless but has an expression of bright anticipation, as if the world has not yet failed to amaze him.

So, miss, my daycare didn't work out this afternoon. Had to skip my other classes. But came back cuz it's so close to the end of term. And I need to talk to you.

Of course. Let's see, what have I got for Jordan to play with . . .

Elin looks around and picks up a three-dimensional model of the atom. She uses it to teach the concept of orbits, spin, wavelike motion. The corpuscular and undulatory tensions of the atom's universe.

Bleak, Principal Preet had said, describing the school's retention in math and science.

All our brains are going to Minneapolis, one conspiracy-prone teacher announced in the staff room after Elin read Preet's latest email. And you know what they're sending us? Long-term-care patients. The expensive ones. Milwaukee is losing its young and becoming a warehouse for the full-time sick.

Two teachers started arguing with him. Elin walked away. Despair was the staff room's black hole.

No. He's good, miss. Has his own stuff.

Jordan takes off his small backpack, fishes out a pad of paper and some crayons.

I dunno, miss. I'm thinking of not writing the exam, taking the fail. I just dunno.

Regina's face is full of emotion.

A week earlier, Elin had bragged to Principal Preet that she had a record number of female students in senior physics. Since then, Mabel Flores has disappeared. And now Regina is losing hope.

Meet your students where they're at. Dilip Preet, fond of educational cant, had added the motivational epigram in italics at the end of his weekly staff email.

That's too many friggin' meetings, Elin thought when she read it. But with Regina, she thinks, I can get this right.

Elin perches on the corner of her desk.

Do you want to sit?

Regina shakes her head. Elin recognizes masked drive: Regina has a lot but has learned to protect it by pretending it's not there. Her ambitious students, especially the girls, approach their senior science courses as if there is no chance of redemption should they get something wrong. They are punitive about missing things: notes, classes, easy test questions. They don't allow a margin of error for themselves, can't forgive slip-ups in others. They are failures even when they haven't failed anything. Group work is personal hell.

Elin had partnered Regina with Mabel for an assignment a few weeks earlier. Two concurrent forces pulling in the same direction. She'd congratulated herself. Oh, the things they could move! After twenty minutes, she'd looked over. Regina had her arms crossed. Mabel's head was bent over her phone. Both of their assignment sheets were blank. Elin had imagined Newtonian forces where she should have seen electromagnetism: the repulsion of like charges.

So, is it your marks?

Miss, I'm not smart enough.

Teachers, the motivated ones, paid out of pocket to attend seminars precisely for this situation; someone with a mitt full of whiteboard markers and a facilitator's certificate would lead a half-day Streaming Girls toward STEM Careers session at a mid-range motel on the city's outskirts. There'd be weak coffee and lukewarm tea and cookies baked from ten-gallon buckets of batter, and gossip about who signed the attendance sheet before skipping out for beers and a hookup between the motel's chafing bleach-scented sheets, their return marked by the fake-gardenia-and-wintergreen waft of motel pump-soap.

I don't get some of it. I have to sit there, and sit there, until I think my brain is coming outta my eyeballs, and I still don't get it.

Partnering students required a fine-tuned sensibility. Elin thought of it like wine and food, how the novel pairing, when it works, opens up both, lets them breathe, makes them more interesting. Each of these two students had qualities the other needed—Regina's no-bullshit persistence and time management, Mabel's intuitive leaps and confidence. Yet they'd left each other cold.

In the Streaming Girls toward STEM seminar, there had been a breakout group on Resilience Strategies. The facilitator asked them for things their female students said about science and math, then taped flip chart papers to the walls with headings such as "My friends don't take it"; "It's boring"; "I'll get laughed at"; "Too much homework"; "For nerds"; and the perennial "I'm not smart enough." They were given Post-it Notes and asked to fill them out with a strategy for each flip chart page, and then stick them up, in a pin-the-tail-on-the-donkey scramble. Elin grumbled. She wrote, "Tell a story about when you felt dumb," on her Post-it Note and pasted it on the last page.

The discussion that followed was exhausting, as the facilitator read aloud each note in succession and invited comments, waiting for one hand to raise among the mute faces. Elin went to the bathroom twice, scanned the news on her phone, texted a series of stupid emojis to Bets, looked at Facebook, Twitter, Instagram, refilled her tea, ate three cookies. She studied the lobby carpet, chairs, wallpaper, and art and imagined her father shaking his head with a Danish *tsk tsk*, reminding her of the importance of a singular vision, how Arne Jacobsen designed every element, facade to forks to fabrics, of Copenhagen's SAS Royal Hotel in 1960—including those iconic chairs. What that man accomplished, Tig would say. He'd shake his head, waiting for Elin to press for details.

When she re-entered the seminar room, one teacher was insisting that you never, under any circumstance, share personal information with students. Another woman put her hand up to say she was offended by the presumption that she'd ever felt dumb or that being dumb at any point in her life was an appropriate thing to model.

Love teaching, hate other teachers, Elin whispered to the man beside her. He pretended not to hear.

Take a few breaths, Regina, Elin says.

She's buying time.

Does the mind know when it is about to miscalculate? Lack of pre-science nettles Elin. She hates getting things wrong, even if later it turns out right.

For her ninth birthday, Bets had asked for a theme, referencing rented bouncy castles and hired Destiny's Child impersonators, and Elin, tight on money, said all right.

We'll do a science birthday.

Her daughter's eyes clouded.

Trust me. Science can be *crazy* fun, Elin said.

Her faith faltered after the exploding Coke/Mentos volcano splattered a shrieky girl in a taffeta party dress. Before she could demonstrate the synchronized balloon dance of static electricity, the birthday guests, restless, popped all her props with the sharp ends of sparklers she'd hoarded from the previous year's Fourth of July.

She wasn't hopeful about the trebuchet competition. She'd pre-built the pivot points and see-saws from discarded wooden pallets, ignoring Bets's wet-eyed worry from the kitchen window. The rubber strips from a deboned broken lounge chair were set aside for slings. Elin filled two plastic potting buckets with tennis balls for projectiles. The eight partygoers were listless, her daughter dismayed, when she divided them into two teams on opposite sides of the yard. But something took hold when they began to test the pivots' force. Elin had demonstrated pulling the short end of the beam down with skipping rope she'd wound around a nail. It didn't take long before one girl realized jumping from an overturned garbage can and grabbing the beam jerked it with a force that made her team's trebuchet exponentially more powerful. A donated sneaker went flying from one camp right over the heads of the others into the yard of the neighbour with the chocolate tulips. That got a cheer.

Elin hadn't pictured the buckets weaponized, filled with dirt, turned into ammo. After the first was launched, disintegrating in soft shrapnel across the other team, a cheer of triumph followed the howls. The haphazard garden was trampled, the shrieky girl discovered the hose, the buckets were plugged with tennis balls and filled with a slurry of water and soil. The skies rained dark guck over her backyard.

The parents who arrived to pick up their children were audibly disgruntled. One boy broke into wails because he didn't want to leave. Elin boasted to his impatient father that he'd grasped some elementary physics. The mother of the shrieky girl in the ruined dress refused to let her take a loot bag. Bets was elated. The science birthday, which right up until the arrival of the parents was by all appearances an abject miscalculation, became that most unlikely thing: epic.

Look, Regina, Elin says, there are still ten days before that exam. I want you to think about staying in class, working with me on the pre-tests. We could set up a few study sessions after school.

Regina sets her mouth, glancing sideways at her son, who is busy drawing. Elin understands: this is a mother who'll be racing out of the last class to shove her way through the end-of-the-day hallway surge before relying on prepaid bus tickets, the promptness of public transit, and green lights at the crosswalk in order to pick her child up without being fined or reprimanded.

Whatever you decide, there's no right or wrong, only what's right for you. You know, I was only a bartender until I was twenty-nine. Then I got pregnant, went back to school later, got my physics degree and finally, a teaching certificate. Had to redo my high school physics first. So the choices you make now are not a life sentence.

Seriously, miss?

Elin gets up from her desk and walks toward the door. She's tempted to ask Regina if she's seen Mabel around, but thinks better of it.

Not a pathway I'm recommending. But not every decision you make right now is your destiny. We don't run out of second chances; we only think we do.

Elin has not, would not, say the same thing to her own daughter: she wants Bets to get her first chances right.

Regina packs up Jordan's toys.

I don't come from the same place as you, miss, she says. I come from where it feels like he and I've one chance to split between the two of us.

A crayon—vivid violet—falls near the desk where Jordan worked. Elin reaches to pick it up.

Use that half a chance for yourself, then. Don't give it away.

Regina Williams hesitates.

He drew you something.

She offers Elin her son's drawing of a large purple tree, clearly the beech. Something's underneath. But it's a child's rendering, his way of seeing. Elin has no idea what it is.

After school, Elin comes home to find the door open again.

Inside the house, she hears noises. The steel wool rub of a heavy object along the wooden floors upstairs, and footsteps, one set heavier than the other.

She stops in the hallway and waits to hear more. The steps thud again now more quickly; she senses them intermingling as if in a tussle, or a foxtrot. There's a giggle—familiar.

Bets. And someone else.

Hello, Elin calls out.

There's a sudden silence; the movement upstairs ceases. She imagines them holding their breath.

I'm making food. Come down when *you* are hungry.

Elin's voice is over-loud.

She was certain Bets was working tonight. But she is glad her daughter has a free evening. She hopes to see the boy. Or the girl.

Whoever's up there. She wants to make them squirm a little. She wants Bets's forgiveness; she'll offer her own.

Mitzi! Mitzi!

Her ridiculous voice again.

The dog moves down the stairs like a bag of loose hammers.

So, Elin thinks, you've been up there with the party.

Mitzi undulates into the kitchen. Even after several days of cohabitation, the animal still unnerves Elin.

The dog stops and looks up, and Elin sees a tentative movement, a subtle sway, easily slowed into stillness. She doesn't want to get ahead of herself and expect friendship or loyalty. But that was a definitive wag. For her.

She remembers the package from Mette that arrived last week: there were dog treats and a toy inside. Elin fishes into the large envelope she'd left on the microwave, touches something soft that whines when she grips it. She pulls out a squeaky toy, a ridiculous pink-and-purple octopus that smells like dollar-store rain ponchos, rips its tag off, and hands it to the dog. Mitzi gums it and drops it glistening with saliva on the floor. She nudges it with her nose and looks at Elin, cocking her head.

What dog desires an eight-armed mollusc made of petroleum product?

So Elin rifles through the junk drawer for scissors to open the treat pouch.

It hadn't even occurred to her. Food, yes, basic and easy on the budget. A soft place to sleep, a regular brisk walk. But the pleasure of a reward, or something spontaneous such as play, even the invitation of companionship—she hadn't thought the dog was capable of wanting it, not with those mustard-gas eyes.

She'd offered none.

Now her hands shake a little holding the Play-Doh texture of the Lamb Berry bites. She won't risk offering the food in an open palm. Elin places them on the floor.

Mitzi leans over, sniffs, and scoops them with her tongue. Then she sits down. Her ears are up. The tail swishes, furling and unfurling on the floor like a lasso.

Every being cries out silently to be read differently.

She'd seen that on a slide—a quote from Simone Weil. It was the most memorable moment of a seminar, called Don't Box Me In: Resisting Implicit Bias and Judgments in the Classroom, taught by an arch, joyless man who she suspected was a frustrated comic.

Elin throws Mitzi another treat and the dog catches it mid-air.

Then it stares right at Elin and lifts a right paw, with a dainty bend.

It's just an animal, she reminds herself, a vector of meat-breathed warmth. Elin bends to scratch her head, surprised that she's welled up.

Mom? Are you all right?

Bets is standing in the doorway. She is flushed and worried all at once. Her bruises a faded cartography. Beside her is a tall, thin man in a dark T-shirt that's silk-screened with an old poster for the Velvet Whip. He's wearing round John Lennon glasses and when he puts his hand through his slicked-back hair, his multiple silver rings wink brightly.

Hi, I'm Curt, he says, Curt Tejeda. We sorta already met.

He offers his hand.

Oh, says Elin. You.

She does not repeat her Simone Weil quote to herself.

Curt was helping me reorganize my bedroom.

Was he?

Elin studies Curt. Up close and in daylight, he's younger than she first assumed. The pitting of his skin distracts from a boyish openness in his eyes, which are big and brown. If she was Bets's age, she'd think he was cool, in an underfed, revenant way.

Mom, were you making hummus?

Bets moves into the kitchen and past her. She starts opening cupboards and pulls out a bag of pita, a can of chickpeas, the food processor missing a lid.

Elin puts away the dog treats and throws the plastic octopus on the back deck and washes her hands. She can tell by Bets's rushed guesstimated pours of oil and tahini that she is unsettled by her mother's weird behaviour: tears followed by spaced-out unfriendliness.

Have a seat, Curt, Elin says.

Bets is chopping the garlic and about to add it raw.

Please let me, she says to her daughter.

Elin reaches for a small pan, throws in a dab of butter, and sautées the garlic, before adding it to the processor with a hefty squeeze of lemon, a dribble of sriracha. Then she gives that same pan a wipe—she's making an effort—puts it back on the heat, and toasts za'tar. She's about to ask Bets why she's reorganizing her room on a Monday afternoon, when she turns.

Bets is squishing the envelope from Mette.

Hey, cool. What did Auntie send us?

Elin spatulas the hummus into a pretty bowl on a platter, surrounds it with cut triangles of pita and baby carrots, sprinkles it with the za'tar and sumac, dumps a few olives in the centre, and brings it to the table.

Dog treats. Stupid dog toy. Card.

Bets's hands outline the hard object.

There's something else.

I haven't opened that yet.

But Bets has already reached inside, removed the card and, finally, a velvet satchel, the mystery item. *Work it out*, Mette wrote. She prods that now.

Ouch!

A red drop fattens on her daughter's finger.

Something's sharp in there. Like a needle or something.

Bets is up running her finger under warm water. Curt's eyes glint like a rock you'd bend down to pick up. She feels a contraction in her chest, an unwillingness to share her daughter's contrasts—fearlessness coupled with a low pain tolerance.

Elin crunches on a carrot dipped in hummus—there's not enough tahini, but the garlic is perfect, the toasted za'tar a nice touch—then loosens the drawstring top of the velvet bag and reaches inside. Her fingertips suss out the prick of something sharp and cool, then weird, bumpy roundness. She loops her fingertip in a smooth metal parabola and draws the object out.

Whoa.

What is it?

Bets is standing up over the table and looking down. Her finger, the tiny wound forgotten, reaches out to touch what looks like a strange heap of stone and silver: loops of wire around a chitinous green thorax. A cloudy gemstone.

It's jewellery, Elin says. I think.

They stare at it as if it is alive, as if it will crawl toward them, fearless as a mantis. Bets's elbows bend over her flattened palms as if she's ready to spring away. Elin considers the object's strangeness, something she should recognize; a mineral that is too murky for jade or raw peridot.

Well, says Curt. It's kinda . . .

He hesitates.

Ugly.

The word that had come to Elin's mind was *obscene*. The brooch is an obscenity.

Aunt Mette doesn't expect you to wear that?

No. I don't think so. Your aunt works in mysterious ways. It means something.

Elin raps the table with flexed fingers.

I just have to figure it out.

Well, says Bets. I hope this isn't her thank you for taking care of the dog. Because if it is, we should keep the dog.

We. The pleasure of that word.

Has she become too accustomed to it being just the two of them?

There are things she might tell Curt about her daughter. How Bets once waited like Jordan Williams had a few hours earlier, except that she was in the back row of a University of Wisconsin lecture hall, lying across two empty seats, where, if she woke needing to pee or got restless, her mother could hustle her into the hallway without interrupting the class.

When Elin discovered the library's fifth floor—a deserted charnel house of shelved scientific biographies—this was where she worked.

They worked.

Bets sprawled under the plywood tables with paper and pens, her little hand resting on the bare skin between her mother's sock and pant leg. Bets somersaulting between the stacks. Bets, wearing a ruffled second-hand dress, dragging an oversized Fano, Chu, Adler edition of *Electromagnetic Fields, Energy and Forces* over the floor to her mother. Elin squeezing twenty-five minutes of focused problem solving into an hour before Bets needed something—a cuddle, a hot chocolate or bag of chips from the vending machine in the basement. A treasure hunt.

I want five books that have faces on their covers, Elin would say.

Buying herself ten more minutes. When they packed up to go home, Elin loaded all the books her daughter had retrieved onto a cart for reshelving, reasoning that a lucky library employee would value the time in the fifth floor's dusty solitude, away from the enervating floors where commerce and media students chatted as if they were in a cafeteria, littering the study carrels with coffee cups, chip bags, and gum wrappers.

She could tell Curt that she'd started her university studies at age thirty-one, while Bets had started before age two.

But he'll have to earn that intimacy.

The stone encased by the brooch is jagged and pocked, with salt-shaped crystalline edges and glassy pools of black-green, its own rough planet.

Why make jewellery out of it? I don't get it, says Bets.

Elin closes the brooch clasp and returns it to the velvet bag, and puts that back in the envelope, which she shelves on top of the microwave.

Her sister has sent the brooch to trouble her, to make her remember.

Curt, why don't you stay for dinner? We'll order something and I'll fetch us a bottle of wine.

She turns to see Curt looking at her daughter: happiness broadens his face, draws attention to the tide pools of his eyes. She wonders if he might be what she wants for Bets after all, an imperfect guy whose dissolute rock-god swagger tarpapers over a furnace of goodness.

She'll work up to saying sorry.

11

S o, Curt has slept over.

On Tuesday morning, there are sounds below Elin. Soft, drowsy murmurs: the tender newness of a first wakening together.

Your house has *aural porosity*, Marty had told her. She'd laughed because it sounded kinky. What he meant was that noise travelled; there was not enough insulation.

Your floors and doors won't shut up, he'd said. You wanna rethink this place's privacy settings.

Elin listens to Bets's bedroom door open, the bathroom door shut, and wonders whether this might have been a point of discussion between them. Or had she tacitly approved of this with the dinner invitation, the bottle of wine, the jokey quips about the Velvet Whip (any of whose band members could be Curt's grandfather), and stories that dangled precariously between embarrassing Bets and making her laugh.

Now that it has happened once, it will happen again. Will she ask them to ask permission? Will she want to schedule, and contain their encroachment on her space, her quiet, her ability to walk around with no bra and unbrushed hair and full aging-woman decrepitude?

And Bets is leaving soon. Elin wonders whether Curt is being left too.

She hears breakfast rhythms next—the grinding of coffee beans, opening the back door for Mitzi (who'd deserted her at the first hint of others' company), and the old refrigerator's suction. She hears kibble falling onto a metal bowl, the snap of frying oil on the saucepan, the radio news turned on. Their laughter.

Elin slips into the vacated bathroom with a change of clothes. Bets will poke fun at her for putting on makeup, but Bets is eighteen, and naturally beautiful.

The bedroom door is ajar, and Elin, taking a sideways peek on her way down the stairs, stops mid-step. All the books from her daughter's bookshelves are gone. The framed art is off the walls. So are the corkboard tiles with their collection of photos, postcards, buttons, handwritten notes. Only the spaceship planter remains. Two large taped packing boxes wait at the end of her bed. The bare walls are dingy with fingerprints and abandoned picture hooks.

She's moving in with Curt.

Elin's foot hovers over the staircase step that leads down; she had been willing to like him. But if Bets moves in with Curt, she will stay in the city, most certainly working in bars for her share of the rent and food. Ambition for a degree, that lodestar which has already dimmed during this gap year, will be doused by another year out of school. And if it isn't, staying with Curt means her options distill into Marquette or UWM.

Mom, are you coming down? We got up early to make you breakfast before work.

Elin finishes the steps slowly. She feels what Mette calls python tension, tightening first around her spine, grabbing her at her throat.

The table is set. There is fresh coffee made. Curt is some kind of wizard with an omelette, because one that's perfectly shaped, a bisected sphere, is on a plate in front of her, garnished with orange segments and cilantro.

There is a vase with a dewy white trillium, a sprig of columbine, weekday grift from the neighbour's garden. Elin hates herself for her contraction, the way it's going to gut this beautiful gesture.

She takes a long sip of coffee to slow herself down.

Yum, she says. But her voice sounds rubbery and overcooked.

Bets flashes her a quizzical half smile and gives her the thumbs-up in the form of a question.

I couldn't help notice you're packing. Up there. Your room.

Oh, yeah, yeah, yeah, Bets looks relieved. Curt's going to help me take those boxes to the basement. Thought I'd clear it out for you.

For me?

Sure. You know, while I'm gone, you can use my room for guests. Or if Aunt Mette comes to town and needs a place to stay. Or if you want to make some money.

Elin looks up, her heart is pounding.

Money?

Y'know, Airbnb or a student.

I'm not going to share this place with strangers. Traipsing in and out of my private space. With a key.

Elin makes the mistake of looking at Curt, but his focus is on the flattened sun sliding from his spatula toward Bets's plate.

All right. Then just a guest room. So you won't be lonely.

But what about when you come back? Don't you want your room to feel like yours?

Elin's voice cracks. Curt turns the heat down on the final omelette, delaying the moment of its perfection.

Bets reaches across the table and places a hand on her mom's forearm. And Elin feels her neck relax; she has gotten it wrong.

They're just boxes, Mom. I can always bring them back upstairs and unpack them.

Elin looks away, embarrassed.

Curt turns around with his omelette already plated in one hand, the coffee carafe in the other, a ballet of hospitality, refilling her cup, passing her the milk jug, offering toast.

I'm sorry.

She has said it finally.

Curt raises his eyebrow. Elin's mouth is slick with perfectly cooked, buttery egg.

For the . . .

Elin slaps the air with two hands, a dog paddle motion with a crazed-mother expression.

For a moment, he is confused and then comprehension smooths his brow. That grin again, full of quicksand warmth. Elin is going to have to watch out for that; he'd get away with anything with that grin.

The Orbits.

The album, its vinyl version, has been pulled out and left on top of the coffee table in the living room.

Elin is shushed out of the kitchen; Curt insists on cleaning up. She hears the snap of a wet tea towel, a shriek, a retributive splash, laughter. The kitchen already messier than she left it.

She wonders who found the album first—a nosy Curt? Or if, after Elin had gone to bed, Bets showed it off: see, this is my aunt, the musician, the quasi-famous singer-songwriter. The long-haired, hilarious, hippie-chick iconoclast. Mette.

She might have sung a few bars of "He Looks Good Leaving."

Jesus. For real? That's your aunt?

Elin imagines them both giggling a little because the song, one Mette recorded at twenty, had become a story separate from her, covered by country artists, drag queens, sampled for EDM. Resuscitated for an episode of a popular detective series—Elin can't remember the title—and used to sell men's blue jeans in the late 1990s, spurring the Promise Keepers to boycott the brand, buoying the song for yet another gust of its undeservedly long life.

She looks at the Narwhal and sees her sister at fifteen sitting on it, leaning into her guitar, willing it to produce a song.

There were two of the chairs in her parents' house. One they had climbed all over as children; pilled and rubbed raw at the arms. It had teal-and-amber stripes that complemented the Sørejse. The other stayed in her father's studio, where he used it for reading John Le Carré novels and completing the *New York Times* crossword. This chair was uphol-stered in a questionable puce bouclé with flecks of magenta. Its wood was smooth and dark and unblemished, the joints steady, as if her father had levitated over it all those years, rather than let it support his weight.

When their parents were gone for the weekend, Mette, flouting rules, holed herself up in their father's studio, sitting on the chair with her guitar, swearing with exasperation, slapping the frets, knocking her fist hard below the Gibson's bridge pins, a muffled sound, as if coming from inside a coffin.

Elin appeared in the doorway holding one of her mother's thin cigarettes, with the elaborate floral-printed filters, so when Mette looked up, eyes smeared with mascara, she'd recognize the offer.

They smoked on the back stoop, passing the cigarette back and forth, before Mette said, Back at it.

An hour later, she whooped with canine glee.

Done!

Summoned, Elin found Mette sitting on the Narwhal, kicking her legs up into the air.

It's good. It's really, really good, El.

That alien assurance of Mette's. As if she concentrated enough, the grit under her fingernails could produce pearls.

Five years later, its melody unchanged and lyrics wizened by actual experience, "He Looks Good Leaving" was first recorded with Mette's earnings from the vegetarian café.

She kept the rights to the song and sold it to the Nashville teen-ager for whom it became a breakout hit. Mette's own version was dis-covered, given airplay, landing with a smaller audience.

That tune opened doors—small gigs and bigger writing credits—a calling card that was lucrative insofar as she never outgrew the moment in which it was written: a young woman watching her married lover leave her bed for his other life.

When the lyrics were interpreted by poptimists as the woman's realization that her lover was unworthy, the leaving as a letting go,

Mette never argued. She recognized the better story, the one that would keep the royalties coming.

Nearly thirteen years after her sister penned her most famous song, Elin returned from her visit with Casper in Boston, determined to have the chair that had produced the serendipitous flash of inspiration, good fortune. If Mette didn't want it, she'd keep it for her. She phoned The Lilli, and when she didn't pick up, Elin left a message saying she was pregnant. Her mother called back and asked if she needed money.

Money was, in fact, the direst of her needs, but Elin bit her lip and said no.

I could use some furniture.

Oh, said The Lilli.

There was an alertness, like a young hound's, in her mother's tone.

I have a feeling you know exactly what you want.

Elin took a deep breath.

Everything in my life is about to change. My house is still pretty empty. It would be good to have a chair.

She imagined The Lilli's eyebrows pulled up toward the ceiling, her chin lowered, lengthening her face into a neckless mask.

Mette had said, Bad idea, you'll pay for it down the road.

But the chair had become not just something Elin wanted but something she deserved, a form of justice.

So, when her mother asked with a precise comprehension, Which one do you want, Elin?, she did not mince.

The one from Dad's studio, she said.

There was silence.

A week later, she opened her door and there was the chair, sitting on the sidewalk in front of her house. There'd been no knock. A light rain had started.

12

Young physicists did their best work when Niels Bohr was not around.

All those brilliants minds congregated in Copenhagen, housed and fed and funded through his unrelenting energy for finding money. Yet he drove them mad. (Home from skiing in Norway, Bohr discovered a mistake in the uncertainty theory Heisenberg devised in his absence and badgered him to tears about it, perhaps hurt that his protegé had waited for him to leave before finishing and sharing it.) A contemporary reading might fix him as a bully, if the loyalties and affections he inspired hadn't been so ferocious. *Kopenhagener Geist* produced the fundamentals of quantum physics and something else, a way of doing science that was open-hearted, undaunted by paradox, the chain reaction he must have hoped for.

Elin thinks he couldn't have known, turning his attention to the nucleus, how far it would take him away from the ideal.

Boom.

Even when it's over, it's not. The energy remains with its invisible consequences, reverberating outward.

She has done something foolish.

Yesterday, at the end of the day, she stood up, quit her classroom, left her bag, her laptop, and her phone unattended, and walked out of the school and over to the copper beech, animated by Jordan Williams's doodle.

Were trees not the portals for spirits, the many worlds? She'd read surprising studies about plant memory and communication.

In the mid-June warmth, the purple leaves cast a dark shadow across the radius of tangled roots. Fallen catkins made it crumbly underfoot, smelling vegetal and wholesome, like a campground, a hike in northern Wisconsin.

Elin's pulse felt jittery. She squatted and fanned her hands over the ground like a TV detective, before sorting through the abandoned butts—there were plenty—and picking up the longest, an elegant, half-smoked cigarette with gold-red braid printed below the tipping paper. Her heart yammered. She pressed it close to her nostrils—had she really expected to smell vintage Copenhagen? There was movement behind her, a whoop of disbelief.

Out on the road beyond the tree was a student. He was holding his phone on its side. He was taking her picture. Another boy behind him, laughing.

Sad teacher.

Always watching each other, students and teachers. But by sheer numbers, the teachers were outsmarted and out-surveilled.

Elin let go of the cigarette butt, stood up, and walked out from under the tree.

She didn't ask for the student's phone or complain about the picture; they were all off school property. And it was too late: the image was already a meme, shared several times. She imagined phones lighting up—short-lived blue illuminances, the smallest of exploding stars. Boomlets.

In the hallway the next day, only a few smirking students offered her cigarettes. The joke was already stale-dated.

The trick was not to let them see you suffering.

Elin wants her senior physics students to understand chain reactions, the nuclear kind.

If it was not a sultry June day, the lesson would be more easily received. The sky is blue lava, the kind of afternoon for being near water: running in, running out, drying off belly-down on a beach towel.

Many of her students are already working their summer jobs at frozen custard drive-thrus, hotels, and the stadium concessions.

You have to, miss, says Eva. Or the university kids get all the hours.

Like her, several of the others have laid their under-slept heads on their desks. Elin scans the room for Mabel Flores. Today, the alert posture, bright-eyed expectancy, open textbook, completed exercises would be welcome.

Mabel would soak up the story of Lise Meitner, who'd discovered nuclear fission when she was in her sixties, exiled by Nazism to Sweden from her beloved Berlin, a woman who was arguably brighter than the German scientist she'd collaborated with for almost half her career, the one who stayed behind to enjoy good meals and consistent funding under the Third Reich.

But Mabel is not in class.

There's a basketball semifinal game later. The final-period classes are cancelled so everyone can attend, an initiative of Principal Preet to encourage school spirit, a face-saving capitulation given so many students skip classes during home games. And June.

But now there's an expendability to the hour leading up to the free period, her attempt at covering material an affront.

Okay, folks, get up out of your seats, push the desks to the side. If we can't imagine the chain reaction, let's be the chain reaction. You've got ten minutes to role-play a nuclear reaction, starting with U-235. Work together.

Her students groan with heat and inertia. The desks move slowly. Elin surveys again for Mabel: definite no-show. Bart Khang is excited; he whispers to Jonas, a gangly boy flirting with felony. Now he and Regina Williams, whose return Elin notes with relief, work together to organize the others. She sits at her desk, pretending to mark. That duo of the undisputed nerd, the mature student with quiet authority, galvanizes the group. Something's afoot.

Six minutes later, Jonas is at the classroom door with a mission-accomplished smugness; he's tucked a basketball into his T-shirt and walks in appearing to be pregnant.

Elin rolls her eyes, and laughs.

You're carrying low. I think it's a boy, she says. Four minutes.

The earless bunny went viral a year after the Fukushima Daiichi nuclear plant accident. Without ears, it looked like a baby seal with strong hind legs. Her students were sharing it the same week a bill worked its way through the Wisconsin State Assembly aiming to lift the moratorium on new nuclear plants, which would open up the state's vast granite shelves as potential spots for dumping the nation's nuclear waste. She'd tried to unpack that in a class several years ago, on a warm day just like this, and those students had wilted with heat and the heaviness of despair. So she told them about the ray cats, felines genetically engineered to change colour when exposed to radiation. A symbol, she said, that would outlive language or lost information to warn future generations about old buried nuclear wastes. I don't get it, a student said. Because those wastes will outlive us all, she added. The students looked perplexed. All their imagined futures included everyone speaking as they did right now, the infinite availability of information. Green cats, though, that got some traction. In the end, they'd returned to the earless bunny picture, though some had gone on to search for ray cats and franken-felines on their phones. Elin had to pretend there was educational value in that pursuit as she clock-watched until the end of the period.

As they get ready, she feels a fizzy energy among the students, who are huddled at the back of the room. There is a lot of laughter, the sound of tearing, and, *Oh shit, that's good. That's killer.* She is thankful for it, though it's the kind of excitement over which she has the most tenuous control.

When World War I broke out, Lise Meitner was almost a decade into her thirty-year collaboration with the chemist Otto Hahn. She left their laboratory, where she'd worked for no or little pay, and trained as an X-ray nurse, using what she understood of radium to assist in amputations of gangrenous soldiers at a military hospital near the Russian front. Hahn was employed by the military, improving poisonous gas. When Meitner returned to their draughty basement lab during Berlin's hungry "turnip" winter, she discovered a stable isotope of protactinium. When the results were published, Otto Hahn's name appeared ahead of hers. She'd sent it in that way. Out of loyalty.

After Meitner was exiled to Sweden, Hahn reached out to her in a secret letter using Bohr as a go-between. He couldn't understand why he'd produced barium by bombarding uranium. In the damp twilight of a Swedish forest, Meitner read Hahn's letter aloud to her nephew, Otto Frisch, another physicist, who'd come to visit. Those strange results. She smoked, letting her fine hands get red in the cold, thinking aloud. Her eye caught melting ice crystals on a branch, dangling fat water droplets over the ground. A hunch. She pulled out a pencil and began scratching calculations on the back of the thin stationery. Frisch helped with the math. They rechecked their numbers. It was the only explanation. The crackle of discovery in that quiet forest. They couldn't believe what they'd figured out: the atom's nucleus had been split. Such a tremendous amount of energy. Meitner was excited, then worried. The Swedish sun had fallen off the edge of the world. Where would this lead?

Now Elin's students are facing her, standing at attention like a dance troupe. She is charmed by them.

Okay, showtime.

Most of the students move to the middle of the room. Except for Bart and Regina, who stand off to the side. Someone broadcasts the *2001: A Space Odyssey* theme from their phone. This touch makes Elin laugh with delight.

Regina holds up the basketball to Elin, who can see it has a large *N* for *neutron* scribbled on it, and she rolls it slowly to Bart, who has written *U-235* on his forehead. When the basketball reaches him, he scoops it up to his chest dramatically, does two travelling twirls that take him into the middle of the large group. Out pops the sign, *U-236*, to signal a momentary absorption of the extra neutron.

This was Bohr's contribution—an intuition that U-235 was the fissile isotope, a picture of the bombarded nucleus having a compound nature, temporarily.

Nicely done, Elin thinks.

And then, just as the music crescendoes, the group splits apart dramatically. They all yell BOOM and raise their arms in the air.

Jazz hands. Witty touch.

Had Bohr fought hard enough for the female physicists who understood fission before anyone else—Ida Noddack, Lise Meitner—to get the recognition they deserved?

He'd begged Meitner and her nephew Frisch to publish quickly. He yelled at Enrico Fermi, who'd build the first nuclear reactor, for not acknowledging them in a radio address. He was in the U.S. at the time; even in an unwired world, the excitement about fission was a chain reaction that couldn't be contained. He rushed his own articles into print that emphatically credited that aunt–nephew duo.

One group runs over to one side, popping up their sign *Krypton*; they freeze interpretive-dance style. Another group runs off in the opposite direction, and holds up their sign *Barium*, repeat the stylistic freeze. Of the students left over, five stay in the middle, and kick and punch the air, throw up antifungal shoe powder like a mushroom cloud. They are the blast. Elin sneezes. In time for the music's second crescendo, three students rush forward with their phones in front of them, streaming videos of epilepsy-inducing flashing lights: thermal radiation.

They stop and throw handfuls of ripped paper at the front of the room: nuclear fallout, ionizing radiation.

Meanwhile, the krypton and barium are melting to the ground, in rhapsodic bends and feints.

We're decaying, Jonas yells.

There was a moment in those first chain reactions when it all could have gone wrong; they'd left out a cooling system in the reactor built under the University of Chicago's Stagg Field in a repurposed squash court. No protection from radiation. It went critical. The woman there, a twenty-three-year-old expert on neutron flux named Leona Woods, liked to swim in Lake Michigan, helped her mother harvest potatoes, and would work on nuclear reactors with Fermi through two pregnancies and one divorce, before becoming a late-blooming ecologist. Unlike Meitner and Maria Goeppert Mayer, two female physicists who were reluctant contributors to the weaponization of nuclear physics, Woods was unapologetic about the bomb. She was proud of her work. Sometimes Elin leaves Leona Woods out of her stories.

The students re-form, laughing and pushing each other, to repeat, so the released neutrons split other nuclei. The papa of the chain reaction Leo Szilard's interpretation: repeat this again and again in a self-sustaining chain, until everything that can has reacted. Which is what happened when Szilard went to work for Fermi.

It's a bit rough, but they're pleased with themselves. The basketball is being thrown around.

Elin stands and claps. More than gratified, she is thrilled by them. Something has sunk in.

When she looks over, the new art teacher—she's forgotten her name again—is standing in her doorway. There's an irritated press to her mouth.

You're being so loud. You're disturbing my class.

Elin imagines the students across the hall, soberly engaged in silent art.

I'm so sorry, Elin says.

How to make the new art teacher see how creative science can be?

We're learning about chain reactions, and they just put together this really clever demonstration of fission. A dance, a piece of theatre.

The new art teacher squints at Elin.

You're talking about a bomb, right? Bombs kill people, right? Show them a diagram. Have some respect.

The new art teacher doesn't wait for a response before she crosses back to her classroom. Elin is cut by this censure. Her earlier regret for not inviting this woman to see her father's famous chair evaporates.

When she looks back to her class, they have gone quiet, their heads hang sheepishly, not because they themselves feel chastised, but she, their teacher, has been dressed down.

Don't worry, miss, says Jonas. Nobody likes her.

Elin wants to accept this comfort, but can't. Her students' fealty is a volatile, unstable agglomeration, forming and re-forming. Plus, the new art teacher has better style. In high school, respect flows toward good shoes.

She's right, Elin says. Science can be so beautiful, utterly elegant and satisfying. Like your performance. But the material reality of that very same thing—in this case, a bomb—is still poison and destruction. That's what we have to wrestle with. Our central dilemma. What will be done with our beautiful theories? Our curiosity? Our perfect equations?

She has become too serious too quickly, another miscalculation.

Still, folks, that was a creative, inspired demonstration of what happens when a U-235 atom is bombarded with a neutron. That was some good fission.

Put the desks back, please. And Jonas, get that basketball down-stairs before anyone knows it's missing.

For homework, Elin assigns them a diagram of a chain reaction. She might be pressing the point: how one small collision begets another. The impact is cumulative.

Two ways to avoid a high school championship basketball game. Option one: circumnavigate the gym. This entails walking four extra hallway lengths—increasing the probability of passing a teacher or staff member witnessing you moving in the wrong direction—followed by a bold, open-air diagonal charge across the parking lot visible to three floors of windows, including the principal's office. Option two: snake along the hallway that flanks the gymnasium's east side to reach the door that leads to the teachers' parking spots. This route is the shorter, but more daring. If the gym heats up, a coach may prop open the door under the scoreboard, making your escape visible to most of the bleachers.

Elin debates which route has the better cost–benefit profile, when the squish of crepe-soled shoes outside the physics room door tells her she's hesitated too long.

Good afternoon, Ms. Henriksen.

Principal Preet stands in the doorway wearing a loose Milwaukee Badgers basketball jersey, forest green and grey, over creased chinos.

Sorry, did I startle you?

Those shoes, Principal Preet. You'll need to lose them if you ever want to be a spy.

Why would I want to be a spy?

Do I bring up the meme before he does? Elin wonders. If he hasn't seen it, then she's alerted him. If he has, what can she say that won't make it worse?

Mette, who never gave up the habit of married men, and every now and then a married woman, would flirt with Dilip Preet if she had him to herself beside an empty hallway. Even if she thought he didn't like her.

But Mette overestimates her hippie charms. And Preet is too well-groomed and serious for flirtation, despite the basketball jersey screen-printed with its gibbous-eyed mustelid.

Something has come to my attention today.

Principal Preet does the hand clap and lean, an early warning system.

There it is, thinks Elin. Damn art teacher. Didn't take her long.

Seriously, she says.

Sorry?

Elin studies Principal Preet. She needs to win him over. If the new art teacher claims she was being loud *and* teaching insensitively, she will have to be extra convincing, even charismatic, for him to see it otherwise.

There's a huge cheer from the gym. He glances in its direction, then turns to her with a new impatience. He can't trade on the jersey's optics in her empty classroom.

My students got a bit energetic this morning, she says. They were having trouble understanding fission in terms of chain reactions. So we opted for a more dynamic learning tool.

A dynamic learning tool?

Yes, they interpreted fission with, um, a kind of collective kinesis.

They danced?

Well, yes, sort of. I guess. It was more of a living, moving diorama.

Principal Preet's mouth flattens and Elin has to fight the urge to sprint down the short hallway. She wonders how many years Lise Meitner was in love with Otto Hahn before she wasn't anymore. They'd shared picnics with Thermoses of tea and cold meats. He'd played the mandolin.

You are a very interesting teacher, Ms. Henriksen. But that's not why I am here.

Oh.

Elin considers other possibilities: someone overheard the terrible advice she offered Regina; a parent complained, again, about her telling stories in physics; she has been nominated for a teaching award; Mabel Flores's absenteeism. The meme.

I understand you have a long weekend coming up.

Elin suppresses a cheery exhale.

Yes. I do. My siblings will be in town—a gallery dedication for my father, organized by my brother. He's an architect. My sister's singing at it. I'm hosting the pre-dedication party.

Your sister's a singer?

Yes.

Omigod. Of course. Henriksen. Is your sister Mette Henriksen? I'd no idea.

Why would you?

That song . . .

He snaps his finger, trying to jog his memory.

"He Looks Good Leaving," Elin says.

Bingo!

He stares at Elin with new regard; she resents his susceptibility to modest celebrity.

All right, then, he says. A few things. Don't do that again—the long weekend—without going through the proper channels with the acting department head. Also, let's talk next week, before exams begin, clear up loose ends before the fall. Next Tuesday. First thing.

He turns away from her. Through most of their collaboration, Lise Meitner continued to address Otto Hahn with the formal *sie* not *du*, though she was friends with his wife and godmother to their child.

Did you want an invite?

Sorry?

The gallery dedication. See my sister sing. It's a private event, so invite only.

Impulsiveness. You'd think middle age would have worn it out of her. Let's throw a party, she'd said to her mother a week earlier. Inspired by a kid's doodle, she combed through discarded butts under a beech tree. In view of students. Now this. She hates that he's thinking about it. An effusive thank you, a polite decline, and they'd both get away unscathed.

Sure. Yes, I'd like that. Already a museum member. Big fan.

That hand clap again. Would he worry he'd been unprofessional accepting her invite? She wants him to.

You coming to the game?

Elin's face hurts.

Of course. Finishing up a few things first.

She watches Principal Preet head down the hall to the gym.

He looks good leaving, she thinks.

Stay away from beech trees, Ms. Henriksen, he yells without looking back.

Elin can't remember who said it first, either Casper or Mette. *Niels Bohr is our grandfather.* It happened twelve days into their parents' longest silent treatment, when The Lilli snapped at her children and glared at Tig, who acted as if *he* couldn't be seen as well as heard, gliding through the house like a dead Danish king.

Said aloud, it seemed obvious.

They needed proof. Or stronger theory. They combed the stories their mother told them the summer Casper found the rucksack.

Pretending to be his daughter to help him escape, said Mette, making quote marks with her fingers. God, we're so thick.

He'd given her something precious. She wouldn't say what that was. Why not? Why be so cagey?

Code—she said she'd understood his code. Remember?

Casper slapped his forehead with his palm. Elin listened, trying to keep up.

Genetic code. Right there in front of us. She understood his genetic code. They shared DNA. He'd given her his genes.

Mette groaned.

The books followed, smuggled in plain sight past their mute parents to the floor of Casper's room, where they were stacked up like the jambs of a Viking doorway.

Rustling pages, the soft animal inhales of treasure hunting. It didn't take long for them to be wholly convinced, using the rough math of children and theoreticians: Every contradiction can be worked around. Or ignored.

Elin found the photo of Bohr and his two siblings, Harold and Jenny. When she made a photocopy, folded it, and kept it in her pocket, Casper taunted.

Jenny Bohr, Jenny Bohr: the sister of, for evermore.

Mette punched her brother's bicep.

You have her hair colour, El, he said.

Her heart sank. Parents, blond. Casper, blond. Mette, blond. Elin, grey-eyed, ash-brown hair.

No theorems or theories to mark her short life: no prizes, no children, she's nobody's wife.

The teenaged Casper had a high-pitched hyena hoot-laugh.

Their hair colour, Mette corrected. We're more fair. Maybe you're our proof, Elin. Maybe what's left of the Bohrs in our blood concentrates in you.

The laughing stopped. Casper looked unhappy.

13

Mustelids, thinks Elin. She's still in the physics room. The basketball game is over; the school has emptied.

Mette and Casper arrive in four days. She's eaten three Moon Pies in a row. And now she can't shake the image of Dilip Preet in an athletic jersey.

The mustelids include sea otters, weasels, wolverines, and badgers. Her first therapist had struck her as badger-like. Which was unfair. But in the long silences when he waited for her to speak, she'd had time to ponder the flatness of his head, his small ears, and wonder if he too had anal scent glands.

Write it down, that therapist insisted. But Elin choked. If she forced what happened into the logic of an account, would the written version change, then replace, what she'd actually experienced?

This very problem—how being both actor and spectator affects the results—preoccupied Bohr.

Start at the beginning, the therapist said, assuming this was the tender spot, most in need of exposure to the healing light.

Elin takes out her phone.

There are things you can say to a dead physicist you'd never tell a lover or some guy with a master's in social work, whimsical socks, and a plump, semi-aquatic solidity.

For starters, the beginning for her hadn't been the worst of it.

———

That came after Bets was five months old, and Mette drove in from Chicago to stay overnight on Fridays through to Sunday afternoons so Elin could work into the weekend's wee hours when tips were 50 per cent better. Sleep past noon.

On one such Sunday, Mette returned from a walk with Bets. Elin, exhausted, had fallen back asleep in the living room.

Knock.

Her sister pressed her face up against the loose pane, rapped lightly as a warning, turned the handle, and walked in. Elin, foggy, registered the sounds on the porch as belonging to another house, another mother waiting for another sleepy child.

She'd fallen asleep on the Narwhal, the one from her father's studio. Under her palms was the puce bouclé upholstery, its dated pocks of pink, like littered pomegranate arils.

The strangest disequilibrium. What had she done?

For a terrible instant, she worried she'd soiled herself. Or her pants were down, and she was masturbating. In front of her child, her sister.

Elin jumped off the chair.

Mette was singing. Of course she was. A bar of melody blew into the foyer with a flutter of fallen leaves.

Bets was still in the carrier on her back. Eyes closed, cheeks starched by the October air, face pressed against the spot between Mette's shoulders.

Elin stared at them as if they were intruders.

Who was this strange person with bulging shopping bags, and a large, wet-faced baby on her back?

Shhhh, Mette said, pointing. Princessa slumbers.

She began to chat about their afternoon: groceries, library, park. Elin realized she was standing, clothed, clean.

But the feeling persisted, a kind of ugliness she couldn't outrun. She stared at the chair, as if something small and hook-mouthed had crawled out from it, burrowed into her damp spots.

Hungry?

Elin mumbled, but stayed in the living room. She could see a line of drool on the back of Mette's jean jacket as she passed, then heard the canvas shopping bag thud on the kitchen table—and the thunder roll of something freed from it, apples or sweet potato. Still humming, her sister opened cupboards, turned on a tap, rattled the crisper drawer that stuck.

Elin smelled the spice of the Narwhal's teak as if it was on her skin. On humid days, it was fragrant with figs and pepper.

She studied the chair and saw herself, a small girl, sitting with her father in his studio, when they both looked up to see The Lilli. Her mother was standing in the doorway, her ashen face knit with a very specific kind of pain.

What are you doing?

Nothing was said, not a word.

Her father tugged Elin's waistband, tucked in her shirt, and lifted her off the Narwhal.

She looked at her mother's face. What exactly had she done wrong?

Bets woke and started to cry. Mette had wrestled the child out of the carrier, and then her baby coat, and carried her into the living room. She lifted Bets and cooed at her gently—Now, now little one—and she tested the bottom of her onesie jumper for dampness.

She's hungry, Mette said, holding the baby out.

Elin shook her head.

Lemme wash my hands.

She ran up to the second-floor bathroom and shut the door. Turned the tap on hot and left her hands under. Then she pulled her clothes off and scrubbed every part of her body until her skin stung.

Bets was bawling loudly. Mette yelled up from the bottom of the stairs.

Hey you! Your kid is hungry. What are you doing up there?

When she came back down, Mette was angry.

Your baby, Elin. Your baby is crying herself into a state.

The heat and heft of that child. Elin sat on the edge of the ratty couch, raised her shirt, unclipped her bra, held Bets to her breast, welcomed the forceful pinch of the hungry mouth, its untied tongue and unapologetic appetite.

She was diagonal from the Narwhal; it sat haloed in a dim afternoon light, so its curved teak angles, the bright fabric, were off-putting, vaguely horrifying.

You all right? You're a bit of a pale zombie mama.

Mette placed a plate with toast, sliced apple, Russian salad on the armrest. Bets was already asleep at her breast.

Elin stared at the Narwhal. There was The Lilli at the studio door, unsure of what she'd just seen. Elin's young life changing in an instant. The next day, she was not left to draw by Tig's studio, nor did he pull her braids at the breakfast table, speaking to her in funny cartoon voices. Suddenly, she was taken everywhere during the day with her mother and not treated like she was a very special child, but held at a distance, as if highly flammable, a pigtailed reminder that everything bad that could go wrong in a good life was right there in your own house, closer than you'd expect.

Elin laid her sleeping child on the couch. Her heart flapped; a small pinhole of light sucked her inward.

She tipped over, hip thudding against the hardwood floor.

Hey, hey, Mette said. What's happening?

Her sister grabbed Elin under the armpits, hoisted her up, then fetched a wet cloth and dabbed it on her forehead.

You okay, kiddo? Getting enough water?

That was when the images became words, falling out of Elin's head like old teeth.

Mette held her. But the more Elin said, the more her sister's arms slackened, fell away.

When she stopped talking, there was silence. Mette stood up, squeezed Elin's shoulder. Some new pinched-nerve tightness in her face.

I should go, she said.

The front door shut before Elin stood or mustered a thank you.

Or, I'm sorry. I didn't mean to tell you like that.

Or, Don't leave me alone.

Mette hadn't said as much as, Oh, El, are you sure? Why now?

Mette hadn't said a word.

There was a playpen in the kitchen. Elin left Bets gurgling happily under her mobile, picked up the canvas shopping bag, put the apples in a bowl, the squash on the top of the refrigerator.

The kitchen's surfaces stared back at her: Mette's face, blank and tense.

She pressed her hands against her cheeks. The house felt small and desolate. And Elin sealed within it to continue an unrelieved orbit around the small, round creature lying on her back kicking at a terry cloth star.

What have I done? she said to no one.

Elin stops talking; the phone records her breathing.

Her morfar fought with words; there were never enough of them. Or they weren't precise. His mother, his brother, then wife Margrethe and her personal assistant transcribed and edited his articles before they were sent to be published, wrangled his wild-windedness into something readable. Otherwise, he'd never have stopped teasing out the contradictions; something always gets left out.

Mette came back the next weekend. To help with Bets. That's what she said. And not much more, other than short, formal questions: Where does this go? Should I buy more wipes? Elin's chest cramped; her mother had taught her that proximity could hold more judgment than love. Yet she didn't want Mette to leave, either.

Her sister made Elin's bed and folded the baby clothes in all the wrong ways. She put Bets on the floor by the blocks, and Elin lay down beside her child on the carpet. Mette found a spray bottle: she spritzed the living room's windowsills as if they were plants.

She moved around until she was at right angles to Elin, still spraying when she spoke.

The probability is low, almost nil, with these cases that it only happens to one child, she said. You know that?

Elin's back was to her.

Yes, she said.

The word hung in the air. Something dark and heavy that didn't know where to land: statistical certainty.

At the end of that week, Mette phoned and suggested they meet in a café. Her voice was friendly but formal, the way she would speak to a songwriter with more ambition than talent—generosity with its trace metal of pity.

Sure, Elin said.

The rendezvous was a block away from her house, an easy walk, a chance to get out with the baby. Bets had been restless and inconsolable without the calming routine of time with her aunt.

Elin brushed her hair, applied mascara, tucked in her shirt, put on pants that had a zipper: made an effort. So she could refuse when Mette offered to pay for her coffee, she ransacked the bedroom bureau and her jacket pockets for change.

Mette was waiting for them when Elin pushed their maelstrom of wind, stroller, loosed hair, falling soother, and whimpering infant into the café.

Her sister's mouth worked into one of her enigmatic half smiles, arms outstretched for Bets. Handing the baby over meant they didn't need to hug each other.

A few seconds later, Bets's little hand was tangled in Mette's hair, their eyes locked. Backlit by morning shining through the café windows, her sister was beyond lovely, her child vibrant.

Mette made a gesture as if to return Bets to Elin, but the child mewed with alarm, clung to Mette's hair, grabbed a little fistful of her sweater.

Leave her, Elin said.

Mette took one of her breaths that seemed to compress whole scenes of dialogue with one exhale.

I'm seeing a therapist, she said.

The cookie Elin had bought for Bets was an embarrassment, nutritionally negligent. She brushed away the granular sugar, peeled off its stripes of caramel icing, fretting that it was still too sweet. Bets was reaching for it, about to fuss. She handed her a piece.

Was there something *you* wanted to say?

The first gulp of her latte was unexpectedly, painfully hot. It burned the tender flesh of her upper mouth, and after swallowing, Elin grabbed Bets's sippy cup, chugged some of its tepid apple juice for relief.

Mette squinted with irritation.

The café was half-full; a woman on her cellphone ordered a prescription cream in a too-loud voice the next table over. Strong espresso, warm panini, souring milk, and street-level exhaust: Elin's head swam.

Bets snoozed in her sister's lap, the little girl's fist still tight around a clump of her aunt's sweater. Mette leaned forward.

Nothing?

Her sister's closeness, the humidity of her whispering, felt like a heat lamp.

I'm angry, Mette said.

At me?

Everything I thought I knew about my own childhood, our family, is changed by this, turned upside down.

If you believe me.

I believe that you believe.

That's not the same as believing.

My therapist says you're being unfair.

That's what you're paying her for.

Goddammit, El. It's the best I can do.

Bets began to stir, and Elin wanted to grab her—to wrest all that pink-cheeked vigour away from her sister's equal, if more oblivious, aliveness.

She stood up and threw things into the baby bag, kicking the stroller brake off and reaching for Bets, who was half-awake. The woman at the next table who'd confirmed loudly she'd pay extra for same-day shipping stared. Her pity, another insult.

Let me help, said Mette.

No!

The buckle clicked into place, and Elin stowed the baby bag underneath, placed a one-eared rabbit stuffy into the now-awake Bets's hands, and pushed the stroller to the café exit. Mette followed, but when she tried to open the door, Elin shrugged her off.

I'm good.

Bets reached out for Mette, whimpering as Elin pushed her hip into the glass door and lifted the stroller over the metal jamb. There were people on the sidewalk moving past the café, and a young man held the door wide for her. When she looked back her sister was picking up her bag and Elin wondered if breathing hurt for Mette in the awful way it did for her.

When Otto Hahn won the Nobel Prize for Chemistry, for his work on nuclear fission, he gave no credit to Lise Meitner. If she was betrayed, she never said so. Not in public, anyway. She remained friends with Hahn for the rest of his life.

I've always been so confused by her story, morfar, Elin says into her phone, staring at the copper beech.

Why? he'll want to know.

Valuing relationships over justice. Over truth.

She imagines his long exhale, the thoughtful stare.

Whose truth, though? he'll say. Lise thought war was indecent. She didn't want to be the mother of a bomb.

———

A card came in the mail a few days after they met in the café. Elin recognized Mette's distinct open loops and felt a small shock of hope. Her sister had exquisite taste in cards. There would be a thoughtful quote and then a short note that would sidestep details. This was how Mette said I'm sorry, let's work it out; this was how Mette made things right.

The card Mette sent that day was more sombre than usual: a small bluebird in an old-fashioned cage. The note was short:

Em,

   I have to take a break from you and Bets for a while. The energy's not good for me. I'm sorry; tell Bets how much I love her.
Me

14

I have a cut, The Lilli says into the phone, her voice rough as pumice. Bring me some hydrogen peroxide and cotton swabs.

This call at work on a Wednesday, so soon after one about Mette's singing, feels uncharacteristic. A shift. As she makes a right out of the school parking lot just before noon, Elin's mind hamster-wheels with worry. She stops at the Walgreens on West National, grabs the antiseptic and swabs, before turning on South Layton Boulevard.

Three days before the party and dedication, and now her mother has a cut. There's a faint threat to this development.

Don't catastrophize, she tells herself.

Her plan is to get her mother's cut dressed and return to school before the lunch hour is over.

She pulls up to the house on the north side of Burnham.

The exterior is exactly as it has always been, right down to the precisely cubed boxwood hedge flanking the front walk and the candelabra espalier of Asian pear under the living room window, babied by The Lilli as if it were a pet.

She parks and walks up to the entrance, uses her key, and steps into the foyer.

Mom? You okay?

The early summer warmth pools in the house's unchanged interior, its museum-grade tidiness, the autumnal palette.

I'm right here, Elin. Don't be dramatic.

In her linen side-slit tunic, statement jewellery, black cigarette pants, and buttery leather slides, The Lilli bullies the decor back into style. She has one leg uncharacteristically propped on the low spare coffee table.

I wouldn't have called you.

Okay.

I tried Casper. He's in a meeting.

Mom, he lives in New York. It's not like he could have picked up peroxide for you.

He would have FaceTimed with me. Walked me through it. Have the pharmacist down the road send it over.

Well, I'm here now. I brought the stuff. You're welcome.

Hmm. You're all I've got, aren't you?

The Lilli doesn't look at Elin. Her eyes have a bleary liquid heat. She's been drinking. Elin peers around for a glass.

So, let's take a peek at this cut.

Her mother grimaces and pulls up the pant from her resting leg to reveal her thin calf. A warm pink streak runs up from an ugly gash that's crusted and dark, just above her mother's ankle.

Jesus, Mom. How long have you had this?

Two days.

What did you do?

I was trimming the pear after it rained. I slipped on my shears.

Elin presses her palms into the streaked flesh above the wound. It's hot.

She won't be going back to school this afternoon, and now a series of negotiations, swaps, and payoffs plays out before her.

Okay, where's your wallet and jacket? We're going to the clinic.

The Lilli makes a thin protest. Tiny seeds of damp make her brow shine. There's a baby-bird translucence to her skin.

Elin's heart races; she senses trouble.

Your brother Casper wouldn't make me go to a clinic.

Mom, I don't give a fuck what Casper would or wouldn't do. I'm right here. Me. I know what I see.

You're so rude, Elin. You've always been the crassest of my children.

Right.

Elin turns and yanks the first jacket she can find from her mother's hall closet.

Not that one, The Lilli barks.

Elin ignores her.

Field trip, she says.

The Christmas after fourteen-year-old Mette tired of Big Bill Lister, there was a foil box under the tree that looked different from the other presents.

Her mother left it for last and then, handling it carefully, held it out to Elin, who was twelve.

This is for you.

Casper and Mette looked up from their gifts. Her siblings' corvid eyes twitched at the wrapping paper's metallic stripes, the elaborate ribbon, the glint of specialness.

It came a long way, The Lilli said.

Elin felt a pressure in her chest; she looked peripherally at her father. He had his face in a new book.

Keep it upright, The Lilli said, pointing one of her long, elegant fingers at the end. Open from there.

Half-unwrapped, the box revealed Danish words she couldn't read. When her mother nodded at her, she tore the cellophane off and opened the lid to find a row of large domes encased in pretty foil, emitting a waft of perfumy cocoa butter.

Elin looked up at her mother for an explanation. The Lilli grinned and pressed her palms together.

Flødeboller, she said. Danish Moon Pies. I had Petrine bring them back from a recent trip to Copenhagen.

Try one, said Casper.

Her insides felt like a tightening fist.

But I like the American ones, she said.

Elin!

Tig clapped his book shut, put it aside.

Don't be rude. Your mother has gone out of her way. And these are a Danish specialty—very high quality.

Elin reached for one of the confections. Not low and flat like a Scooter Pie, but tall and mounded like a Royal Guard's bearskin hat, robustly un-sandwich-like. She unwrapped it with a painful, self-conscious deliberation. Her mother's face, a fuse of anticipation seconds earlier, had already dimmed into something smooth and inscrutable, her dark star opacity.

What met Elin's mouth was different from a Scooter Pie. The chocolate tasted meatier, the marshmallow creamier, not overly sweet, in the way that certain pleasures are problematic for being exactly right for you. She worried about disguising her enjoyment, until she bit through to the cookie base and tasted marzipan.

The half-chewed mouthful of *flødeboller* disgorged in one gag, a pulpy flotsam in the palm of her hand.

They were all watching.

Geez, El. Grow up, Casper said.

Her mother stood up and fetched a napkin for Elin, wiped her hand roughly. Then she put the lid on the box and disappeared with it, the tentacles of its specialty shop wrapping paper wiggling from its underside; a rare and shimmery cephalopod that wouldn't survive a Wisconsin winter.

Her father put his book down and followed The Lilli with a long sigh. No one would see the *flødeboller* again.

Elin looked to her sister for understanding. Moon Pies were their thing, a sister thing, an American thing. She wanted a cookie sandwich with a parsimonious dollop of marshmallow smothered in cheap chocolate that would be washed down with a cola by someone wearing a new pair of overalls and thinking about freight trains. She did not want to be like her parents, retreating into their Danishness to hold themselves above Americans, the same people from whom they expected success.

She would die happy if she never ate marzipan again.

Oh, El, Mette said.

Which meant her sister understood only part of it.

In the clinic waiting room, Elin leaves The Lilli while she rearranges her afternoon, sitting in her car in the parking lot on her phone.

Rather than call the school office to inform them she can't teach her afternoon classes, Elin phones Gary, the teacher who was planning to cover her Friday morning physics class, and who Elin knows has a Wednesday second-period break.

Missing or cancelling a class near the end of term is considered bad form; there's no budget left for substitute teachers, so the students will be made to sit in the library. If the librarian resists, they'll be sent home. Parents are sure to complain. Complaints go to Principal Preet.

If you take my class now, you have your Friday morning free again, Elin says.

Gary's eagerness deflates her.

The waiting room in Dr. Hou's office is packed. It's a joint practice, an interdisciplinary team of family physicians, social workers, physiotherapists, dieticians, and even a personal trainer. There are heaps of magazines and three dispensers of hand sanitizer and two television screens playing a loop of health videos. The walls are taupe, the carpet olive, and the chairs upholstered in a washable grey.

The Lilli hates going to the doctor. She wears a succession of expressions: scared child, disoriented hostage, trapped fox.

Elin reaches over for her mother's hand, surprised at its balsa lightness, its papery bundling of bones and sinew. Her thumb against The Lilli's palm has a battering ram's heft.

Can I weigh you? the nurse asks after ushering The Lilli into an examination room. Her mother is a pointillism of sweat.

The Lilli shakes her head.

I have a scratch, for Godsakes.

Standard procedure. You haven't been here in a while. Helps us when it comes to treatment.

No, says The Lilli. I want to see Dr. Hou. I want to see my doctor.

The nurse frowns.

Soon enough. I have to look at your wounds.

Wounds? I have a single gash on my ankle.

The nurse asks The Lilli to climb onto the examination table, take off her shoes and socks, and hike up her pant leg. Elin assists. Her mother does not wear socks. The slides fall off her feet. With a small shock, Elin notes her mother's toenails, usually beautifully pedicured, are unpainted and yellowish, in need of clipping.

The nurse's finger traces the angry pink snaking up The Lilli's leg.

If you'd waited a few hours longer, you'd be in an ambulance heading to the ER, she says to The Lilli.

She leaves and there are murmurs outside in the hallway.

When Dr. Hou comes in, he looks grave.

The Lilli is still on the examination table, shoulders hunched like a morose teenager. He doesn't make small talk, but peers at her ankle and its marauding lines of sepsis.

It's too late for oral antibiotics, I'm afraid. The nurse is calling across to the hospital. Set up intravenous.

Elin reaches out and clutches Dr. Hou's forearm.

How long will that be? Are you admitting her?

He ignores Elin.

You'll need to stay overnight for observation, Ms. Henriksen. You've let this go a bit long.

Dr. Hou looks at Elin.

I'm going to ask you to step out for a minute so I can talk to her.

Really? Is that necessary?

In the hallway, she hears what sounds like arguing. The Lilli's voice is pitchy and frightened. A long train of tests and specialists, hospitalizations and IV feedings chugs along in front of Elin. The Lilli grim-faced, strapped into a seat, bony and frightened.

The door clicks open and an unsmiling, furrowed Dr. Hou enters the hallway.

How long has this been going on?

The cut—two, maybe three days ago.

Your mother's obstinacy. Her lack of reason, meanness.

Oh, that, says Elin. That's been forever.

Her mother made bombs. Starting at age thirteen. If they were short on fuses—and often they were—she filled a cigar box with calcium chlorate, covered it with wax paper, dribbled sulphuric acid over it. And ran.

We used IEDs before they called them that, The Lilli said proudly, when the U.S. invaded Afghanistan for Operation Enduring Freedom, and then again when Desert Storm was all over the news, and Milkwaukeeans argued about WMDs in Iraq while waiting in line at Starbucks.

You're identifying with the enemy, Mom, Elin said. But The Lilli didn't see it that way. Politics were irrelevant; she couldn't cheer for the side with bigger firepower.

Once a guerrilla, always a guerrilla.

Yet in the hospital, her mother cries.

She lies back in the adjustable bed, as if pinned by a shock wave. Her palms dig into the sheets, girding against the unknowns suggested by the invading IV tube curling parasitically from her wrist.

Elin folds The Lilli's beautiful tunic and pants and puts them on the table beside her bed. The leather slides are stored in a plastic bag underneath. Her mother's jewellery is safe in a pocket in Elin's purse.

I'm alone, she whispers. Tears flow down her high cheekbones and hit her lips.

I'm so very alone.

No, Mom. You've got me.

Elin wraps her arms around her mother, tormented by the sharpness of her shoulders, the bumps of her spine, the weightlessness of her.

I'll be back. I'm letting the dog out, swinging by your place to get your toothbrush, hand cream, fresh undies. Okay?

Her mother shudders.

I wish Casper was here.

I do too, Mom.

Bring my better jacket, would you, Elin?

Even The Lilli's stories of danger were ones where good taste prevailed. Elin imagines her mother as a skinny preteen pulling Niels Bohr and his wife through Sydhavnen alleys reeking of smoked chestnuts, beer piss, fish guts, unable to keep her eyes off Margrethe Bohr's clothes.

She wore a beautiful trapeze coat, the colour of wild cherries, The Lilli told her children, the summer Casper found the rucksack. To escape in, of all things.

The Lilli's assignment was to get the couple safely to the gardening shacks at the edge of the water where they'd wait for a signal from the fishing boat that would take them to a ship, deeper in the sound. From there to Sweden. Bohr's brother, nephew, some architect rumoured to be a Communist, were already there. They acted like it was a cocktail party, The Lilli said. I saw the flicker of light and yelled at them, *You have to go now!* A thirteen-year-old ordering a Nobel Prize winner to his knees so he wouldn't be seen. And oh, his wife didn't like that. The crawling.

It was awful seeing her beautiful coat ruined.

———

The nurses' station is bright but solemn, the patient rooms dimmed and hushed, when Elin returns.

The Lilli has fallen asleep sitting up in bed. Elin empties the items she's taken from her mother's home onto the small table: lavender-scented cream, mint toothpaste, deodorant, mouthwash, reading glasses, a bedside paperback, bruxism guard, hairbrush, dental floss, Cherries in the Snow lipstick. (For all your mother's airs about style, Petrine said, she's a cheapskate when it comes to makeup.)

A folded bathrobe and slippers.

It's too much: Elin has no measure of what will make her feel less alone. This is The Lilli's first hospitalization.

Elin leans on the button that lowers the bed, and her mother stirs, and rolls on her side. She looks childlike, her legs bent up and inward, her sleeping face released from the grip of her frustrations, her disappointments in others.

Mette should be here, Elin thinks. She should show up for some of the hard stuff.

A text from Bets brightens her silenced phone: All cool with gran? You stayin' there?

Alone, The Lilli had said, the first time Elin had heard her use the word since Tig died.

Elin texts a thumbs-up emoji, followed by a heart, to Bets. She hates emojis. But which words were as precise?

She tries to sleep on the hard chair beside her mother's hospital bed. Her feet balance on the bed rungs, but there is no turning radius for her body, nowhere to rest her lolling head. Her torso slouches so the edge of the chair's backrest cuts into her neck.

Something good and solid and beautiful for people to sit on, her aunt Petrine had said about her father's modest accomplishments. His chairs were his best work. That's not a bad thing to contribute. More than most of us do, right, darling?

Elin capitulates, sits up, but she is so tired. The rooms have gone quiet with the drowsy hum of the automatic floor scrubber in the hallway. Her mother's IV will last through the night. She slips off her shoes and crawls onto the bed without disturbing the long, thin woman.

Her mother reaches behind her: Elin lays her fingers lightly over the transparent, freckled skin. The Lilli pulls her daughter's hand forward over her hip, where she can hold it with both of hers.

I hate you.

I hate you.

I hate you.

After his escape, Niels Bohr sent a message, in code, asking specifically for The Lilli. He wanted her to fetch something important he'd left behind.

On an overcast day in early November, Mette left a message for Elin. A different kind of code.

She wants to talk to you. Come soon.

Elin had just turned thirty. She drove to Burnham and left Bets in the Hyundai, where she'd fallen asleep. The front door was open just a crack.

It was such a small thing, but so uncharacteristic for a house that was usually vacuum sealed. She couldn't hear anything. She looked back at the car and she thought twice about leaving Bets there. The window was halfway down. It was a cool day. Bets was sound asleep, bundled in fleece.

Mette's retreat several weeks earlier had been both polite and seismic. Elin was already feeling shakier, unmoored without her sister's regular help.

She only made one step inside when her mother came running at her, face streaked with rage and tears.

Hateful, hateful bitch. That story again. How dare you?

Mette stood in the far room, arms crossed, facing out the back window. Something had happened. Something had been revealed that wasn't hers to tell.

Don't you come here. You're not part of this family. You're not one of us.

A numbness held Elin in place. She saw a wild fear in her mother's eyes, her skin raised with blossoms of rage.

If she protested, she cannot remember what she said. She does recall looking past her mother, trying to catch her sister's eyes.

Why?

She got in the car. Her body shook. She couldn't get the key in the ignition. She was about to lay her head on the steering wheel, to give up. Don't do this, she whispered. The car's oxygen thinned.

If I fall apart, one of them has to come out, take over, she promised herself.

She heard a sound. Bets was waking up, emerging gently from a dream, giggling.

Elin jammed the key in the ignition, rolled the engine over, drove away.

Now she stares at her mother's back, the dinosaur bumps of her spine through the thin hospital gown.

I love you.

I love you.

I love you.

The monitors whoosh. There's quiet laughter at the nurses' station. An electric kettle whistles.

I love you too, Elin, her mother says.

Half-asleep, Elin's unsure of what she's heard.

15

M a'am, ma'am.
    Someone shakes Elin's shoulder. She's having a dream that she wants to remember.

You can't sleep there, ma'am. I'm sorry, but you'll have to get out of the bed.

It's after 2 a.m.

Elin climbs off, and mouths Sorry to the nurse. Her mother has wrapped her sheets around her like a body about to be immolated on a sacred river.

The effect is disrupted by her sound; The Lilli breathes like a slightly congested child.

Elin can still feel her warmth, and it conjures a better time, when her mother's tonic-sweetened breath mixed with July pollens and the city's cindered air. She'd unlocked the back door with a wordless *tink* to find her children grimy and panting. Her hair was swept up and she wore a fresh cotton sheath of bright coral. She'd put lipstick on.

Dinner was made. There was a jug of ice water, garnished with mint sprigs, on the table. Rounds of fresh, cold cucumber. She sent them to wash up and change their clothes. They returned smelling of carbolic soap, dizzy with relief.

The Lilli drank G&T with bitters and watched them eat.

You're never lonely when you're necessary, she said after she told her stories.

At the nurses' station, Elin asks when her mother will be discharged.

A woman in a dark-magenta uniform and a long black braid looks at her dully.

Not until a doctor sees her first, the woman says. Sometimes we get one up here by 7 a.m. More likely nine.

Elin wonders how late she can be for her morning class; she's counting on an early-rising doctor.

The lights are on at the house when Elin pulls up. Inside the door, she hears laughter. Bets's. She stops at the doorway. Her daughter, as Elin once did, now stays up all night, falls asleep at dawn. Elin's too tired to worry about it.

The entrance is open but for the screen door. There is another voice. Curt's. He is doing an imitation. Bets is giggling uncontrollably. Her foot is stomping to relieve the buildup of her mirth; her hand is hitting a wall. This is Bets, employing her whole body to transmit delight.

As a new mother, after Elin figured this out about the strange creature she'd brought into the world, she was alert for things that would make her child laugh: a dog licking her ice cream cone, the squishy sound of feet in rain-soaked sneakers, around-the-world on playground swings.

Curt must be entranced by that laughter—how could he not?—and works to elicit it again and again, as she once had.

They are in the kitchen; she hears the clink of glasses, the soft gurgle of an emptying beer bottle, the smell of freshly made popcorn.

Leave them be, she thinks, aching for her own bed. Mitzi slides out to greet Elin, ears down, making a slow switchblade swish with her tail.

Mom, is that you? Is Granny okay?

Elin turns midway up the stairs.

Bets stands at the bottom, looking up. Her eyes are huge green stars. She's radiant.

Oh no, Elin thinks, she's in love.

Everything's fine, hon. The Lilli is sleeping. She'll be discharged in the morning. I'm going to grab a few hours then go back.

Do you want me to come with you?

She looks at the dog, who is moving past her on the way up the stairs to the attic.

No, hon. I need you here.

At 8:15 a.m., Elin hovers around the nurses' station, much to the chagrin of the new woman on shift, whose uniform's an unappealing kelly green.

The prospect of an early visit, and discharge, by the doctor on rounds has come and gone.

I'm sorry, says the nurse. But some of the other patients on this ward have more acute conditions than your mother. You'll have to wait.

Elin makes the call; she has left it until the last minute. Dez, the teacher covering her Friday afternoon class, has a Thursday morning break. He too is eager to swap again and regain the early start to his weekend. Now it is all gone, the luxury of her entirely free Friday; she will give Joy back her free second-period, there's no point wasting a future favour if she has to come in and teach her other classes. She'll fit all of her errands for the party into her lunch and the break period that follows.

The Lilli—once more in her precise tunic, black pants, stylish shoes—sits on the edge of the bed, a portrait of majesty held captive. She's no longer attached to the IV, but the port is still in her wrist; the charge nurse is irked that she has changed out of the hospital gown.

If the doctor orders another bag of drip, you're taking all those clothes off again.

Don't talk to me like I'm a three-year-old, Elin's mother tells the nurse. I'm perfectly fine. This is a waste of my good day.

How to explain The Lilli to others? She'd have to reframe her, lean on something like quadratic equations with their double real, real and imaginary solutions, each of them right, if occupying different locations.

But where to locate The Lilli's working truth if she had trouble finding her own?

The scab on her mother's foot looks less ominous, the flesh around it only faintly rosy. She presses her palm once more against The Lilli's calf. The temperature feels normal.

Get your hands off me, Elin. You're not a doctor.

Be quiet, Mom.

She feels less charitable now that her long weekend has been foreshortened and her mother's infection is stanched. The Lilli's predicament fits like a compression stocking, the entirety of Elin girdled by duty.

If her mother had fixed Elin in the amber of flightiness, when was the last time Elin saw The Lilli as anything but problematic?

Once, she'd asked Mette, Why do you love her?

They were adults. Just a few months into talking again after their long estrangement. Mette didn't hesitate.

She has those stories, right? All a parent needs to be loved is to tell one good story.

The best, for Elin, was how The Lilli stole Denmark's last supply of heavy water—it fit into a beer bottle—right out from under the Nazis. At the request of Niels Bohr.

Dressed as a girl making deliveries from the market, she walked into his sprawling Vesterbro property, passing under an arched gateway held up by huge stone elephants, and beside an immense copper beech, before climbing the steps to the House of Honour, where the physicist and his family had lived right up to their escape.

The hallway smelled of oiled wood, cigar smoke, and chrysanthemums. There was an arcade with tropical plants and a glass roof. An indoor fountain. The wonder of that, The Lilli told them as children. She wanted to spend the whole afternoon staring at the paintings. More Gestapo than mice, though. Her job was to be as inconspicuous as possible. So, she moved directly to the kitchen, as if she knew the place.

The cook had hidden the heavy water, a colourless liquid, in a bottle of beer in the larder. She made a small mark on its glass lip with a filleting knife, took cheese and bread from Lilliana's basket, replaced them with the bottles, and handed her a few *krøner*.

On her way out of the kitchen, Lilliana locked eyes with the Gestapo officer who'd taken over Bohr's office. He was rifling through the physicist's papers.

What are you looking at? he snapped.

The art, she said. Beauty makes us better people.

She didn't blink.

The doctor arrives after 9 a.m. She is young and flustered and Elin can tell she has an authority issue with the nurse in the kelly-green uniform, who snarls at her.

She looks at The Lilli's calf and rolls her bottom lip under her top.

You could use another bag of vancomycin.

I don't want to stay, says The Lilli. I have plans.

Hmmm, the doctor says. But if you show up here again because we didn't get rid of the infection, you'll have to stay longer.

I'll take my chances, says The Lilli. Please give me my bill, whatever it is I need to sign. I'm not staying.

Elin's mother makes an imperious wave with her hand.

There isn't much the doctor can do. And Elin won't protest; she's determined to return to school in time for her afternoon classes.

Okay, the doctor says. There's an extra release for you to sign, and you can go. I'll write you a prescription.

They are not out of the hospital parking lot when they begin to argue.

I think we should cancel the party, Mom. You're not up to it.

Don't tell me what I'm up to, Elin. I've had a cut. I got some drugs. It's Thursday, there's plenty of time.

You haven't had a lot of sleep. And you'll be wiped out by the antibiotics. I just think we're pushing it.

It was your idea, Elin, this party. Too late for second thoughts. What's going on? You and your sister arguing?

Her mother's tone is brazenly hopeful.

No, Mom. I'm just worried about you.

Well, don't be. I won't be calling to uninvite people now. If you're so worried about me, you can come over earlier to the house and help me set up and clean.

This is not what Elin wants to hear. It will eat further into the little time she has to get shopping done. She turns toward the expressway that will take them over the valley, and down 94, so she can exit on Mitchell and get her mother home quickly.

What are you doing, Elin? I want to go downtown. I'm meeting your aunt Petrine for lunch.

Mom, you just spent the night in the hospital.

I didn't get a chance to call her. The old dear will be waiting for me. Besides, I'm fine.

You don't even like her. You always call her a snob.

That's the kinder version.

Her mother's jaw moves clockwise like a dry rotor.

But I don't have the luxury of choosing my friends now, do I? she adds.

Her tone sounds newly frayed. Elin glances sideways and sees that the straightness of her mother's posture, so necessary for upholding impossible standards, is finally rounding into a subtle concavity.

That woman needs something to resist, Petrine once said to Elin at a meal when there'd been a stormy exit after The Lilli argued with Mette. First, her parents. Then, the Germans. Finally, anyone who's stupid enough to love her.

We're meeting at the Pfister, her mother says. Your aunt's choice—pretentious as ever.

The Lilli was easier to understand if she herself was a secret. Bohr's secret. And someone else's.

But who?

When they were younger, there'd been some discussion of Margrethe. But Casper, whose room had books stacked like bar graphs, said it didn't make sense that the mother of six sons would give up a daughter, not raise her as her own.

They made a list. Secretaries, personal assistants, Tisvilde painters and poets, colleagues' wives.

Why not a physicist? Elin said.

They considered Lise Meitner. She was seven years older than Bohr. There were photos of them together. How could he resist her kindness, her tenacity, her beautiful mind?

She may have been in love with Eva von Bahr. That's who she was visiting in the Kungälv, Mette said.

Casper was losing faith.

Bohr strikes me as pretty buttoned down. Long-term marriage. Feels unlikely.

But they all cheated! Einstein loved women. Marie Curie had an affair. And Schrödinger lived with his girlfriend *and* wife. I mean, shit, they travelled together. Think about it—they're unravelling the nature of light, the contradictions of particle and wave, the insides of an atom, the whole damn nucleus. Marriage must have seemed kind of backward. Limiting.

Maria Goeppert Mayer, Elin said.

Who's that?

Second woman to win the Nobel Prize for Physics.

Seriously?

Can't our grandmother be brilliant too?

She was also fun, but Elin couldn't admit this to her siblings or that Maria, a golden-haired flirt who loved dancing and racing her bike along Göttingen's cobblestones, turned fifteen the year her city held a festival to celebrate Bohr's visit.

Later, when Elin still wanted it to be true, she went back to the books. Found her own sources. If her grandparents were two physicists with families of their own, then a mutual connection to Max Born, opportunity, even shared ideas of the universe, would not be enough to make them lovers.

Grief and the need for consolation, however—that had its own eros.

The years leading up to the Second World War were marked by loss for Bohr: his mother passed away, Paul Ehrenfest killed himself and his son, Jenny died alone in a psychiatric hospital, and Bohr's youngest boy was institutionalized after being afflicted by meningitis.

And then Christian, the oldest Bohr child, was lost in a sailing accident.

It was easy to imagine how a beautiful young physicist, fresh off remarkable work for her Ph.D., a woman who laughed loudly, loved champagne and dancing, elaborate holiday parties, morning-after break-fasts of Bloody Marys and white asparagus with hollandaise and boiled ham, a woman who had mastered quantum physics and was, like Bohr, turning her attention to the mysteries of the nucleus, how she would be hard to resist. Impossible, really. For a middle-aged man stooping under the weight of laurels and grief, unsure if his best science was behind him.

Petrine wears a quilted silk bomber jacket, slim white jeans, and silver sneakers. Elin spots her immediately after they enter the Pfister's colon-naded lobby (its golds and blues make Elin think of a Fabergé egg). Her aunt's hair, still faintly blond, is waxed flat into a neat bun, and she has applied a luscious burgundy lipstick, daring it to bleed into the lines around her mouth in an apparent fuck-you to being eighty-eight. She is frailer than when Elin saw her last, but her eyes are bright with fun.

Elin suspects Petrine's actual offence was having a wealthy husband—a regional hotel developer named Evan Walmsley, whom she met when she was a stunning nineteen-year-old working at Fritz Hansen and he was on a post–ww ii furniture shopping spree in Copenhagen, and who later gave Tig his first real work in the U.S.

She has chosen a table with two chocolate leather club chairs nestling against a square column, and she's already nursing a martini with a helix of lemon.

Oh, Elin, you've come too, Petrine says after she and her mother exchange dry pecks on the cheek.

Just dropping Mom off. She's had a bit of a medical misadventure. I'll let her fill you in.

Her aunt surveys The Lilli hungrily, looking for the breach.

Do you mind making sure she takes a cab home?

Don't talk about me as if I'm senile, Elin.

She leans in and gives her mother a hug and then her aunt.

I have to go back to work. See you at the party, Petrine.

What party's that, my dear?

Petrine tilts her neck with feline curiosity. The Lilli's eyes flash at her daughter.

Elin spins on her heel and leaves. She'll let them figure it out. When she looks back, they are leaning into the space between the chairs, two widowed foes alert for territorial advantage: Mutually Assured Dishonesty.

Even in that, there has to be some comfort.

Outside the Pfister, Elin has double-parked her Hyundai. There's no ticket on the windshield. For an instant, she feels jubilant. As though she's beaten the system. She opens the door, sidles into the front seat, and puts her key in the ignition before she notices the white bag on the passenger seat with a typed label: her mother's antibiotic prescription.

For once, she'd like a clean getaway.

16

The gymnasium's back door is open. With fifteen minutes to spare before her first afternoon class, Elin uses it to sneak into the school rather than out.

She is hungry. There isn't enough time to hit the first-floor vending machine or forage in the staff room refrigerator.

The warm weather primes the gym's odours: the coal tar floor polish fumes, the composite leather of cheap basketballs, a faint bubble gum and rotting banana skin smell from un-emptied trash bins, the cat-pee swoon of the open change rooms.

Summer, almost.

The smells make Elin woozier. She wonders if she can bargain with the tough grandparents who work in the cafeteria for some left-over french fries or pizza.

In order to eat, she'll risk an encounter, at different rates of probability: Principal Preet or one of his administrative assistant spies, the new art teacher (whom she either has to apologize to again or who owes her an apology), and the acting head of science, who is peevish, eager to see his fellow teachers stumble.

She's least willing to risk seeing Principal Preet. He will have reviewed the call logs and noted there have been replacement teachers in two of her classes. She failed to show at the Spirit Day basketball game. Now their Tuesday morning tête-à-tête is freighted with new things she'll have to explain.

Elin goes around the cafeteria and straight to her ISM class on the ground floor. A gnawing stomach can be ignored. Lately, she has been anxious-eating. There's a sourdough-starter bloat pushing against her waistband.

The students file in and she finds herself happy to see them, their Island of Misfit Toys deflation, their bottomless need for attention and encouragement fixing her in place, giving her a steadiness. I know what to do here, she thinks.

Teach them a little. Befriend them a little. Give them a break from out there.

She hears a sound through the closed window, a faint split followed by a crash, a lightning–thunder call-and-response but for its closeness.

She picks up the lesson where they left it, an open chapter in the exercise book, before she peers out the window.

Two boys, both of whom are supposed to be in this very class, have dragged an un-emptied cafeteria trash bin outside and are whipping bottles at the windowless brick wall that faces the parking lot. Each crack is followed with a whoop as shattered glass rebounds off brick like ignited fireworks.

Elin watches. Such primal glee. So shitty and infectious.

How, then, to pull them back into learning, make them care?

Glass, she might tell them, is an ancient contradiction. Sand, lime, and soda. Apply heat. Let cool before the atoms properly crystallize. What results is a tactile solid that's structurally a liquid. Atomically disordered.

Now build a culture around it: windows, fibre optics, smartphone screens.

Crack goes the paradox.

She hears her mother's voice.

Bad weather.

Elin's eyes follow the ballistic arc of a shard that misses one boy's soft cheek. It lands on the asphalt with a *tink*.

Eureka.

————

Later, when she arrives home, she beelines to the kitchen, retrieves the opened envelope left on top of the microwave, pulls out the small velvet sachet, loosens its drawstrings and reaches inside for the weird brooch before cradling it like a petrified bug.

Ahhhh, she says.

The gemstone is not a stone at all. It is a dirtied heap of silica fused by ionizing radiation.

An obscenity.

And now Elin sees her sunburnt sister in a seersucker blouse and loose shorts with large pockets in the Burnham garage, pulling out all the items from an old rucksack. Her mother's heels cracking against the cement before they had a chance to open it. In the instant, before the rucksack was yanked away, there had been a little velvet bag.

Oh, Mette.

My twisted sister.

Mitzi comes up from behind, nudges the backs of Elin's knees expectantly.

The late-day light is still abundant. She clips the dog on her lead and heads toward North Avenue.

Now that university students have decamped for the summer, the wooded Milwaukee River embankments behind the residences are quiet and freshly rinsed. It's the kind of fragrance that would seem inevitable if a person didn't know how the city has abused its rivers in the past, dredging and draining them, turning them black-green with tannery and pig-iron effluents, until they were sulphurous and sickening. The culprits, the industries that built Milwaukee, are no longer here. Forgiveness, it seems, is a natural process. There's a family of beavers in Riverside Park being live-streamed by the ecology centre. Bets has seen a young fox on this very trail.

Mitzi is terrible on a leash. She yanks and strains and gets underfoot. The path is empty. Elin considers unclipping her. How far could a

Chicago mutt go? Or was she from Texas? She remembers her sister's consternation, the tang in her voice when she smiled and teased Elin about forgetting the cat all those years earlier.

She could use a good run, Elin thinks, distracted from a sound she might have recognized. A loud crepitation followed by an attenuated sigh. Elin hears it as if it's in the distance, something from above the underpass, a problem of traffic or construction in the city's other life above its verdant valleys.

Except that it's right above her: a huge branch.

And it's falling.

Mitzi yanks Elin with a surprising force. Elin stumbles first to her knees, scraping their flesh through her light summer pants. Then, because the dog bolts and she still holds the leash, she lurches forward, chin thudding into the paved path with a sharp sting, arm overextended painfully.

The branch explodes upon impact. It has dropped from the highest arc of the canopy, shattered across the asphalt, so that a shrapnel of bark, pointy chips, small twigs, and seed pods bounces along the back of Elin's calves and spine. Cabbages of dust and pollen rise up from it, in a sharp exhale of relic moisture.

Gymocladus dioicus, Elin thinks, flat on her stomach, staring at one of the seeds. Kentucky coffee tree. She has been almost killed by a rare species whose genus name means "naked branch."

The leash is pulled taut. Elin's right arm throbs. She gasps and rolls over onto her hip, sensing the little yips of breaking seed pods, with their mildly toxic payloads of cytisine, under her weight. There is grit on her face and in her mouth, a cut on her lip, the meaty iron of blood in saliva.

There had been no wind, not even a breeze. And the dog sensed the branch before it hit: it saved her.

But Mitzi is still straining and frantic. Elin pushes herself up onto her stinging knees using her palms, the leash wrapped around her right wrist, her shoulder whingeing at the new pressure. She has twigs in her hair, one tickles her cheek. The dog keeps pulling and Elin reaches for Mitzi's collar, to bring her closer. For a hug. She wants to reassure her. But this new stricture panics the animal, which turns and nips the soft flesh of Elin's wrist.

No! she yells. BAD DOG.

Mitzi tugs and pulls her head out of the collar.

Realizing she's untethered, the dog runs off. Her escape is sudden and nimble—yet more of that shitty glee—up the embankments and into the strip of woods.

Mitzi, no! Come back!

Elin stands and looks up to where the bough has come from. There's a bright oval like an expression of surprise in the tree canopy.

Behind her, the branch blocks the path; its bark is darkly fissured and amphibious. The spot where it ripped from the tree's trunk is the colour of fire.

In a parallel universe, her skull is crushed, daggers of coffee tree poke from her back in a sylvan carapace.

In another, the dog pulls her but not far enough: her leg is T-boned by the branch. She will never walk again.

In yet another, she dies after lingering painfully for hours, her mouth dried by wood dust, her eyelids knit with bark chips, her body swollen with heat and pooling blood.

Probability has made a choice for her. She isn't cut out for the freak accident. Not this one. The problem with parallel universes is you can't feel anything—stings, aches, sore joints—the way you feel them right here, right now. With mass.

Still, the dog, who has both saved Elin's life and wounded her, is running free, in the mutt-verse, where surely she's happier.

Which means Elin should run too—after a dog she can't see, a dog she could pretend was never in her life, a dog who had just appeared without a conversation, without her consent or any rationale for being hers.

Her eyes scan the wooded embankments, hoping for a Mitzi flash.
Instead, she sees a nurse log bridging a shallow forest culvert, its mossy
hips slowly sinking into the soil.

Mette will be here in two days. Elin has lost her dog. Casper will
at least get a kick out of that.

Yoda, the sequel, he'd say if he were here.

Adolescents again, they'd race to the log, already laughing. He'd
walk its length, forward and backward, goading. C'mon. 'Fraidy cat.

Elin stops on the trail and discerns only the chirp of a chickadee,
the susurration of the spring-plumped river, traffic from the overpass
behind her.

Her arm and knees hurt. She has no idea which direction to go.
The dog has more street smarts than woods savvy.

And the river is so close, shouldering along the trail in a muddy
boil. Can Mitzi swim?

Come back, asshole, she whispers.

She continues along the path. New plan: keep moving and something will work out. When had that not been true?

In the final year of her undergraduate degree, Elin's theoretical physics
professor, Mark Higgs, asked her to pick up her paper in his office. If
only her sister and brother could see her, she thought as she ran up the
stairwells to the physics department. That's what she wanted—her
success witnessed.

Come in, he said, sit down. In his expression, she read contained
excitement. Her forehead cramped with gratitude. He's impressed. He
wanted to ask her about her thought process.

It had taken so long for something good to happen; she was going
to soak up every detail of this encounter. The book spines behind his
desk that leaned at different angles in drunken cuneiform. The under-
watered spider plant, its brown-tipped pups loosed down the window

length. The smells of unwashed floors, perspiration, burnt coffee. In one corner of his desk, the turkey mustard sandwich that sat open, its yellow-pink nakedness curing in the dry heat, as if he were about to add mayo or lettuce. And him, wearing a jacquard sweater stretched wide at the crew neck, worn at the elbows. His face with its wry, anemic benevolence behind smudged eyeglasses: a possibly good-looking man, had not his preoccupations rimed him.

Early-onset shabby, Mette called it.

What are your plans after graduation? asked Professor Higgs.

Arrival. Finally. She drew in a breath.

There was a new flutter in her chest. She hadn't considered he might offer to supervise her graduate work or recommend her to another program, a prestigious one. Surely, he expected her to take herself seriously.

Elin surveyed the office again, telling herself: I will be spending a lot of time in here. Journal papers. Funding proposals. Hypotheses. Collaborative proofs. She'd eaten up his lectures, could quote verbatim the stories he told.

He noticed the turkey sandwich. His face flushed. He covered its innards with the top bread slice, rewrapped and bagged it, with a controlled precision she recognized as a feint for impatience.

You have a small child, Ms. . . .

Henriksen.

Right. So, moving out of state will be difficult. The years and privations of graduate work, more difficult still.

I'll figure it out. I'm resourceful, she said. The brakeless locomotion of her future headed straight for her.

He pushed back from his desk, folded his brow, pulled in his chin so it layered against his neck. They were destined to be friends; she'd make fun of his corporal origami.

Have you considered that undergraduate work might be enough for you?

Elin drew in a sharp breath. The room had a sudden din. A phone rang unanswered in the graduate office next door. The hallway photocopier whirred awake, began an allegretto click and slide. Letters of acceptance? Laughter volleyed down the hallway; someone was being congratulated.

She had not heard him properly.

I want to be a theoretical physicist, she said.

His mouth twitched as if she'd administered a small electric shock.

Indeed. We all do.

I'm a very hard worker, professor. Very determined.

You are. I've seen both. These are estimable traits. This is why I wanted to talk to you.

He looked around the office, as if he could find an aid, a diorama or diagram, that would dig him out of this moment. His eyes landed on her, her body. Not a sexual look, the way he took her in. No. He studied her as if he'd found a specimen, the very thing he needed, right in front of him all along.

Physicists are like gymnasts, he said. You take a group of gymnasts, all young, and most of them will work hard, expect to compete at an elite level. But only a few will make it. Hard work and ambition, yes, they are required. But it's not enough. An elite gymnast has a genetic predisposition, a body type, innate flexibility, which, recognized early, and exploited with all the right attention at the right time, will blossom. Most elite physicists are the same. Somebody notices something early about them and supplies that attention. I'm guessing that hasn't been your experience, Miss Henriksen?

Did I fail my paper, professor?

No. You did okay. But just okay.

This last word landed like a life sentence. Elin shifted in her chair. She'd left Bets in the cafeteria with a young woman, a polymath on a full scholarship whom she'd met in her biological physics seminar and who'd informed Elin, with a preferred sibling's assurance, that among her many exuberant talents was a natural connection to children. They were eating tater tots and building bridges with takeout coffee cups when Elin, en route to Higgs's office, glanced back.

I've sacrificed a lot to be here. To do this degree, Elin said.

She wondered if he could raise a small child alone while paying the bills, completing Advanced Thermodynamics, and submitting an okay Contemporary Interpretations of Quantum Mechanics paper. On time. After working into the morning's wee hours at a downtown bar. She wondered if he was the kind of man who would call a woman flighty, and never be able to see her any other way. Even if it turned out she not only had a genetic predisposition for this subject but the very best kind. She might have told him—had he gained her trust—that bloodlines tied her to the best generation of physicists, who were also the most destructive. So far.

He pulled himself back to his desk, leaned on his elbows, softened his expression so it read like a sympathy card blandishment: my sincerest condolences. She noticed the flakes of dandruff along the part of his hair, the faintly xanthous hue of his skin, the deep labial ruts of his smile.

Have you considered teaching? At the secondary level? I'd be happy to write a reference letter for you. There are so few women teaching physics in high school. What a role model you'd be. And think: you could give that extra attention to someone who doesn't yet realize the level of her own talent.

Elin stood up. Her chair skittered backward.

Thank you. But I don't need a reference to go to teachers' college.

Professor Higgs stood also, held out his turkey-mustard hand to shake. She imagined the nitrate tingle of luncheon meat and mustard's waning pungency on his palm.

She nodded but did not extend hers.

Elin smells the balsam poplars and sugar maples, vibrating with insects in the sticky curls of their tender leaves. A former stray such as Mitzi may run for hours before realizing she is nowhere familiar. The old programming will return. She will scrounge to survive and trust no one but herself.

How long will it take her to forget these few weeks, this small attachment of sharing the same ten cubic gallons of air with two human strangers?

She'd had a dream about Mabel Flores. Her student was not in class because she'd jumped off a Marquette Interchange overpass with a note in her pocket calculating, perfectly, her force of impact and where she would land, given drift from that day's prevailing winds and the predicted amount of traffic. Before dying, Mabel hit the roof of a Nissan Rogue knees first, bouncing to the asphalt, where she was promptly run over by a half-empty delivery van returning online purchases to be landfilled. The Rogue was bringing home seniors from the Potawatomi Casino. The delivery van was driven by a father, working three jobs. Mabel's parents wanted to know why Elin hadn't done more.

What more could I do? She had a 98 in my class.

Talked, said her mother. You think you're the only one who needs a friend?

Elin's gone farther than she'd intended; she turns and heads back the way she came. This too feels irresponsible. If Mitzi continues in a linear direction, Elin is moving away from her: opposing forces.

She freezes, unsure of what to do.

Mitzi! Christ. Just come!

It is Mette's fault. She's failed to teach the dog basic commands.

What if the dog prefers her liberty?

There it is again. This desire for certainty, a compass.

Mette will come, be applauded and feted, and ask for the dog. Casper will be polite but distant: they've exhausted the kinship they'd had as children, her failure to offer the Narwhal to The Art Museum another slight. Bets is in love and leaving. The Lilli gets older, frailer, more needy and unkind. And Elin is organizing a party, as if it might fix something, though she can't say what.

———

One day in class, Professor Higgs went on a tear about the injustices done to female physicists. Elin held her breath through all of it.

When Chien-Shiung Wu arrived to do her graduate here, the University of Michigan didn't even let women use the same entrance as men. Maria Goeppert Mayer had finished her Ph.D. at the University of Göttingen, with a doctoral thesis showing the mathematics of double photon absorption and emission that was way, way ahead of its time. Still, she couldn't get a professorial position in America. Both Wu and Goeppert taught at girls' private schools. And eventually, both found their path to Harold Urey and the Manhattan Project. Urey gave them titles, paid work. Wu distinguished herself through pure nose-to-the grindstone, top-drawer experimental physics. Graduate students called her many unkind things; the Chinese Madame Curie was the least offensive. But she didn't win a Nobel Prize for Physics. Eighteen years after the end of ww ii, Maria Goeppert Mayer did; the second woman, after Marie Curie, to do so.

He clasped his hands loosely, so they were as open and receptive as a satellite dish.

It's well past time, he said, for another woman to win.

Elin walked out of the lecture hall that day with an expansion she couldn't name. She carried Bets to where her car was parked, wrapped her daughter up on the back seat—she was drowsy—and parked at Bradford Beach to stare into the boundlessness of Lake Michigan. City of deep rivers and broad bays.

Invincibility.

That was the feeling. She'd wait all her life for it.

There's a ripple of colour in the woods. A figure steps out of the forest: an older woman with a singular thinness, her pelvis sitting like the head of a shovel on the stems of her legs. Elin's chest tightens. At her side is a dog. She's put a bright head scarf around Mitzi's neck, and has two fingers looped through it. In her other hand, she holds a cigarette.

Elin takes long strides toward her. As she approaches, the angularity of the woman's face, the way skin fastens like wet silk to her skull, is familiar, but she can't say why. The dog wags its tail at the sight of Elin. She cries out.

Oh, thank god!

The thin woman turns and waves. She is pleased with herself. Mitzi has pulled her ears back: she's sitting between the woman's legs, shaking. The low rumble of a train builds in the distance.

Thank you so much, Elin says, trying to catch her breath.

Oh, you big baby, the woman coos to Mitzi.

I think she's scared of the forest, of being alone out here, she says as Elin gets closer. This little doggie's had some trauma in her past.

Elin stares at the thin woman and nods her head. She pushes Mitzi's head through the dog collar, clips it back to her leash.

The stranger's eyebrows tip into dump trucks of concern. She eyes the blood drying along Elin's forearm.

Are you okay?

Elin wonders if her face is smeared.

A branch fell and scared the dog, Elin says.

She's not willing to blame Mitzi for the blood.

The stranger places a frail hand on Elin's forearm, close to the crusted wound. The woman's palm is light and dry, as if it were only hollow bones and eider, a duckling's wing. Elin is jarred by the delicacy of this touch.

I heard it, says the woman.

Sorry?

I heard the tree fall, she says, winking. A tree fell in the forest. It made a sound.

Elin opens her mouth but has no response.

Great dog, by the way. Not sure she's ready to be off-leash.

The woman turns and walks away from them with a messianic gait down the trail, blading the air with her sharp arms.

Elin swears she hears singing, a joyful, warbling matins.

She pulls Mitzi homeward. They cut through the woods on a foot-path that takes them up to the street sooner. Tiny slivers of wood scratch against Elin's hips as she moves. Her gait is hobbled by holding the leash in her left hand to protect her right shoulder. She has to believe what she knows of the dog: that she bit Elin out of instinct, out of panic, out of fear. But saved her out of love.

17

S he's checking the mailbox too often. A nervous tic.
　　Elin does it now on the way out of her house, as well as in.
Card.
Package.
Card?
Patterns, the soul of science.
Mette had sent a bluebird card to take a break from her sister and her niece. Five years later, she got back in touch with a piping plover, a bird that nests by water, on rocky ground, and so must work extra hard to protect its young.

Em,
　　I'm sitting in a lighthouse on Michigan Island, working on the most important album of my career.
　　At night there is just the lake—that other Great Lake, the greater one—breathing in and out, in and out. The water is blue-black-green here; a vast light-absorbing sink.
　　There is only this.
　　I have a small hut with no running water or electricity. The place is crawling with black bears.
　　But there's room for you, for Bets, and Casper.
　　Come.
　　What have we got to lose, that we haven't already lost?

You always said you wanted to swim in Lake Superior. It is cold, Elin, it is beginning-of-time cold.

I've enclosed instructions.

Me

That card had been such a relief.

This Friday morning there are no cards nor packages, torments nor offers. Elin leaves the lid of the mailbox open.

She's running late.

I thought I would hear from you last night.

Her mother puckers when Elin stops by on her way to school.

I had to walk the dog after seeing you, Mom. Mette's dog. Then, you know, dishes, marking, lesson prep. I'm trying to make sure things don't get on top of me.

You'll survive, Elin. I did.

She accepts one of the takeout coffees Elin has brought with her. Her mother's lips flatten, and she looks at her watch. (The silver ligature on her crepe wrist is a sleek, unfussy Vivianna.)

Your mother was hospitalized, remember?

Mom, I drove you from your hospital room to a lunch with Petrine. You can't have it both ways.

I can and I will, Elin.

Her mother pokes a cheese Danish from the same coffee shop with one of her elegant fingers. Elin buys them for the sake of this ritual rejection. She'll eat it in the car on the way to school.

I'm going to need your help today, The Lilli says, shoving the Danish away from her.

No can do. Have to teach. Sorry.

Elin, you said you would take the day off. You promised. There's so much to do before your brother and sister arrive. Casper has shouldered all the work for the dedication. I can't ask him for another thing.

Yes, but because of your infection, I missed a morning and after-noon of classes. All my favours are used up.

The Lilli waves. Mad Santas: that's what Mette called her moth-er's hands, when her skin reddened up to the little white cuffs of her French manicure.

Elin stands up to leave the backyard patio table where they have been sitting in the sun. She re-bags the uneaten Danish and drains her coffee.

You can't! There's silver to polish and glasses to wash. The house needs cleaning, and there are so many things I have to buy. You prom-ised, Elin. I should have known you'd pull this.

The Lilli stops. The colour drains from her face. Her voice is newly shrill, some old collisions of grief and regret in it.

Who can I count on anymore?

They lock eyes.

Her mother turns away. Elin could slap her. Elin could hug her.

The clock inside the kitchen doorway tells her she's going to be late.

Write a list, okay. Write down everything you need to get done. Then we'll divide it. Maybe Petrine can help?

Petrine!

Her mother scoffs. A spittle of coffee lands on the collar of her beautiful white blouse.

That woman doesn't do things for others. She has them done for her. I will *not* be calling your aunt Petrine for any favours.

Whatever. I gotta go. Write out a list. I've already started getting some of the food together. At lunch, I'll come by and head to Milwaukee Public Market. What I can't do then, I'll get done tonight. Sound good?

She's using her solicitous voice; her mother is insulted.

The Lilli stares beyond the patio, lost to her new petulance. As Elin leaves, she remembers she has agreed to dinner with Bets this evening. She'll have to get as much as possible done at lunch, the rest tomorrow.

Back in the car, she takes a huge bite of the Danish before starting

the engine. The cheese is sour-tasting, the pastry dry. Whatever sweetness it has can't mask its overall failure. She thinks of the look in her
mother's eyes and recognizes an old fear of slipping standards.

Against all predictions, Elin has assumed the role of a reliable child.

A week after she found the piping plover card, Casper picked them up
at 6 a.m., arriving in a sporty rented convertible with a good-sized
trunk. A car the colour of plums.

Jammy, Elin said.

She'd not slept the night before, worrying. It was a seven-hour
drive. They hadn't talked for five years. And those packages, reports she
could quote from, refute. Teach him a lesson.

But the Casper who stepped out of the car, tanned and fit, was
newly divorced and sadder around the eyes.

Bets ran to him, as if he'd been in her life all along, and threw
herself into his arms.

You're so big! he said, and twirled her around. She was breathless
with enchantment. Elin smarted with the unfairness of it: the way a
child collapses an absence into seconds.

Casper reached for Elin next, held her tightly, let her go quickly.

Michigan Island on Lake Superior, he said. Quintessential Mets,
right?

Elin nodded.

Bring hats and sunscreen. Once it warms up, we'll put the top
down.

It was a clear, perfect day. The sun was shining, the radio on, her
child holding her arms to catch the wind, in love with the quicksilver
quality of life: Saturday morning turned into an amusement park ride
in a purple car with the handsome uncle who made her laugh.

Tucked into Elin's back pockets were cue cards. At 3 a.m., she'd
relented to her insomnia, got out of bed, and wrote out the main points
of what she wanted to say to Casper and Mette when the moment arose.

This was not it.

Elin wondered if it was a moral failure to slip back so easily into the familiar, less painful versions of themselves. She couldn't resist the sun-saturated sky, its frothy lip of cirrus, the air's piney tang, the anticipation of roadside french fries and homemade pies. Relief from the routine of the city.

Besides, Casper's music made her smile. He must have known this. He must have imagined nostalgia working like wood lice, chewing away the smallest chunks of her resistance, so she didn't see what was happening until it was mostly done.

What is it?

In first-period physics, Bart Khang asks before Elin loosens the drawstrings on the velvet bag.

She reaches in.

I want you to tell me. Pass it around. Watch out for the pin. It's sharp.

She pulls out the brooch that Mette sent, and gives it to Bart first; he has his hands open. He's itching to investigate it.

Weird, he says, looking closely, before passing it along. It's jewellery.

Yes. But what's it made of?

Gold.

Perhaps. What's in the middle?

Hands start reaching out for the object. Her students hold it as if it were alive, a scarab that could make a slow dash up their forearms.

The door of the classroom opens and in walks Mabel Flores. The same as ever: backpack sliding off one arm. Eyes focused on her empty seat, the shortest route. A quality of blankness in her expression that is also ferociously aware. Her glance lands on the brooch working its way down the row.

Jade?

No, it's a good guess. Pass it along.

Elin tracks Mabel's movements peripherally. For some students, attention is the worst thing you can give them if it's poorly timed. She'll have to pretend Mabel has never been gone.

Emerald?

I wish!

It's a crystal.

No. I like what you're doing, though.

A kind of salt?

Interesting. I didn't see that coming. You're on to something.

The brooch lands on Regina's desk. She holds it up to the light, touches the prickly centre.

It's glass, fool, she says to the boy beside her.

Nicely done, Regina. Now, why would somebody make jewellery out of a hunk of glass?

Ugly glass, says Bart.

Precisely. Ugly glass. Keep passing it along.

There's a gleam of satisfied wickedness in Bart's eyes. Elin inhales an old longing for her brother, not for the adult Casper whom she barely knows, but the Casper who had been eight, and eleven, and fourteen, and at all those ages vindictive and admirable, contemptuous and smart like Bart, someone she adored and hated all in the same forty minutes.

Does he miss another Elin, a younger one, in the way she misses him?

Casper parked the convertible in Bayfield. They had to hire a private water taxi to get to the island. The water had a muscly choppiness. It felt huge and northern, a big ol' badass glacial pothole. In contrast, Lake Michigan seemed domesticated, even lazy.

When she caught sight of the historic lighthouse, whitewashed against the green of forest, she regretted agreeing to only four days.

Mette was at the small dock waiting for them. She was wearing adult OshKosh overalls with conductor stripes, and her hair, its

sun-bleached curls, fell out of a red bandana. She was ruddy from wind
and hiking back and forth to check on the island's single campsite, part
of her duties as a volunteer lighthouse keeper.

She looked as if she had always lived on this island; there was a
capable way in which she hauled bags off the boat and held out her
arms for Bets.

The possibility of the conversation Elin hoped to have with her
siblings—after Bets, worn out from hours outside, was tucked in her
bed, sleeping solidly, and a wine bottle had been opened and a fire
started—began to slip the instant Elin accepted the hand of her sister,
so robust, so eager to bring her ashore.

What had Einstein said about splitting the atom? *It would be like
a blind man in a dark night hunting ducks by firing a shotgun straight up
in the air in a country where there are very few ducks.*

Elin had seen blue-winged teals and ruddy ducks in a marsh they
passed on their way to Bayfield. She didn't know birds could have blue
beaks, or feathers of bluebell, robin's egg, and turquoise on the same
wing; she imagined they'd melt into the sky at dusk and be even harder
to shoot.

They swam in the livid and lavender of Superior, tentatively
wading in where Mette had found a protected inlet with forgiving
rocks. It was cold, a thrilling cold because it was so ruthless, spearing
through the soft flesh to that little cauldron of heat at the body's core.
Afterwards, they wrapped themselves in towels, and shivered on the
rocks in the sun. They fished off the dock, pretending they were luring
the Paleogenic giants—pike—but hoping for a pretty sun-dappled
bass at best. They hiked and found unripe raspberries. Bets climbed the
towers with her aunt, the old lighthouse, the new lighthouse. When
the braver sea kayakers docked, she ran down to offer them a tour of
the island for a dollar.

At night in the cabin, Mette picked up her guitar to test out the
songs she was working on, Casper read a novel left by an earlier volunteer,

the first book he'd read in a year, he announced, and Elin sat on the edge of her chair watching her child triangulate, over and over, running from Casper to Mette to herself, interrupting what they were doing to show them a fossil she'd found, or a dead *Cecropia* moth, or the pimpled purse of a milkweed pod. Bets, the charged particle of light bouncing between three dark planets, absorbed in their own troubles.

When Bets went to bed, smiling sweetly into the cedar-scented must of the small room off the kitchen, the adults talked in whispers around two Madeira bottle candles.

Mette confided her struggles writing the songs for her first new album in ten years, and the bridges she'd burned to make time for it.

Casper complained that Shahr had been too precise, too noble a partner: he thought he might suffocate. Now that he'd left, he was racked with guilt whenever she called crying, yelling at him for wasting the best of her child-bearing years in their marriage.

Elin had one story to tell, the one in which they'd disappointed her, the one outlined in key messages on the cue cards, so she couldn't be led off topic, get lost. But on the second morning there, Bets had fished a cue card from the back pocket of Elin's discarded jeans and started drawing on it, presenting it later to Mette, who had looked perplexed at the palimpsest of Crayolas and discernible printing. Elin found that card in the firepit. She convinced herself not to start the conversation, risk breaking this new spell, the one in which they were all together again, and had learned their lessons. They were smarter now. Not everything had to be said aloud.

And there was Bets, who fused them all, who glowed brighter, longer in their presence, who vouched for the narrative in which they were all connected.

On the last night, Casper had too much wine and fell asleep on the couch. Mette pulled her sister outside to look at the stars.

Elin squeezed her hand, marvelling at the strength of her sister, her preternatural vigour, her homing signal for water, as if she were one of the Scandinavians who'd landed in the state's flat middle and slowly worked their way up to the Superior coast to fish and build cabins on a lake that looked and acted like a sea they once knew.

The sky was bright with quartzy clusters.

Endless tomorrows, Mette said, looking up. *De nova stella.*

Elin followed her glance.

One explodes every second, somewhere out there, in the universe. Few humans have seen it in action. Most of us witness the aftermath: the beautiful death.

Elin waited a beat; this was the moment. Her sister and she alone. But Mette took in a deep breath first.

He's afraid to have children, she said.

Mette reached her free hand up into the sky as if to smear the stars.

He says a childhood is too much like a Jenga game: you build it up, and then one piece is pulled, makes it come apart, everything you think you've known.

What are you saying? Elin asked.

Mette turned to her sister.

He's sad. I'm just a witness to it, El.

Silence.

Do you only believe what you see?

Elin points at the stars.

His sadness. These balls of gas, collapsing under their own gravity.

Mette let go of Elin's hand.

There's something there.

Where?

Elin looked around in the dark. Her pulse quickened.

No, in those words, El. The ones you just used. His sadness, these stars. Collapsing under your own gravity.

Mette put her hands on her cheeks, shook her head with a slightly manic giggle.

All month I've been stuck. Working and reworking it. And there it is. Your fuckin' brilliant words.

She wrapped Elin in her arms, squeezed, and moved away. All in one motion. She hurried toward the cabin, already singing the words, reversing and refining them, her voice a soft, sweet churring, a nesting animal oblivious to the abrupt quiet around her.

Elin listened to the lake, heard only its monumental reproach, and gasped.

She turned to follow.

There was a shadow on the lawn between the old and new light-houses and she wondered if this, finally, was one of the many black bears Mette had boasted about.

The movement was all wrong, especially when it stepped toward her, slowly, its head bent low to the ground. No bulk to this animal's shoulders.

Yellow eyes floated in the darkness like lit wicks.

Elin had never encountered a wolf before, not in a zoo, nor in the wild. If she was scared, she was too numb to feel it.

It stopped moving. Elin wondered if the wolf realized it was being watched as much as watching. The witness to its own witnessing. A crackle in the woods behind the cabin alerted the animal. It turned and trotted off, not giving a fuck about the easy kill, the soft meat of her broken heart.

Maybe the best part of being a wolf was recognizing what to spend time on.

Inside the cabin, she didn't tell Mette, absorbed with guitar and paper, about the wolf, or Casper, still asleep on the couch with his book on his chest and a glass of wine on the floor at his side. She checked on Bets, who had come so alive on this trip, who'd run and explored and asked dozens of questions, and entertained them at night, her captive audience of three adults, before falling hard and happy, lungs stretched by good air, into sleep. Elin knelt by the fire and took the remaining cue cards out of her back pocket and let them burn slowly. She didn't mention the wolf in the morning as they waited on the dock or share it with Casper during the long silences on the ride home, when Bets slept in the back seat, and the purple convertible's top was closed because it rained lightly, then hard.

Mabel moves noisily. She can see the brooch heading toward her down the row. There's a ready-to-pounce smugness on her face.

Mabel knows exactly what the brooch is made of.

Trinitite, she says when it's finally in her hands.

Her own cleverness paints her pink.

It's from Trinity, New Mexico. A place they tested the bomb.

Elin looks at Mabel and is startled by the difference in the girl: Her usually sallow skin is sanguine, glowing, burnished with health. Her posture is straight. She has energy. Being away has been good for her. Better.

Bravo, says Elin.

Regina's eyebrows arch.

July 16, 1945. The first nuclear bomb test sucked the sands of the Jornada del Muerto up into the air where the heat was most intense. Liquefied them. It rained beads. Left a jade-coloured crater of wormy, knobby glass. So why would someone make jewellery from it? Seems a bit creepy? Right?

Elin looks around the room. It is going to be a stinker of a day. Her students are like wet lettuce left in the sun. She glances out the window, for half a second, at the copper beech.

C'mon. Four more days of classes, folks. Let's get through this unit. What hasn't happened yet?

Hiroshima, and Nagasaki, says Mabel. The bombs fell in September.

Elin throws a picture up on the projector screen: Robert Oppenheimer with his foot plunged into the sand of the Trinity site's ground zero. There are journalists around him.

Yes. Eight weeks after the plutonium bomb was tested at Trinity, one uranium bomb fell on Hiroshima, one plutonium on Nagasaki. Little Boy and Fat Man. Tens of thousands of people died instantly. What else happened?

Radiation.

Right. Thousands of others were getting sick. The American and British governments could justify killing people but not poisoning them. So, they attempted to convince the U.S. public there was no poison. They got old Robbie to pose for this picture. And they let all those journalists take bits of glass with them. They filled their pockets.

Propaganda, says Elin. You are holding a piece of propaganda.

Mabel has handed the brooch across to the last row.

Sly, says Jonas.

When they could no longer deny the Japanese radiation stories, the army bulldozed the trinitite under, restricted public access to a few visits a year, criminalized pocketing the glass. By that time, there was a lot out there.

Is it radioactive?

Bart drops the brooch on his desk.

You should know better. Remember our calculations for the half-life of radioactivity? Review, folks. Sure to be on the final. There's very little radiation left in that glass, now that seventy-three years have passed.

Bart, pass the brooch around one more time, says Elin. I want everybody to take a good look. This stuff is dense with information: the kind of atomic device and the metals used for its casing, where detonation occurred, under what conditions. The glass captures it all. Takes some forensics to tease it out. But it's there. And there are geologists who believe this glass holds clues to a larger narrative, you know, how meteorites may have caused ice ages, and mass extinctions. It's all there, encoded at the level of the particle; a unique story, big and small. Fused together, made into an ornament.

So why do you have it, miss?

Elin looks at Mabel. She will have no trouble resuscitating her physics mark, but the other courses might hold her back.

It has something to do with World War II and maybe my parents, Mabel. Indirectly, my grandfather. Or the man I think he is. I'll let you know when I figure it out.

She's lost the attention of the rest of the class. But Mabel's face is a tungsten filament. Elin wonders if she can convince Mabel's parents to let her repeat one semester of final year at another school more suited to their daughter's outsized talents: what would they risk for possibility?

Nobody had wanted, or expected, a full concept album from Mette Henriksen.

Except Mette.

The album cover shot for *The Orbits* is Lake Superior in a storm. The clouds are heavy and ominous, black-green, and the water reflects the sky. Both surge. In the bottom of the centre third, off to the left, is the small, slender beacon of the lighthouse, whitewashed with a red crest and a yellow eye, like a seabird.

The lighthouse, that little symbol of purposeful hope and safety, was meant, Elin was sure of it, to be Mette. She was too angry with her sister to ask if she was right. Because the title, the image of a roiling Lake Superior adorning it, told Elin what she needed to know.

Had Mette used Bets, even Casper, and most especially her, to finish writing the album? Elin's discomfort, her unspoken hurts, her desire to be together, the momentum of habit outweighing courage, Bets running between them, enclosing them, gentle as a drawstring.

This was turned into elegiac melodies, cryptic, moody lyrics, the undertow of minor chords. Too intimate and exposing.

What looked like a reconciliation had been a creative enema.

Elin felt vindication when the critics came out swinging:

guitar-centric earnest

auteur pop-rock

late to its genre's funeral.

Mette, devastated.

In the two years following *The Orbits*, her sister hollowed out physically and financially. Grew thin. The loss of some of her frontier robustness was mirrored in the more tentative way she inhabited the world. She had to downsize the life she'd mortgaged to pay for the album production. Gone were her leases for apartments in Branson and Brooklyn. Her Victorian farm outside Naperville was sold so she could keep the River North townhouse. She reduced her recording trips to Montego Bay and Berlin, all of it penance for insisting on putting the album out on vinyl, at the very moment CDs were losing steam to digital playlists, and the audiophiles were still a few years out from reviving the LP.

Mette still moved around, her restlessness her only excess for a life and body reduced to romantic spareness. Had the album dimmed her or humbled her?

Staring into the album cover, Elin notices the way the dark paint catches the dining room light, creates a schiller, a kind of iridescence that is common to blue-black-green minerals. Labradorites. Moonstones. All the wavelengths.

Her sister had collected rocks for a while. She believed they were good for her, removing certain energies, attracting others, helping her to reach her full potential.

Perhaps the brooch contains such a trick, a piece of spectrolite, changeable and in need of sunshine to be understood.

Or is the brooch a reminder of four days when they were all together, the three of them?

The last time they had done that.

18

Her mother has written an impossible list and it starts with Danish blue followed by six other cheeses.

In her suddenly compressed lunch hour, Elin steals a glance at her mother's handwriting, sprinkled like insect legs on a crumpled note paper.

Three traditional marzipan *kringler* will be ready on Saturday morning for pickup from the Danish bakery in Oak Creek. A forty-minute drive.

Seriously, Mom?

Be sure to take the special order, not those horrible bastardized *kringles*. *Please* insist. Planning, El, is the difference between mediocrity and success.

Anything else?

You'll need to source six bottles of aquavit (remember to freeze the night before). The amber. Brennivin, if you can find it.

She feels a surge of adrenalin. It's a daunting inventory of tasks for thirty-two hours, especially when she has under two (a lunch and a spare) to dedicate now.

There is a glorious cross breeze as she moves down Mitchell Street. Elin flips on the radio to stop herself from clenching and white-knuckling the steering wheel.

Gritty air wafts into the car from the driver's side, scoops up her mother's list, and carries it out the opening in the passenger-seat window.

Why hadn't she just taken a picture of it with her phone?

The light turns green, the car behind her honks. Elin inches forward slowly, debating for a half second whether she can afford to pull over and chase the piece of paper, still visible in her side-view mirror; a solo murmuration swooped into an updraft, it curls and scallops above the street, and Elin thinks of starlings and how vast numbers move cohesively in intricate, breathtaking patterns because each bird pays attention to the seven others that are closest. They turn uncertainty into beauty.

When she gets to Milwaukee Public Market, she has a moment of hesitation: it bustles with a lunch crowd on the second floor. The din reaches up to the steel girders.

As she waits in line at the automatic teller, her armpits dampening, she formulates a new plan, the listless one.

Wine first, store in trunk. Then cheese, six kinds. Drop off at The Lilli's for refrigeration. Crackers, dry goods at Glorioso's en route back to school. Store with wine in trunk. Flowers, *kringler*—tomorrow. Beer—text Bets to pick up at work, cab home.

An hour and fifteen minutes later, she's back in the car heading to Glorioso's, trying to conjure the specifics of what The Lilli wanted from there. There's no time to return to her mother's house to drop off the cheese, so Elin decides she'll risk the staff lunch room refrigerator. She'll make a DON'T TOUCH sign. She will cross her fingers no one opens the fridge looking for a windfall, as she does each day.

Beside her on the passenger seat are three pints of early strawberries and a big bundle of rhubarb, two items most definitely not on the lost list, but ones that cheer Elin. They are a whim, an idea of delighting her sister and brother with a dessert that had been their favourite, yet another task added to her impossibly pressurized schedule. Elin thinks they are her best purchases of the day.

Ten minutes later, in the school parking lot, she is rifling through the trunk with the wine and bags of crackers, looking for the cheese. The back seat is empty but for her purse, the front seat is fragrant with the smell of sun-warming strawberries. But the cheese—brie, blue, Benvenuto, whey, Wensleydale—is missing even though the receipts are crammed in her wallet.

Her eyes land on the rhubarb's thick stalks, the frilly, elephantine leaves, with their dangers for compost and young dogs. She sees herself place the cheese bag daintily off to the side of a plywood shelf as she sorts change for the tender-fruit seller. It stays there as she juggles the newly purchased pints, a second bag, her purse over her shoulder, opening her glasses case—Just wear the damn glasses, Mom, Bets inveighed the last time they shopped together—in order to see properly.

She'd failed to pick up the bag again.

Now she imagines the next customer, or even the thirty-something tender-fruit seller—sunburnt and hale from hours among the berries—discovering the bag.

Opportunists. How tempting to integrate expensive wrapped cheeses into one's own groceries, or to take the unintended manna, a month's worth of ploughman's lunches, to share in the market's staff lounge.

She slams the car's trunk shut. Pulls out her phone and calculates. The buzzer for the next period rings in the hallways.

Can she return to the market, find the cheese, and be back at school in fifty-five minutes?

Ahem.

Bart Khang comes up behind her in the parking lot.

Elin's face opens in a question.

It's Friday, miss.

Yes, Bart.

Physics Club, he says.

She's forgotten.

One Friday lunch hour, once a month. A club that Bart Khang organized, and for which he's recruited the members—his three friends Dunston, Mabel, and Jorge.

What does a physics club do? she'd asked when he first proposed it to her eight months earlier.

I dunno. Just sit around and talk about stuff.

Elin had looked skeptical.

No competitions. No bake sales, he said.

She was sold: he'd read her correctly. A low-effort extracurricular was a shield against the constant assault of volunteer requests for coaching, field trips, grant writing, fundraising, and event planning.

Perhaps this is why the new art teacher is so hostile. She'd started the Street Art Club (which, to many students' disappointment, involved talking about the aesthetic movements within graffiti rather than hitting the underpasses with Kilz cans). She'd taken over prop and set design for the yearly musical. She's coaching girls' softball and is petitioning the school for a positive space.

In contrast, Elin must seem like the very worst of the already troubled public school system, a complacent middle-ager who's leveraging its meagre perks, riding on the relevance of her subject matter, taking up space that a younger teacher might want.

Of course. I'll be there soon, Bart.

When he's out of sight, Elin kicks her rear car tires. She can't catch a break.

There's never been more than three people at Physics Club, including Elin.

Today, she's surprised when Mabel and Jorge are waiting with Bart in her physics room, opened lunch bags already emptied. Dunston follows her in, hair damp with sweat against his forehead.

She wonders if they even like each other, these four students, if they travel together like particles with weak attractions, unstable bonds, a temporary state until they're free of high school.

Caf's insane, he says.

Elin can imagine. The school's atmosphere sings right now, a tinnitus of stress, excitement, revealing summer clothes, pollen and smog grit wafting in the doors. The four of them huddle—refugees from an abundance of energy.

She usually starts them off with an idea, and then sits back. They have talked about the tension between a theory of nature and a theory of knowledge, and how the *Kopenhagener Geist*, because it embraced uncertainty, leaned toward psi-epistemology—the idea that the observer is inextricably tied to what we know as reality.

If you believe we need our perception to exist, she said once, then all three possibilities of Schrödinger's Cat—dead kitty, alive kitty, partly dead kitty—are objective truths. They're all real. Then you're an ontologist or, for the sake of this debate, a psi-ontologist.

A Scientologist, miss? said Dunston. Is this a cult?

Is Tom Cruise a physicist?

I am thetan: creator of all things.

They started to giggle.

Then the conversations took turns she couldn't keep up with: holons, branes, gravitational waves. The singularity, inevitably.

Today, she is torn: gratified that Mabel has come, fretful about cheese.

Classes end at 3:20 p.m. and Milwaukee Public Market closes at 8 p.m., but on a beautiful June afternoon some of the vendors will be packed up and gone before 4 pm.

Because of Physics Club, she'll have to let her last class out ten minutes early, too. It's against the rules. But it's the only way she can get back in time.

What have you got for us?

Jorge stares at her with impatience.

Elin feels empty; an old gourd.

An infinitely expanding universe of notifications in her inbox: articles she has to read twice in order to still not understand. *Was ist Der witz?* Ehrenfest, a friend of Bohr's, had said when his mailbox similarly overflowed with journal articles concerning the fundamentals of quantum mechanics, and he got depressed and stopped attending conferences. Elin struggles with string theory; can't really say if loop quantum gravity is any better, and prays her students won't ask.

She wonders if they should talk about falsifiability, and the new thrust of theory that appears post-empirical. The idea frightens her: science without experimental evidence. As if to say Thomas Kuhn had it right, our ideas about the natural world are worked out through committees stuck in historical paradigms. Hadn't Bohr intuited this? *The Structure of Scientific Revolutions* was published the year he died.

But it feels too heavy and the day already presses on her. Elin opens the second drawer of her desk looking for a dry-erase marker, thinking she will give herself a break and diagram an idea about colonizing Mars she'd heard on a recent podcast. But her grip closes on something else, a soft leather case with a solid lump. She pulls it out. The hide is stamped with gold ink. Inside is something solid.

What's that?

Dunston's chameleon eyes lock on her hands, as if she's cradling a locust.

A year ago, she'd bought herself a pipe. Physicists smoked. It was that simple. One of Einstein's pipes was sold at auction for $65,000. Another was in the Smithsonian. Bohr had a pipe but switch-hit with cigarettes. (He was once so distracted he didn't notice his pipe chamber missing: two young physicists watched him try to light the stem.) She'd had the sudden urge to smoke one—she thought it would calm her down and also make her sharper. An impulse she shoved to the back of her desk drawer.

Why do you have a pipe?

Mabel: confused and censorious.

Whim. Something about all the greats in the golden age of quantum physics smoking them.

We have to, says Bart. The Physics Club should smoke a pipe.

Inside the case, there are two small jars of tobacco and a lighter. It's irresponsible and possibly immoral to smoke the pipe. But god knows, it's wholesome compared with what their peers and siblings do.

The truth is, they've already talked about terraforming Mars with nuclear bombs in order to make it habitable for humans.

Okay. Let's give it a go. Close the door, Dunston.

Jorge stands.

I know how, he says, taking it gently from her. Saw it on YouTube.

He double-wads the bowl with an unexpected expertise. Then he adds flame, sucks, adds flame until the bowl smoulders.

Oh, crap, he coughs. That reeks.

The other three reach for the pipe.

Elin opens a window. She studies the beech and hopes for nothing, no witnesses.

I feel smarter already.

Bart laughing, puffing, coughing.

They pass it around. Finally, they hand the pipe to her with conspiratorial expectation.

Elin puffs, but doesn't cough. Faintly, through the abruptness, she tastes rum raisin, cocoa. There's a strong hit of nicotine: she loves the duality of this sensation, how it made her thinking both more acute and dreamlike.

You're badass, Ms.

Thank you, Dunston. A few more each. Then we're done.

After her second puff, Mabel looks at Elin as if she's a stranger: opting for a lapse in judgment rather than disappoint them.

You could lose your job for this, miss.

Elin brushes her left hand under her mouth. She'd been so

furious at Bets for throwing a punch that might get them sued. Possible answers appear to her as mental flash cards:

That's unlikely

It's between us

I trust you not to tell

Mabel blinks. She's also weighing the options. They share this habitual overthinking.

You're right, says Elin and nothing more.

A pall, like a spring storm, passes over Mabel's face. Confirmation of something she suspected or feared: Elin values teaching so little that she'd risk it on a whim. But the other answers were worse, weren't they?

Jorge takes the pipe.

I used to work in the groundskeeping crew at this cemetery. And you know how everybody has their nice little granite headstone aboveground? Like it's all, this is where so-and-so's body is, and over here is someone else's? Well, underneath the soil, it's a friggin' orgy—bones and decomposition. All grandpa's particles mixed with a baby that died from scarlet fever a century earlier and the kid from the car accident last week. Full intermingling. Like, centuries of it. Time and space entangled.

Mabel tucks her lunch bag into her knapsack and reaches for the pipe.

That's not what entanglement means, she says. In physics.

Live hard, die young, says Dunston. In the multiverse, you just get another crack at it. Don't even have to be nice to each other. You just keep getting another simulation.

Quantum physics isn't saying everything is up for grabs, Bart says.

Elin experiences an unexpected constriction at the top of her chest that almost hurts. God, she loves the weirdos. The very ones who could deep-six her career.

Good place for us to wrap up.

Dunston hands back the pipe and she taps its chamber against a lab table sink, and then throws a glass of water on the still warm tobacco. Fragrant steam rises, the whiff of felony.

I'll see you next month.

They all turn to look at her.

This was our last meeting, miss, Dunston says. 'Member, classes are over, like, next week. Then exams.

Oh, Elin says. Of course.

She looks around. There should have been pizza. She has a trunk-load of overpriced crackers and aquavit, rhubarb and strawberries, a wormhole where the cheese should have been. None of it shareable. Elin plunges her hands into her bag and feels the salvation of humidity-softened cardboard: Moon Pies. She counts with her fingers—four—and pulls the individually wrapped cookie sandwiches out one at a time, so they look like an intentional surprise.

Thanks for a great year!

Dunston takes one first; his thumb sinks into it. Elin watches a surge of chocolate darken the wrapper from the inside. They slump out in single file, loosely waiting for each other.

If I'm going to fall apart underground, y'know, become part of the soil and the water all over again, says Jorge, opening a Moon Pie with his teeth on his way past the door, I want my shit figured out. I don't want my bitterness about being a fat virgin fuck-up ending up in someone's vegetable garden.

You know gravitational waves are going to totally wipe out relativity, says Bart.

He turns and gives a little wave to Elin.

Mabel tears hers open and takes a big bite.

So glad to see you, Elin says as she passes. Let's talk about what you're doing next year after class Monday.

The girl's expression is unexpected: melted-chocolate smile, crumb-speckled cheeks, eyes pulsars of gratitude.

———

Smelling of pipe tobacco and humidity, Elin arrives again at Milwaukee Market at 3:36 p.m., her hair like a smashed wasps' nest, half sprinting for the stall where the tender-fruit seller is packing up for the day.

More strawberries?

He seems surprised, delighted that one person would have so much appetite for something he's grown.

Ah, no. I left something here. Any chance you found a bag full of cheese?

She points to the side where she remembers putting her bag down and where it no longer is. His eyes scan in the direction of her hand and he hesitates.

Guilty, Elin thinks.

They were special cheeses. I'm in a bit of a panic about them. They're for a party for my sister.

He's stacking empty pint boxes, whisper-counting them.

She's a singer. Bit of a local celeb.

Elin is tempted to hum "He Looks Good Leaving," but the man looks too young to know or care.

Oh, says the fruit seller. He hoists up an empty palette polka-dotted with berry juice. She wonders at his manners. What is he in such a rush about that he can't listen to her for a moment?

When's the party?

Odd question, Elin thinks.

Tonight. In a few hours, actually.

The lie makes her face twitch with heat. She sees a worried flicker in the fruit seller's eyes.

Sorry, ma'am. I haven't seen it. No one turned it in.

Her shoulders slump. Of course. It's hard to resist eighty dollars of cheese.

He darkens and she turns away from him, pulls out her phone. Had she spoken aloud?

It's eighteen minutes before 4 p.m. She senses the drift of vendors. Repeating her cheese purchases requires a latticework of movement between purveyors. She has no cash.

At the ATM, Elin clears her throat and shuffles her feet behind a bent old man who can't see the numbers as he presses them in. She sprints to British Baked Goods, where she picks up cheese nips, a pound of sixteen-year-old Lake District cheddar, and a jar of onion jam. She dodges two motorized scooters and an overloaded dolly to beg the short *nonna* at Bella Fromaggio's to please, please, please dip into the packed bucket of baby bocconcini and fill a half-pint tub for her, in addition to the last hunk of their lush *robiola rocchetta*.

Next, there is the Dutchman's Finest, where she grimaces at the price of a Wisconsin blue cheese smoked over Oregonian hazelnuts.

There is no Danablu, he tells her curtly.

Fine, she says. Never liked it anyway.

She hands over a wad of bills for the state version.

Her final stop is Jensen's for the jar of herring and brick of Ski Queen—a sweet brown whey cheese that as a child sat in her mouth like some terrible tease, not quite butterscotch, not quite peanut butter, not quite cheese. She's never known anyone to be able to stand more than a few slices. Except Mette.

Mrs. Jensen—two decades of intermittent visits hasn't put Elin on a first-name basis with her—has removed her apron and is turning off the lights of the refrigerated display case. Elin flies as fast as her sore knees and canvas shopping bag will allow her and comes to a full stop just as the woman is about to exit from behind her counter.

Sorry, dear.

No! I have to have whey cheese. And herring!

I would if I could, but everything is locked up and cashed out.

You don't understand. I lost my bag of cheese earlier. It was eighty dollars' worth of cheese. And I don't have eighty dollars to waste. I ran back here, and it was gone.

There's more to confess: she dismissed her last class of the day ten minutes early just so she could buy this cheese, on a week when she was already on the principal's radar. She had to ask her students to leave by the back way, in exchange for ten minutes' less physics on a Friday afternoon, rather than risk them being stopped and questioned if they walked past the administration office.

She asked twenty-eight students to help her break the rules and keep it secret.

And she knows that some of them didn't. It was so much easier to go out the front door.

Which is how her mother had done it. She'd delivered bread and cheese to the Bohr kitchen, and picked up the bottles of beer—*if you're stopped, tell them this is how you get paid*—and then left the mansion through the front door, passing the officers without a second look, a scrawny girl holding a fraying basket with chipped bottles, one of them containing the ingredients for a bomb.

Mrs. Jensen gives her a blank look with several generations of Walker's Point Norwegian indifference concentrated in it. The Norwegians had had their own heavy water plant in World War ii, and their cross-country skiing guerrillas descended then scaled a deep ravine to blow it up, wrest the supply from German control, and establish themselves as the true badasses of Scandinavian resistance.

I put it down on the berry stand. And now I have to buy it all again. I had no cash. So, I went to the ATM.

The weary vendor flicks off the booth light, turns over the CASH ONLY sign, rubs her palms along her butcher's apron and unties it. She folds it in a very precise square.

My sister's coming for a memorial. My father's. There has to be whey cheese. We're Scandinavian! It's her favourite. It was his, too. I would have come here first—but you're at the back. And the ATM is that way. I can only move so fast.

I'm so sorry. A few grocery stores in town stock it.

Elin bursts into tears. She is not sure if it's despair or her inability to complete the task. The tears stream down her face, and they keep coming. Her breaths are short and stunted. Mrs. Jensen looks at her with more curiosity than pity, as if deducing Elin is definitely not Finnish, but one of those softer Scandinavians, like most Danes, some of the Swedes.

Okay.

The older woman sighs loudly. She turns, throws her bag on the counter, pulls out a large key chain with a fuzzy troll attached, and starts to unlock the case.

She fetches a brick of whey cheese—it's the cheaper brand. Elin stifles her protest. She plunks it down on the counter, locks the display case again, and opens a cupboard where the herring has been put away.

Fourteen or twenty-six ounces?

Twenty-six, please.

Mrs. Jensen walks out from behind the counter with a brick of cheese in one hand and a large jar of herring in the other and pushes them toward Elin.

How much do I owe you?

She shakes her head.

Not worth it for me to reopen my cash. They're on the house.

Oh no. I couldn't.

But Mrs. Jensen picks them up and places them herself in Elin's shopping bag and turns to go.

Thank you. Thank you so much.

Market closes at four on Fridays, Mrs. Jensen yells back without turning. Next time, plan better.

When she looks up, a moon-faced man under the THAT EGG GUY sign and the teenaged counter help at Seafood Terminus have stopped working to stare at her. She sniffles, but inside she feels a small thrum of triumph.

If nothing else today, she has won at cheese.

B ets dials the radio button, lands on a station, listens for three seconds, moves on.

Just choose already.

Elin can't think of the last time they drove together.

The smell of warm strawberries lingers in the car's interior, with its dendrochronology of grime and crumbs and memories:

late dashes to school

dance recitals

birthday parties

grocery stores

11 p.m. pizza runs

mental health days

road trips.

Years of drives just like this, the compressed insularity of mother and daughter in its movable terrarium, just enough air for the both of them and sometimes not enough. Laughter and singing and stony stares through the front windshield, the asphalt's yellow lines rolling past on each side, holding them together.

Soon, the car will lie down like an old, rusted dog, spent. Elin holds her breath each time she turns the key in the ignition, waits for the engine's reluctant pant.

Bets hears a few bars of a song, doubles back, finds the station, tunes it and turns the volume up, leans back. Elin had watched her daughter for signs of trauma after the fight; now she suspects Bets's perfectionism and civility *is* the trauma. Bets with her big smile, her quickness to put others at ease.

The windshield is grimy. There isn't much fluid left. It spurts.

Bets has settled on a big-lunged ballad with an obvious hook.

Who's that?

The windshield wipers are only spreading the dirt, clouding her view. Elin toggles.

Sara Loud.

You like this?

Bets peers in the side-view mirror with a co-pilot's alertness.

I like that Sara Loud is working again, she says.

Was she the one who had the whole thing with her former manager?

Elin stops playing with the windshield wipers, convinces herself she has enough clear glass to drive.

He assaulted her. Then trashed her career when she spoke up.

Jeesuz, Elin says.

Bets turns the volume down.

Aunt Mette reached out to her.

Who?

Sara Loud.

She did?

Yeah, on Twitter. Couple months ago.

Mette tweets?

Bets sighs.

Yup. Got a bit of play. All these trolls were ganging up on Sara. And Mette said she believes her. That kind of bullshit was all over the business when Mette was recording.

She said she *believes* her?

Yes.

Just like that.

Of course.

Has Mette even met this pop star?

Not the point. She's standing up against the misogyny of the business.

Elin inhales deeply.

But do you know if they've met? If they even know each other?

I dunno. Doubt it. Different generations. Different music. What does it matter? They friended each other on social media. Even talked about recording a duo version of "He Looks Good Leaving" together. Updating it. Cool, right?

Bets uses a new tone of voice: the one where she controls her irritation with someone less enlightened than her.

Also updates your aunt. Sounds like pretty shrewd marketing on her part.

Bets twists her body in the car seat.

That's a shitty thing to say. She's your sister.

Elin presses her lips together.

I don't understand how your aunt can truly believe someone she's never met. How do you make that call?

Her daughter takes in another long breath and taps out three beats on the windowpane with her fingertips. When she speaks, her tone is parental, calm.

Because it's the right thing to do.

Elin can't listen. Why is her windshield so filthy?

She grabs the lever to release the fluid and yanks it back, holds it there angrily. Nothing happens. She slams the windshield wipers on high to see if they can move the dirt.

Her foot lifts off the accelerator. The car hiccups and abruptly slows. A horn brays angrily behind them.

Mom!

Elin corrects herself. The driver following them pulls out and yells through an open window as he passes:

Learn how to drive. Stupid cunt.

Elin uses her palm to slam the radio button off.

Cunt Eastwood. That's how Mette handled hecklers using the C-word after the disappointment of *The Orbits* left her playing small bars where the crowd was unsure of her semi-Buddhist banter and her revived love of bluegrass.

You're right, buddy, she'd say, I'm Cunt Eastwood. Dirty 'n hairy. So make my day, and shut the fuck up.

Then she'd pluck her guitar and launch into the first verse of a song like "If You Were a Bluebird" with a voice as sweet and clear as lavender syrup.

Bets has chosen a café-diner in Cudahy just beyond a row of puddlers' cottages with an easy atmosphere and comfort food. It is intimate and appealing, the kind of place you'd go to break up with a lover or fire an employee, because a scene would be so conspicuous here, and if he or she left in a huff, it would feel okay staying, finishing their meal and yours.

Sitting across from each other, Elin and Bets are over-polite. They comment on the heaping plates of food being delivered to a couple at the bar. Elin pretends to be interested in the quirky art on the walls, the decent wine and beer list, the strangely uncomfortable chairs, and a display case of homemade pies.

But what she thinks about, with a rash-like itch of fear and curious hurt, is the large brown envelope sticking out of Bets's purse.

Elin can't see how she missed it, with her new obsessive mailbox checking.

They are relieved when a server who is a few years older than Bets arrives and takes their drinks order. Elin reminds herself that the kinds of good things she's wanted for her daughter also come in envelopes.

While Bets studies the menu, Elin takes another peek. The face of it—with return address, postal marks, logos—is turned away from her. All she can see is the envelope's perfectly intact tongue, neither dimpled nor torn, folded over the top end. This is so like Bets, this meticulousness, opening an envelope without destroying any part of it. How can it not be something precious to her, some fulfilment of a secret wish?

Over and over, Bets has said, I'm travelling. I'm starting in London and then I'm wandering Europe for a while. If my money lasts, a whole year. The ticket's bought and paid for.

Elin has not believed her. Ideas change. Money never lasts as long as you want. Those European capitals, so enthralling at first, gradually weary travellers, ultimately disappoint. (Though she's never been, Elin has overheard another teacher say as much.) Moving around can be lonely and fail to elevate. Now, at least she has a fallback; the envelope's shaped for something serious and grounded: adulthood.

The server is back with their drinks and asks if they'd like to order. Elin has her eyes on the menu, but nothing is registering. Where? she wonders. Which school? She's hoping for science. All those hours coaching Bets through binomial theorem and differentiation. And physics: the subject for which she had the most help, and which caused the most tears.

Mom? Are you ready?

Elin senses the server shift impatiently from one foot to the other, and eye the door where new customers enter.

I'll give you a few more minutes.

Pasta special.

Elin blurts it. Bets will wait until the ordering is done before she starts a conversation about the envelope.

Anything to start?

She wants a salad, but its delivery will be another interruption. But then Bets orders a starter, something with hot cheese and rosemary bread cubes, that will postpone the substance of their conversation until later.

There's a palpable hollow in the server's cheeriness. Her eye twitches with impatience. Restless, Elin thinks. This is not where she imagined being at this stage in her life.

Elin lifts her glass of wine.

A toast to new beginnings, she says.

Bets smiles a bit warily and raises her beer.

They make small talk about Curt (his band is doing so well), about The Lilli (she's cranky) and what needs to be done for the pre-dedication party (too much).

When the server returns to pick up the finished appetizer dishes, Elin orders another drink, and Bets heads to the bathroom.

She could reach over so easily and just steal a look at the envelope's front, gird herself at least for the question of where. She'd have thoughts prepared about the money issue. How much. How soon. But the idea of her daughter catching her doing this from across the restaurant stops her. Bets could retreat behind a smouldering civility in a way that reminded Elin of her mother.

They wouldn't recover before the dinner was over.

When Bets returns, the server brings another wine for Elin, and informs them in a flustered voice that she's made a mistake in their entrees; there will be a delay. Dessert is on the house.

They both reassure her that it's not a problem, and finally Bets reaches for the envelope.

Without thinking, Elin presses her hands together in a little clap of delighted anticipation. Bets's eyes quicken with concern.

Mom, what are you doing?

I was just . . . I dunno.

She grabs her wine and takes a big swig. Now she is heating up. What if it's not what she thought?

So, says Bets. I paid to do a little test.

Test, repeats Elin, bunching up her fists into gleeful maracas.

She can't help herself. This is good news. Law school, medical school, certain mathematics programs, elite science institutions. Entrance examinations are required. But how? How did her daughter study and take them without Elin knowing?

I've had the results for a while.

Bets pulls three separate sheets of paper from the envelope. Elin expected more: a letter of acceptance, a scholarship offer, followed by a thick welcome package, glossy coloured ink, pictures of rolling lawns and neo-Gothic halls. A fridge magnet—at minimum—and a campus map.

She slides the pages over to the space on the table between Elin's cutlery. The first appears to be the printout of an email.

To: Bettina Henriksen
From: FT GENE-y:
Subject: Mitochondrial sequencing and autosomal test results

Below is a map, not of a campus, but with coloured circles and a legend of percentages, followed by a bar chart, and a long list of names under an x-axis of headings. Two rows of these are highlighted and flagged in yellow, another three in orange.

Bets reaches her hand across the table and places it near the sheets. Elin feels her face being watched. The pressure makes her temples burn.

A cold well of disappointment starts in her gut and seeps upward. The bar chart and map colours blur. She knows what she's looking at. Not why.

I don't understand, she says finally.

She won't make eye contact.

It's my DNA, Mom. Look.

Bets reaches across and points to the map. Her finger is shaking.

I'm almost 40 per cent Iranian. I mean, how weird is that? And I have cousins, Mom. Strong matches for third cousins—four of them. One of them, she lives in L.A.

Elin looks over the sheets again and goes back to the email header and sees a date.

You had these results months ago.

Bets exhales quickly.

I think I know where he is.

Who?

My father.

The waitress approaches with their meals. Elin knows she's disappointing her daughter. The pasta special looks oily and unappetizing, its salmon strips red as abrasions.

But Denmark, right? You're still planning to visit?

Why would I go to Denmark, Mom?

Because you're part Danish. It's part of who you are. As much as anything.

She swishes her right hand so it arcs over the papers, as if she's telling them to go away.

Bets snatches the sheets, shuffles, and pulls out a page. Her face is flushed.

She pushes the map back in front of her mother and points to the blooms of colour on Denmark and Germany.

According to this, you might be more German and less Danish than you think. Just saying.

Elin leans back in her chair, lays one hand across her belly and shoves the opposite fist into her chin. She needs a second to collect her thoughts. She takes another sip of wine, and it makes things worse.

Why now?

Bets's forehead accordions.

Geez, Mom. When have I not asked you about him?

You could wound a child with too much information. *Omission lies with us*, Elin had joked to Joy, should be the motto on her parental coat of arms.

She'd seen him again, once, after walking in the door of McGillicuddy's for her afternoon shift. Bets was two years old. Elin had a deal with another mother on staff, spelling each other off for child care. He was sitting at the bar: she recognized the shape of his closely shaved head, its elegant, muscular slope into his good shoulders, and the contrary fineness of his long fingers gripping a recently poured pint. She stopped mid-stride and moved back into the hallway by the washrooms. There'd be no avoiding him if she walked in behind the bar; the place was nearly empty. Saying hello meant saying other things. What's your name again? How have you been? And even, Remember that night? Crazy, right?

She was making assumptions. He might not be back here for her, but simply because of a vaguely warm association with the place, or that it was close to his hotel, or this was an easy spot to meet his friends. He'd be embarrassed to see her or, worse, that she remembered him, and by doing so exerted an obligation over him. He might not even recognize her; motherhood and loneliness had made her pouchier, darkened her hair to dun, dimmed the mineral startle of her eyes.

He turned to catch a game score and she saw again how brazenly good-looking he was—aghast she'd had the nerve to get naked in front of him.

The more difficult dilemma was if he responded warmly to her, was glad to be remembered. How to have a light, flirty conversation and not mention the wild intimacy they'd shared, the child who'd resulted? Elin had lifted Bets onto the very bar stool where he sat, on a few afternoon shifts when she couldn't find a babysitter, and entertained her with orders of deep-fried mozzarella sticks, colouring books, and music videos on the overhead televisions. A regular could come in at any moment and ask, How's that little darlin' of yours?

His interest. His kindness. He might not be shocked by a child.

There was a flash of gold on his wrist: a nice watch. His sneakers and jeans smarted with weekend newness. His body testified to gym regimens and dinner-plate restraint. He took care. A professional.

Elin had been working in bars since she was seventeen; she'd been groped and kissed and choked more times than she could count. Once, a line cook locked her in a walk-in freezer with two of his friends and switched the light off, for forty minutes. She blacked out. Men had stuffed dollars in her bra, thrown beer down her top, fingered her pussy, pinched her boobs, grabbed her ass. Told her what to wear and how to talk and how to suck their dicks in between ordering Pabst, Schlitz, Miller, Old Milwaukee. She kept showing up for her shifts, pocketing tips, smiling, and cheerily upselling appetizers. She hadn't believed she had options.

A busboy carrying a rubber bin filled with ice hip-checked her, and a few cubes bounced off her shins. She yelped with surprise. The customer's head wheeled around. Elin moved further into the shadows. His eyes had a worry she didn't remember; the mouth was more boyish, his hair receding up a thoughtful forehead. His kisses, she recalled, were remarkably plush. She was not the kind of woman he'd build a life around. Maybe he'd come hoping for more anonymous sex.

Elin walked back down the hallway, in through the kitchen, out the back door. She sat in her Hyundai and phoned in sick. She apologized three times.

I just can't get out of bed, she said.

The other bartender swore with disbelief.

Fucking busboy just saw you, El.

I must be haunting the place, she said and hung up.

She drove home telling herself she'd made the right choice. Yes, on occasion she wanted to have sex with a kind man, a handsome man, a man who was into her. But she didn't want to live with one. She didn't want to ask for money, or give money, or debate paint colours or TV programs or why she was so nice to the boy at the checkout counter.

She didn't want to wait to find out how mad he had to be before he took a swing, or that he couldn't get off unless she was hog-tied and gagged, or thinner or blonder, or with a thin blonde. She wanted to talk to a man and laugh with a man, and even, yes, feel pretty to a man. But she didn't want him in her house, living with her, where she would always *always* have to worry about leaving him alone with her child, her baby. Because even a decent man, a good man, can't necessarily be trusted, may not be who everyone else thinks he is.

Elin pulled into her driveway. Her bank account was $318 in overdraft. There were no shifts she could afford to miss.

That one time she woke up with Bets's father, his hand was resting on her hip, the warm top of his foot was tucked into the cool skin of her left arch, and she could feel his exhales along the back of her neck, where her low hairline ended in wisps. The bedroom smelled not of her or him, but them, their intermingled breath and uric sweetness. She wondered if other people got to feel like this over and over again. She hoped it was possible.

The next week, she took a back-breaking double to make it up to the bartender she'd left without coverage.

Bets's father didn't return.

Elin hears her pulse in her ears now, sloshing like a scow taking on water. Her vision pinholes inward. The rotini wriggles in old sauce, shiny with amoebas of oil.

She'd gotten ahead of herself; seeing the envelope, mentally reworking her finances, imagining weekend road trips to visit her daughter out of state, bragging about Bets to others. See, see, see what I have done.

And the wine—she'd guzzled that.

Her breath quickens. She starts to sweat. There is a pain, a jellyfish cramping at her left shoulder, the kind they warn women about, its first faint twinge arriving as she smoked the pipe with her physics club that afternoon.

Mom. Are you okay?

Elin shivers.

You broke my dental mirror, Bets. The one in the rosewood box in the bathroom. You broke it and didn't tell me.

What? What are you talking about?

She senses her daughter's face collapse, in that way that makes her chest pound harder. Now it is too fast, and her vision is almost gone, Bets's face is a blur.

You shouldn't have done it. I'm pissed that you didn't have the guts to admit it.

Mom, I have no idea what you're talking about. Or why you're accusing me.

My mirror! In my box on the back of the toilet!

Bets shakes her head.

This is crazy, Mom. I didn't do it. This is batshit crazy.

Her daughter's face with its dark brows and big eyes, incongruous freckles, wild mass of black curls, was still the face Elin saw herself reflected back from; she didn't know who she was if she wasn't working toward something for her kid.

I didn't break your dental thing, Mom. I've never seen it.

Liar!

Elin pushes back from the table and holds her palms against the edges. Don't pass out, she tells herself. Don't. Don't. She wants to finish the first conversation.

Jenny Bohr had died alone. Cause of death: *psychosis manio depressiva in manitonem.* She had just crested middle age.

What's happening?

She was supposed to get it right for her kid, protect her from the tawdriness and terrors of adults and their selfish choices.

The air in the restaurant thins: there's too little oxygen for her lungs. She hears her mother's voice.

Don't be dramatic, Elin.

There's a hand on her shoulder, a sudden reassuring firmness.

Here. Breathe in. You're going to be okay.

The server has brought her a paper bag, placed it gently near her mouth.

Bets squats beside her.

Elin breathes. She breathes and she breathes, and she breathes.

It's over. She's alive.

Thought so, says the waitress. Panic attack. Have 'em all the time. Just keep breathing.

Twenty minutes later, they stand on the sidewalk outside the restaurant.

Elin's eyes water.

Bets has her arm linked in her mother's.

So that's one way of changing the subject.

We never got our complimentary dessert, Elin says.

She could kill for a pipe right now.

In the Kungälv, all those years ago, Lise Meitner had removed her gloves to smoke, and read the letter from Otto Hahn, the man who'd betray her.

She watched a snow crystal melt and she thought of the indefatigable Niels Bohr, who'd begun his career with a virtuoso's paper on the surface tension of water.

What if the nucleus stretches like a drop of water prior to splitting?

Something can only stretch so far.

Carrying takeout coffees, they find a park with a pond, pavilion, and picnic tables.

Seated across from each other again, Bets looks at Elin apologetically.

I'm going to find him.

Elin nods, presses her top lip over her bottom.

One cousin in L.A.—my third cousin—we've already been talking. She says they'll help me out. Her mom is my dad's second cousin. They think his father remarried. So, I'm either looking for J. Ghorbani or a J. something else.

In Chicago?

Maybe not. I found a couple of J. Ghorbanis on LinkedIn. Both had worked in Chicago for a few years. One seems to be in Oregon. The other is, get this, living in Solvang.

Solvang?

Funny, huh? I'll get a bit of Denmark in after all. It's only a few hours out of L.A. This cousin will help me out if I'm based there. She's almost certain my father, if he's my father, grew up in the city. On top of that, his parents are still alive and still in the family home. Mom, I might have a full set of grandparents!

Oh. Bets. That's great.

Elin reaches over to pat Bets's forearm and senses the coolness of her palm on her daughter's warm skin.

Did you say you'll be based in L.A.?

Yeah, Mette has set me up with a place to stay, a summer house-sit for a friend of hers.

You've been talking to Mette about this?

I didn't want to upset you. I wanted things lined up.

You're not going to Europe at all?

Switched my ticket.

Or school?

Not a priority, says Bets.

Her eyes are wide with excitement; even now, they can startle Elin with their peridot clarity.

I want to know who my father is. I want to meet my cousins, and whoever else is out there. I want to meet people who look like me, are like me.

Elin squints into the dusky sun. There are geese on the pond, with fuzzy, greenish goslings gliding behind. Her eyes tear up.

I look like you.

She wonders if the young geese are amazed at what they are doing, this trick they so recently mastered. Every new intrepidness will go so fast for them now.

Bets squeezes Elin's hand.

Sorry to break it to you, Mom, but we look nothing alike.

It wasn't true; Elin saw the best part of her life in her daughter's face.

Tehrangeles, Elin says.

Bets drops her head.

You know the mirror. I didn't touch it, right?

Elin can't meet those eyes.

Curt is sitting on the stoop when they get home. Elin can tell by the way his eyes widen at Bets and then her, he's received several texts already. A play-by-play.

She's irritated that Bets and Curt live in an infinite set of present moments, theirs and others', including those that don't belong to them. Nobody ever gets the retrospective account anymore. Batshit crazy, Bets had called her. Liar, Elin had yelled at her daughter. It was not a matter of how much Curt should know, but rather how much truth was sacrificed for clarity.

We're taking off to hang out with my band. Are you going to be okay?

They both look at her in a way she's not ready for, the same way she looks at The Lilli, as if ever more fragility is inevitable.

I'm fine. Go!

When the door closes and the house is empty, Elin opens the refrigerator. She has spent more than a hundred dollars on dinner without achieving satiety or getting dessert. The strawberries, ruby-coloured, soft-fleshed, and fragrant, are losing their vitality by the minute. The worst kind of obligation. She pulls the pints out, empties them into a colander to wash them, before transferring them into a larger bowl.

Elin carries them to the attic, the same bedroom where almost two decades earlier she brought a baby home. Mitzi's nails chirp on the stairs behind her. The dog curls up at the end of the bed, her paws cradling the plastic octopus, which she'd snuck back into the house after being let outside. It glows in the dark, pink-and-purple phosphorescence, as if they are underwater together. Moonlight slows and diffuses around them; Mitzi's breath is a gurgling current.

One after the other, Elin eats the fresh strawberries. She sprinkles black pepper on them.

She won't make her siblings' favourite dessert after all.

Fuck Mette, and her meddling ways.

Elin falls in and out of sleep, fingertips stained pink.

2 0

The Lilli's oat-coloured skin has a rusty stain. Like a red sky in morning.

In place of hello, she clears her throat.

Where on earth have you been? It's after 10 a.m.

Elin's arms are weighed down with grocery bags. Her mother walks away into the house.

My list! Where is it?

Elin drops the bags in the vestibule. Her trunk is open; the wine is there. She hurries down the steps for it.

When she returns, holding a heavy box, her mother is peering into one of the bags with cheese.

Elin, this roquefort smells like a damp basement. And you haven't bought nearly enough.

Have you got coffee made, Mom? I could use a cup.

Elin goes back to the car. It takes four trips to empty it and fetch her purse.

As she hangs up her jacket, The Lilli comes up behind Elin.

Where's your change of clothes?

I'll go home, grab a shower, come back.

We might not get everything done, Elin.

The Lilli points to the kitchen.

Your work is there; the list is tacked to the fridge.

Rinse glasses

Polish cutlery

Cube cheese

Arrange platters

Plate desserts

Put spreads, olives in serving dishes

On the counter, her mother's Christer Holmgren wineglasses teeter on impossibly elegant stems. Their smoky hue matches the overcast light. Beside them are the squat Per Lütken rocks glasses, and the delicate Sasaki champagne coupes. All of them in perfect condition, all more than a half century old.

Elin pulls out the coffee maker and starts a fresh pot.

Your sister, her mother says, leaning in the kitchen door jamb, has arrived. She's staying at the Pfister.

Nice.

Extravagant. I put clean linen in the guest room for her. She could have warned me.

You were worried Mette would be too much for you. Remember? You'll have Casper. And the Pfister's close to The Art Museum. One less person to drive.

Her mother stops listening and turns.

Candles! I'll want the votives out. The Kubus lit.

Elin watches her disappear around the corner into the living room.

The Lilli has laid out Michelsen sterling flatware—solid and primitive. Elin dislikes how it lands heavily on plates, sounding like hailstones on a clay roof. She throws the flatware in a large roasting pan with baking soda, vinegar, and boiling water, lets it sit. The Lilli says she has a shortcut for everything, but The Lilli can't complain. Elin will make her brutalist cutlery gleam.

A polished fork cannot reflect uneaten food, Mette said the year she experimented with her own Zen koans. Elin started writing them down.

When she runs to the washroom, she hesitates for a moment by her father's studio; the drafting table has a drawing pad on it, a clean ashtray, and sharpened pencils, as if he has just stepped out for lunch, one that has lasted twenty-four years. The old Narwhal, reupholstered to match the one Elin has, commands the corner. A louvred Poul Henningsen pendant lamp hangs over it, an odd bird hovering over its frangible nest. Elin closes the door so it shuts with a definitive *tink*.

Why hadn't Casper asked for that chair?

Their father's most iconic design was named for a mystery, her brother told Elin the summer before he started high school.

Dad said people didn't believe in the narwhal.

She was nine and he was fourteen; neither knew it was the last year they would be close.

The hunters who caught them in the Arctic harvested the whale's long ivory tooth; when they brought them back to Europe, they let people believe they were unicorn horns. Made more money that way.

So, the chair's named after a lie.

No. Don't be an idiot, El. Dad said a Danish scientist had proof the horns came from narwhals. Eventually, they accepted he was right.

How long did that take?

A century. So, it's named for truth. Right?

Or waiting, said Elin.

He ignored her.

They work for three hours solid, Elin in the kitchen, her mother vacuuming, dusting, polishing, moving tables and chairs with a manic vigour.

Mom, ask for help. You were just in the hospital a few days ago, remember?

The Lilli harrumphs.

I wish you hadn't mentioned the party in front of Petrine.

Elin has emptied and reorganized the refrigerator twice to fit in stacked trays of meatballs, cheeses, sausage rolls, shrimp, herring, antipasti, more cheese, cakes, post-dessert cheese. Other dessert trays are on the counter.

More than enough food here, Mom.

Elin!

The Lilli's face pokes around the corner. Pelican-sharp, ugly-gorgeous.

Enough is not enough, she says. It has to be better than enough.

Elin finishes wiping the glasses with a damp linen cloth. She's holding a Sasaki Coronation Smoke coupe with a fine crystal stem.

Do you know how rare those glasses are? It's a mistake bringing them out. You won't be careful.

Elin places the glass gingerly on a tea towel. The Lilli's face is bloodless and perspiring.

Mom, take a seat. You're about to keel over.

The refrigerator door opens with a dry pucker.

Don't you dare touch those trays.

They're overloaded. It's a ridiculous amount of food. I'm making you a plate and you're going to eat it.

She puts a slice of herring, a chunk of *rochetta*, fresh raspberries, and a lemon mini-tart in front of her mother. She runs the water so it's cold and fills two glasses, placing one by The Lilli's blue-veined hand.

You're having tea too. Eat.

Stop fussing, Elin.

You look like death.

Very kind.

There's time for you to nap.

I'm not an invalid.

That wasn't a recommendation.

Don't be pushy, Elin.

She makes a plate for herself. The water boils. Elin sits across from The Lilli, watching her mother's colour return with each sip, realizing the knot between them has worn her out.

I want to ask you something.

Hmmm.

The Lilli raises an eyebrow, but she doesn't look up. A fingertip hovers over her lunch plate, doing reconnaissance.

Remember the day Dad died?

The Lilli's finger stops moving; its tip rests lightly on the soft underbelly of a raspberry. She need only exert the tiniest extra pressure to crush the fruit.

What a ridiculous question. Of course I do. Why bring it up?

Her mother wraps both hands around her tea mug. She blows on the liquid's surface.

I always wondered about the choice you made that day. I mean that cab ride.

Your father fell. I panicked. Needed help. You were the only one around.

But if he was breathing, that was time he was still alive. An ambulance would have been quicker.

I panicked, Elin. It was just a fall. I thought he'd fallen. I didn't want strangers in the house.

Was he breathing? Did you check his pulse?

The Lilli pulls her lips slowly from the edge of the cup. Her hands tighten around it.

I need to understand. Was there a chance to save him?

Elin's mother puts her mug down on the table too quickly; its nicotine-coloured liquid splashes. A gulpful slops onto The Lilli's hand, some landing on the lunch plate so the raspberry floats a safer distance toward the rim.

What are you getting at, Elin? On the weekend of your father's dedication. When we have a party to throw.

Did you want him to die, Mom?

Elin watches the scald grow on her mother's knuckles, a psoriasis of pink that seeps into the thinly skinned bones and greenish veins on the top of her hand. The Lilli does not wince. Her hellish wilfulness, Petrine calls it.

How dare you! He was my husband. He was my business partner. He was the father of my children. I built a home, family, business around that man.

But you thought he was an asshole.

The Lilli pushes back from her chair. Her face, a bruising carmine.

I will take that nap. And Elin?

Yes?

Don't confuse your feelings with mine. You made a choice. Nobody forced you back into this family.

She leaves with a straight back, and a slight wobble.

I'll see you at seven, she says.

Elin hears the rear bedroom door shut.

Mette had said once that a story's mostly untrue by the time it's told. But why not risk trying? Even if the telling has cruel failures? Otherwise, we'd never say anything at all.

With her mother resting, the house is both quiet and clamouring. The kitchen is as sanitized and overstocked with its prepped stations for food, implements, resupply.

Elin stands in the dining room where the Sørejse once was, now replaced by a smaller, more pedestrian-looking table and chairs, attributed to Arne Jacobsen, a choice that amused and troubled her children.

That table has a tasteful runner, and artful fans of cutlery, small plates, napkins. The effect is of a mothballed aircraft carrier, quickly retrofitted, launched in the direction of a campaign it wasn't designed for.

Elin hears music.

When Mette was eleven or twelve and first learning to play the guitar, she announced at dinner, in this very room, that she wanted the family to be her first audience, right there, right then. She'd been working on a song by the bluegrass singer Kat Bunch, determined to master it, playing it over and over, sitting on the edge of the bed, straining her young, sweet voice, repeating the chords until her fingertips were pulpy, eyes watering with each press against the strings.

She dragged her chair away from the Sørejse, picked up her guitar tucked close by, and began to play.

Even Elin, who'd heard the song so often—*if my heart weren't already breakin', be you who'd get it achin', before breakin' it all over again*—could tell that Mette had achieved something admirable: her voice, though thin and green, matched the recording, and when it didn't, it wasn't a mistake, but something extra: a faster tempo, a cheeky joyfulness.

No one, including Mette, had anticipated her mother joining in. From the end of the dining room table, a low, rich voice caught the refrain in harmony.

That The Lilli could sing, or wanted to sing, especially American bluegrass—this felt electric.

Elin remembers it as a kind of pain; being both upset and thrilled. There was her mother, eyes half-closed, soulfully, tunefully, not her mother. The right words, the right notes, emanated with innate musicality out of The Lilli's throat, chest, mouth, which in that specific moment, the one that Mette had laboured for, was as wrong as it was beautiful.

When it was over, Tig, Casper, and Elin clapped wildly, partly out of astonishment, partly out of embarrassment for Mette, who looked pale and distraught.

Tig rose. Both his daughter's and his wife's faces turned up toward him.

He hesitated before he squeezed Mette's shoulder.

You played so well, he said.

He moved over to where his wife sat, kissed the top of her head.

Lilliana. I had no idea you had such a beautiful singing voice.

Her mother emblazoned with unrestrained delight.

That night, as she listened to Mette in her bed, facing the wall, trying to hide her hurt in short inhales, Elin was wakeful with rage. Her father's too-careful response. Her mother hiding her own talents, revealing them at the worst time.

She couldn't sleep for fear her sister would stop, would give up. Because that's what she'd do.

But Mette was a different animal. She woke up the next day as if the dinnertime performance hadn't happened, except for some new tightness in the way she gripped the guitar. She sang all the time after that, in every space where she wasn't told to stop: bathroom, basement, garage. She began writing her own songs almost immediately, but she didn't perform them for the family first. If The Lilli's theft was an instance of glory, the gift she'd given Mette was focus, singular and slightly ruthless.

The last item on the party to-do list is picking up the custom-ordered *kringler* in Oak Creek. She has two hours before the bakery closes.

Instead, Elin drives from her mother's house to the high school. To get into the building on a Saturday, she waves her teacher identification in front of the security guard, the same one who dragged Rosa Wyzcowski's brother down the hall ten days earlier.

He tells her he'll have to record her visit in the logbook.

Of course, she says to him. I misplaced a copy of a final exam. Give me fifteen minutes.

He starts to follow. Elin stays on the first floor and heads to the ISM room. The security guard lingers at the door as she boots up the old desktop computer.

Machine takes forever, says Elin. Funding cuts, right?

He waits a few more seconds; they both stare at the dark screen. When he lumbers down the west hall with ponderous footfalls, the poster above the whiteboard peels away from the wall finally and drifts down to Elin's feet. Einstein's sadhu eyes look tired. His Davidoff pipe chamber long emptied. She thinks, okay, enough with the tree-climbing fish, and folds the laminated page to an eighth of its size before stuffing it in a baseboard crevice widened by marauding mice.

She pulls the power plug on the computer—it had yet to load— and heads out the door to the second-floor stairs.

The guard will circle back to the ISM room in five to seven minutes, find it empty, and debate whether she has signed out and left quietly or is somewhere else in the building swiping supplies and guerrilla photocopying. Since Principal Preet's moratorium on spending, there has been misbehaviour. Somebody will review the guard's log on

Monday morning, noting that a teacher who's not a theatre director or coach had entered the building: an outlier, an aberration. The kind of thing that gets noticed, mentioned to the principal.

Elin slips into the second-floor physics room, opens the desk drawer, and finds the pipe. Better that the evidence of the Physics Club's last meeting be hearsay rather than material. Just in case.

But she isn't ready to go. Oak Creek is a twenty-minute drive. What is she rushing toward?

She'd gone back to the Pfister after she discovered her mother's forgotten prescription. Elin pulled the Hyundai up a block, swore at herself, parked even more illegally than before, and ran to the hotel clutching the package. When she entered the lobby, the sight of a nearly empty manhattan glass in her mother's hand before noon and within an hour of her being released from the hospital without breakfast caused Elin to perforate the paper bag with her grip. Both The Lilli and Petrine were liquor-loud with a specific boisterousness, one they used to collapse several decades, reanimate their past lives with horsetrades of art for accuracy. As Elin moved toward them, she heard her aunt say, Bohr. She was sure of it.

Pissed off and overheated, she stopped, stood beyond their sightlines, and eavesdropped. Neither had good vision.

So did the great man talk to you, Lilliana? Before he got to Sweden? Realized his wallet was stolen?

Very funny. He asked me how old I was. Why my father let me work for the resistance. I said I was safer here than with that bastard. That shut him up.

Oh, Lil.

He told me he'd blown his own glass for his experiments. Early on. How he etched dates and formulae into the rims. It was such an odd thing to say, waiting in a shack to escape. Oh, he's scared, I thought.

Just a befuddled old man. And then he said, Find us. We'll take care of you. He hugged me. I've always wanted a daughter, he said. He smelled of tobacco, juniper, and allspice. Like a Christmas market.

Can I smoke, darling?

You're a terrible listener, Petrine.

You mentioned tobacco. Put it in my head.

Petrine lit a cigarette and held out another.

We're not supposed to.

There's hardly anyone here. Let's see how long it takes two old ladies to get in trouble.

Petrine tapped her ashes into one of her two empty martini glasses rimmed with the mashed pink caterpillars of her lipstick. Her mother lit the other cigarette.

Did you see him again?

No. In the late fall of '43, I went to his home, the Aeresbolig, to sneak out a bottle he left behind.

Ah, I've heard this one before. That water story. You know, they needed a lot to make a bomb. Maybe the old physicist was giving you a way to contact him instead. A chance to scratch something into the rim of that bottle he wanted. Fix a note to it. Seems obvious.

Think it didn't cross my mind? Drinking tea in china cups with Margrethe Bohr, teasing her sons about spooning too much remoulade on their sandwiches. Papa Bohr bringing me a beachcombed whelk, explaining the harmony of the universe with it.

They would have given you a good life, Petrine said. A very big life. The kind you always wanted, Lilliana.

Ice tinkled against The Lilli's glass.

Yes, but the same day I delivered that heavy water to the resistance, I chased a woman suspected of sleeping with Gestapo around Frederiksholms Kanal; tore off her silk stockings in front of a jeering mob. Left a bomb on a collaborator's porch that afternoon. Explain that in the House of Honour.

Finish your cigarette, Lil. I want to order another drink.

Besides, I was thirteen and had a thirty-year-old lover.

He was twenty-seven, darling, said Petrine. You're exaggerating again.

You sure about that? What a complete and utter asshole.

Petrine cackled with surprise. Her mother's laughter resounded like something old and hard, splitting then re-splitting.

Bracelets jingled. Petrine waved her hand for service.

Elin intercepted the waiter and pointed to the club chairs. She asked him to deliver the white prescription bag to the taller woman in the linen tunic and cigarette pants, threatening to report him if he served either another drink and slipping him a twenty-dollar bill as reparations for the ash-filled glasses.

Her hands shook when she plucked the parking ticket tucked under the windshield wiper before getting back into her car.

2 2

E lin's experience of late is that time runs away rather than runs
out.

She tapes a page of graph paper over the classroom door's small
window, locks herself in and sits on the ledge, and prepares the pipe
with a shag-shred combo, triple-wad. For her students' sake, she'd pretended not to know.

The leaves of the copper beech are almost at peak purple, ebonized
in the sun. Elin has never witnessed the metamorphosis that follows,
but by July those leaves will be dark green, like kale, and the tree,
though magnificent, will seem less otherworldly.

But for that one Kat Bunch song, her mother did not sing again. That
voice—robust, musky, intuitive—had gone somewhere, swallowed,
into a place already expert at not saying much.

Perhaps that's what made The Lilli's use of silence internecine: her
commitment. For two days, what Elin overheard at the Pfister confused and rattled her. Disproving her theory about being Bohr's grand-
child—had she only ever half believed it?—turned out not to be as
upsetting as discovering that the basic premise held some truth.

Was she the only one who hadn't known what could have been?

She pulls out her phone, presses Record, and places it on the desktop, watching the flat line of her voice memo, the small diastolic flutter of her inhales and sighs.

What is there to say to him now?

There were always holes. Every theory has a few. But you *did* want a daughter. That makes us something to each other, right?

Elin bats the red button. She is too careful. Too concerned about *his* feelings. Perhaps it is time someone lets him know he didn't make it onto the school posters, the memes, the lists of hundred best quotes about anything.

History had buried Niels Bohr. Except to the nerds.

Even in Los Alamos, they hadn't needed him for science. Such a production was made getting Bohr out of Sweden when it swarmed with double agents and sympathizers. A low flight in a Mosquito over enemy waters. A Baker Street alias. All so he could join the Manhattan Project because he was good for morale: the estimable Nobel Prize winner brought in to jolly along the more essential scientists struggling with their consciences. One of those was Enrico Fermi.

Another was Maria Goeppert Mayer, who was close friends with Fermi's wife.

Elin turns on the voice memo again.

You must have met.

She was away from her children—they resented her preoccupation with physics. She was away from her husband; war shook that marriage. By then she smoked too much. She drank too much. Yet in Los Alamos, she finally had a title and salary that acknowledged her talents.

Elin takes a last puff of the pipe. Her mouth feels ashy and dry. How much to say? What would he already know?

Maria Goeppert Mayer had been unhappy in Los Alamos, despite its importance to her career. Painfully aware of being German, she thought helping build the bomb would prove how American she was, while at night she imagined that same bomb cratering Göttingen, where her cousins and old aunts still lived, and a street was named for the barefoot Franciscan monks who'd built a monastery there, and one summer afternoon she'd looked right into a solar eclipse wearing special glasses her adored father made for her.

There's a telltale heavy-footedness in the hallway outside the physics room. The security guard is on the second floor. Elin spits into the pipe chamber quickly, taps it out in the garbage, and covers it with a crumpled candy wrapper. The phone is still recording.

Who was there for a brilliant, underappreciated, troubled woman to talk to? If not you, morfar?

Elin read somewhere that Goeppert Mayer's health deteriorated in Los Alamos, as if not talking to someone was making her sick.

End memo, she says.

On North Bremen, the mailbox lid is shut. Elin hears actual music and voices inside.

Her porch, her door, and for a half second she's tempted to knock. That would amuse her and no one else. And there's the two large boxes of *kringler*, balancing on her forearms, to consider.

She had not amused the security guard after removing the paper from the window of her locked physics room to reveal him fiddling with his master key.

Found it, she said, swinging open the door.

She tucked the folded graph paper into her bag and smiled with such gratitude, he couldn't doubt the great kindness he'd performed for her.

Excuse the smell. Science rooms always reek.

In the North Bremen hallway, she kicks off her shoes and feels the barometric squeeze of her sister's unmistakable presence.

Mette fills space, she requires air. Never does she wear one distinct scent, but many:

matcha tea

organic cotton

vintage leather

cumin

satsuma

sea salt.

Not one distinct sound but an aural collage: the soles of her feet on wood, laughter, whispers, humming always humming, and then a breakout note, a line of poetry, hands slapping beats on her thighs, tabletops, her wet finger teasing C-sharp from a glass rim.

Elin wants to run up the stairs, hide. Her whole day has been spent getting ready for siblings. She wants some control over these few free hours. Two hours of quiet in her house. Take a bath. Consider an outfit.

El! Em? Is that my sister?

Mom? You home?

The stereo is playing *The Orbits*. Talk, laughter, singing from the kitchen, climbs over the album's easily frayed silk. They are drunk or high. The happiness exaggerated, giddy. Bets, Curt, Mette.

Elin walks into the kitchen, unloads the *kringler* on the counter, turns, and is enveloped by her sister, the lean length of her, strong arms and shoulders, the hempy fug of her long hair, salve-soft kiss on the cheek.

El, have you been smoking?

Mette's eyes are bright with mischief. Elin's head shake is stern.

I've missed you, little sis, Mette says. Her arm swoops extravagantly. Come sit. We have wine.

Curt pulls out a chair between Bets and her sister. He's at the end of the table. They have glasses in front of them and they are flushed, the excitement of theatre kids before opening night. The table is littered with presents: Pacari chocolates, mala bead bracelets, Sri Lankan beedies, street market T-shirts. Bets's face, with its new radiance, has barely perceptible traces of last week's bruises. Mitzi is under the table. She thwacks her tail against the hardwood at the sounds of Elin's arrival.

I hear you've been at the Frank Lloyd Wrong all day. You're a hero. Put your feet up, girl. How's Mama?

Mama? You've spent too much time in Missouri.

Elin pours herself a glass of wine; she can never reconcile the contradictions of her sister. Comfortable and uncomfortable with her.

Mette reaches for the bottle.

Are you pacing yourself? Long night ahead.

It's a party, El. Besides, I've got time to go back to the hotel and stand on my head. Sit!

Aunt Mette has something to ask you, Mom.

Elin plunders the open chocolates. She might as well get heartburn. She hopes Mette leaves soon. She'd been counting on their reunion to have cheese trays, bite-sized desserts, lit candles, atmosphere-controlled levity.

Okay.

So, Mette says. You know my place in Chicago?

Yup.

I've decided to downsize again, but instead of selling my property, I'm going to repurpose it.

Elin's favourite song on *The Orbits*, "Breathing Ashes," is playing. It was an odd tune for Mette, the guitar stripped back to childlike chords overlaid with a harpsichord melody, and multiple tracks of Mette's voice in cool contralto harmonics.

El, are you with me?

Sure.

Some old sadness, dust in rafters, Mette sings, *all our afters, ashes of befores.*

What I mean is, I'm going to live in the upper half of my townhouse and completely blow out the bottom floor, turn it into a community meditation centre.

Quiet tenants, says Elin.

Exactly. Feels like something good to do. And I can live in a smaller, more rational space on the top floor. Strip it right back to the essentials. You know, room, bathroom, study, deck, kitchen.

So still pretty sizable, right?

Yeah. Sure, it will take some getting used to. So, while the renos are going on, it could be three to four months, I thought I'd move back to Milwaukee, and hang out a little more with you and The Lilli.

You're going to live with Mom?

Mette laughs.

That's a very bad idea.

Breathing in ashes, Mette sings. *It all collapses, under your gravity.* So where?

With you. Mette will come live with you, Bets says. She can have my room. And you won't be lonely. It's kinda perfect.

Oh, says Elin. She holds her mouth open for a half second too long. Since when has her life become something for others to remedy?

As long as it's good for you, says Mette, though Elin hears finality in the way her sister and her daughter have preordained the arrangement.

I won't be in your way. I'll be recording with a friend of mine here. Should be a blast. Get me used to living a little lighter on the land. Staying put. Fewer flights with all the carbon. I'll be a better daughter, too, spend time with The Lilli, take some of the load off.

Elin gulps the wine. She imagines two small hands stretching her mouth. What Mette calls her funhouse smile: faked and baked.

Of course. You're welcome here.

Think about it. We haven't lived together since we both moved out of Mom's house.

When?

In high school, El. We lived together right out of high school.

No, when will you be coming?

End of the month.

Two weeks, then.

I'm leaving on that Saturday, says Bets. I'll have my room super clean for you.

Elin straightens. Losing Bets and gaining her sister. No room to accept one change before the next was on her doorstep. With a new cat.

Mitzi might as well stay till I get here. She seems at home.

Okay, says Elin. Sounds like a plan.

Her voice is fey, breathy.

She holds up her glass of wine, they all toast.

"Breathing Ashes" has ended, and Elin didn't get to hear the second refrain. The next song has too many competing ideas, contrapuntal melodies; Elin never could follow it.

Hey, El, says Curt. Me and Bets'll walk the pooch before the party. Since you've been working so hard.

Elin's head tilts. El. Bets. Pooch. Who'd given him permission to be so familiar, so quickly? She looks at her daughter and sister, who don't seem to have noticed.

That good, Mom?

Great.

Elin drinks her glass of wine and listens to Mette talk about all the things she'll do while back in Milwaukee. Bets and Curt laugh. They are refilling their glasses and debating ordering food, and they have moved on to Sara Loud.

Mette says she's offered to change the title to "She Looks Good Leaving." Curt and Bets whoop and clap. They suggest ways to rework the lyrics.

Ten long breaths, Elin tells herself. I will take ten long breaths, I will smile and kiss my sister on the head, excuse myself, go up to my bedroom. Cry if I need to.

If Mitzi has any fidelity, she will follow.

Though Elin knows, if the dog stays, she will love her still, against her better judgment.

Elin pushes her chair back from the kitchen table.

You're not going, says Mette. I wanted to show you something.

She digs into her purse, a woven leather hammock bag, and pulls out a yellowed snapshot, curled at one edge, a bluish tinge to the image.

Elin leans in and sees herself at six in a black bodysuit and a small, sparkly skirt, nude tights, tap shoes. Her brown hair is loosely braided, matted to her forehead with sweat. Her cheeks round, eyes stormy.

Beside her, in the same outfit, but a foot longer and leaner in all her proportions, is Mette, a corona of braids around her serious face, eyes glaucous as northern lakes. Her mouth is pinched self-consciously. She holds an arm diagonally across her body.

You were such a funny kid, El. Refused to do the lessons. You were more interested in your outfits and spent all the time looking in the mirror. Mør was appalled.

Laughing, Bets reaches for the photo.

No, says Elin. You mixed that up. That was you. I was a good dancer. I took it seriously. Those were my only lessons.

Mette slaps the table with feigned outrage.

Revisionism! Fake news!

I have an excellent memory, Mette.

Bets rolls her eyes and Curt's enjoyment subsides. Elin takes the picture out of her daughter's fingers and stares.

Were her and her sister's childhoods so interchangeable? How unlikely to have taken on Mette's story as her own.

It was a long time ago.

No, Elin thinks. She can sink back too easily into the memory, remembering how hard she worked at those steps, whispering the pattern under her breath *brush-drag-toe-heel right stomp, brush-drag-toe-heel left stomp, slide tap, slide tap, stomp stomp* until the teacher, whose onyx hair was blunt cut, said, Elin, try it without sticking your tongue out. While Mette, bored, hanging back, sang at herself in the studio mirrors, her hip cocked and one hand wagging a finger at her reflection.

Mette, see how I'm all sweaty. You were the one too busy admiring yourself.

Okay. Whatever works. Still. Cute, right?

But you must remember you threw a fit about having to go to those lessons.

El, it's just a photo. Found it while cleaning up. Thought it was a blast. Didn't mean anything by it.

Not saying you meant something by it, Mette. But you mixed things up. Those dance lessons were important to me.

Her tone is scolding, louder than she'd intended.

Mom. Let it go. Aunt Mette was just having fun.

Elin bites her bottom lip. She picks up her wineglass and rinses it.

I'll grab a shower before the rush.

The awkward pause in the kitchen doesn't last. By the time Elin's feet hit the second floor, she hears Mette belting out the lyrics to the last song of the album.

On the first stair to the attic bedroom, Mitzi presses against Elin's calf, matching her step.

Elin leans over and hugs the animal's warm barrel of ribs too tightly.

23

Let's steal some, Mette says, elbowing the boxes of *kringler*. C'mon.
The kitchen is empty but for them, now that Bets and Curt
have taken his car to pick up The Lilli for a pre-party dinner at a pub
on Kinnickinnic, a plan that has Mette's high-spirited signature all
over it.

Elin has been invited. And declined. Which was part of Mette's
intent, her generosity.

Uh, uh, Elin says. She'll see.

Will she though?

Mette picks up a lighter and her phone from the table, throws
them in her bag, and grabs her *bleu de travail* jacket. She's going to
check in at the Pfister and cab to join the others for dinner.

We're getting old, she says on her way out the door, blowing kisses.
When *did* that happen?

At her mother's house, Elin has the food trays unwrapped and on the
sideboard, the red wine decanting, the ice buckets filled, the Kubus and
other candles lit, the back screen door open for ventilation, in under
thirty minutes.

She is standing in the middle of the living room and she feels a
bubble of anticipation, just as she had before a busy night at the bar,
when the *mise en place* of her trade—lime mix, maraschino cherries,

celery, rim salts, lemon wedges, mint leaves, grenadine, ice, orange wheels, fresh juices, whipping cream, cocktail napkins, toothpicks, ice, ice, ice—was plumped, jewelled with condensation, tidy. And she was caffeinated and ready to hustle.

If she'd overreacted to Mette's photo, the party's sublimity would be redemption.

At 8:45 p.m., she's in her mother's bathroom reapplying lipstick, considering how to tame the frizz of her hair. The thin gold legs and mantis body of the trinitite brooch perches on the sink's edge as if considering flight.

Knock.

She wasn't expecting anyone to arrive for another twenty minutes. Elin unfolds the brooch clasp and pins it to the chest of her dark bateau neckline top; she will keep it on long enough to see the flash of humour in her sister's eyes, their shared joke.

The knock repeats, light as a child's.

She'll have to accept the state of her hair.

Aunt Petrine holds her cashmere wrap out for Elin to take without saying hello.

I'm early. It's my gift to your mother.

She brushes her dry lips against Elin's cheeks; heliotrope's almond-cherry notes rise up from her old skin.

Then she pulls away suddenly and Elin feels a sharp prick in the flesh above her heart.

Petrine's long fingernail is pressed into the brooch.

Where did you get that atrocious thing?

When Elin has her settled in with a double martini—*How dry? Open the vermouth, tell it a dirty secret, screw the lid back on*—her aunt smiles with a cryptic sensitivity.

That brooch, she says, that ugly, ugly brooch. The one time I truly felt sorry for your mother.

Elin watches the door.

Your father bought that thing days after your parents landed in the U.S. Evan and I met them in New York.

There are a dozen things Elin could be doing, including pulling out her mother's ancient curling iron, giving her hair some vivacity. Her aunt has her cornered.

A show at MOMA featured the work of a former Parisian, a jewellery designer—what was his name? A bit of a darling of *Harper's Bazaar*. Among his designs were pieces with that horrible stuff, delivered straight from the Pentagon's public relations department.

Your father had no money. I mean, not a dime. But somehow, while he was making arrangements for his conquest of L.A., he found his way to this designer's atelier on 48th. Koven! That's his name.

Petrine slaps her hand on the sofa arm: Elin notices the chicken-paw colour of her aunt's flesh, the contrariness of a gaudy ring.

What if Mette invites some handsome musician she knows to the party? The idea thrills and horrifies Elin. Her hair.

Now Petrine is glaring at her, pinning her in place.

They must have hit it off, the two of them; swapping war stories. Koven had a shop in Paris for a while. Ended up doing something top secret in the Loire Valley. Odd duck: a covert-ops jewellery designer. Who knows how Tig exaggerated his own adventures in Denmark.

Your father walked out of that studio with a plug of nuclear fallout on a palladium nest. He began his new life with an instalment plan for an overpriced luxury item. How American.

And he insisted your mother wear it on her dress that night for dinner. Seventeen-year-old Lilliana, slender and ferocious from war. Can you imagine? She made heads turn. But I knew by the way her mouth twitched she was furious; not just about the money—that was bad enough—but the thing itself. Ugly. She was going to spend a lot of energy curbing her husband's impulsiveness. Her first taste of disillusionment. Emphasis on first.

Petrine drains her martini.

Another! And take the damn thing off. Some things are too painful.

Five minutes alone in the bathroom, Elin thinks, that's all she needs to reset herself.

She picks up her aunt's glass, rushes to the kitchen. She's pouring gin when the front door opens and she hears her mother's voice, scraping the octaves of surprise.

Petrine! You've arrived before the host. How like you.

The party goes well.

Until Elin gets drunk.

Mette has a circle around her in the dining room, including Bets, where she talks and erupts into a cappella lines of her old songs, in a call-and-response with one of her admirers. The living room seats are full. Guests have arrived with surprising appetites and are balancing plates and drinks with breathtaking carelessness.

Casper enters without fanfare, stows his bag in the guest room, pecks his mother and sisters on their cheeks, fills up a large glass of wine, falls into conversation with an old neighbour. His entrance is a piece of cinema, the long continuous shot.

Elin moves back and forth, deftly picking up emptied glasses, her mother's treasures, and taking them back to be rinsed and safely air-dried in the kitchen. Bets and Curt come in to say goodbye: there's a show at an underground club they want to see.

Bets squeezes her arm, kisses her cheek.

Mom, you did good, says Bets. Great party. Take a cab, okay?

Curt gives her a hug, and Elin realizes she's getting used to having him around. Even with his presumptions.

As she refills the dessert and cheese trays, she starts to hum, and it's because of this abandon, this high of getting things right, that she shoves a square of warm *kringler* in her mouth at the very instant The Lilli comes to the doorway holding a Sasaki.

The pastry's warm, buttery lightness, the subtle marzipan—a taste she'd re-evaluated as an adult—the shaved almonds and granulated sugar crunch, is so much to savour, now that her mother's eyes have landed on her.

You better watch that, Elin. You're getting hefty. I will have to tell people you're my old German nurse soon.

The Lilli cackles. She puts her emptied coupe by the sink, ready to be washed.

I'm going to take a pill and go to sleep. No need to rush everybody out. Except for Petrine. I've called her a cab.

Elin holds her breath. When her mother exits, she swallows the *kringler* without chewing. It sits in a painful, buttery mid-chest lump. She replenishes an empty dessert tray, comes back to the kitchen, and fills up a tippy Holmgren wineglass from an open bottle of Malbec, takes two large gulps to flush the lump down. It is stodgy and unmovable. Elin refills the glass and takes another long pull.

The room is already swaying by the time she wanders toward the smaller group around Mette that includes Casper.

Elin stands just slightly outside the circle. No one moves to let her in; how do they not see her? The one who has rinsed and refilled their exquisite glasses, layered their open-faced rye toasts, portion-controlled their sweets.

Casper and Mette interrupt each other laughing, charming the guests around them, retelling the story of how her mother snuck into the Copenhagen Forum to sprinkle their father's ashes. More than ever, her brother strikes Elin as an artful blend of The Lilli's architectural bluntness and Tig's sun-bleached hues, thoughtful and precise.

Flighty.

He'd repeated that word as if he believed it even though she'd moved out of the family home years before him, bought her own house, raised a child alone, put herself through school.

Paid the bills.

Paid her dues.

Paid the piper.

Paid for her mistakes (with her ambition).

Elin drains her glass; something dangerous and inevitable slouches toward her. Her plan for the evening had not included tipsiness listing into stupefaction.

She hears the name Sara Loud. They are talking about the pop star. She can't quite make out the words they are saying, though the self-conscious murmurs of assent, the piety of appall, make them cluck like pigeons under a bridge.

Another gulp of wine slides with a sulphurous heat over her tongue, down her throat.

She thought she'd done better than to stay wounded; she thought she'd let it go, and willed herself, read herself, recorded herself out of that state, the forever hurt. She'd winced at the sound of another's woman's sorrows, telling herself she would not do that, remain caught in the helplessness of that first injury, holding her bruises, keeping them fresh, so she could never recognize herself without them.

And yet this party, what had she really wanted from it?

And now her mouth is moving, though she doesn't recognize the voice as hers.

Weird, though, isn't it? How you believe a pop star you don't even know.

The alcohol has dulled her ability to modulate loudness or choose her words. She knows this because the circle rips away quickly like wet paper, as if discovering her there, finally.

What do you mean?

Elin's not sure if Mette asks or someone else. She's beyond caring.

A complete stranger. Not a family member.

Mette freezes. A few of the guests shuffle nervously. Elin swigs.

Some stories are just too close to home, right?

She moves her hand to mimic Mette's earlier ash-sprinkling gesture, forgetting she's holding a glass. She lets go of the Holmgren, and it follows the shortest upward trajectory before it falls, splits hard in the middle of the circle. Two of the guests move back with a gasp as the wine dots their legs like the gush of a nicked artery.

Seriously, El, says Mette.

The broken Holmgren's elegant stem rolls on the hardwood, marking the parabola of a wagging finger. Elin laughs. The others back away from her, their eyes cast down. Casper comes from behind, grabs her elbow, guides her around people.

I'll get a dustpan, she tells him.

You do that, he says.

Elin stops at the kitchen entrance, at the very same spot where her mother had watched her earlier. Her vision reels.

My old German nurse, she'd said.

Sitting on flattened tea towels on the counters and kitchen table, her mother's dainty coupes and Christer Holmgren wineglasses balance on their bowls, their thin stems thrust to the ceiling, hemmed in by a fortification of rugged Per Lütkens. All of them in perfect condition, all more than a half century old, all of them the colour of an overcast November: ten thousand dollars' worth of smoky Danish glass.

As an eight-year-old furious with her mother, Elin had stared at the very same glassware in its tidy rows on the credenza, willing herself to smash it. She walked around with clenched fists and a sore stomach for an entire afternoon. The distance between the imagined destruction and the visceral, material doing it was surely measured in units of satisfaction.

Somewhere in the world, there was a volcano erupting, the lava burning a path to the ocean, where it sizzled into acidic steam studded with tiny glass slivers. Elin heard that on the radio.

She lobs a Sasaki coupe—exquisite and fine, so admirably designed—against the ceiling. Its little *tink* against the plaster, followed by a rain of thin shards across the counters, is rash, infatuating. Forty-eight years, *pffsssst*. Elin feels the shitty, infectious glee. She moves into the centre of the kitchen and throws another glass into the high corners, against the Fog & Mørup hanging pendant lamp, which makes a brassy clunk. Another at the maple cupboards. It sounds like an old man's fingers breaking, the settling of accounts. She claps her hands.

And then the sink, the backsplash, the kitchen window, the ceiling again.

Tink. Tink. Tink.

Bad weather. A glass-studded volcanic cloud.

The Lütkens have a dull sound. The coupes are dainty, pianissimo. The Holmgrens shatter with a rough gusto, satisfying her the most. A large shard lands on her scalp.

The Forum's glass ceiling exploding, its slivers landing on her bare flesh. The snap of the dental mirror. The loose pane cracking up toward the centre. Glassy ashes. She's a saboteur, a Dane ruining Danish things; the House of the Future, the house of the past. The bomb in the desert; its rain of glass beads.

She reaches up and feels blood.

What the fuck.

Mette rushes in. Her feet crunch on broken glass.

Stop, El. Stop right now.

But there are only a dozen glasses left; she is drunk on adrenalin, Malbec, and Rioja. Elin reaches for another stem and tosses it to the ceiling.

This is what you want? Embarrass us. Wreck things. Trash the place.

The next glass Elin throws right at Mette. She dodges.

Grow up, El. Grow up.

Elin grabs another glass. Mette picks up the one closest to her and tosses first. It bounces off Elin's cheek. She winds up to respond and Casper is there, grabbing her wrist, twisting it painfully, until she lets the glass drop into his hand.

Great party, he says. You cleared the place.

Mette steps forward. It's uncharacteristic of her to cry.

What do you want, Elin?

24

After midnight. Elin walks from Burnham to North Bremen, choosing the well-lit routes. It is balmy and the revellers are out. She feels painfully sober yet intoxicated.

Mette and Casper argued before she left: who would stay over, clean up the remaining mess, face The Lilli in the morning.

She was surprised when Casper accepted the key to Mette's hotel room at the Pfister.

She imagines her sister not sleeping in order to tweeze glass out of the kitchen's corners, where it knit into the table runner, made rivers of granulation in the floor tile grout. When The Lilli shakes off her Ativan fog after 7 a.m., she will be alarmed that it's Mette, not her son, bringing coffee to her bedside. Elin has no idea what her sister will say.

She'd hesitated at the front door, and Mette shook her head.

I'm all about forgiveness, El, but if you forgive too soon, it's not good for anyone.

Now, in the dark solitude, broken by the occasional hollowing of a passing car and the soft scald of sodium street lamps, drunken shouts at a bar entrance, Elin feels a surprise jimmied in between shame and regret: perspective.

She looks up.

All those years earlier on Michigan Island, she'd stood with her sister under a sky gaudy with stars, in air so cool and clean it made her nostrils hurt.

We'll never see this many stars again, Mette had said.

The shadows of spruce and the monster of Lake Superior made the world feel suddenly too huge, too vast for one mind, one heart, to contain.

That was the time for her to speak.

My eyes ache, she'd said instead.

When she gets to North Bremen, she sees a faint blip emitting from her bedroom window—she's left a lamp on for the dog. She has to try and retry her key. She turns the light on in the kitchen, fills a water glass, roots for the vitamin B capsules, and heads toward the stairs. The house is dark now, quiet. Elin squints at herself in the hallway mirror as she swallows the vitamin.

There'd been another moment, when Casper quit the house for the hotel, leaving Mette and Elin in the kitchen that sparkled with broken glass, a bit stunned, like two survivors of a flash flood, who can't face how some of what destruction creates is beautiful.

Elin took the trinitite brooch out of her pocket and placed it in front of Mette.

I thought you might want this back.

Why?

Nostalgia. A good part of our childhood.

El, I don't even know what that thing is. Casper gave it to me a few months after Dad died. Said I would figure it out. But I didn't. Hung on to that piece of junk all these years.

Casper gave it to *you*?

Elin tries to imagine her obedient brother pocketing the velvet bag as The Lilli charged across the garage floor. That he had secrets, that he was unknown to her, felt surprising.

I sent it to you as a lark.

A lark?

They went quiet. Elin unhooked the brooch clasp and pressed the pin into her fingertip until a crimson bubble formed.

There was a sharp sting, and Elin stared at the puncture, its tiny red jewel, surprised to feel pain.

Mette stood up, windshield-wiped her foot across the floor, made a path to the broom closet. The crunch of crystalline exoskeletons, whole bodies, disintegrating.

El?

She turned to her sister, who looked forlorn, as she had sometimes when they were kids.

Yes.

It should have been said earlier. I know who you are, Elin. I know you like myself. I could have done better by you.

Elin hesitated: the sensation of something she'd wanted for so long hovered just above her palms, smaller than she'd expected, more evanescent, so delicate. It couldn't be held for long.

Okay.

Now Elin's face stares back from the hallway mirror.

Better, she repeats to herself.

Her image bears the wear and tear of disappointment. She can see it, thanks to all those reflected photons, exponentially more than she can imagine, individually invisible.

Yet she cannot see what makes her see.

We observe using a mechanism that itself is unobservable at its unit of action, a professor told her third-year physics class. Seeing really *is* believing.

Weirdly, unexpectedly, an act of faith.

Elin won't sleep with this much alcohol in her bloodstream. In her early twenties and working in bars, she'd made a scientific study of hangover prevention. But being an inebriated subject meant she collected some of her data drunk too. Despite this, one regimen seemed to outstrip others in its efficacy:

Three glasses of water

Hottest-bearable shower
One hundred jumping jacks
Hot cup of lemon and cayenne
Warmest pyjamas under duvet
Sweat for an hour
Repeat once
Vomit if necessary
Ibuprofen and rest.

If she's going to make it to the dedication, it's worth a try. To collect her thermal pyjamas, she takes the stairs to the attic in measured swoons. At the foot of the bed, Mitzi raises her head and casts an uncharitable glance toward the unsteady woman gripping the handrail at the top step. Elin has one arm out of her dress when she leans back into her duvet, bargaining for ten quick breaths with her head on the pillow before showering.

She gets halfway.

25

Twelve years earlier, Elin couldn't get out of bed.

The weight of not having done any of the things she'd told herself she would do with her life pinned her to the mattress.

She hadn't become a physicist.

She hadn't found love.

She hadn't lived in a city other than Milwaukee or created the kind of life that was filled with art, liquidity, rarefied conversations, good taste, epic meals, spiritual growth, amazing sex, impossible fitness: a radiant halation of success that her cool friends would fucking hate her for if they didn't love her so much.

Elin had a six-year-old daughter.

Elin had an eighty-six-year-old house.

Elin had eighteen thousand dollars of school debt.

Elin had a detritus of decapitated Barbie dolls, earless teddy bears, plastic cars, board game dice, dress-up wands, coin purses, sparkling hair scrunchies, gel pens, scented notepaper, candy wrappers, playing cards, ticket stubs, Halloween eyelashes, mini snow globes, bracelet charms, lacy socks, tortoiseshell barrettes, porcelain giraffes, broccoli elastics, and bread tags covering the North Bremen home's formerly spare floors and furnishings.

She was drowning.

Her weekdays started at 6 a.m., when she rose, showered and dressed, made a pot of coffee, and watched the phone, hunched like a raptor.

Three out of five days, it rang before 8 a.m.

That left ten minutes to think about how she was going to teach the substitute class, pretend to have authority on subjects she didn't—English Literature, Geography, Man and Society, Music, or Phys. Ed.—and perhaps grab something, anything, from her bookshelves or her stack of educational guides to help.

She was rarely asked to teach her specialties of mathematics and science. Either male teachers were called first or science teachers were less sickly.

The calculus of making each morning work burned her chest like acid reflux. Her day went better if there was a 2:3 ratio between the time it took to get Bets to school (not always a constant) and the time it took to drive to where she was to teach (always a variable). On a good day, that ratio bought her enough time to check in at the school office, find the classroom before the period started, and take a breath, so she appeared organized and in control when students bulldozed in, glancing sideways at her, elbowing and winking at each other. Late and flustered was a state that never augured well for a winning lesson, a good substitution.

The other two days of the week, she got the call at 8:45 a.m.

They're already in the classroom, a breathless assistant would tell her. How quickly can you get here?

She considered these her straight-to-hell assignments. There would be no connection, no moments of shared laughter, no learning. Her objective was to arrive, contain the chaos, and secure the furniture.

Occasionally, the call came later than 9 a.m., for a substitution that started after a first-period spare or lunch.

Those calls were worst of all, because by that time Elin had adjusted to the idea of a day off. She agreed to these assignments reflexively—Bets needed a new winter jacket and she'd been making noises about piano lessons and karate. But after Elin hung up the phone, she was coated in a treacly disappointment, the sensation she had chosen poorly.

Exhaustion, its tougher rind of sadness, crept up on her slowly during that first year of substitute teaching. She couldn't stop moving long enough to register it was there, not until it had become something heavier that wouldn't reflect light, a tarry hopelessness.

So, when the day came that Elin couldn't rise at 6 a.m., get dressed, make coffee, and she didn't answer the ringing phone, she was almost unsurprised.

There it is, she thought. Knew you were coming for me.

We're taking a mental health day, she told Bets. They curled up on the bed, dipped Cheerios in a can of chocolate frosting, and watched daytime talk shows, singing lazily to jingles during the commercial breaks.

By 11 a.m., they were still in their pyjamas. Bets got quiet.

Can I go back after lunch?

Elin pulled on a pair of jeans and a sweatshirt, drove her daughter to school with a note, ducking at the sight of other adults, and noting the Hyundai's quarter tank of gas. She hadn't brushed her teeth.

The next morning, she ignored the ringing phone again, pulled on the same jeans over her pyjama pants, took Bets to school, came home, and went back to bed.

Two days turned into three, three into a week, a week into two.

You working today, Mom?

I'll be better soon, hon.

Elin slept until noon, washed down Kraft Dinner with oxidized Merlot for lunch, and went back to bed, waiting for the alarm to tell her it was time to pick up Bets from school.

They ate takeout chicken chimichangas from twenty-four-hour Taco for dinner and watched public television until 10 p.m. The mailbox filled up and was neglected.

The first day of the fourth week arrived. At midday, Elin rose from her bed, un-showered and still in the same pyjamas she'd been wearing all week, and lumbered to the kitchen. The wine bottle was drained. She opened all the cupboards looking for something analgesic: a bag of cookies or a bottle of amaretto or Irish cream given as a gift, promptly dispatched to the back of a dark shelf and forgotten.

Knock on wood.

Elin shut the cupboards guiltily. She poked her head into the hall-way, to assess the shadow cast through the door's frosted glass.

A tall, lean figure with long, wild hair waited on the porch.

Elin considered not moving, letting her sister believe no one was home. Except that the Hyundai was parked outside. And an alarmed Mette might phone her mother, or go to collect Bets at school, creating a Rube Goldberg machine of distress.

She approached the entrance, slowly working out a dissembling, evasive response to her sister's inevitable interrogation.

But when she opened the door, Mette simply looked her up and down and barged her way in.

Uh uh, she said. No, no, no.

What happened next was unexpected but, when she thought about it later, typical too.

Mette breezed into the living room. She pushed the Narwhal back and moved the coffee table out of the way, and shook the kilim, so that a shower of hard plastic bits rained like fallout onto the room's hard-wood, before she folded the carpet up, kicking it to the side so it swept the floor clear.

Elin watched, arms limp against her thighs.

Mette shoved a mixed tape into the stereo and rolled the volume dial with the palm of her hand.

"Dance Little Sister," by Terence Trent D'Arby, thumped into the room.

Mette grabbed her sister's hands and pulled her from the hall onto the emptied living room floor, ignoring Elin's deflated beach ball whimpers.

Each time Terence Trent D'Arby sang, Dance Little Sister, Mette yelled, Dance!

She wouldn't let go of Elin's arms: she pumped them as if they were levers. She pulled Elin, who was lumpy, all torpor, into a jerky box step. There was no resisting Mette's strength, her lean forcefulness.

Dance!

Elin's arms moved like rusty pinions. Mette grabbed her waist, as if trying to force her to bounce.

"Dance Little Sister," the 1973 Rolling Stones B-side, played.

Elin felt her body move, but she hated the movement, and the body doing the moving, and finally the sister making her move.

The tape was a disaster, a thoughtless pile-up of danceable hits— the Smiths, the Cure, Talk Talk—followed by Outkast, Tower of Power, the Gorillaz.

The choices infuriated Elin.

Mette swooped and gyrated. Elin tried to sit down. But Mette was too quick, her grip on her sister's wrist too strong.

She picked up a paperback with her free hand and slammed it into Mette's shoulder. Her sister didn't flinch.

Mette grabbed Elin's free wrist, so she had both, and jerked her shoulders back and forth. The more Mette made her dance, the more Elin's fury grew.

Mette did a twirl and released her grip. Elin took a swing. Mette dodged like a featherweight.

More!

She said this as if it was part of the dance.

It was the pretending that made Elin snap.

They were always fucking pretending everything was okay.

Mette grabbed for her sister and clutched her shoulders.

Her father had held her like this, the way you would hold a frightened bird to keep it from damaging its thin-boned wings; he pressed his lips, martini wet, onto the child's, wiggled his tongue like a warm goldfish in a small mouth, a feeling that was strange but not entirely unpleasant, except that it amplified the other sensations—the whiff of

KRISTA FOSS

vermouth, 3 p.m. sunlight, cigarette smoke, wool, body heat, and oiled teak—so she was overwhelmed with something inexplicable and tortured, easily mistaken for love.

Elin yanked her sister's hands away with a surprising force and kept dancing; she was going to keep moving, against the inertia.

Finally, she fell to the couch; murderous, confused. The tracks switched again, into something moodier: Radiohead. Mette was still dancing, but now tears streamed down her face.

We are so fucked up, Elin thought.

She kicked the coffee table with her foot so it jammed into Mette's shin.

Ouch!

Mette grinned through her tears. Typical, again. She launched herself over the table and landed so she straddled Elin.

If only one sister was chosen, what did it mean about the other?

The pillows she grabbed were small but dense. It lasted ten minutes, her sister's ferocious pounding. Finally, Elin laughed. She laughed so hard she dry-heaved.

Later, she'd find small claw marks on her cheeks where the pillow's glass beads had ripped at her skin.

Mette pulled her off the couch again. The Violent Femmes were playing. The Hives. Hoodoo Gurus. Coo Coo Cal.

Mette's music was psychotic.

Now Elin danced. Mette was the child who sang throughout the family home, but she, Elin, was the dancer. For a while, she'd danced in every corner of that Burnham house, up and down its staircases. When she danced, she was not herself, she was someone else, anybody else. Beautiful and whole and weightless. Flighty in the way that meant able to lift off.

Mette was covered in a dew of exertion, tears, and snot when finally she shut the music off. She poured Elin a big glass of water and left. Just like that. Not saying a thing.

The next morning, Elin answered the phone on the first ring.

26

Had it been her choice, the devil's ivy, *Epipremnum aureum*, would have been the first to go. But it's the *dieffenbachia* that's missing. This makes no sense. By two measures—aesthetics and health—it was the better plant. A simple repotting would prevent its heliotropic contortions, the unnecessary expense of plant energy.

The shelf in front of the window has been cleaned but sits empty. The devil's ivy still nods sleepily along the sides of the bookshelf, its bearded vine and waxy leaves wanting attention.

Principal Preet takes a call in front of her, giving her time to think about plants and how certain choices subvert the democracy of sunlight. She wonders if he buys his shirts in Chicago. And who gets up first in his house to make coffee in the morning, him or his partner. They haven't had kids yet; somebody's resisting. Or they can't. How trying for him—he'd be the kind of parent determined to raise a child better than the ones he sees traipse through his office every day. That conceit wears thin after a decade. She could tell him that.

Excuse me, he says, putting the phone down. So, I expected to see you yesterday.

Sorry?

Your father's dedication. The Art Museum.

She raises an eyebrow.

You were there?

You invited me.

I did. Of course.

He tilts his head, invites her to explain.

I'm a big fan of the museum.

You said. I remember.

He is waiting for the reason that would have kept Elin from an event of such importance: the naming of a gallery for her father in the city where she lives. Something attended by the rest of her family.

Your brother gave such an impressive speech—moving, thoughtful. Smart man. Met your daughter and mother too.

Elin chews the corner of her mouth.

And your mother's hilarious. She said you got drunk and smashed thousands of dollars' worth of her crystal. Delivered that totally deadpan. Almost had me.

Elin looks at him blankly.

Well, tough break, missing that moment. And I'm sorry about your dog getting hit by a car. Milwaukee drivers, right? Your daughter filled me in. You've got quite the family.

Thanks.

So.

The hand clap again.

Your request for class trip funding. I left it late. And now it's the last week of classes.

She won't tell him that the last eight principals have denied her funding, that she pays for the trip herself every year, that she actually plans for that.

If I ever get funded for that trip, it's time for me to go, she had whispered to Joy in the staff room last week.

It distracts her, picturing Dilip Preet in summer-weight wool and a crisp shirt open at the neck, holding a flute of sparkling wine and swanning around the gallery newly dedicated to her father. Women in sundresses and heels, buffed and glowing. The light reflecting from Lake Michigan across the galleria. The Lilli, stiff-necked, imperious, and bleary from the night before, yet still formidably elegant in vintage

Oscar Gundlach-Pedersen chunky silver bracelet, matching necklace, and wedge heels paired with tuxedo pants and a dark-pink blouse. (Those clothes, pre-curated, were set out in her mother's bedroom the night of the party.) Mette hanging back, still in ripped jeans, long hair twined in a loose braid, her makeup-free face flush with lack of sleep, winking at Bets, who has slept over at Curt's and is wondering where her mother is. Her father's Sørejse, the Arne Jacobsen chairs, the security guard standing at attention in his ill-fitting uniform. Elin realizes with a faint happiness that she doesn't entirely regret her absence, beyond waking late Sunday morning, one arm still in her party dress, with a pounding head, a crust of drool, her pillowcase twinkly with glass slivers shaken free from her hair.

I understand you've booked the trip already.

I have, said Elin. But it's okay.

No, he says. He holds a hand up to interrupt her.

We're going to reimburse you. Though next year, I would like you to apply properly, at the beginning of the year, file your request as part of the science department's budget.

Elin nods absently. How long had he stayed at the dedication? Had he brought his wife along or come solo, slipping out to meet her for a late lunch? Did he look into Bets's eyes and see the kindness there, the goodness Elin had a hand in?

You'll be here in the fall.

Of course I will, Ms. Henriksen—Elin. This is a good fit for me.

His voice trails off at the end of the sentence. She's happy to hear this—she likes him, wants him to see the best of her, the better her. She won't ask him about the iPads; the push-back from staff has been withering. She won't complain about the moratorium on supplies, and she'll resist commenting on the missing *dieffenbachia*, jumping to conclusions.

There *is* something about the fall we should discuss.

Okay.

Elin has ideas; she'd like to be freed up from Introduction to Secondary Mathematics to teach more physics.

It's actually a three-pronged discussion we're having today, he says.

Like a Scandinavian fork, Elin says.

That unbreakable Michelsen flatware. The uneaten food it won't reflect. On Sunday morning, Mette had texted: Come. Cas is pissed. The L won't talk to you. But I will.

Better not, Elin texted back.

So, we've dealt with the class trip and proper procedures.

Is he looking at a piece of paper? Elin wonders. Does he need notes for three items?

She remembers her first meeting with him, how he'd rested his hands and elbows on her employment file the entire time. Her eyes assessed the strength of those hands but couldn't decide what they made manifest: wilfulness or willpower.

The second thing we need to discuss is what you'll be teaching next year.

I wouldn't mind teaching fewer ISM classes. Perhaps just one semester of it.

He clears his throat.

Well, unfortunately, that's not how I'd like to leverage your skills at the school.

Oh.

Elin's pulse quickens. He knows she talks to herself, possibly that she smokes in the physics room; now he has met every member of her family. She feels enmeshed.

She'd lied to her daughter about losing Mitzi yesterday, when Bets texted her from the dedication ceremony for the third time. Bets must have added the part about the dog getting hit by a car when she explained Elin's absence to Principal Preet; a dog lost in the woods had not sounded like a good-enough excuse. After answering the text, the analgesic of staying in bed vanished—she hated lying. Why couldn't she just admit to Bets she'd messed up? She imagined her brother clearing his throat, flattening his palms across the wood of a little lectern, placing a glass of water off to the side, and calling the crowd to attention. He'd be wearing something Danish and well-made, but still fun, approachable: a Martin Asbjørn jacket, with a splash of yellow in the plaid, a beautifully detailed Sten Martin dress shirt underneath. There would be no fishing in his pockets for notes. He didn't use them.

This thought had made Elin sit up in bed. She ran down the attic stairs to the shower.

I think we want to get on board with career and technical training at this school, while there's good funding and political support, Dilip Preet was saying. You know, make pathways for our students, who aren't so academic, to get apprenticeships or into community college trades programs. Do you have any idea what some of these kids could be making as machinists or tool and die makers?

Elin looked at him with curiosity.

No. But I'm sure it's good money. I just ... Weren't you worried about retention in academic science just two weeks ago?

Yes, but as you know, I'm new here. I'm figuring the place out. And ...

You've decided that this school should be vocational.

No, not entirely, Ms. Henriksen.

He's sounding defensive. Elin feels a dampness in the small of her back, behind her knees. There's something turning in her, whining like a Dremel.

A day earlier, Dilip Preet had craned his neck around the dedication ceremony looking for her. Not imagining Elin haphazardly dressed, wet-haired, in her basement, opening a plywood locker, pulling out a small, dusty banker's box. Finding the studies, the ones Casper had sent her all those years earlier, dog-eared and striped with highlighter, dimpled with tears and coffee rings, held together with pink produce elastics.

Elin had shoved them into an oversized kraft envelope.

False Memory Syndrome: Collateral Damage from Damaged Accusers
Eating Disorders, Sibling Order and Disordered Memory
Suggestibility and Recovered Abuse: Case Studies in Memory Distortion

The reports had stacked up, a house he built around her, which, like all theoretical structures, was tidier than the real one.

So, when Elin received the fourth package, she'd started to read; she went back and read every one of those articles, reports, studies, journal editorials. She brought them to her kitchen table at night, when Bets was sleeping, and used her school highlighters and Post-it Notes to underline, to note unstated assumptions, or poorly designed research questions, confirmation biases and weak associations in the meta-analyses, the footnoting of earlier works that had been discredited. She noted who sponsored the studies, and the affiliations of the authors and the conferences they presented at, and read deeply on the crisis of replication in social psychology.

Physics helped her understand something essential: results are only as good as the questions being asked, the methodology used. Who observes, who is observed. And what framework shapes the observations.

She became an expert in her own unbelievability.

At the bottom of the banker's box were answering machine tapes and several of the notecards Mette had sent her over the years, alive with fading spoonbills and grosbeaks and jays. She'd fished out the one with the bluebird, opened it, and tore it in half, letting the side with Mette's note, its gregarious cursive, fall back into the box.

In the kitchen, she hesitated: an uncapped Sharpie wavered over the blank underside of the ripped card. And then she wrote.

Cas,

I'm returning these. Held on to them hoping we'd talk it out one day. Think I waited too long. Yours to carry now.

Xo

El

Elin was about to cap the pen when she noticed the soft brown nap of the small velvet bag that had spilled from her purse, drunkenly tossed onto the kitchen table hours earlier. She grabbed it, took one last look at the twinkly murk inside, then pulled the drawstrings taut and shoved it inside the envelope so it bulged like an Adam's apple.

P.S. Hideous brooch also coming back to you. It might be worth something. Sell it?

She taped the card to the envelope's front beside Casper's full name in all caps, and c/o Pfister Hotel, before grabbing that same purse and running out the door to her car. Before she could change her mind.

What I'd like to do is cultivate a smaller, more focused stream of academic students here, Dilip Preet was saying. Have a squad of teachers specialized in working with them: inclusive and brain-based learning approaches, blended and team-based modalities.

And you want me on this squad?

He coughs into his fist.

Well, no. I'd like to see you focus more on the ISM and mathematics side of your specialty. We could get you in on a development team I've put together with the math department: we're going to roll out a Math for Technical Careers course in second semester.

But physics is my specialty. I love teaching senior physics. My ratings are good.

Your ratings are solid, Ms. Henriksen. But your approach is not the most conventional, right? It's a bit, er, off-grid.

Off-grid?

Yup. And we need our students as plugged-in as possible. Get them ready for this big ol' digital world. So we're absolutely going to leverage your skills. But we'll also broaden our pedagogical expertise to include those with depth in game-based delivery.

The dampness that started in the small of Elin's back has crept upward, a Rorschach of wet under her shoulders that threatens to join leakage from her underarms.

She wants to protest the importance of what she teaches, and that, yes, dammit, taking students to a 400,000-square-foot facility demonstrates the scale of what can be hidden from people, or what people can choose not to see. There is no way to gamify it.

As it turned out, she had a better excuse than a lost dog. She'd raced through Milwaukee's largely empty Sunday afternoon streets, double-parked on Wisconsin Avenue, barrelled into the Pfister lobby with limp hair, and delivered her package to a prim front desk clerk, insisting it be given to Casper Henriksen before he checked out, unspooling a twenty-dollar bill, which the woman refused with a half smile, raised hand, and eyes cast with disregard. Rankled by this treatment, the declined tip—realizing outside the hotel that her puffy face hadn't so much as a coat of lipstick—she returned to her illegally parked car and pulled out into the street abruptly.

The crunch to her rear fender was instantaneous. That loudness of its metal-on-metal pitch chewed right past her insurance deductible into some new territory worth several hundred dollars unreported or a guarantee of punitive new premiums.

A tall woman emerged from the green RAV4 behind her. She was wearing an orange, white, and black baseball uniform. Through her side-view mirror, Elin read *Manitowoc Mudhens* across the front of the woman's jersey as she approached, yelling and purple-faced, waving large hands.

Elin stayed in her seat, hung her head. She started to laugh; she couldn't help herself. Now the woman was at her window, calling her a bitch, thwacking her baseball cap against the driver-side window. And Elin was immobilized, with tears running down her face as the Mudhens logo—surprisingly well-designed—splat on the glass near her face over and over.

So, if I'm hearing you correctly, she says to Dilip Preet, the majority of our students will be streamed into technical careers except for an elite squad. Some kind of STEM ninjas, who will game their way to big scholarships, improve our numbers. Is that right?

Her face is hot. She feels a sharp stab in her chest. Principal Preet flattens his mouth as if to push her question away from him.

You do know that in the long run, over the length of a student's life, general education serves students better, Elin says. Not just as employees, but as citizens. As fulfilled *human beings*. There are *studies*. It gives them the skills to adapt to changes.

Yeah, but Ms. Henriksen, we get funded on those short-term numbers. Those are the ones that have to matter for us.

We're sending some very bright individuals into industries that are in constant flux. This city's fucking history is littered with industries that leave.

Up comes Principal Preet's hand again. Elin doesn't want to cry or spiral. Yet the spinning has begun, whirring and whirring.

Sorry about the f-bomb.

Her voice sounds like a croak. She swallows, reduces her volume.

But wonder, Dilip. Don't we have the responsibility to instill wonder in our students?

His surprise at this question hardens almost immediately: the quick-dry cement of the utilitarian.

Wonder is a luxury, Ms. Henriksen, for those who know their rent will get paid. Besides.

He stops speaking for an instant, as if cutting out an immediate thought and pasting in its safer replacement. Redaction in real time.

The studies on long-run adaptability are inconclusive, by the way. The data is not very granular.

He straightens his back, re-folds his hands. They are a closed vise on his desk.

This is the direction we're taking, Ms. Henriksen. Why don't you get through exams and marking, let it settle with you, and we'll have another quick chat before summer break? Sound good?

Elin wants to say, No, fuck you.

She gets out of her chair and looks at him. She's going to make it out the door without yelling or fainting or breaking anything, when she realizes they are not finished.

There's a third prong. You forgot the third prong, she says.

Yes, you're right. Almost forgot.

He clears his throat.

I've decided not to grant any accommodations to full-time work in the fall. That's across the board: I want all hands on deck as we work through this transition period. I understand you had applied for an accommodation for . . .

Credentialling.

Right, says Principal Preet. I'd like to keep you at full operating capacity for the fall, but maybe we can find some money for you next summer. If your professional development dovetails with our new direction.

The girls' second-floor washroom hasn't had a working sink for two years, says Elin. So there are other priorities for any money you find.

The hand clap again.

That girls' washroom is on my list, he says with a tone that aims at buoyancy, trying to get the heaviness to lift before he ushers her out.

Elin nods. She moves to the door and turns. Principal Preet is standing up behind his desk; his cellphone is in his hand and he's midway into a text.

She wants to tell him that the best part of her Sunday had been not having to live with a lie. With her car's back fender dangling onto the street, Elin had cried with relief at having an even better reason for not making it to the dedication. And because of this, she'd found the words to convince a very angry third basewoman, a returning champion late for her season opener, not to throw a punch or call the cops.

Quick question, she says. What happened to the *dieffenbachia*?

My wife saw it. Took it home.

Elin stares at the empty ledge.

We'll chat in a few weeks, Ms. Henriksen. And by the way, good work with Mabel Flores.

Hmm?

Her attendance. Might have to do some upgrading. But she's back with us.

Elin lingers midway between his desk and the exit. She wants to tell him that Mabel Flores has come back to write her physics exam only. She has a meeting with Mabel's parents in two days. The reference letter for a school with a program for gifted science students has been written.

Tell your wife both plants have potential, she says instead.

Excuse me?

By then, she's halfway out the door.

She wanders into the staff room in a daze. It is mostly deserted, the frayed furniture soured by dust and June heat, the sink smelling vegetal beside a rack of rinsed, stained mugs. Summer rhythms: teachers disappearing, relocating their desks to their back porches. She's glad for the loneliness. She opens the refrigerator; there's a waft of mildew.

Inside are a few forgotten Tupperware containers and a single can of Diet Coke, left by one of those who've already decamped, for someone who needs it more: her.

She yanks at the cutlery drawer. Elin's going to waste the hour she planned to use for marking exams, staring into space instead; there's no point fighting it. The drawer is a mess of coloured rubber bands and bread bag ties, plastic forks, and soy sauce pouches. No thumbtacks that can catch soft flesh.

She thinks Mabel will struggle adjusting to that other school, with its longer bus rides, its coddled students, their easy contempt, and the extra pressures it will put on the whole Flores family.

Whether it was the better option was neither clear nor evidently true. And yet.

On Sunday afternoon, after Elin exchanged numbers with the baseball player, called her insurance company, and manoeuvred the Hyundai with its dragging fender into an empty parking space, she got out of the car and stared down Wisconsin Avenue toward the water. The Art Museum was in the way.

The wings of its *brise soleil* opened slowly in the distance, more manta ray than bird, scalding white. They widened, undulated, fell downward, rested. Unnatural and breathtaking. A feature that could be requested for special events.

Guests in the newly dedicated gallery were, at that very moment, decamping for the sunlight-drenched café a floor below, where the patio doors were opened to the waterfront. Where Mette would pick up her guitar, give them all permission to loosen their clenched politeness and laugh.

Elin wondered when she'd last heard her sister sing live.

She started walking toward the museum; she broke into a trot.

What is it with your generation of middle-aged women and leggings? The Lilli had asked her more than once. Elin wore ones she'd grabbed from the floor that morning after shooing away Mitzi, who'd curled up to sleep on them. Overtop, she'd layered her favourite oversized denim smock, faded and frayed from years of washings. Buttons were missing.

At the Windhover Hall entrance, Elin veered to the outside, skipped over the pathways and lawns that circumnavigated the museum, coming around to the café's glass prow that pointed to water. Only one set of patio doors was open, for ventilation. Lake Michigan was frisky, all cat paws and frothy wavelets. The wind off the water was crisp, which had discouraged an outdoor crowd. Lucky. She slid behind a huge planter, with a direct view of the dais Mette had climbed up with her Gibson L-200 slung by a hand-beaded strap over her shoulder.

The café was at capacity. Elin spotted her aunt Petrine, The Lilli, Casper's distinguished forehead, all at the same table near the front. Bets and Curt were farther away. There was the high hum of chatter, clinking glasses, and guests braiding and unbraiding like rogue proteins.

Mette cleared her throat at the microphone and hit a long note at the top of her range, before singing a raunchy, raw, stylized version of the state song.

On, Wisconsin! On, Wisconsin!
Grand old badger state!
We, thy loyal sons and daughters,
Hail thee, good and great.

Some wary laughter. The crowd went quiet.

Thank you for coming. For the gallery dedication upstairs and a celebration of my father and his legacy.

A hum started in the arches of Elin's feet, moved quickly into her knees. She stole a glance at her mother and saw a sudden pale alertness. Don't sing that song, Mette. Not that one.

But her sister's fingers moved over the rosewood frets and found unrecognizable notes.

Gonna sing a little somethin' by Kat Bunch. For someone else I'm missing today.

If it's the last time that we talk
Let's choose the places that we walk

Elin relaxed. Mette's eyes half closed, her timbre still so high and sweet, the guitar work nimbler than she remembered. She'd always thought Mette soaked up the audience like a sponge, not the other way around. But at a distance, Elin recognized the tidal force of what people take from those onstage.

The song ended with Mette's voice landing on a pure note, a northern kid with a heart as wide as a borderless south. The well-dressed people broke into a not too showy applause. But Bets and Curt hooted. The Lilli looked appalled, Casper charmed.

Elin listened until the first chords of the next song began. She glanced again at Mette, her mother, brother, and aunt, and realized she had no story without them. *Becoming is all we have,* said the lyrics of one of Mette's songs. Elin searched for Bets, and she was still there, among them, for now.

She turned and moved to the waterfront trail. The sun was high; the breeze whisked the water's slumbering coolness through her clothes, into her face. She walked along the lake all the way to North Point, the refrain of the Kat Bunch song repeating in her head:

The two of us aren't bound by home
Without you sister, I'm all alone.

Finally, she wanted to feel it. All the parts that got chased to the corners.

———

The staff door opens. It's the new art teacher. She's carrying her lunch, a bright, chunky salad, in a round glass dish with a press-on plastic lid.

She sees Elin and hesitates, but there is no escape. If the art teacher backs out of the staff room now, she will be making a point, and the point will be disproportionate to whatever injury Elin has inflicted.

Elin relaxes her face, makes a decision. She is going to tell the art teacher about her father, the modernist designer. She will crow about his accomplishments and place him squarely in the context of his early influences, Denmark in the golden age of modernism, the war, Arne Jacobsen's escape from Copenhagen and return, her father's missed opportunities and his Milwaukee years, in which he produced his best designs, including one that she has loved, and loathed, and loved again, for a while.

Most of this the art teacher will already know, will politely endure. So Elin will give her something more: the story of how Tig Henriksen, on a late night supplies pickup for the Danish resistance, encountered a not-quite-adolescent girl named Lilliana Brundson sleeping in a cabbage field, guarding airdropped ammunition and guns. And it would be this girl, already hardened to difficult choices, who'd encourage him to escape Denmark early, follow Jacobsen around Sweden, emigrate to America to work as a designer. And then, as his wife, chase down his commissions, negotiate with suppliers and craftsmen, keep his books, raise his children, and sometimes, late at night, slip into his studio to perfect a sketch, with her natural eye for the interesting, unfussy line, the balanced curve, which is how Elin, an early insomniac, caught her mother at her father's drafting table one night the year she turned ten, reworking the Narwhal, uncovering its genius, refining its mythic creature movement that elevated it above her father's other designs.

She hopes the art teacher—her name is Jaia—will snatch at this confidence, its unexpected comity. Elin is late to nurturing friendships in the present.

27

Wednesday morning breaks with heat and smog. There are a dozen senior physics students waiting for her in class, fifteen minutes early as instructed, already panting and lethargic, a few holding grease-stained bags with breakfast. Regina has brought Jordan in a stroller, and Elin considers how long a four-year-old will last.

She hands out bus tickets, and asks them all to fill up water bottles and wear their baseball caps.

We have a bit of walking after the bus drops us off, she says.

A refrain of groans.

An hour later, when they are in front of the sprawling former Hawley Plant on South 60th Street in West Allis, she hands them a one-page fact sheet on its dimensions and what was once manufactured there.

FEMA once declared this a disaster area, Elin tells them. After the government coughed up money for brownfield rehabilitation, this part of the facility has undergone an award-winning redevelopment and design for Johnson Controls.

She wants them to bake a little, because the inside of the building, where she has scheduled a tour, will be cool and eye-popping. The past, the future, the revisionism in the middle. She's always impressed when historic ugliness is transformed. Underneath the sandblasting, cladding, drywalling, history lurks in the dimensions.

The young woman with green hair who meets them at the front desk knows she's Casper's sister; her access is a favour to him, one of the consulting architects who conceived the award-winning redesign that shows off the former defence manufacturing plant's scale and yet smooths over its rough beginnings, with chrome and glass, floating staircases, and low, sleek neo-modernist lounges.

She wonders if this will be the last time she can leverage her brother's name for such a favour.

On the way into the building, the students get mutinous—we could be doing exam review, Bart Khang says—but inside surprises them: human ingenuity, its insidious and magnanimous impulses, both scale upward.

The tour guide is funny. A recent engineering grad with a Turkish accent, she charms them into docility, and takes them to the staff lounge, with its table tennis and foosball tables.

Twenty minutes, she says. Try not to break anything. I'll be back.

The rest of the building is not as beautifully redeveloped, but its footprint and height impresses. They meet Elin's actor friend, who's dressed as a *circa* 1940s Allis-Chalmers foreman, complete with grime swipes and beer breath. He delivers his soliloquy in a booming, alcoholic rage inside the lobby of the insulation company. The students pay attention. Right to the last line.

You can't outlive a bomb. It's forever reaching backward and forward in time. Damn thing never stops going off.

He wipes his brow with his cap, and his voice cracks.

Elin worries he's veered to the maudlin; she's embarrassed by the ridiculousness of him, reciting the monologue of a play that never gets staged.

But her students clap with brio. The actor is grateful for it. He beams, and gives her a big kiss on the cheek, which makes them clap more.

It's too hot outside to walk the perimeter of the building and map its dimensions. The lobby where she normally has her students work out the Frisch/Meitner calculations for nuclear fission is closed off: a new bank is taking over the space. She tells them that Frisch was responsible for the formulae that, using gaseous diffusion, showed enough U-235 could be separated from uranium to make a bomb. Later, Chien-Shiung Wu and Maria Goeppert Mayer would be hired by the Manhattan Project to make it actually work. Male students had complained about them both for their high standards. Wu was called Dragon Lady.

On a cooler day, she'd told other senior physics students to walk across to 70th Street and grapple with the sprawling acres of the other Allis-Chalmers buildings. She usually finishes her story there. How, after the war, Wu would get an associate position at Columbia University and help two scientists win the 1957 Nobel Prize for Physics by designing and conducting the experiments that proved their theory. And Maria Goeppert Mayer would land at the University of Chicago, eventually studying "magic numbers," and showing that inside stable nuclei the particles mirrored what was going on outside it, organized in shells with orbits and spins just like the electrons. She compared it to a room full of dancers, twirling in a waltz, spinning and circumnavigating at the same time.

Maria, like Elin, had loved to dance.

Years later, after she was lured to California with the late-to-arrive offer of a full professorship, she had a garden where clouds of hummingbirds mobbed the feeders; it was here she received word she'd won the Nobel Prize for Physics.

Wu lost her brother, father, and mother and wasn't permitted to return to China for their funerals because of a travel ban to Communist countries.

Elin wants her students to see that it is all interconnected, that the wonder and guilt of the bomb is shared, and knit with stories we know and don't know, and ones that continue. Including how, in Milwaukee, in the sprawling acres of the Allis-Chalmers site, the machining that made gaseous diffusion possible was built.

She likes to leave her students to think about that—the discomforting paradox.

But it's not a cooler day.

I'm buying everyone lunch, she announces instead.

They take over most of a nearby sub shop's tables. For the next two hours, before she hands them each a bus ticket home, they sit and eat and chat, sharing bites of cookies and chips, spoiling Jordan, who eventually nods off for a nap in his stroller, talking eagerly about their plans for university and college, for summer school upgrades and late acceptances, and where they'll get the money, and who in their family can help, and who won't.

For a small window of time, they all breathe in the future's helium lightness, its hoped-for abundance.

Then they are done: a few of them package up the half sandwiches, bags of chips, extra pops, for a mother, sibling, aged grandparent, live-in boyfriend, and they scatter in different directions.

Regina and Jordan wait at the same bus stop as Elin. There's a moment of awkward quietness. Out of the context of the classroom, they're two overheated women, one young mother, one middle-aged one, waiting for their buses.

You finished senior physics, says Elin. You realize there's no way you can't pass now.

Regina shifts on her feet. The stirred-up grit from manic cars, the shadeless bus stop, is choking.

Don't get me wrong, miss. But this course was a headache.

You worked hard.

Well, no disrespect, you do some weird shit. But today was kinda cool. Like a light went off for me. This happened *here*. My city.

Her hand sweeps through the hot air along the horizon of the industrial park, its monumental bleakness.

I hope this means you'll stick with science.

She shrugs.

Regina's bus arrives with an agitated deceleration. Elin helps lift Jordan's stroller up the steps.

At the bottom step, Regina turns.

Thought the biggest thing I could reach for was nursing assistant. Now it's like, I'm gonna pass motherfuckin' senior physics. Might as well aim for being a doctor.

A second later, Jordan presses his face against the bus window and they are gone.

Another bus takes her back to V.H. Phillips, where she's parked her car. Elin slips the receipts for bus tickets, lunches, and the actor's case of beer into an envelope marked *Principal Preet*, scrawls *Regina →
scholarships* on her to-do list, before she takes a peek at the copper beech. The purple dapples with spinach.

After years of writing letters, meeting with generals and diplomats, winning separate audiences with Roosevelt and Churchill (who was suspicious of him), fighting for openness with nuclear science, arguing knowledge was less destructive if it was public, the bombs were dropped and Bohr, back in Copenhagen by then, sought solace in the shade of the huge copper beech on the grounds where he lived.

There is nothing underneath Elin's beech. But among its boughs, she notes a splotch of flammable brightness.

The Baltimore oriole has returned.

It sits in a low branch.

28

In the bad dream, she and Niels Bohr are in a see-sawing sailboat called the *Chita*, bucking against the roiling waters of the Kattegat strait between Denmark and Sweden.

Elin is at the stern when Bohr hands her the tiller so he can look through his binoculars at a bank of dark clouds moving toward them. Bets sits on the bow near the pulpit, her hands gripping the gunwales, knees bent into her chest. The boat lists starboard.

Elin yells out a warning. A large wave bullies in port side. By the time she turns, Bets has lost her grip, disappeared.

Elin drops the tiller. Her mouth is dry. She thinks it can't be real.

Man overboard!

Niels Bohr looks around.

My kid. Over there.

Elin grabs the lifebuoy, moves along the side deck, slipping.

Turn leeward, she yells at him.

He won't pick up the tiller; he's too absorbed in something, looking at the horizon.

She sees her daughter's thin arms above the churn of sea water.

Hold on!

The suck and drag of waves. In one instant, she is far, the other near.

Summers, all those summers. Yet Bets was never a strong swimmer.

Her daughter cries out, saying something she can't discern through the mewling wind. She throws the lifesaver in the direction of the voice. Its white sclera bobs near the girl.

Help me, Elin screams at Bohr.

He grabs the tiller and jerks it, so the boat turns toward Bets, whose dark curls are strewn across the waves like winged kelp, the jade amulets of her eyes sinking.

Bets! Grab it.

But she is popping in and under the crest and boil of waves. Close. Reach. It's right there.

The water changes.

It becomes an undulatory sediment of ash-coloured corpses. All the adults surrounding Bets's young life are there, entangled: Mette, Casper, The Lilli, Tig, whole generations of Danes she doesn't know. Elin herself is ragged and soaked, falling apart, every version of her, a young child, twenty-four-year-old, new mother, middle-aged teacher. Cinereous casings, disintegrating and wet, milling closer to the boat with each swell.

Bets swims strongly now, but into the leviathan of dark sea instead. No!

She sees her daughter's head turn, and there is a hesitation in her glance that Elin knows is full of love.

The dark tower of water sucks her child into its vertex, and folds. Swallowed. She is gone.

Elin pulls off her slicker, steps on the bow, and is about to dive in after her when she is grabbed on the sides of her shoulders.

Held.

She shoves Bohr roughly. He slips on the deck, pulls her back with him, and she hears the snap of a bone, an anguished cry of pain. With no one at the tiller, the boat turns on its own, curving away from where she'd met her daughter's eyes.

Elin pulls herself up, throws the lifesaver again, aiming it aft, then rights the boat so it moves toward she does not know what.

The water calms abruptly. There is nothing. Just a wet seabird banking upward into the wind and rain, moving out of sight.

Nowhere to dive but into the vast, clueless blank. No trace of a ragged, storm-stewed child she can pull back on board, wrap in a blanket. Save.

Bohr is lying on his side whimpering for his son, for all the griefs that can't be consoled, the trail of blood from his leg milky with seafoam.

The boat moves closer to land.

Elin holds the rails, shouts wretchedly into the wind.

She's tiring out, the light is gone, shore's in sight now and windward. Land means facing every day, the rest of all her days, knowing who's lost.

The sailboat hits the dock. Bohr limps out. Yet Elin can't move. She won't fasten the moorings. The boat drifts back into the strait, chasing the storm. The panicked cries from shore are muffled by the wind. She will keep looking. She will keep looking and looking and looking. Never sure.

That's when she wakes up. She is drenched.

Sea water. Sweat.

The house is quiet, so quiet the light outside her bedroom window is a creamy-rose quartz, a pre-dawn watercolour. Mitzi stirs; it is early for breakfast, but the dog is game for a change in schedule. Elin peels herself off the bed, a soaked rag of a woman.

She drags her body into a tepid shower, changes into jogging pants, a hoodie. She remembers it's Saturday in June. In Milwaukee. The City of Festivals. Yet she is sodden, waterlogged. She hears the landslides of sleeping breath, an extra set of lungs, Curt's, pulling air in, pushing it away.

Elin hooks Mitzi to her leash and heads outside. There is nothing else to do. She is waiting for the day to begin, to move through the dread she felt upon waking.

They walk through Kilbourn Park, take in the panorama of the city under a pinkish-violet light, and then keep moving down North Avenue.

Twenty minutes later, they are standing by the old water tower, staring into Lake Michigan's broad, flat face, its implacability.

She wonders if she is losing her mind. But there is the Michigan, the same old lake, untouched by her insanity, its infinitude of thereness. All the tiny slivers of truth crowd her; Elin imagines their dark, dendritic edges around a warm thrum, pulling her in. A centre that will hold.

Mitzi butts the back of her knees with her sharp skull, then nuzzles her shin, reminding her she has yet to be fed.

The radio is on. Elin hears laughter and movement in the kitchen. She pulls off the hoodie, unleashes Mitzi, and notices her daughter's luggage lined up at the bottom of the stairs.

Bets charges out of the kitchen. Over her street clothes, she is wearing her old bathrobe, its once eye-smarting pink washed and tumble-dried into a greyed rose. Her eyes are clear, her face bright for adventure.

There you are, Bets says.

She wraps Elin in a big, protective hug.

You're leaving your robe?

Bets looks down at it.

Belongs here. But, Mom, keep it, okay? I wanna have it when I'm back.

She has never told Bets that Casper sent the robe to her, Elin, as a present, a few months after she'd visited him in Boston to tell him she was pregnant. The gift mixed up in her mixed feelings. Mette was there when she opened the package to find a plush, oversized candy-pink robe printed with tiny eyeless white cats, a tag from a Newbury Street boutique tucked into its front pocket. They both laughed at the absurdity of it, for Elin, hormonal and gravid, nearly thirty years old, frantic and unprepared for raising a child on her own.

It's so . . . young, Mette said.

Elin never wore it. She kept it tied in its pretty grosgrain ribbon, wrapped in the original tissue paper, at the bottom of a dresser, for more than a decade. One Christmas Eve, when Bets was eleven and the presents under the tree were rushed and underwhelming, a tired Elin retrieved the robe. It was slightly musty but ostensibly new. She rewrapped it. Her daughter squealed when she opened it the next morning, wiggled into its oversized luxury, wore it for the rest of the day, not noticing the stale smell, and then for the next seven years, growing into it after it was stained, faded, threadbare. Gradually, begrudgingly, Elin accepted her brother's obliviousness and genius: Casper had understood the need to remain a child, safe and untroubled, if only for a while.

We're making a feast, Bets says. Hope you have an appetite.

Then she turns and races back to the kitchen, the belt of the robe untethered and flopping.

For an instant, Elin is back on the sailboat. This is what she's dreading: the unmoorings.

They have agreed: Curt will drive Bets to the airport since Elin's car is in the shop.

She straightens herself. Bets is singing along to a song. It's hard to resist, all that nervous, gleeful excitement, the tremulous anticipation of self-discovery. A journey.

Her daughter doesn't act like someone freighted with the disappointments of the adults in her life, or at least as heavily as Elin fears. Did she misread all those bodies entangled in the water in her dream? Perhaps, like sea otters, they'd been holding on to each other.

She hears Curt imitate Bets's vibrato. He's saving up to join her in a few months. There are places he wants to see, music he wants to hear, opportunities he wants to take before, you know, he loses his nerve. Elin moves toward the kitchen.

She is jubilant. She is sad. She is hungry, so hungry.

At 3:20 p.m. on a Saturday afternoon, Elin pulls the Narwhal from its corner in the living room, gives it a quick wipe, and heaves it upward so its weight is on her thighs.

She carries it to the front porch, sits on a top step beside it, waiting. Mitzi squeezes around it to join her in a patch of sun. In daylight, the chair, a theropod of teak and puce bouclé, has a reptilian awkwardness. Beautiful-ugly.

Ten minutes later, Jaia pulls up in a borrowed pickup truck. Elin is grateful for the punctuality: she'd warned her that if she had to wait, she might change her mind.

Jaia's girlfriend is tall and athletic and the more avid collector of the two. She jumps out and, with no introduction, approaches the chair as if it were something rare and timid discovered in a virgin rainforest.

Omigod, omigod. You can't be serious. It's in perfect condition. Are you sure?

Yes, says Elin. You're doing me a favour.

What's the deal? Is it cursed? Is it stolen?

Babe.

Jaia uses her classroom voice. She looks at her girlfriend, her eyebrows arched with censure.

Sorry. It's just so great. Do we need to sign anything?

Elin laughs.

No, just take it. Enjoy.

Can we buy you dinner? A bottle of Scotch?

Elin shakes her head and moves up on the porch behind the chair.

Thanks, but no thanks. I'm a little behind on grading.

Jaia carries the chair gingerly. The girlfriend jumps into the truck bed and lifts the Narwhal's end up, barking instructions at Jaia, who rolls her eyes.

Elin watches as for an instant the Narwhal takes flight, a Jurassic bird. She feels a sense of awe.

It was, is, a beautiful object.

They coddle the Narwhal under blankets and bungee cords. Fully covered, it appears smaller, a poached and smuggled specimen.

The art teacher is in the passenger's seat, and when her girlfriend steps into the cab, shuts the door, they begin to talk urgently in half whispers.

The engine does not start. Moments pass before Jaia steps out of the truck and approaches Elin where she sits on her porch steps.

Don't hate me. She put me up to this.

Okay, says Elin.

Is there any way you would sign an affidavit testifying to the chair's provenance—maybe even retelling that story you told me in the lunchroom?

There's a prickle behind Elin's ears.

Provenance?

It's just that Nicky's got this thing about having our collection certified. In case we ever sell.

I just gave you that piece for free.

I know. I know. I didn't want to ask. But the provenance thing is big with serious collectors. They're a bit obsessive.

Elin draws back. She wonders if she'll ever get the modulation of forgiveness right. Too much, too soon: too little, too late. She lowers her head and gives it a shake.

No, she says. If you don't mind. You'll have to trust the story's true.

Elin holds out her hand, it hangs in the space between them, before Jaia clasps it.

Understood, she says.

The truck pulls away with the new art teacher mouthing, Sorry, thank you.

When she steps into her hallway, she notices Bets's pink cat-spotted bathrobe left hanging on the banister, and puts it on.

Elin stares at the space in the living room where the chair had been, the not-empty emptiness. Unexpectedly, a set of moments, clear and perfectly preserved, return to her:

The way her father held a drink.

The snap of his newspapers.

The ridiculous Danish scat he'd improvise to his worn copy of "Weather Bird."

The precise jackknife he did from the diving board of the Washington Park pool.

Black pepper on everything, even strawberries.

Gammel Dansk and soda at the breakfast table.

The bathroom after he'd had a shower and vacated: steam pungent with lemony cedar, the faint smell of anise.

His voice on the phone behind a closed door, a low Morse code with long pauses.

How he could get utterly lost in a design at his drafting table, becoming all angles like his furniture, shoulders hunched, elbows bent, jaw thrust forward, working like that until the only light was the bulb shining down on his sketch, the rest of him disappearing in shadow but for the chiaroscuro fuse of his face.

———

These moments feel separate from the others she can't forget, reminding her that among all the feelings about him that had been so hard to carry, the hardest had been love.

She hears the truck's engine fade and she is grateful for what's left. Mitzi licks behind her ankle.

The late afternoon sun drops a scalene of burnt umber on the wood floor where the chair had stood. A cat might curl up there. Or a woman.

It looks warm.

Her parents' epic silent treatment, the one that lasted nearly three weeks, ended without reason, without cause.

The Lilli was in the kitchen and her father called from the upper level asking if there was any coffee made.

She answered. Just like that.

Her mother's voice was neither singsongy nor resentful, but workaday, orderly, normal.

It was over.

Elin arrived at the breakfast table after her siblings, disoriented. Mette looked glum. Casper, expectant. Her father joined them.

The radio was tuned to WPLX. Their mother hummed to the jingle.

We've invaded Grenada, Tig said from behind his newspaper.

The kitchen was fragrant with crisp, warm waffles, raspberry coulis. A fresh pot of coffee urned.

The Lilli arched an eyebrow.

Denmark?

No. Us. The U.S.

Oh.

Elin studied her mother as she poured waffle batter into heart-shaped moulds. Her mouth pursed with fresh lipstick: Cherries in the Snow.

Other than faintly red-rimmed eyes, The Lilli seemed unchanged, unapologetic, beyond acknowledging how scorched they all were.

She came to the table holding a platter of fresh waffles, sat down, and served herself.

They're calling for snow. It's not even November.

Tig grunted.

Wisconsin's insufferable.

They both chuckled; this thing they'd dully complained about many times.

Elin tried to eat the waffles. Her throat felt impassable.

Mette's face was leonine and watchful.

Then her fork—those hateful pewter Michelsens—dropped from the height of her chin so its tines *tinked* against the thick porcelain like thrown nickels. Berry blood splattered the white linen. The Lilli eyed the precipitate red across her tablecloth. Tig peered over his newspaper momentarily. They both resumed chewing.

Mette pushed her chair back, standing.

Twenty days, she said. Twenty fucking days!

Face poached of colour. Chair overturned.

The silence ending, something else starting.

Mette didn't go to school that day. She never went back. She moved out six months later; she wouldn't let them celebrate her six-teenth birthday.

Casper returned the books to different libraries. Elin argued with him.

We're not done yet.

Just a game, El, he said.

But he was wrong. She'd find every one of those books again. And again.

Elin lies on the hardwood in the sun, wearing Bets's tatty old robe. And pulls out her phone.

classroom windows
museum floors
stairwells
carports
sun patches
She's been talking to herself for so long. And in too many places.

You've been good to me, she says. Always there. I think you saved me, more than once.

But maybe it's time.

Time, he'll say, corrugating his immense brow. Time.

It's a comfort she can anticipate his every move, trust him.

Elin scrolls through the voice memos. Her thumb hovers over each little trash can.

Oh, physicists are in love with time, he'll say.

S he doesn't see the brown envelope sticking out of the mailbox. Not at first.

The cab driver empties her bags, remarkably few.

Ma'am, I'm leaving the cat here.

Oh.

She'll expect the front door to be open. She'll pick up the cat in its travelling case, whisper some words of assurance to the overfed feline, thank the driver, turn to see the door still closed.

Hmm.

That's when she'll notice the envelope. Still, it's not like her to take things out of someone else's mailbox.

She'll bang on the door with more vigour the second time.

C'mon, sleepy. Get your ass out of bed!

She'll put the cat box down and carry her bags up the stairs to the porch.

Third time's a charm. She'll see that envelope sticking out of the mailbox again, and this time she'll notice the big *Me* written in black marker in the far-right corner, like an element in a periodic table.

All these years in Milwaukee and Elin's never taken the ferry. By 6 a.m., she's on the Lake Express watching the city shrink from view. Then it's just her and the lake for another hour, alone, the emptiness of gunmetal water and ozone, before the Muskegon shore pops up to the east out of the morning haze.

She's not being a hero about the drive: Toledo, Cleveland, Pittsburgh. There are a number of places she'd like to see; it will take her two days to reach Baltimore.

She'd debated calling The Lilli.

Mette left a message warning her that she wanted to be paid back for the glasses. In full. But then she added that Petrine had double the size of their mother's collection—the exact same glasses. So, y'know, *swapity-swappity*. That's what she said. Those very words. Elin had no idea what Mette would have to sacrifice in such a trade.

First rule about truancy, Marty had said over the phone, don't give advance notice.

He'd offered her a key to his family cabin in the Ocooch Mountains. She looked at the pictures on Facebook. The unspeakable beauty of it, hidden in plain sight.

I can't say when, she'd said.

Of course you can't. That's the point, right?

Mette has a way of opening an envelope that is so like Bets's, it's uncanny: the alien deliberateness, the attempt to preserve the envelope's integrity. She'll sit on that disintegrating wicker chair.

There's another, smaller envelope inside the big one. Before opening that, she'll feel the two hard outlines beside the card. Like her daughter, her sister will make a game of guessing the objects—keys—before confirming it by opening the smaller envelope and finding the card with its illustration of a Baltimore oriole. (The Audubon version doesn't do the bird's colour justice.)

Maria Goeppert Mayer received the Nobel Prize for Physics in 1963. Niels Bohr had been dead less than a year. In the photo Elin found, she's holding the crook of the Swedish King's elbow. Her dress is floor-length floral print, with a matching shawl that hides the paralysis in her left arm, the result of a stroke soon after she became a full professor at the University of California, San Diego. Her hearing is poor. A lifetime of chain-smoking—she did it during lectures while simultaneously holding chalk—means she tires easily. The strap of her dress has fallen down her shoulder. She is a woman who grows orchids and throws elaborate dinner parties, as her own parents had.

She is ordinary and remarkable, complicated and simple. Her approach to physics was to view it as a set of puzzles; to approach with a child's joy, wonder.

Elin has plans. She is going to wander around the red-brick buildings, vast green acres of Johns Hopkins's Homewood campus, the country's first research university, one whose motto is *The truth shall set you free*. She'll imagine Goeppert Mayer there, her first nine years of life in the U.S., being pushed outside the work she loved, and yet still doing it.

Elin feels this is a good spot to make her promise: she'll visit Copenhagen, finally. The year another woman wins a Nobel Prize for Physics.

She figures she has some time.

The afternoon she was supposed to have her final chat with Principal Preet, she reached out to an old physics professor instead, because she had an idea that still needed refining. He surprised her by responding quickly, with fond remembrances, and forwarding her his contact at Johns Hopkins, who has cross-appointments in history, physics, and philosophy. This woman has cleared an hour for Elin on a Wednesday afternoon when the campus will be half-empty for summer. She's excited to talk—her exact word, *intrigued*.

———

About forty-five minutes out of Baltimore, in a suburb of Washington, D.C., is an institute of physics, with a public library and archives named for Niels Bohr.

Before her meeting at Johns Hopkins, Elin's booked a day alone with its photographs, oral histories, recordings, textbooks, letters, not about physics, but physicists. How they grapple with the profundity of their unfathomable selves, and their place in a barely fathomable universe.

She isn't quite sure how to articulate her ideas for graduate research; they'll need sharpening. Still, when she'd rhymed off a working title over the telephone—"Narrative, belief, and the female physicists of the quantum revolution"—her old professor hooted with encouragement.

And she'll look for a picture, proof that Bohr and Goeppert Mayer met, hung out, maybe got on each other's nerves. Two inveterate mumblers. Why not? If she finds one, she'll take a photocopy, if only to remind herself there's magic in the hypothetical.

She thought she was interested in the blurry line between knowledge and belief, and how belief and disbelief have their own unique proportions of beauty and destruction. This she'll save for her graduate work. What she really hopes to discover is what to do with love. Hers.

Elin's not even off the ferry when she's smiling: the fulvous spittle of early sun on Michigan's water, the way Mitzi curls in the front seat of the Hyundai with one baleful eye half-open, the teenaged stevedore who'd winked at her before she got in the car.

She has part of her life left to live; not the biggest part, nor the part when her mind is most elastic, her body unmarked. Yet there remains possibility, and possibility is a surprise, just enough grace.

After she gets the signal from the dockworker wrapping mooring lines around a grey bollard, Elin turns on the car engine and rolls off the ferry.

If it's foolhardy to go back to school—in a year, Bets may also be ready—perhaps it's time to be more of a fool. She's over-relied on hardy.

Five minutes later, the lake disappears from her rear-view mirror.

Knock on wood.

A shadow's cast through the frosted glass and it lands on the small lobby's wood floor that lost its lustre decades earlier.

The pane won't rattle; she's had it reglazed.

There is no one to see the shadow, or to worry about the trouble it brings, to feel her heart flutter weirdly, to take a deep breath and open up.

Finally, she's not there.

She's left with the yellow-eyed dog, the dirty car, her last two paycheques, her aching hips, and what remains of her uncertainty.

Her daughter is raised: a strong, open-hearted person who's a lot like her.

Yet better.

Me,
     I've kidnapped Mitzi; you meant for me to have her, right?
     Keep The Lilli away from pruning shears.
     Back whenever.
     Xoxox
     Em
     P.S. Let's be better too.

She guesses her sister's already shaking her head. And if she doesn't laugh right away, she will when she finds the freezer full of Moon Pies. Perhaps she's known all along this was how it would go.

Explore the new place, Yoda Jr., she'll say.

Then she'll let the cat out of the box.

ACKNOWLEDGEMENTS

WORKING CLOSELY WITH an editor is one of the great privileges of having a novel published. Kelly Joseph took a chance on this story and her thoughtfulness and intelligence shepherded it here, making it better at every stage: she is an utter delight to work with.

There would be no novel without my agent, Samantha Haywood who is a wonder of encouragement and smarts.

Thanks to novelist Sally Cooper for her astute feedback, laughter and the sustenance of friendship. Nancy Sullivan modelled the kind of science teacher my main character wants to be—filled with wonder and heroically compassionate. Early readers kindly kept me on course: Lisa Borkovich, Nancy Sullivan, Jeffrey Rosnick, Sally Cooper, Jeff Griffiths and Tor Lukasik-Foss. Fehn Foss and John Martin read more versions than humanly possible. Much gratitude as well to the open-hearted folks in Milwaukee: editor and writer David Bowen for showing me his town; Barbara and her Little Bohemia digs; Sheldon Sisk for an unforgettable January walk and writer Scott Mashlan for his keen eye and insider's knowledge.

Publisher Jared Bland and everyone at McClelland & Stewart offered the gift of their support. John Sweet's incisive copy-editing and Wendy Thomas's eagle-eyed proofreading improved the manuscript immeasurably. Lisa Jager designed a stunning cover.

As a writer-in-residence for the County of Brant Public Library, I penned an entirely different novel that led me to this one, and I'm grateful for the friendship I found there, including that of the talented Christine MacArthur. Funding from the Canada Council for the Arts and the Ontario Arts Council freed me up to create and so made it all possible.

Fehn Foss saw this story circling the perimeter of another manuscript, and said, Write that. Her courage, talent and generous spirit elevated this book and bless my life outrageously.

Finally, thank-you to John, for loving, believing, and being my home.

DISCUSSION QUESTIONS FOR *HALF LIFE*

1. "You can't outlive a bomb. It's forever reaching backward and forward in time. Damn thing never stops going off." (page 27) "Elin wants her students to see that it is all interconnected, that the wonder and guilt of the bomb is shared, and knit with stories we know and don't know, and ones that continue." (page 296) How do these quotes relate to Elin's story?

2. In the opening section of the book, we witness Elin confronting her father's death. What do you think of The Lilli's actions surrounding Tig's death? Why do you think she went to Elin instead of calling paramedics?

3. What did you think of Elin's relationships with her siblings, Casper and Mette? How have these relationships, and their pitfalls, affected Elin's growth? How does Elin compare with her siblings, both in reality and in Elin's own views?

4. Throughout the story, we see Elin seeking small ways to self-harm, particularly with her use of thumbtacks. Why do you think Elin behaves this way? What other, more discreet ways does Elin display this self-harming behaviour?

5. Why does Elin, as both a child and adult, focus so much on her imagined relationship to Niels Bohr? What does this relationship offer Elin?

6. The story weaves in Elin's own relationship to physics and incorporates stories of the accomplishments of many renowned physicists, including Chien-Shiung Wu, Maria Goeppert Mayer, and Lise Meitner. Do you see Elin's experiences mirrored in these stories and in these historical figures? In particular, how does Lise Meitner's story, and the idea of being "the mother of a bomb" relate to Elin's story?

7. Why do you think Elin reacts so strongly to Bets's search for her father? How does Bets's search differ from the one Elin and her siblings took to find their own family lineage?

8. *Half Life* is told in pieces, jumping between timelines and histories. What does this structure tell us about the nature of memory? How does the title, *Half Life*, relate to Elin's story? To memory? To trauma?

9. Examine the ways food is used throughout the story and in relation to different people and relationships. Specifically, how do Moon Pies with Mette, the *flødeboller* from The Lilli, and Whippets with Marty play into the story? What do they tell us about Elin and her relationships?

10. Elin often thinks of Niels Bohr's sister Jenny. In what ways are Elin and Jenny similar? In what ways are they different?

11. Throughout the novel, we see the recurring motif of broken glass (the cracked window pane, Elin's broken dental mirror, the trinitite brooch, The Lilli's shattered glassware). Why does this imagery

continue to appear in different ways throughout the story? Examine each instance and discuss its importance.

12. "But if seeing is believing, then perhaps, she thinks, not seeing is another kind of believing, equally powerful." (page 43) How does this quote relate to the reactions from each member of Elin's family?

13. How do you feel about the relationship between Elin and The Lilli? How does this relationship shape Elin? How does Elin's parenting style stem from or veer away from her own experiences with her parents?

14. At the end of the novel, we see Elin striking out on her own and pursuing her own growth. Has Elin changed over the course of the events described in the novel?

KRISTA FOSS'S short fiction has appeared in *Granta* and has twice been a finalist for the Journey Prize. Her first novel, *Smoke River*, won the Hamilton Literary Award. She's an award-winning essayist who has worked as a bartender, journalist and teacher. She holds an MFA in Creative Writing from the University of British Columbia and lives in Hamilton, Ontario.